SHOW BUSINESS IS MURDER

MYSTERY WRITERS OF AMERICA PRESENTS

SHOW BUSINESS IS
Murder

EDITED BY
Stuart M. Kaminsky

BERKLEY PRIME CRIME, NEW YORK

A Berkley Prime Crime Book
Published by The Berkley Publishing Group
A division of Penguin Group (USA) Inc.
375 Hudson Street
New York, New York 10014

This book is an original publication of The Berkley Publishing Group.

This is a work of fiction. Names, characters, places, and incidents either
are the product of the author's imagination or are used fictitiously, and
any resemblance to actual persons, living or dead, business establish-
ments, events, or locales is entirely coincidental.

SHOW BUSINESS IS MURDER

First edition: August 2004

ISBN: 0-425-19652-6

Library of Congress Cataloging-in-Publication Data

Mystery Writers of America presents show business is murder /
edited by Stuart M. Kaminsky.
p. cm.
ISBN 0—425-19652-6
1. Detective and mystery stories, American. 2. Performing
arts—Fiction. I. Title: Show business is murder. II. Kaminsky,
Stuart M. III. Mystery Writers of America.

PS648.D4M96 2004
813'.087208357—dc22

2004045137

PRINTED IN THE UNITED STATES OF AMERICA

10   9   8   7   6   5   4   3   2   1

Contents

Introduction

STUART M. KAMINSKY

"**THE PLAY'S THE** thing wherein we'll catch the conscience of the king."

Hamlet was playing detective and using show business, a troupe of traveling players, in an attempt to get the killer to give himself away. Hamlet, being Hamlet, can't resist the urge to step in and tell the actors how to do their job.

Shakespeare was not the first to use a show business/mystery tie-in. Hamlet wasn't the first would-be show business detective.

But he may have been the first truly famous one created by a major author. Excuse me, *the* major author in the English language, if we ignore George Bernard Shaw's somewhat disingenuous dismissal of the bard.

But I digress.

The icons of mystery fiction have always been drawn to show business. An actress took in Sherlock. Poirot was constantly running into theater people. Dorothy Sayers wrote a novel about murder in a publishing house.

It's hard to think of a mystery novelist who wrote more than five books who wasn't drawn to show business.

And then came Hollywood.

Show business mysteries went far beyond and deeply into Hollywood. In his novel *The Little Sister,* Raymond Chandler set the tone of fascination with, and repulsion by, Hollywood. Ross MacDonald . . . I could go on with a list that would include almost every major mystery writer of the last century, but let's focus, at least for a paragraph or two, on one quirky byway of the show business mystery.

A popular, and generally forgotten, young readers' genre in the 1930s and 1940s featured the movie star as detective. I read books with detectives like Bonita Granville and Shirley Temple. I think Jackie Cooper even solved a murder or two.

Andrew Bergman picked up the idea of using real show business figures in mysteries with his LeVine novels, and I, George Bagby, and others kept the books coming. The public that loved mystery movies also seemed to love mystery novels about movies and stars.

This is not to say that other sides of show business were being neglected by the fleet fingers of those of us who like to kill performers and artists on our pages.

Let's jump to this collection of stories. If it has a design, besides the obvious one of show business as focus, it is variety—variety in style, subject matter, media, and seriousness. Some of the stories, like John Lutz's tale of a talking dog and mine about an inept vaudevillian, are meant to be funny. Some, like Annette Meyers's tale of a failed show business marriage, are clearly tragic.

Just for fun, we've included a script by Gary Phillips and Ed Hoch's near-fantasy about a performance artist whose act consists of her being a roulette ball.

And media? We have stories about television, movies, theater, the music industry, and even a woman who hires a private detective to find Elvis. We have actors, producers, writers, and musicians who solve the crimes or become the victims.

We have stories set in England, Germany, Chicago, Los Angeles, Las Vegas, and an imaginary small town.

We have traditional first-person private-eye novels and third-person not-so-traditional tales from the perspective of killers and victims.

Our tales take place in time over the past 70 years.

If anything else holds this collection of whimsy together, it is that show business is possibly at its most interesting when it is, indeed, murder.

—Stuart M. Kaminsky

Small Time in His Heart

CAROLYN WHEAT

THEATRE 80 ST. MARK'S
The Movie Musical Theatre
Screening Schedule, September–October 1972

SUN-THURS:

Girl Crazy
11AM, 3:30PM, 8PM
Mickey and Judy put on another show, this time at a Western college. Great Gershwin songs stitch together a paper-thin plot; Judy shines as always.

For Me and My Gal
1PM, 6:15PM, 10:15PM
Gene Kelly's first feature for MGM has him high-stepping with Judy and then breaking her heart by dodging WWI draft (ahead of his time?). Great period fun.

Birch Tate, 1972

WALKING ALONG EIGHTH Street from the Village, you first crossed Sixth Avenue, under the benevolent eye of the Jefferson Market Courthouse Library. With its turrets and narrow leaded windows, it looked like a fairy-tale castle. You could picture Rapunzel letting down her long thick hair, which made Scotty laugh when Birch said it, because Scotty remembered when the old Women's House of Detention was there and prisoners leaned out of barred windows, yelling at boyfriends and girlfriends on the street below.

Rapunzel, Scotty said again, and laughed.

If there was one thing Birch was getting tired of, it was being young. Too young to remember the Women's House of D. Too young to remember Busby Berkeley. Too young to care much about seeing Judy Garland in a movie; to her, Garland was a boozy concert singer with a drug problem and a ruined voice. Which was cool when it was Joplin, but Judy Garland was *old.*

She was not, Scotty had decided, going to spend one more day in this abysmally ignorant state. Theatre 80 St. Mark's in the East Village was running a Garland double feature and Birch was, by God, going to know by the end of this afternoon precisely why Judy Garland was the greatest star Hollywood ever produced.

They passed Orange Julius and the wedding-ring store, pushed through the crowd at Macdougal, and met the boys on the corner of Sullivan. Patrick and Stanley were even crazier than Scotty when it came to old movies. Patrick liked to say he was the reincarnation of Ann Miller, which was supposed to be funny because Ann Miller wasn't dead. Stanley preferred somebody called Lubitsch whom Birch had never heard of, and then Scotty said, "But he didn't do musicals," and Stanley arched his eyebrow and asked, "What about *The Merry Widow?*" and Scotty said, "Oh, you mean that blatant ripoff of Mamoulian's *Love Me Tonight?*"

Who cares? was what Birch thought, and wondered how long she could stay with Scotty if all they were going to do was spend blue-sky Sunday afternoons watching old movies with a couple of—

Queers.

The word popped into her mind before she could stop herself. It wasn't a nice word, and it was especially not nice because what were she and Scotty? But somehow it was different when it was boys.

The trouble was, she was new at this. She'd "come out"—and in her mind the words were always in quotes—only a few months earlier, and not by choice. She wasn't even sure she really was one, except for one thing: there had never been a boy or a man, in the movies or in real life, who made her feel the way certain girls did. First Enid and now Scotty. She felt a stirring in her jeans just looking at Scotty—her elegant short hair with its slight curl, her long legs in those tight jeans, the silk shirt, the studded belt, the Frye boots—Birch looked down at her own feet, clad in moccasins, peeking out from under frayed bell-bottoms and wondered for the fiftieth time what a really cool chick like Scotty saw in her.

"My baby dyke," Scotty called her. "My little tomboy from the Catskills."

Birch didn't mind being called a tomboy; she'd spent her entire seventeen years of life answering to that description. But "dyke" sounded so ugly. It had sounded especially ugly in the mouths of kids she'd known since kindergarten. When some of her former friends caught her holding hands with Enid at the Tinker Street Cinema last summer, they'd thrown stones at her, called her dyke. Now Scotty used the word with amused affection, as if it could never hurt.

Scotty, present

"ALL SINGING, ALL dancing" it said on the long red awning that stretched from Theatre 80's double doors to the curb. You could see that awning from as far away as the Bowery, and you walked toward it with heart high, knowing that no matter how dreary the day or how low your spirits, the double feature at the end of your trek would change your mood more rapidly and surely than any of the illegal substances being thrust at you along the way. Who needed grass when you had Busby Berkeley? Who needed uppers when Fred and Ginger were dancing cheek to cheek?

Patrick I still miss every day. He was the brother I never had, and yes, I'm well aware that I have three brothers, thank you very much. Three brothers who hate me for three different reasons: Brian because he's a Christian now and I'm going to hell, Ian because he's a stuffy old fart and I embarrass him, and Colin because I had the nerve to be born at all. The only saving grace to Colin is that he'd feel that way even if I liked men.

So Patrick was my soul-friend, the girl I should have been.

Birch, 1972

"LIKE THAT PLACE in Hollywood," Birch said, and Patrick rolled his eyes. Usually she liked Patrick, but she could tell she was about to get another lesson in how little she knew.

"That one's Joan Blondell." He pointed to the square of sidewalk with handprints and a scrawled signature. As if she couldn't read. Of course, who Joan Blondell *was* and why her handprints belonged in cement outside the theater was unclear; still, she thought she recognized the name Ruby Keeler.

"I was here when she came," Patrick said with a rapturous sigh. "Oh, she's put on weight and her hair can't possibly be that color in real life, but just to see her, to stand next to her—it was a dream come true."

Scotty came back with the tickets and they walked through the double doors into the narrow hallway that led to the seats. The white walls were covered with posters and black-and-white glossies signed by the stars personally to the theater's owner, Howard Otway. Patrick always made a point of blowing kisses at his favorites as they made their way to the coffee bar, a little black-painted cubbyhole just off the screening room.

No popcorn, just movie candy and tiny little cups of very black, very strong coffee. Everyone but Birch bought a cup; she decided on Milk Duds because they lasted nice and long. She suppressed a sigh. The little theatre reminded her of the Tinker Street Cinema back home, where she'd spent so many happy hours—until last summer.

Scotty, present

WHAT WE DID at Theatre 80 was buy our coffee in the ante-room, push aside the heavy red velvet curtain, and walk across the stage to our seats. Theatre 80 hadn't started life as a movie theater. It was a legitimate stage once home to *You're a Good Man, Charlie Brown.*

This meant that not only did the theater have a little foot-high stage, but the seats were nice and plushy, set wider apart than usual. There was also a real curtain that opened and closed, giving the showings a special touch you just couldn't get at the Quad or even the Regency uptown.

The regulars were there: three old ladies I privately thought of as the weird sisters, a little matched set that reminded me of salt shakers. The old man with the liver spots and the burgundy-colored beret who sat by himself in the fourth row. Groups of gay men wearing sheepskin coats and laughing loudly. Black-clad film students from NYU, who discussed the social implications of the musical in not-hushed-enough voices. Patrick made it a point to steer us to seats as far away from them as possible.

We loved each other very much, Patrick and I, but we

never actually sat together during a movie. He favored the center seats, and I had to have an aisle. No idea why, just an overwhelming need to know I could get up and run out if I had to—not that I ever did. It was just that the thought of being trapped in the center brought on a panic I couldn't control. So I led Birch toward the extreme right side of the theater and found us two seats in the seventh row while the boys edged past a plus-sized couple who glared at them.

The lights dimmed and then darkened, the red curtain was pulled back, the projector began to whir, and a thin blue vapor emanated from a tiny window in the back, projecting an image onto the screen.

And not just any image: The MGM lion roared, and the audience clapped. We were notorious for applause. First the stars received their due (Judy most of all), and then the director got a hand, and the choreographer, and, from the gay men especially, the costume designer.

For Me and My Gal contains one of the great movie lines of all time. Judy and Gene play vaudevillians in 1917 or so. Just as they get the booking to play the Palace—that ultimate cliché of vaudeville musicals—Gene gets his draft notice to fight in World War One. He injures himself to beat the draft, and Judy, whose brother has just died in battle, catches him at it. She turns to him and in a voice dripping with contempt, says: "You'll never be big time because you're small time in your heart."

Patrick and I loved this line. We repeated it often, cracking each other up every time. Of Richard Nixon the unspeakable, we said only, "He's small time in his heart."

So of course at intermission, when we met for a shot-glass-size cardboard espresso, we said the line in unison and laughed. Next to us, the weird sister with the whitest hair turned to her companion and said, "I remember the war. I was in high school. We were supposed to knit socks for the soldiers."

"I knitted three pair," the other said with pride. "My brother was a doughboy."

"I only finished one sock," white hair admitted. "And then the war was over."

The little old man with the burgundy beret stepped into the room on light, dancer's feet. When he saw me looking at him, he winked and did a little dance, humming "For Me and My Gal" under his breath.

He did a nice soft shoe, his leather soles gliding across the floor, no taps, just thumps of emphasis with the heel. His lithe body was perfect for the moves and the twinkle in his eye told me he was enjoying the little burst of applause that greeted his impromptu performance.

When he was finished, he bowed low and removed his beret. Long wisps of yellow-gray hair barely covered a scalp dotted with liver spots. He stepped to the counter next to me and ordered a double espresso.

Blinking lights in the lobby signaled the end of intermission and the start of the second feature. We made our way back to our seats, but the conversation, and the old man, was not forgotten.

Birch, 1972

GIRL CRAZY HAD maybe the dippiest plotline of any movie Birch Tate had ever seen. This playboy from the East, Mickey Rooney, gets sent to a Western college so he'll shape up. Judy Garland works there because her grandfather owns the place or something, and she falls in love with Mickey even though he's the biggest goofball on the planet. Mickey and Judy decide they need to put on a big show to make money for the college, only Mickey has no idea that Judy loves him, so he's always making out with some blonde or other. It was really stupid, and Mickey Rooney struck her as a guy even straight girls would have a hard time finding sexy, but Judy Garland—well, Scotty was right. Judy was amazing.

There was that incredible voice, for one thing, and the big brown eyes and the way her face changed to show exactly what she was thinking all the time. When she sang "They're writing songs of love, but not for me," Birch found tears on her cheeks. The plot, Mickey Rooney, none of it mattered when Judy sang. The song went clear out of the stupid movie and into a whole world of its own, a world of love and pain and compassion, a world of someone who'd longed for love and wondered if she'd ever find it.

Birch knew that feeling. Back in her freshman year, she and her dad agreed that it was no big deal that nobody asked her to the school dance. She was only fourteen, and there was plenty of time to outgrow her tomboy stage. They both kept saying it as dance after dance came and went without anyone asking Birch (which was not her name back then but the name she took for herself when she realized she had to bend or she would break).

The junior prom was the first one that hurt. Not only had nobody asked her, but the boys she asked turned her down flat. Boys she'd known for years, gone hiking with, played baseball with, told her they wanted to ask other girls instead of her.

Then she took the dainty little watch with the real diamond chips her dad gave her for her sweet sixteen and exchanged it for a waterproof sports watch. For the first time in his life, Sam Tate allowed himself to say what Birch guessed he'd been thinking for a long time: Did she want everyone in Woodstock to think she was a lesbian, for God's sake?

She wasn't exactly sure what a lesbian was, but she knew it wasn't good and it meant no boys asked you to dances.

Then she met Enid and the truth dawned. They *were* writing songs of love, but not for her, because nobody wrote songs of love for two girls.

So that was why the tears were there, not because Judy couldn't get a stupid twit like Mickey Rooney to look twice at her.

FRI-TUES

Golddiggers of 1933
12:30PM, 5:00PM, 9:30PM
Remember your Forgotten Man at this Depression-era classic. Powell and Keeler, Blondell and McMahon—can musicals get better than this?

Golddiggers of 1935
2:45PM, 7:15PM, 11PM
"Lullaby of Broadway" makes this the only noir musical in Hollywood history. Do boo Adolphe Menjou, but not during the movie, please.

Birch, 1972

THEY DID BOO Adolphe Menjou, first when his name came up on the credits, and again when he appeared in the movie. The booing was loud, long, and enthusiastic, and Birch was determined not to ask why.

The little man in the wine-colored beret who looked like a garden gnome gave a Bronx cheer when the dapper actor came on the screen. "Right on, Pop," someone else yelled.

Birch remembered his cheerful tap-dance in the coffee room the last time she was at Theatre 80 and wondered what would make a nice old man behave like that.

When the double feature was over and she and Scotty rejoined Patrick in the lobby, he and the little man were deep in conversation.

"Busby Berkley was a tightass little shit," the old man said, spittle gathering at the ends of his lips. "Little tin god—

the way he treated Judy was a sin and a disgrace. And no," he added, turning to Patrick, "he wasn't one a youse, boyo. He liked girls all right—except when they were dancing."

Birch didn't wonder how the old man knew Patrick was gay. Everything about Patrick, from the open way he laughed, to the theatrical gestures, to his graceful walk, to the color-coordinated scarf he so carefully arranged around his neck, to his candid, flirty blue eyes told the world who he was. Birch admired that about Patrick; he never seemed to pretend or to feel ashamed.

"Remember that number in *Golddiggers of '38?*" Patrick turned toward Scotty with a nod, inviting her into the discussion.

" 'I didn't raise my daughter to be a human harp!' " Scotty quoted and both broke up laughing, neither bothering to explain the joke to Birch.

"Which was the one where Ruby Keeler danced on the giant typewriter?"

"*Ready, Willing, and Able.* Ruby's last Warner's musical."

Birch turned to the old man and asked, "Were you in the movies?"

"Girlie," the old man replied, "I started at Metro when its mascot was a parrot. The lion came later, after Sam Goldfish took over."

Patrick's face lit up with a combination of awe and amusement. "That's Samuel Goldwyn to you and me," he explained to Birch. Scotty just nodded; of course, she'd already known that.

"So you were in the Freed Unit," Patrick said in a breathy voice. "You knew Arthur Freed? And Gene Kelly? And Vincente Minelli?"

"Freed Unit." The old man shook his head. "There was no goddamn Freed Unit. That's all made up by a bunch a people want to think the musical was more than it really was. Freed was a producer like all the rest, nothing special."

The man in the beret might as well have tried to convince Patrick that Cary Grant wasn't gay.

"Can we buy you a coffee?" Patrick asked. "We usually go to Ratner's after the movie, and we'd be delighted if you'd—"

"Sure," the little man replied. "My name's Mendy, by the way." His accent was deepest Bronx and his breath smelled of pipe tobacco. "Short for Mendelson." He laughed without humor. "Of course, it was changed for the movies. Too long for the marquee, they said. Too *Jewish* for the marquee, they meant."

Once inside the steamy dairy restaurant, he ordered borscht and when it came, sipped it loudly, smacking his lips in obvious appreciation, dunking hard pumpernickel rolls into it until they softened into an orange-colored mass.

Now Birch, her mouth nicely puckered from juicy dill tomato, asked the question she'd been trying to avoid. "Why did they boo that man? I thought he was okay in the movie."

The old man's answering smile was as tart as the dill tomato. "He was a Friendly."

"Yeah," Patrick said, his lips white with powdered sugar from his blintz. "He ratted on people he thought were Communists."

"Only most of them weren't," Scotty added. "And even the ones who were—I mean, being a Communist wasn't illegal when they joined the party back in the thirties."

Birch spent the next five minutes being lectured to about the House Un-American Activities Committee, the Hollywood Ten, the blacklist, the graylist, *Red Channels,* a man named Dalton Trumbo, another man named Walter Winchell, and a lot of other ancient history that meant absolutely nothing to her.

Mendy sipped his black coffee, grimaced, and reached into his pocket for a tiny pillbox. With yellowed smoker's fingers, he lifted the lid, took out a small white tablet, and slipped it into his coffee. He stirred, drank again, and smiled at Birch, who was watching the operation closely.

"My grandfather had nitroglycerin pills for his heart," she said in a low voice. "But his doctor wouldn't let him drink coffee."

"These aren't nitro, kid," the old man replied. "Just saccharin. I'm a diabetic, gotta watch my sugar."

"Ginger Rogers, too," Patrick said. "Wasn't she a Friendly?"

"No," Mendy said, his sharp eyes narrowing with bad memories, "that was her ma." He shook his head. "Poisonous woman. Had a tongue on her so sharp it's a wonder she still had lips."

"I always liked that Gene Kelly tried to fight the blacklist," Scotty said. "Him and Bogie and Bacall."

"Don't forget the divine John Garfield," added Patrick. "They all went to Washington to protest the Committee. But then the studios cracked down and they all folded."

"The whole thing scared the hell out of Kelly," Mendy agreed. "The First Amendment committee, Bogie, Bacall, Eddie Robinson. They make their big statement and then come back to Hollywood and find out they'll be fired unless they tell the world they were duped by the evil Commies. It killed Garfield, the whole mess. Friends on one side, friends on the other, people going to jail—it ate him up inside, and one day he just died."

Patrick asked the question on everyone's mind: "Did you get called before the Committee, Mendy?"

"Believe it or not, I did. Went to a couple meetings, next thing I know I'm Public Enemy Number One. They hauled me up there, wanted me to name names. I said, hell no, I wasn't gonna rat out my friends. Never worked again in the Industry. Not one day's shooting did I get after that."

"Wow," Birch said, impressed. "But why didn't you just tell them you were a Communist for a while but you didn't want to name anybody else?" For some reason, she didn't mind showing her ignorance before the old man. It was okay to know less than a guy who must be eighty years old.

"What you have to understand," Mendy said, "is that you couldn't do that. Once you answered one question, you had to answer them all. That's why the Ten took the Fifth."

Birch nodded as if this made sense. She supposed she knew what taking the Fifth meant, but who were the Ten?

"The Hollywood Ten," Patrick whispered into her ear. "A bunch of writers. They refused to answer and they went to jail."

"So if I'd gone in there and said, hell, yeah, I was a Commie and proud of it, or if I'd even said, I was a Commie and I'm ashamed of it now, they'd have asked me for the names of all the people I'd seen at meetings. Everybody I'd ever known in the old days would have been in trouble on account of me."

"So you were blacklisted?"

"Made no sense to me. I mean, sure, some of the writers tried sneaking pinko lines into their movies, but I was a hoofer, for Chrissakes. What was I gonna do, *tap* Marxist slogans into my scenes?"

"How did you feel about that?" Birch thought the question was stupid; how would anybody feel about that? But then she realized Patrick already knew the answer, wanted the emotion, not the facts.

"Kid, what do you love more than anything in the world? How would you feel if you had that taken away from you for no good reason? Like they passed a law saying you'd go to jail if you—"

Patrick's blue eyes glinted. "Honey, they *did* pass a law. I don't need a blacklist to feel like a second-class citizen—I'm a faggot."

Mendy lowered his eyes. "Sorry, kid. I kind of forgot."

"That reminds me," Patrick said with a snap of his slender

fingers. "Did you know a dancer named Paul Dixon? He came out to Hollywood from Broadway, they wanted to make him a big star. He started rehearsals for, I think it was—"

"*Summer Stock* with Judy Garland," Mendy replied. "Yeah, I knew him a little. In fact, he and I were up for a couple of the same roles."

"Wasn't there a rumor that he—" Patrick began.

Mendy nodded. "Yeah, that was almost worse than the blacklist, the way it killed his career. He coulda maybe beaten the Commie rap, but the other—that killed him dead."

"What happened?" Scotty asked the question, which meant Birch didn't have to.

"Westbrook Pegler—big columnist back then, not as big as Winchell, but big enough, writes a column calling Dixon 'a mincing twerp with twittering toes.'" Mendy raised a bushy gray eyebrow. "I bet you can guess what he meant by that crack."

"I could maybe think of something," Patrick replied, his lips in a thin smile. "It's one way of saying 'swishy.'"

"I'm not saying that was the end of his career," Mendy said, "but it was the end of any talk of leading roles. Your Astaires, your Kellys, your Donald O'Connors—they were all straight boys. You kept the swishers in the chorus, you didn't team them with Rita Hayworth or Judy Garland."

"So we never got to see Paul Dixon show what he could do," Patrick said wistfully. "Tragic. Really tragic."

WED-SAT

Take Me Out to the Ball Game
1PM, 5:30PM, 9:30PM
Fun with Kelly and Sinatra as baseball player vaudevillians. Berkeley directs; Esther Williams stays dry; Betty Garrett and Jules Munshin get the laughs.

An American in Paris
3:15PM, 7:15PM
The Oscar-winning, best musical of all time! Gershwin music, glorious dances, and Minnelli's amazing color palette make this a feast for eyes as well as ears.

Scotty, present

"IF I WERE going to die in a movie," Patrick said as we passed Second Avenue and the former Fillmore East, "I think I'd want it to be *An American in Paris.* Doubled with *Footlight Parade:* Jimmy Cagney and Joan Blondell. I love the energy of that movie, the complete conviction that putting on a show, anywhere, anytime, anyplace is just about the best thing anyone can do."

It was a measure of our madness in those days that nobody said, "What a sick idea." We all gave the question serious thought.

Stanley, Patrick's on-again-off-again romance, opted for *Pal Joey.* He had a thing for Kim Novak, whom he declared the closest thing to a transvestite he'd ever seen on the screen.

"The Bandwagon," I said without even thinking twice. "Doubled with *It's Always Fair Weather.*

"I want *Peter Pan,*" Birch said, a dreamy look in her eyes. "I always wanted to be able to fly."

"My dear child," Patrick said in his archest, most condescending tone, "you are speaking of *cartoons,* which, no matter how much music they contain, will never be taken seriously as musicals."

Birch thrust out her chin and said, "What about when Gene dances with Jerry the mouse in *Anchors Aweigh?*"

Patrick threw back his head and laughed. "You've been teaching her at home, Scotty. Point taken. If the great Gene thinks cartoons belong in musicals, then you shall have *Peter Pan* if he makes you happy. After all," he said, throwing out his arms in a campy, graceful dancer's arc, "that's what musicals are about: happiness."

Birch, 1972

THE BASEBALL MOVIE was corny, although Birch had liked Betty Garrett, the lady with the husky voice who chased after Frank Sinatra the same way she'd chased after Enid the summer before. It made her blush to think of how young she'd been then, what a fool she'd made of herself. Frank Sinatra looked so different, young and skinny and kind of innocent and sweet, not like he was today, all tough-guy.

In the intermission she waved at Mendy, who raised his espresso to her. It was too crowded to get to him so she mouthed "Ratner's" at him several times. He gave a vigorous nod and she turned away, satisfied.

She hoped it would be okay with the others that she invited him, and then decided, hell, she was as much a part of the group as they were and she could invite whoever she wanted. And besides, they liked hearing his stories, so what was the harm?

Scotty, present

THE OLD MAN stood out the first time I noticed him. Not that being old called my attention to him; many old people loved Theatre 80 for taking them back to a time they'd been young and in love.

But that was what set him apart: He didn't look happy to be there. He looked grumpy, as if his wife had dragged him to see a musical and he'd grumbled all the way, telling her he couldn't understand what she saw in a lightweight like Gene Kelly, not a real man like John Wayne or Kirk Douglas.

I had the whole dialogue worked out in my head. I knew this guy; he was my father, a man who never admitted enjoying anything if he could help it.

Funny part was, no wife ever showed up to sit next to him.

When the twenty-minute ballet that closed *American in Paris* ended, there was silence for a solid minute, and then the theater erupted in loud, sustained applause.

All except for the man in the last row. He sat stolid, his face a mask of indifference.

So why had he paid three-fifty for a seat? If he only wanted to warm up, the subway was seventy-five cents.

Then I noticed something else. His eyes were fixed, not on the screen, but on a man who sat three rows in front of him.

Mendy. The man's attention was wholly occupied in watching Mendy, who clapped with apparent enjoyment, oblivious to the fact that he was being stared at so persistently.

The curtain's close had us racing for the lobby, hoping to beat the crowd. The boys were already there, putting on leather jackets and wrapping scarves around necks in preparation for the cold October evening. Patrick was gesticulating, showing Stanley something he'd noticed in Gene's dancing. Unusually clumsy in his exuberance, Patrick bumped into the man who had stared, and received an unusually harsh epithet in return.

"Pardon *me*, Mary," he said with an archness I would have advised against.

The old man glared and replied, "You stupid fool. You made me—" He broke off, and I realized with a shock what he'd been about to say: "You made me lose the man I was following."

It was true. Mendy, easily visible earlier in his wine-colored beret, had disappeared. I'd had my eye on him, hoping he'd come out with us again for coffee, but he was gone. Had he slipped out to avoid the man who was following him?

And why would anyone follow him?

Roberta
TUES-FRI 11AM, 3:30PM, 8PM
"Smoke gets in your eyes" when Fred and Irene Dunne run a dress shop in Paris. Ginger's "hard to handle," but oh, so much fun to watch.

Funny Face
1:15PM, 6:15PM, 10:15PM
Yes, Fred's too old for her, but Audrey Hepburn makes us believe. The real gem is the elegantly butch Kay Thompson and the Gershwin score.

Scotty, present

WHAT WAS IT about musicals that grabbed me so in those days?

The boys—well, the boys loved the fashions, the campy lines, the red lipstick, even though neither was a cross-dresser. They loved the romance, too, and so did I in spite of myself. I might identify more with Fred the wooer than with Ginger the wooed, but still, the act of wooing, of loving so completely at first dance, had me in its thrall. I was, after all, a child of the fifties, of Loretta Young and her swirling skirt.

I'd always pictured my ideal lover wearing that skirt, a

little Kim Novak evening sweater over her creamy shoulders, hair piled into an elegant French twist.

Instead, I had Birch, whose knees had barely healed from childhood skinnings, whose frayed bell-bottoms picked up the dirt of Manhattan streets, whose sad eyes reminded me that she'd lost everything dear to her when she came out: home and father, friends and family, everything she'd ever known. It was up to me to fill all her empty places, to show her a new life beyond the village of Woodstock, to buy her egg creams at Gem Spa and introduce her to Twyla Tharp's dance company.

There were times I wondered if I'd taken on too much.

Birch, 1972

BIRCH HAD MISSED Mendy at Ratner's the time before. With Stanley along, Patrick and Scotty had really done a number, remembering old movies Birch had never heard of, talking about favorite scenes, quoting lines, arguing about which studios had the best stock companies. Birch had gazed out the window into the crisp fall night, watching people walk past Kamenstein's hardware store across the street, wondering what the hell she was doing here with these people.

She didn't belong with Scotty and never would. She was only staying with her because she had no place else to go, nobody else to turn to. Scotty didn't love her and never would. She was only being nice to a waif from the country.

The mood passed as soon as they left the dairy restaurant; Scotty took her hand as they walked home along Bleecker Street, past the welfare hotels and jazz joints, and Birch felt okay again.

But still, she was pleased to see that tonight Mendy was

in his accustomed seat in the fourth row right, two rows down from where she and Scotty sat.

Scotty, present

THE SONG I love from *Roberta* is "Yesterdays." It's a wonderful Jerome Kern ballad, filled with a very Russian sense of longing for the past, and it's sung by Irene Dunne just as her mentor, played by Helen Westleigh, lies on a couch dying one of those picturesque Hollywood movie deaths.

And perhaps Mendy died while that number played on the screen. I don't know. All I do know is that when the curtain closed and Birch and I went over to him, he was no longer alive.

I'd shaken his shoulder after saying his name brought no response. He was slumped as if in sleep, but too still, too eerily silent, for death's younger brother.

"He must have had a heart attack," Patrick said, no trace of campy playfulness in his reedy voice.

We hung around the corridor, oddly reluctant to leave, yet having no real reason to be there. Sure, we'd known Mendy, shared food and stories of Hollywood, but we weren't really friends. Still, leaving wasn't an option any of us considered, at least not out loud.

The police arrived after the ambulance. I waited to be questioned, wondering whether I should tell them about the mystery man who'd followed Mendy.

But what did it matter who was following him if Mendy died of a heart attack?

The words "bitter almonds" caught my ear, reminding me of English murder mysteries set in enormous country houses. What did bitter almonds smell like, anyway, and how were they different from ordinary almonds? For a wild second, I wanted to ask the nearest cop if I could go in and sniff Mendy's breath so I'd know for good and all.

I restrained myself. This wasn't a Dame Agatha story; it was the real death of a real man I'd known and liked.

Correction: it was the real *murder* of a man I'd known and liked.

Because Mendy wasn't a suicide. This I knew. He'd been wholly alive, not a thought of death in his head. He'd reveled in the discovery that there were people like us out there, people who wanted to hear his stories and relive his Hollywood glory days. People to whom the blacklist was an outrage and he a hero for enduring it.

Next question: How did you get cyanide—because that was the poison that smelled like bitter almonds—into someone's coffee? Had Mendy put his cup down somewhere, just long enough for the killer to slip in the poison? Was it liquid or solid? Mrs. Christie's *Sparkling Cyanide* made it sound liquid, which would be easier to administer—but wouldn't it make the coffee taste bad?

The biggest question of all was *why*. Why was someone following Mendy? Why would anyone want him dead?

I went over to one of the cops and told him what I'd seen. The response I got was less than satisfactory.

How did I know it was Mendy he was following? How did I know he was following anybody at all? Couldn't he have just been annoyed that Patrick bumped into him?

It wasn't just that the police weren't listening, I realized after a few minutes. They weren't listening because of who we were. One cop kept looking at Patrick as if viewing a giant cockroach, and his partner asked me several times just how old Birch was. I had a sudden realization that in the eyes of the law, I was taking advantage of a minor.

I wound up the conversation quickly, leaving the theater dejected because of Mendy's passing, but also frustrated that the police were going to call it suicide.

But what could I do about it?

Birch, 1972

GOING TO RATNER's was like holding a wake for Mendy. At least, that was how Birch Tate saw it. They were eating Jewish food and talking about the old man and how much they'd liked him and how his death wasn't suicide, and that was as close to a memorial as they were ever going to get.

Scotty and Patrick were deep in discussion about how somebody could have slipped poison into Mendy's coffee when the guy at the counter took out a little pillbox and popped a tiny white pill into his coffee and then stirred. Funny way to take a pill, Birch thought and then realized: saccharin. People put saccharin in coffee when they wanted to lose weight or if they were diabetics or—

"That's it," she said, so loudly that even the man at the counter turned around. "Because you would," she added, turning to Scotty.

"Would what?"

"Take a saccharin tablet if somebody offered it to you. Just like you'd take a joint. You wouldn't say, no thanks, and take out your own because that would be rude. Mendy was a diabetic, remember?" Now Birch had Scotty's attention, and Patrick's too. "He put saccharin in his coffee the night we talked to him."

"That is sheer brilliance," Patrick said, and Birch blushed.

"That means the killer was in the theater," Scotty pointed out. "Mendy always had espresso from the coffee bar."

"Yeah, somebody walked up to him, opened his little pillbox first and offered him one and he said, sure, thanks, and didn't think twice."

"Which means one more thing," Patrick said, his blue eyes alight. "The killer was somebody Mendy trusted. Or, no, maybe not trusted exactly, but not somebody he didn't trust. Does that make sense?"

"I think so, Watson," Scotty replied thoughtfully, her chin resting on steepled fingers.

"Why do I have to be Watson?" Patrick said, polishing off the last of his potato pierogies with onions. "What makes you think I'm not Holmes?"

"What makes you think *I'm* not Holmes?" Birch cut in, surprising herself at her own boldness. "I thought of the saccharin thing."

"If you're Holmes, then explain what Patrick just said."

"It's like the dog in the night-time," Birch began.

"My God, you're a Sherlockian!" Scotty reached over and took Birch's powdered-sugary hand, lifted it to her lips and kissed it.

"If you mean, have I read the Canon, then I guess I am," Birch replied, deliberately (and for the first time) using the term she'd read in *Ellery Queen's Mystery Magazine*.

"It's love, folks," Patrick said with a wide smile. "Birch, honey, Scotty here has been looking for you all her life. A girl who gets Sherlock. When's the wedding?"

The warm feeling coursing through Birch like heated maple syrup wasn't a bit dimmed by the dirty looks she received from two old ladies at the next table. Who cared what anybody thought about her and Scotty being together? Who cared whether or not some guy named Gershwin was writing songs of love for two girls—what mattered was the love itself. And this, thanks to Sherlock Holmes, she had.

"Right now, I think I'd rather come up with Mendy's killer," Scotty said, releasing Birch's hand. "And I suspect we've all hit the same mental obstacle. If the killer is someone from Mendy's blacklist days out to avenge an old wrong, why would Mendy take a saccharin tablet from him?"

"Exactly." Birch leaned back in the booth with a satisfied expression on her face. "Just like the dog not barking. If

Mendy didn't recognize the guy who gave him the poison, it couldn't have been an old enemy."

"Unless Mendy didn't realize the guy was an enemy." Patrick's voice was thoughtful and he gazed into the distance. "There were people who testified in executive session, secretly naming names and never getting the rap as informers. Poor Larry Parks, the guy married to Betty Garrett, had to do that."

"But Mendy didn't name names," Birch objected. "He was a victim of the blacklist, so why would someone want to kill him?"

"You're supposing he told us the truth," Scotty said. She reached for a cigarette and Birch wrinkled her nose. Smoking was one of the few things about Scotty she genuinely disliked.

"What if he lied to us?" Scotty blew smoke into the air and waved out her match. "What if he did name names and somebody he named killed him out of revenge?"

"We're back to the old problem," Patrick said, irritation wrinkling his smooth forehead. "If Mendy ruined some guy's life by giving him up to the Committee, why would he accept a pill from the guy?"

"Who expects somebody to poison you, for God's sake?" Birch wasn't sure why she'd decided to become devil's advocate. "Maybe Mendy recognized the guy but thought bygones were bygones."

"Not those people, honey." Patrick shook his head and his long blond hair fell into his eyes. "Elia Kazan, to name just one, will never be forgiven for naming names. People who lived through the blacklist have long memories and there are no buried hatchets that I know about."

"What if Mendy didn't recognize the guy? It was a long time ago, and frankly, one old guy kind of looks like the next to me."

"Wow." Patrick gave a long low whistle. "Imagine. Ruining somebody's life and then adding insult to injury by forgetting you'd ever done it. Heavy."

"Heavy indeed," said another, deeper, voice.

It was the man Scotty said had followed Mendy out of the theatre. Birch might never have recognized him out of context, but in Ratner's, while they were talking of Mendy, he was in context.

"Sit," Scotty said, moving over in the booth. "Sit and explain."

"You can't think he's going to confess?"

Patrick looked at the old man and his blue eyes widened. "Are you who I think you are?"

"Paul Dixon. The former Paul Dixon. The present Paul Damrosch, not that it matters. I can't keep a job under any name."

"You blame Mendy for that?"

"He wrote the letter." The little old man's breathy voice held a world of sadness. "My best friend, and he goes into executive testimony, talks just to the committee, no publicity, names names, and my name leads all the rest. Then he plants that phony story with Pegler, calls me a faggot. Makes sure I'll never work again. To this day, to this goddamn *day* I got FBI guys following me around."

"How do you know it was Mendy?" Scotty's voice held a note of pleading. "Couldn't it have been somebody else?"

"You ever hear of the Freedom of Information Act?" Dixon looked around the group. Patrick nodded and Scotty started to speak, then closed her mouth.

"I got my files. I looked close, and even though they put black ink over all the names, I thought about where I was when, who I was with. Who took me to those so-called Communist meetings. I took out my old diaries I used to keep when I first got to Hollywood. Kept them so I could write home to my mother, tell her all the glamorous people I was meeting."

"And you figured out that Mendy ratted on you," Scotty said. A long blue cloud of smoke emanated from her lips; she crushed the butt into an ashtray. "He destroyed your career—but is that a good enough reason to kill somebody?"

"My wife couldn't stand it. She was high-strung when we married, I knew that. But when we sold the house in the hills and moved to Compton, when I couldn't even hold a job in a bakery, when she started seeing guys in black cars everywhere she went, she lost control. One night she took too many pills and died in her sleep and I will never, so long as the sun sets in the West, forgive Mendelson for that. He killed her with his big mouth."

"If you were married, how could anybody believe you were gay?" Birch thought it was a good question, but Patrick rolled his eyes and Dixon gave a short, mirthless laugh.

"Kid," the old man replied, "Rock Hudson was married. Every faggot in Hollywood—" he gave a brief, apologetic nod in Patrick's direction—" pardon my French, makes damn sure to get married."

When Birch blurted, "Rock Hudson is gay?" Patrick almost fell out of the booth laughing.

Scotty brought them back to the matter at hand. "Maybe he was just trying to save himself. Maybe he named you thinking the Committee already had your name."

"That doesn't excuse the call to Pegler," the old man replied. "Mendy was jealous—he wanted the breaks I was getting and he thought if I was out of the way, he'd be cast in the roles I was up for. Happiest day of my life was when Gene Kelly said yes to *Summer Stock,* because that meant Mendy was screwed."

"We figured out that you offered Mendy a saccharin tablet and he took it," Patrick said. "Do you mean to tell us he didn't recognize you?"

A slow, sweet smile crossed the wizened face. "Oh, he recognized me, all right. That's why I'm not afraid you'll tell the cops what I'm telling you. He recognized me and he knew he had two choices: take the pill and go quietly or let me tell my story. One thing about the old ham: he really liked putting on that 'I was a victim of the blacklist' crap, and he didn't want anybody knowing him for the rat he was. I expected him to take the poison, the dirty coward. At least now I can go tell my Stella the bastard is dead."

"Your wife?"

"Yeah. She's buried out in Woodlawn; I brought her home to be with her family. So I'll take her a bouquet to-morrow and tell her that Mendy's gone and she'll maybe forgive me for going to those stupid meetings and screwing up my life."

Scotty, present

THE COPS HAD Mendy's death down as a suicide, and now it looked as if it really might have been one. There was nothing for us to do but drift home and make a date to see an-other double feature next week.

The newspapers reported the death of Paul Dixon, black-listed "onetime movie hopeful," about four months later. I figured he'd already been diagnosed with the emphysema that killed him; one more reason he wasn't afraid of jail.

There's a strange undercurrent of sadness in movie musi-cals. Judy's addictions, Mickey's pathetic eagerness to please, the frenetic tone of thirties musicals, the ones that packed as many chorus girls onto the screen as possible, per-haps just to keep them eating during the Depression. And what the blacklist did to a couple of young hoofers.

I once went to a church basement with an old friend and her deaf sister to see a silent movie. Before the film, a man made a speech in sign language, which Beth kindly interpreted for me, saying that the great days of silent film were still alive in the church basements and libraries where, as he put it, "The lights are turned down, the projector is turned on, and the deaf watch."

It was a strangely moving experience, seeing Lillian Gish and John Gilbert with people who saw their movies as whole, not soundless. I think of that when I recall the days and nights we spent at Theatre 80. The movie musicals were made for Main Street, for families and "kids of all ages." Old people and gay people bought the tickets at Theatre 80. We were an audience not planned for, but perhaps especially sweet because unexpected. We kept the musical alive in those lean years between *Brigadoon* and *Saturday Night Fever*—not that even Patrick, with his huge crush on Travolta, ever accepted *Fever* as a true musical.

Patrick died a year ago today. He was our cruise director, our emcee, our encyclopedia of all things Hollywood. Gay Hollywood was his specialty, and like so many of us, he took great pleasure in claiming the brightest, most incandescent stars for "our side." As if straight America would come to tolerate us if they learned that some of their favorite stars were "that way."

Oh, Patrick, I do miss you!

My life back then had more Patrick in it than I knew. I breathed him like air, and it never occurred to me that one day he would cease to exist, like the musical itself.

No, not AIDS; he hated clichés, except when they were lines from old movies. Plain, ordinary, vanilla cancer, the kind straight people get, too. And, yes, I brought a VCR to the hospital so he could watch all the musicals his heart desired and I think, I hope, *Footlight Parade* was the last one he saw.

So tonight Birch and I will gather together all the people

who loved him. We'll make buttered popcorn, toast him with champagne, and celebrate the life of a man who was completely and totally big time in his heart.

And perhaps we'll raise one of those glasses to the late, never-great Paul Dixon.

Money on the Red

EDWARD D. HOCH

"SO YOU'RE A performance artist?" the Las Vegas reporter asked. Wanda figured he was about twenty-one, probably on his first assignment covering the more bizarre aspects of Vegas nightlife.

"That's what I am, Sonny," she said, taking her costume out of the closet.

"Name is Rick Dodson," he said softly.

"Yeah, Rick. You're a handsome young man. This is for the *Vegas Weekly?*"

"That's right."

She peeled off her blouse and jeans. He wasn't the first man to see her in her underwear. "I have to dress while we talk. Hope you don't mind."

He moistened his lips but kept a firm grip on his pencil. "No. Go ahead."

"What was it you wanted to know?"

"Is Wanda Cirrus your real name?"

"It is now." She held the costume up to the light, inspecting it for stains.

"Are you married?"

"Not now. Not for years."

"As a performance artist, do you feel you're closer to the artistic world or to show business?"

"When I'm performing in a museum it's art, when I'm in an Off-Broadway theater it's show business. What more can I say."

"What is it here in Vegas?"

She slipped into the snug red and black cat suit, zipping it up the front, and pulled up the hood to cover her hair. Then she slipped her feet into the shiny black boots and picked up the black gloves and blindfold for later. She pressed the button to arm the apartment's security system and replied, "I don't know. Why don't you come along tonight and decide for yourself?"

COVERING HER COSTUME with a long cape, she talked about performance art as she led him downstairs. "It only dates back to the 1970s, really. It was an outgrowth of the so-called happenings during the sixties, when I was still a child. These usually were collaborative efforts involving a company of performers in a non-structured theater piece. Members of the audience were invited to take part, and there was often a good deal of nudity involved. In the mid-seventies some individuals or smaller groups began to appear on stage. A few became quite well-known in places like New York and San Francisco. I remember a woman who daubed herself with paint and rolled around nude on a canvas. She even sold some of the resulting paintings. I believe there's a man in New York today who sits on a ladder eating the Wall Street Journal. He's also been known to crawl through the Bowery wearing a business suit. There's usually an implied message of some sort in performance art."

"What is the message in your piece?"

She gave a little shrug. "Chance. One writer viewed me as a personification of Lady Luck."

At the car she suggested he follow along in his vehicle. "It's not far."

Ten minutes later Wanda pulled into the parking garage at one of the older hotels, just over the city line. Rick followed along as she led the way through the lobby to a private meeting room that had been converted for use as a bar and casino. A tall man with a mustache was waiting for her at the door. "Hello, Wanda. How are you feeling tonight? Black or red?"

She laughed, handing him her cape. "I haven't decided yet."

"Who's this?" he asked, indicating the reporter.

"Rick Dodson from the *Vegas Weekly*. Rick, meet Judd Franklyn. This is his operation."

The two men shook hands. "Doing a little story about us?"

"Well, about Miss Cirrus."

Franklyn slipped his arm around the young man's shoulders. "Sure, you can tell what she does. But call it a performance. Don't mention the betting aspect. I don't want the Gaming Commission after me."

"All right," Dodson agreed.

"Between ourselves, they know what goes on, but we can't be too blatant about it. We don't run ads. We depend on word-of-mouth."

"I understand."

Judd Franklyn looked Wanda up and down. "You're in great shape, girl. Go out and do your stuff."

"Nobody's called me a girl in twenty years." She slipped on the black gloves and followed him to the platform, still carrying the blindfold. The hood was in place over her hair and neck. The clinging cat suit was basic black, but with red lightning bolts that gave her the appearance of some sort of comic book superhero. Miss Roulette, perhaps.

The platform indeed was a huge roulette wheel, its diameter almost equal to a boxing ring. Close to a hundred players were crowded around it. Wanda stepped over the numbered slots to a small turntable at the center of the wheel. "Ladies and gentlemen," Judd Franklyn announced, "it is my honor to present the famed performance artist Miss Wanda Cirrus as the human roulette ball. She will blindfold herself, and while the wheel spins clockwise her little turntable will move in the opposite direction. She will roll off the turntable and reach her hands into one of the numbered slots. You have one minute to place your bets."

Wanda smiled at them and pulled the padded blindfold over her eyes. Then she crouched down, linking her hands around her knees, and waited. Almost at once the turntable began to move. She knew the wheel itself would be spinning, too. After several seconds, when she started to grow dizzy, she pitched forward off the turntable. As she hit the padded wheel itself her two hands shot out blindly, clasped together, and found one of the numbered slots.

"Twenty-nine black!" Judd Franklyn called out.

As the wheel slowed its spin Wanda pulled the blindfold from her eyes. "It is fate," she told them with a graceful bow. "I'll be back in fifteen minutes."

Dodson was waiting for her in awed amazement. "How often do you perform?"

She gave him a smile as she pulled back the hood from her head. "Every fifteen minutes from nine till midnight, Monday, Wednesday, and Friday nights. The wheel action doesn't stop, of course. When I'm not on they use a white volleyball."

"That's unbelievable! Is this the wildest thing you ever did?"

Wanda shrugged. "Once at a performance art festival in Boston I stayed curled up in a birdcage the entire day. And I crawled naked down a tube filled with glop. It was supposed to depict my birth. When I turned forty I decided it was time I kept my clothes on." Remembering when she changed into her costume, she amended, "At least some of them." She wondered why she was telling him these things that she'd never told anyone else.

"Is this sort of work profitable?"

Wanda shrugged. "I make a living. Off-Broadway I get a percentage of the gross. They work it a bit differently here, but it still depends on the business my performance brings in."

He watched her for the next hour, every fifteen minutes, as she rolled in a ball off the revolving turntable and stretched out her hands to blindly find one of the slots. Seven red, one red, twenty-two black, eighteen red.

"Thanks for your help," he told her as he left.

"I'll watch for your article. If you need anything else, give me a call."

The rest of the night was routine. Thirty red, double zero, two black, seventeen black, another seven red, thirty-six red, eleven black, twenty-one red. Thirteen performances in all, nine to midnight. Five black, seven red, and the double-zero. Seven odd, five even. Only one repeat. She liked to keep track of the numbers and colors, seeking a pattern that didn't exist. The big betting always came at midnight, her final performance, when Franklyn raised the limit from five hundred to five thousand.

She performed again on Friday night, and this time after her ten o'clock appearance one of the bettors who was having a good night wanted to buy her a drink. "No thanks," she told him. "I get dizzy enough doing this routine thirteen times a night."

"How about after you knock off at midnight?"

She looked him over more closely. He was probably in his early forties, about her age, "Do I know you from somewhere?"

"Sam Dole. I'm here often. You maybe noticed me in the crowd."

"Maybe," she agreed, wondering what he wanted. Maybe he just liked the way the black and red cat suit fitted her body.

"So how about that drink?"

"Why not? It's Friday."

"I'll meet you in the parking garage right after midnight."

"What's wrong with the bar here?" she asked.

"They probably don't like you drinking with the customers."

She thought about that and decided Judd Franklyn might find cause for complaint. "OK, the parking garage it is."

The next number she hit was a zero.

BY TEN AFTER twelve she was out of the hotel, walking toward her car in the garage. Her hood was down and her costume covered by the cloak. She wasn't looking for Sam Dole but she knew he'd be around.

"Wanda?" a voice spoke her name, quite close.

"Hi, Sam. I thought maybe you found something better to do."

"Not a chance. Want to go in my car or follow me?"

"Where to?"

"I know a little bar outside of town."

"I'll follow."

He avoided the Strip, where the midnight traffic made it seem like high noon, and headed instead out the route 15 expressway to Enterprise, just south of the airport. The bar he chose was called the Landing Strip, a small place by Vegas standards with only a dozen slot machines along one wall. At this hour there were just a few customers at the bar and the tables were empty. Wanda had never been there before.

When the bartender brought their drinks Sam Dole came right to the point. "How'd you like to make some money?"

Wanda smiled at him. "I couldn't tell you how many times I've heard those words in my life. Look, Sam, I'm no call girl. If you're looking for one, you're in the right town but I'm not one of them. I'm a performance artist, period."

He reached across the table to touch her hand. "I'm not talking about sex. Just listen to me, will you?"

Glancing around to make sure they were out of the bartender's line of vision, he took something from his pocket. "Put this on."

It was a blindfold with an elastic band that went around the back of the head, just like the one she wore in her performance. "What's this all about?" she asked, but slipped on the blindfold as he requested. She realized at once that part of the inner padding had been cut away, leaving only a black gauze covering over her eyes. From the front she appeared blindfolded, but in actuality she could see quite clearly through the gauze. She took it off almost at once. "If you think I'm going to spot certain numbers for you, you're crazy. It wouldn't even work. When I land on that padding and stretch out my hands to a winning slot, there are only a few within reach."

"Not a certain number, just a certain color. The colors alternate from black to red around the wheel, except for the zero and double zero spots. So no matter where you land and reach out your hands, you're never more than one—or two at most—away from a red number. With this blindfold you could pick red every time, or black."

Wanda snorted. "And end up buried out in the desert somewhere. Judd Franklyn is no dope, you know."

"I'm not talking about winning fifty grand a night or anything like that. Franklyn has a five hundred dollar limit anyway, except for your midnight appearance. But if you picked blacks or reds in a pre-arranged rotation for your thirteen spins, at even money that would mean winnings of six thousand for the first twelve and five thousand for the last spin. That's eleven thousand for the night. We'd give you three thousand a night, nine thousand a week."

"Who's we?"

"I can't win it all myself. I'd need a partner making some of the bets. If it works out we can keep at it."

"In Vegas that's small change."

"It adds up."

Wanda shook her head. "Not me. Get someone else."

"Someone else? There is no one else. It's your act!"

"Look, Sam, I don't know you. I never saw you before tonight. Why should I trust you and go along with this harebrained scheme?"

"Think of it as another performance. It would even top what you're doing now."

"No."

"Here's my phone number. At least think about it over the weekend and give me a call."

FOR SOME REASON she kept the card and did think about it. On Saturday night she went to see the Blue Man Group at one of the casinos on the strip. They were the best known of the performance artists and sometimes she envied them for their success. Maybe she needed some partners. Thinking about Sam Dole, she finally decided that what he'd said about another performance was right. It was still her creation, whether or not she could see through the blindfold. "Just one night," she told him over the phone. "This Wednesday. I'm nervous about it."

"Beats spending the day in a birdcage."

"But it's a lot riskier if Franklyn finds out. Make sure he doesn't."

"Don't worry. We'd better not talk or see each other again until afterward. This is what I want you to do. Just colors, because they're easier than numbers to see accurately through the blindfold. Forget the zero and double zero because you may not land near enough to them. Pick the colored slots in this order for your thirteen appearances. You'd better write them down. Red, red, black, black, red, black, red, black, black, red, black, black, red. That's seven black, six red. Got it?"

"Yes."

"I won't see you Wednesday night. Thursday night I'll be in my car behind the Landing Strip at midnight to give you your cut and talk about the next show."

"I don't work Thursday," she reminded him. "We can make it earlier if you want."

"No, midnight's best for me. I'll see you then."

Wanda hung up, wondering what she was getting herself into.

ON WEDNESDAY JUDD Franklyn greeted her at the door as he always did. "Good to see you, Wanda. Feeling lucky tonight?"

He'd never asked her that before. "What good does it do me to feel lucky? I don't bet."

When she mounted the turntable at the center of the wheel at nine o'clock, she glanced casually around at the faces in the crowd. At first she didn't see Sam Dole, but after she donned the doctored blindfold she spotted him with a short young woman who was making a bet. Then she crouched down as the turntable started to spin. She rolled off the padded wheel and stretched out her joined hands. Just ahead of her was eighteen red. She didn't even have to cheat.

There were the usual cheers and groans from the players, and then applause as she took her bow and promised to return in fifteen minutes. She didn't see Dole, but she assumed he or his friend had collected their winnings. The evening went along routinely after that. Once around eleven o'clock, between performances, she went to the bar for some tonic water and found herself standing next to the young woman who'd been with Dole.

"Having any luck?" she asked casually.

"Off and on," the young woman replied. "You do this for a living?"

"I've had some Off-Broadway gigs and I was at the Brooklyn Museum last year. Performance art is hard to define sometimes. This is my first experience as a human roulette ball. I suggested it to Judd and he bought it." She drank a bit of the tonic water. "What's your name?"

"Minnie Brewer. And no jokes about a short beer. I've heard them all."

Wanda chuckled. "Do you come here a lot?"

"This is my first time. I heard about your performance and I had to see it for myself."

"Well, I'm on again in a few minutes. Good luck with your betting."

This time she had to slide a few inches to hit the proper color, but it was hardly noticeable. By midnight when it was time for the five thousand dollar limit, she didn't see Minnie at all. But Dole was in the front row of bettors, looking pleasantly surprised when thirty-six red came up. It had been a good night for them both.

On the way out she saw the reporter, Rick Dodson, lingering at the bar. "When's the story running?" she called over to him.

"Soon as I can get a good angle," he told her. "My editor was hoping for something a bit sexier."

"I'll perform nude next week if it'll help," she said and kept on walking.

She slept late on Thursday morning and woke up remembering she had to meet Dole that night. For a few minutes she considered forgetting about the whole thing, letting him keep all the money. But she'd earned her part of it, why not collect? Driving out to the Landing Strip a little before midnight she decided she'd take the money this one time and give him back the blindfold. She'd experienced the rush of it and needed no more.

Dole's car was parked near the back of the lot and she could see him seated behind the wheel. She opened the passenger door and slid in beside him. "It went smoothly, but that was the last time. Pay me off and I'll say goodbye."

When Dole didn't answer she thought he had dozed off waiting for her. She gave him a jab to wake him up and that was when she felt the knife in his side, buried up to the hilt.

WANDA LEFT THE car quickly, pausing only to wipe her fingerprints from the door handle. If Judd had found out about the scheme, she could be next. She could be in big trouble. She drove to her apartment and went quickly inside, remembering to enter the code and disarm the security system.

They found his body about an hour later, and it was a story on the morning news even before they'd announced his identity. Wanda spent most of Friday debating whether she should show up for her performance that night or hop the next plane back to New York. She wanted to get out of town fast and forget the whole thing, but fleeing might appear to be the action of a guilty person. And Judd paid her for the week on Fridays, when he could calculate the handle for the three nights she worked. She hated to leave without her week's pay.

So she showed up as usual on Friday at quarter to nine. For once Judd wasn't at the door to greet her, and the bartender pointed toward his office. "The cops are questioning him about that killing."

"What killing is that?" Wanda asked innocently.

"Fellow named Sam Dole, a small-time operator from back east. He tried to shake down some Atlantic City casinos and they think he was trying something out here that got him killed."

Wanda shrugged. "You never know." She hung up her coat and pulled the hood over her hair, then climbed up to the turntable with the real blindfold. In total darkness once more, she had no idea what number she hit until the croupier called out, "Nineteen red." Double zero came up the next time and it wasn't until nearly ten o'clock that Judd Franklyn reappeared with the two detectives.

One of them watched Wanda go through her performance and as she left the wheel he stopped her and asked to examine the blindfold. "Sure," she said and handed it over.

"Fine," he said after holding it to the light and poking at the padding. "Just checking."

Judd Franklyn came over to her as the two detectives left. "Some punk got himself killed last night so they're checking with the casino owners. One of my chips was in his pocket and they came here. No cash on him. It was probably just a robbery."

"Did you know him?"

"Not by name. They showed me his picture and I think he was here a few times. Hell, am I supposed to remember every face I see?"

She performed the rest of her appearances until midnight, then received her week's check from Judd. "Maybe I'll take off next week," she said, testing the waters.

"Take off? You can't do that. We got a contract!"

"Do you really need me?"

"Damn right I do! I got customers only come here on your nights."

"We'll see how I feel on Monday."

She walked out to the bar and was surprised to see Minnie Brewer at the wheel, placing a bet on the spin of the white volleyball. "I didn't get here in time to see you tonight," she told Wanda. "I was over at the Sands."

"You didn't miss a thing." She asked the bartender for a tonic. "Sorry to hear about your friend."

Minnie gave her a puzzled look. "Which friend is that?"

"Sam Dole, the man who was killed. I saw you talking to him one night."

"You make friends fast around a roulette wheel, especially this one. Watching you is like, I don't know, watching an Olympic gymnast."

Wanda laughed, deciding it was meant as a compliment. "Well, thanks."

"Anyway, I didn't know that Dole person you mentioned. If I was talking to him it was just idle conversation."

Wanda nodded. "Can I buy you a drink?"

"Thanks but I just finished one. Got to concentrate on the numbers." She put some chips on Even and was rewarded when six black came up.

Wanda got her cape and went out to the car. The traffic always seemed heavier on Friday nights and it was close to one o'clock before she turned into the apartment parking lot. Someone was waiting in the shadows near her door and she grew apprehensive until she recognized young Rick Dodson.

"When's the article going to appear?" she asked, repeating her usual question.

"Sunday, I think. Can I come in?"

"It's pretty late for socializing."

"I've got another question for you."

"All right. Come on in." She unlocked the door and turned on the lights, tossing her keys and purse on the table. "Do you want a drink?"

"No, no thanks."

She settled down on the couch opposite him. "Now what's your question?"

He took something from his pocket and showed it to her. It was a blindfold, a mate of the one she'd worn for Sam Dole. "Do you want to keep on, working with me instead of Sam?"

Wanda took a deep breath. "You killed him, didn't you? You were never a reporter writing a story. You were getting information on me for Sam, so he could decide if I'd be likely to go along with his scheme."

"Forget about Sam," he told her, waving away her words.

"Why did you kill him, Rick?"

"I'm the one who thought of the idea and he was cutting me out of my share. I was supposed to bet the final five thousand but he was on the other side of the wheel placing a bet, too. We won sixteen grand, not eleven, and he wouldn't give me the cut he'd promised."

"I should have known when I saw you there again the other night. You were Sam's betting partner. I thought it was a young woman he was talking to."

"Sam was always talking to young women. That was another problem between us. But never mind him. Are you in this with me?"

"No, not when there's been a murder. You're on your own."

He took the knife from his pocket and the blade sprang open. It could have been a mate to the one that killed Dole. "You don't understand. If you're not with me on this you're against me. I can't have you talking to the police."

"I already have, Rick. When I saw you waiting for me just now I suddenly knew you were Dole's partner. He mentioned once that this roulette wheel stunt was better than sitting in a bird cage all day. But you were the only one I'd told that to, and your article for the magazine hadn't yet appeared. He could only have heard about the bird cage from you."

He was shaking his head, playing with the knife. "You didn't talk to the police. You haven't gone near the phone."

"I didn't need to. I simply neglected to punch in the code to deactivate the security system. The police should be here right about now."

The knocking came right on cue, and a voice called out, "Police! Are you all right, Miss Cirrus?"

"No I'm not, officer," she said, hurrying to open the door before Rick Dodson could decide what to do. "I'll tell you about it."

DODSON WASN'T THE sort to keep secrets. He waived his rights and confessed to the murder as soon as they got him downtown. Wanda slept all day Saturday and part of Sunday, then got up and thought about the future. Instead of heading for the airport, she had her costume dry cleaned and went back to Judd Franklyn's wheel on Monday night. It may not have been art, but it sure was show business.

Razzle Dazzle

ANNETTE MEYERS

HE BEGAN EMPTYING the pockets of his suits methodically, collecting the scraps of paper, napkins, receipts, all of which he'd dropped, stored, left, forgotten but not, sometimes crumpled, one time or another in various pockets. He made several trips into the kitchen and only after studying each piece of paper did he put it in its proper place on the kitchen table. The order was important. It explained everything.

"No, it doesn't, David."

Miranda stood with her brutal back to him, staring out at the fog that made their rooftop seem adrift. From the river came the nasal honk of a foghorn.

"But it does, love. You'll see." He'd done what he had to do.

The kettle let out a shrill shriek, and he shut it down. He turned to Miranda. "I forgot to grind the beans." But Miranda was gone.

His glasses were stained. He took them off and held them under the faucet, rinsing. The water stained the porcelain a rusty color. He dried the glasses thoroughly and put them on again. He saw with such clarity now. It was amazing.

Back to sorting. Here was the note on the flap of Sardi's matchbook. *Twenty-five. Silver.* Where was his Mont Blanc? He went back to the bedroom. Miranda was in bed, pretending. He stood watching her.

He'd done the right thing. Planned it down to the last minute, waited till Patrick left for school. She'd given him no choice. He had to put a stop to it.

It was a while before David remembered why he'd come to the bedroom. His pen was in the inside pocket of the dark blue Hugo Boss. In the kitchen again, he crossed out "silver" and wrote "diamonds." Diamonds for Miranda.

MIRANDA. SHE WAS the most beautiful girl he'd ever seen. With his legal pad ready, David stood in the dark theater in front of the orchestra pit beside Bob Fosse as the girl dancers auditioned for *Chicago*. Chita Rivera and Gwen Verdon were already set for the leads, so this was chorus. But it was not news that Fosse was a control freak, right down to the last bit of costume, to the understudies in particular because Gwen was no kid. She'd be out a lot the way she was when she was in *Sweet Charity,* and that was nine years ago.

Bobby, Buddha-eyed, arms folded, watched as his assistant showed the first group of dancers the combinations, then stepped back and signaled to the accompanists and the dancers began.

She was a head taller than any of the others and another chorus dancer might have gotten lost in the back row. But not Miranda. She gave off a kind of glow. A blonde iridescence on long, elegant legs.

David looked over at Bobby. No reaction. Was he blind?

When the dancers finished, Bobby said, "Thank you." The dancers felt the rejection, took it personally. David could see the slump in the shoulders as they left the stage. But not Miranda. She edged out as the next group of dancers came on and took their places.

Bobby said, "That one."

"The tall blonde?"

"Yes."

So like Bobby, David thought, as he raced for the stairs to the wings. He liked to make them suffer a little before he gave them the good news.

She was on the street, her heavy bag hanging from her shoulder, when David caught up to her. "He wants you," he told her.

Her eyes were a deep gray-blue, confused now. Her brows pale as her hair. "Who?"

"Bobby. He wants you. I need your name, and your agent's name, address, and phone number." I need you, he thought.

"I don't have an agent," she said. "I haven't been here long enough." It was just starting to sink in. "He wants me?"

"Yes. Rehearsals start in four weeks. Are you available?"

She began laughing, a deep throaty laugh, which is when David fell for her big time.

"My name is Miranda Donnelly," she said.

She gave him her phone number. "Find an agent and get back to me," David said. "You should have an agent, although the dance contracts are usually minimum. I'll find you an agent. Leave it to me. You're going to be a star. You need someone who knows how to do it. And I'll help you."

She was waiting, looking at him expectantly. "I don't know who you are," she said.

He felt himself flush. "David Sharp," he said. "I'm the assistant stage manager."

She thrust out her hand and smiled at him. "Well, I'm pleased to meet you, David Sharp. Thank you for the good news."

DAVID SET THE matchbook cover down. Twenty-five years. He would shower her with diamonds. Yes. It would be really big. He'd take over Sardi's for the night. Let's see, who owed him? Half the world owed him, though they wouldn't admit it.

"I don't want diamonds," she said. "I just want it to be like it was."

"I do, too. And it will be, you'll see. I'll make it right."

"Oh, David, you always say that." She covered her mouth.

It had been wonderful then, when they were both beginning. Fosse, the brilliant Bob Fosse, had created a number just for her.

"He saw me as . . . what did he call me, David?"

"His perfect instrument."

The show was a big hit. And David became production stage manager, calling the cues. And after the show every night, Miranda was his. All his.

They were married the week before rehearsals began on Bobby's new all-dance musical *Dancin',* with Miranda as lead dancer. This was when David decided he had to break out, become a producer.

He had a connection—the father of his Rutgers roommate was president of the teamsters N.Y. local. The connection greased the way for David to get an apprenticeship in ATPAM, the Association of Theatrical Press Agents and Managers. His short term goal was to become a general manager. He would learn the business of producing this way, then do it himself. And he would do it better than anyone had done it before. There'd be no stopping him.

"You were so intense," Miranda said. "Sometimes it frightened me."

"You were getting what you wanted, why shouldn't I?"

David studied the scraps of paper in front of him on the table. It was something specific he remembered making a note of yesterday or the day before.

Their first apartment. It had been in this building. A small one bedroom, third floor rear, right next to the elevator. Dark as hell.

"Now look what we have," he said.

"A penthouse. Sixteen floors up. You wanted a penthouse."

"So did you. Who's the genius in this family? Who's the deal maker? Who gave you the best?"

"David . . ."

"Yes. David." He liked to hear her say it. She had that throaty voice. She was so beautiful and she was his. He reached for her now and she slipped away from him.

He went to the sink and splashed water on his face. He had to call the office. There were things to be done. He hit the direct dial button.

"David Sharp Productions," a strange voice said.

"Put Betty on." Betty Carbone. Not much of a looker, but a great gal. Loyal. When he began producing plays, he made her his general manager. She'd been with him for years. She was like family. He loved her like a buddy. He trusted her.

"Who is calling please?"

"The man who's fucking overpaying your salary," he yelled.

The girl was flustered. "Oh, oh, I'm sorry, Mr. Sharp."

Betty came on. "David?"

"Listen, Betty, there's something I have to do."

"Yes? Is everything okay?"

"We're working things out. And Betty?"

"Yes?"

"I love ya, pal." He hung up the phone.

Where was he? Oh, yes. He was sorting his papers. Ticket stubs. So many. They wouldn't mean anything to anyone else, but it made sense to him. It was their life together.

Miranda went on the road with *Dancin'* and he flew out to see her every weekend.

"I loved touring," she said. "We'd go dancing after the show. I met so many people. It was so much fun."

"I hated not seeing you every day. I hated that you were with them."

"Them, David? Who is them?" He caught the exasperation in her voice. Didn't she know he adored her?

"Anyone you were with when you were not with me."

He placed the stubs back in their place. All except one. *The Naked Truth*. His play. A review with sketches written by a dozen famous writers on erotic subjects, the performers either all or semi-nude. It had been done before, and it hadn't been successful. But that was because he wasn't involved. It needed someone with vision. He would do it better.

"And you did," Miranda said.

"Yes. And then I bought the theater, too. You have to own the real estate," he said, "otherwise, you're always paying the man."

"Where did the money come from, David?"

"What difference does it make? I have friends who believe in me."

"Why the hell not? You were laundering their money."

"I didn't hear any complaints from you. You have the best of everything. Clothes, the penthouse, everything you could ever want."

"Yes." She gave him a sad smile. "Like the hot tub."

"You loved the hot tub."

"With you sitting in it doing business, a phone on each ear, making your deals, raising money, negotiating with the unions. Oh, yes, I loved the hot tub."

"I was really something. Admit it." He made another grab for her, but she eluded him. "I never understood how you could let Bobby talk you into going back. You had everything."

"That was part of the problem. I felt as if I was just something valuable that belonged to you—"

"Oh, come on. I never heard anything so crazy."

"And I missed dancing." She raised a long elegant leg and rested the back of her heel on the table without dislodging the lines of scrap paper. "You never—"

"There wasn't any work for you."

"You never let me talk. You never let anyone—"

"Talk? Anyone who wants to talk can talk. I'm the one with something to say."

"You see what I mean? You finish my sentences. You do it to everyone. Bobby's offer to be his assistant choreographer was perfect timing."

"You wanted to get away from me."

"You chased me away. You chased our friends away. You compete with everyone, even to the point of where to buy the best focaccia."

"Your lousy friends couldn't handle how successful I was."

"They were our friends once."

"They were jealous."

"That's not true. You made them nervous. You talk non-stop right through everyone."

He took the coffee beans from the refrigerator and poured some into the grinder, then ground them to drown out her sound. She was gone when he finished, back to the bedroom, back to her barre. She was always walking away from him.

He poured the hot water through the grounds. "There's coffee," he called. She didn't answer. He could hear her singing as she worked. "Razzle Dazzle." She'd replaced Ann Reinking in the revival of *Chicago*. Bebe Neuwirth herself had called and asked Miranda to do it. And Miranda had been a sensation.

David had hated it. He put his hands over his ears. He didn't want to hear "Razzle Dazzle." It reminded him of Fosse and the old days before everything got so complicated, when you knew who your enemies were.

THEY'D JUST BEGUN to live together. She was sewing elastic across the instep of her new ballet shoes and the needle kept piercing her fingers.

He licked the blood from her punctured fingers. "You can buy them with the elastic already there," he said.

"It's not the same," she said. "It has to be perfect. That's why I do it myself."

He knew in that moment she was what he wanted. It was how he felt his life should be. But in the end she was not perfect.

"DAVID," SHE SAID. "What will you tell Patrick?"

"I'm working on it," he said. He began looking through the scraps on the table for a clean piece of paper. Patrick was fourteen, almost a man. The best part of Miranda and him.

The jagged corner of a receipt caught his eye. He knew what it was though no one else would. Dick Boodle & Associates. Boodle was a former cop who'd set up a detective agency. David had used his services for body guards and stage door security for *The Naked Truth* cast.

"You've been having me followed," Miranda said, an aura of sweet perspiration surrounding her. "Since the spring."

"I found out who he was. Advertising. A loser. You fucked me over for a loser."

"David—"

"After everything I did for you. How we live, the clothes on your back, and it's not enough for you."

"What you did for me? Having me followed for the last six months? I haven't seen him in—"

"You saw him yesterday." David knew all about it. She'd met him at the Mark Bar. He shook the memo at her. "It's here in black and white."

"I had a drink with him is all—"

This time it was David who walked away. He opened the door to the terrace and stepped out on the roof. The fog had lifted but the sky was gray and dense, and the temperature had dropped. Snow was in the air. At the edge of the terrace was a low brick wall that separated the terrace from thin air. Below was the closed courtyard, earth and stone now. In the spring, grass and daffodils.

He heard the phone ringing. He charged back into the apartment. He didn't want Miranda to get it. The answering machine picked up and the ringing stopped. He listened. She said he had a love affair with the phone. But it was like an extension of his personality. When the *Times* did the feature on him, they took his picture with a phone on each ear and another on his desk. God, he loved it. But lately, since he'd stopped going to the office, he'd just let it ring, or let the answering machine get it.

"Miranda?" It was Nora, the bitch, her sister. Always butting her nose in. "Are you there? Pick up. I'm worried about you."

He got hot, seething, began screaming at her, though she couldn't hear him. "We're working everything out, not that you care, you trouble-making bitch."

"You say that, David," Miranda said, "but we're not working anything out. It's too late for that." Her cheeks were pale, her eyes distant.

"I swear, Miranda, I'm turning over a new leaf."

"Yes. Like when you don't let me go to the dentist, and to even the supermarket by myself."

"I don't want anything to happen to you. Most wives would be thrilled to be taken care of like I take care of you."

Miranda sighed. "We've been married twenty-five—"

"Wonderful years—"

"Some wonderful years—"

"You turned everything we had into shit."

"I broke it off with him."

"You saw him yesterday, don't you remember?"

"I told you, for a drink. That's all."

"It's not all. It's never all." He went back to the terrace, slamming the door. Gratitude. No one had any anymore.

Miranda was ungrateful for anything he'd done for her. There'd been a scene in Philadelphia—what the hell was the name of the show? His brain was fuzzy. Anyway, they'd cut her number. He'd come down after a tearful phone call, but first he'd made his own calls. The number was put back in.

He couldn't lose her. She was his whole life, more important even than *The Naked Truth*. Why didn't she understand that? It was for her own good. Yes, he'd had her followed, yes, he'd had the phone tapped. How else would he know what was happening in his life? He'd done what any good husband would do.

One more call. Ruben Bronson. He'd trained Ruben from scratch. Ruben was production stage manager on *The Naked Truth*. When was the last time David had talked to him? Once more to the speed dial. "Listen, Ruben—"

"David, I was just going to call you. Can you come in tonight? We have a problem."

"I have some things I have to do."

"It's Jenny's replacement. You haven't been around. She's not working out—"

"You handle it."

"Okay, if that's what—"

"I love ya, kid." David hung up.

In the kitchen he scrawled the letter to Patrick on the phone bill. He had to write around the notes he'd made about the people Miranda called and the numbers he didn't recognize.

"Why have you stopped going to the office?" she said.

"I want to be with you."

"You're driving me crazy, David. You've got to give me some space."

"So you can sneak around and meet your friend, the loser?"

"I have other friends."

"Yes. Like Linda Marshall who warned you that I was dangerous."

"If you listen to my phone calls, you have yourself to blame. Linda is a therapist. She thinks you need help."

"She's just a dyke who wants you for herself."

Miranda stared at him, weeping. Her tears made red streaks on her cheeks. She was tormenting him. Why didn't she just stay where she was? He closed his eyes and made her go away.

The quiet became oppressive. He went into the bedroom. She was back in bed, where they would find her.

He returned to the kitchen and rinsed his hands, stacked the dishes and utensils in the dishwasher, all but the bread knife, which he dried carefully and put in the oak block on the counter.

The afternoon was waning.

"Please, David," she said, "Patrick will be home soon."

"We were working it out," he said. He was on the terrace again, walking around. He looked at the canvas-covered hot tub with its blanket of withered leaves and crusty pigeon droppings, the Adirondack chairs around the table. The empty mug someone had left under the table wore a moldy crust.

He took off his glasses and placed them on the table.

He looked at his Rolex. There was blood on the face. He raised it to his lips and licked the blood off. It was four o'clock. Patrick would be home soon.

He listened to the sound of the elevator, the key in the lock.

"Mom? Dad? I'm home."

For a brief moment David stood on the low brick wall that enclosed the terrace, then he stepped off.

Arful

JOHN LUTZ

"**ARE YOU TRYING** to tell me dogs can talk?"

Braddock had been in Hollywood three long years now. He hadn't been able to sell a screenplay, but he was sure he'd heard and seen just about everything, much of it right here in Savvie's bar, within spitting distance of Wilshire Boulevard. But here was something he hadn't expected, like an opening scene from an old *Twilight Zone* episode.

The old man sitting across the table from him smiled, wrinkling his seamed face even more and giving him the look of one of those dolls with heads and faces made from dried apples.

"No," he said, "not every dog. But some dogs sometimes, if a certain operation is performed on their palates and if they are properly trained." He took a swig of blended Scotch and twinkled an eye at Braddock. "I know how to train 'em."

Braddock was barely in his twenties, but he knew he was no fool. "Who trained *you?*" he asked.

Mitty—that was the old man's name—twisted his lips in an odd mobile line that changed his smile to a tight grin. He had small, even teeth that were yellowed and probably false. "Dr. Darius," he said, "the veterinarian surgeon who discovered and perfected the operation."

"Sure," Braddock said. "I think I met him once."

"Doubt it," Mitty said. "He's been dead for over fifty years. But before he died he taught me not only how to develop the facility of speech in certain dogs of a particular combination of breeds, but the operation that makes it possible."

It was dim in Savvie's. Outside the tinted windows only an occasional pedestrian trudged past in the ninety-degree heat. This time of the afternoon there were no other customers in Savvie's. Braddock, Mitty, and Edgar the part-time bartender had the place to themselves. Braddock considered what Mitty had told him. How naive did the old joker think he was?

"I suppose you're a rich man," Braddock said.

Mitty raised bushy gray eyebrows high on his deeply furrowed forehead. "I wouldn't be sitting here with you and Java sipping this cheap Scotch if I was rich, now, would I?"

"Java?"

Mitty nodded and glanced down and to the side, toward a dog that had been so still and quiet that Braddock hadn't noticed it. Java was a small black and white pooch sitting patiently on its haunches near his chair.

"I didn't see it there," Braddock said.

"Java's a *he,*" Mitty corrected.

"Sorry, fella," Braddock said to the dog. For only an instant, he half expected the dog to answer.

Java resembled one of those miniature collies, only his hair was shorter. And he did have a funny look around the mouth, as if he were sort of smiling. As if he knew something.

"Why didn't Java introduce himself?" Braddock asked.

"Introduce yourself, Java," Mitty told the dog.

At the mention of his name, Java woofed.

"That's talking?" Braddock asked.

"Not at all. You can't expect a dog to know the English

language without learning it. And I didn't give him the proper commands. What he is, he's shy, not much of a performer. That's why I said he wouldn't talk here and now. But he's getting better, more outgoing."

"Where have you performed?" Braddock asked, being careful to look at Mitty when he asked. "I mean, you and Java?"

"Nowhere yet. We're working up to it."

"Uh-huh." Braddock sipped his drink, a club soda with a lime twist. He never drank before evening, keeping his mind clear to write. He'd soon discovered that many of the powerful people in the film industry were blatant con men, not to be believed. If he'd been naive when he arrived in L.A., he was long over it. Now there were calluses on his cynicism.

Mitty leaned back and regarded him. Braddock regarded the old man right back. He had to be in his eighties, and he dressed like a racetrack tout in *Guys and Dolls,* tan checked sport coat, red shirt, redder bow tie. The tie had a sprinkling of tiny black polka dots and was perched in an oddly rapacious way at his Adam's apple like a brilliant exotic butterfly, carnivorous and going for the throat.

"As I recall from seeing you in here before," Mitty said, "your first name is James."

"Correct."

"Like James Braddock, heavyweight champion of the world."

"Never heard of him."

"He was long before your time. But shouldn't you still know yours is the same name as a heavyweight champion?"

Braddock almost pitied the old man for the question. "That kind of ancient knowledge is useless now. It's a new world. Linear logic is dying. If something comes up and I need that kind of information, I can always get it from the Internet."

Mitty shook his head with unexpected violence, as if trying

to jar loose the persistent butterfly tie clinging to his throat. "You have to be able to think, to synthesize, not just have a lot of facts at your disposal. Everything's connected to everything else."

"That's what I'm telling you," Braddock said. "The Internet."

"But the world didn't start when the Internet was invented. Or just as you were born."

"I think it pretty much did," Braddock said. "At least, when it comes to useful information."

Mitty appeared saddened by this statement. He looked down at Java. Java looked back. He still seemed faintly amused and, yes, rather shy. A strange thing in a dog.

A fat man in oversized Levi's and a tropical-print shirt waddled in from the heat and breathed in the air conditioning with a smile as he wiped a wrist across his perspiring forehead.

"Glad I could find somewhere to get a drink," he said. "Everyplace else is closed because of the election." He settled his bulk on a bar stool that seemed to bend beneath his weight, though that was probably an optical illusion. "How come you're not closed?"

Edgar, who was a huge man himself, in his sixties with the build and misshapen ears of a former pro wrestler, said, "'Cause last election day, we knew who to vote for. Fact is, though, we were about to close."

Mitty winked at Braddock and smoothly and slowly tugged on Java's leash until the little dog was out of sight on the other side of his chair. Then he raised a gnarled forefinger to his lips in a signal for Braddock to be silent.

"What's the big secret?" Braddock whispered across the table.

"Java," Mitty said. "Even if you don't believe me, he's a valuable piece of show business property. But I must trust you with him for a few minutes."

No one spoke, not even Edgar, busy behind the bar, as Mitty wrapped Java's leash around the table leg, using an elaborate kind of slip knot. He hand-signaled for the dog to sit and stay, then went shuffling off toward the men's room. Java didn't move or make a sound. Braddock had to admit the pooch was well trained.

The fat man finished his beer and made his way back out into the heat.

Edgar looked over at Braddock. "You ever hear of Mitty and Buddy?" he asked.

"No. And are you really getting ready to close?"

"Naw, I just said that to get rid of that guy. If he'd stayed around, he would have thought Mitty was nuts. I like Mitty. I don't wanna see that. And Mitty was bound to start bragging again about that dog. You can't shut him up for long."

"That's for sure," Braddock said. "But I don't know why he'd brag about the dog."

"Not *that* dog," Edgar said, "Buddy. Mitty and Buddy used to be one of the hottest lounge and resort acts in the country. But I'll tell you something: that dog there, Java, looks a lot like the photos I seen of Buddy."

"Come off it," Braddock said with a laugh. "You mean this Buddy was a talking dog?"

"I mean it," Edgar said, stone faced. "He even talked to some scientists the government sent when they heard about him."

"Funny I never read about that," Braddock said.

"Well, it's kinda like UFOs."

"How so?"

"The scientists didn't believe it even after they heard it. 'Cause they didn't want to believe it."

"But I've heard of UFOs."

"That's 'cause there are more of them than talking dogs."

"So why's Mitty telling me all about this stuff?" Braddock asked.

"Because he's dying."

Braddock sat back. "What?"

"He's got something bad wrong with him, some kinda rare blood disease nobody can do anything about. I think he wants to sell you the dog."

"Buddy?"

"Naw! Buddy's been dead more'n forty years. Java. Mitty knows a smart young guy can work up an act and make a fortune with Java. He likes you, thinks of you as a son. He told me that."

"I only met him a few months ago."

"He says that right away you reminded him of himself when he was young, full of ten kinds of malarky and burning to make some kinda smash in the business."

"Ten kinds of malarky?"

"I'm only repeating what—"

Edgar broke off what he was saying as Mitty emerged unsteadily from the men's room and returned to the table. There were wet spots on the front of his pants and his fly was slightly more than half zipped up, just far enough that Braddock decided not to bring it to his attention and embarrass him. As Mitty sat down, he drew from an inside pocket a folded, aged envelope.

"Look at these," he said, lovingly spreading the ancient contents of the envelope on the table so Braddock could examine them.

There were old playbills, press clippings, and grainy black-and-white photographs. Several of the photos were of posters extolling the virtues of Mitty and Buddy. On one of the posters they were headliners at some Catskills resort Braddock had never heard of. The only photo of Buddy was a grainy black-and-white of the dog with his leash wrapped around a post, much as Java's leash was wrapped around the table leg, with the same distinctive kind of slip knot. Buddy and Java did look a lot alike.

"You think I wasn't big in show business at one time?" Mitty asked. His complexion was sallow. He dug in a pocket and deftly swallowed a pill with a swig of Scotch, waiting for Braddock to answer.

"I believe that," Braddock said.

"But you don't believe about Buddy."

"I didn't say that . . . "

"And you don't believe Java here is trained to speak."

"Listen," Braddock said, feeling sorry for Mitty, "I've gotta be honest. I'm like all the rest of them out there. I don't believe dogs can talk."

"Not *dogs!*" Mitty said desperately. "*Certain* dogs. Maybe one in a hundred thousand. *If* they're trained."

"And have been operated on," Braddock reminded him.

"Only some of them. Now and then there's one that has the proper palate formation and doesn't require the operation. And to tell you the truth I never even tried the operation. I love dogs, can't cut on 'em like I was a trained surgeon. After Buddy died I gave up show business. Then, when Dr. Darius's widow died and the family let me look through his papers, I was overjoyed to learn there were rare dogs that didn't need the operation in order to learn a facsimile of human speech."

"Dogs like Java?"

"Like Java," Mitty said. "It took me years to find him."

"Maybe Buddy and Java just happen to be similar," Braddock said.

"Certain breeds . . . " Mitty said mystically.

Braddock looked again at the yellowed newspaper clippings and photographs on the table. "I've got to admit, you were impressive, you and Buddy."

"It could be Braddock and Java," Mitty said. "This is a way for you to beat this business, Jim! This is opportunity knocking, if only you'll believe it's out there!"

"Opportunity usually has a price," Braddock said, remembering this was L.A.

"It does this time, too," Mitty told him. "I'd never lie to you. Java is valuable and he's all I have to sell. I've gotta get six thousand dollars for him."

"Six *thousand?* I don't have that kind of—"

"Yes, you do! I heard you say you sold some foreign rights to a screenplay you wrote four years ago, when you were only nineteen."

"That's the only thing I ever sold," Braddock said. "And if it weren't for that money I'd have to get a j—j—"

"Job," Mitty said.

"I have difficulty even saying the word," Braddock told him, feeling a chill.

"So did I when I was your age. That's because our kind knows our calling, our business. Don't you understand? I'm offering you the way in! Chaplin with his tramp outfit and cane! Laurel with Hardy! The three tenors! Braddock and Java!"

"Why six thousand dollars?" Braddock asked.

"It's the cost of a fu—It's the exact price of something I need."

"But I've never even heard Java talk."

"But he *can!* I swear to it!"

"So show me. Make him perform."

"You can't make a shy dog do something like talk if he doesn't want to."

"Make him want to, if you want to make me want to buy him."

Mitty glanced at Edgar, who looked away and began polishing glasses with a gray towel.

Mitty turned his gaze on Java, who also looked away.

"I do not wish to appear the fool," Mitty said.

"That isn't my intention," Braddock said honestly.

Mitty sighed, then tugged on Java's leash and signaled with his hand for the dog to sit. Java settled back on his haunches, staring expectantly at Mitty with watery brown eyes. Spaniel eyes, Braddock suspected.

Mitty looked around. He didn't seem to want any more witnesses to this than was necessary.

"He can't pronounce just any words," he said to Braddock.

"Of course not." Braddock wished he hadn't started this. There'd been no reason to dare the old geezer, to humiliate him.

Mitty found a sheet of yellowed paper from the assortment on the table, unfolded it, then put on a pair of half-lens reading glasses and referred to it. Braddock saw that it contained a handwritten list of about twenty words.

"He can't say all of these yet," Mitty said, noticing Braddock staring at the list. "They're Buddy's old words. There'll never be another Buddy."

"Of course not," Braddock said, feeling smaller than Java. "Start with something easy."

"Awful," Mitty said.

"What?"

But Mitty was staring intently at Java, who still had his moist brown eyes fixed on the old man. *"Awful!"* Mitty suddenly shouted.

Java turned his head, looking away as if embarrassed.

"Awful!" Mitty shouted again, with a note of desperation.

"Arful!" barked Java.

Mitty, his face flushed in triumph, looked at Braddock. "You heard! You heard!"

Braddock was stunned, yet dubious. He remembered what Edgar the bartender had said about the government scientists. It was natural to be skeptical. "It might have been a bark. I mean, it started with the word *Arf*. But dogs say that all the time, even ones who can't talk."

"A *bark?*" Mitty was incredulous. "Not a bark! No! You said start with something easy!" He stared hard again at Java and shouted, "AWFUL!"

"*Arful!*" barked Java.

Mitty beamed. "Awful!"

"*Arful!*"

"Awful!" Mitty was consulting his list, not even looking at Java.

"*Arful! Arful!*"

"Tree!" shouted Mitty.

"*Tree!*" barked Java.

"Car!"

"*Car!*"

"House!"

"*House! House!*"

"My God!" said Braddock.

Edgar was leaning over the bar in shock. "I read about it, but I never seen it."

Mitty hugged Java, then collapsed back in his chair, breathing hard, exhausted but wearing his seamed smile. "I've got to be honest, that's as good as I've ever heard him."

"He talked!" Edgar was saying over and over. "He really talked!"

"He talked," Braddock admitted, not knowing what to think, how to feel.

"That's why we were big, Buddy and me. It's why you and Java can be big, Jim. Jim and Java. That's even better than Braddock and Java!"

Braddock's heart was hammering as he stared down at Java. "Awful!" he shouted at the dog.

"*Arful!*"

That did it. "Will you take a check?"

"From you, of course," Mitty said. "Just make it out to Mitford Chambers for seven thousand even."

"You said six thousand!"

"Did I? Make it five thousand then, Jim. I don't want you to feel bad about this day. Not ever."

THAT NIGHT BRADDOCK folded a soft blanket in a corner of his tiny apartment for Java to sleep on. But the next morning Java was in bed beside him. The dog had drooled on the pillow.

At breakfast, after Java had finished his dog food, Bradford swallowed a bite of egg and shouted, "Awful!"

Java barked back something that sounded like *Arful,* though it wasn't as clear as it had been yesterday at Savvie's.

"House!" shouted Braddock. "House!"

"Shut up!" shouted Maureen Waters, his unemployed neighbor in the adjacent apartment. She was an aging character actress prone to violence.

Braddock sighed, looked at the list of command words and instructions Mitty had given him, then made sure Java had plenty of water. As he left the apartment, he carefully locked the door behind him.

Savvie's wasn't like yesterday. There were half a dozen customers at the bar and tables even though it wasn't yet noon. Lou Savvie himself, a slender, jovial man who looked like the aged Frank Sinatra and knew it, was tending bar.

"Ring-a-ding-ding," he said, when he saw Braddock.

Braddock sat at the far end of the bar and ordered a coffee with cream. "Edgar working today?" he asked.

"He was supposed to," Savvie said. "He didn't show. That's why I'm here."

Something stirred uneasily in the pit of Braddock's stomach. He tried to ignore it. "Mitty been in?"

"That old character? Nope. Haven't seen him for a while."

"He was in yesterday," Braddock said, sipping coffee.

Savvie looked at him with his head cocked to the side. "Place was closed yesterday, election day. The law."

"But I was in here. Edgar was tending bar. Mitty was sitting at that table right over there. I sat with him."

Savvie grinned, as if wondering if this was a joke. "I think not, pally."

"But I bought a—"

"What?"

"Never mind. Mitty was telling me about his early show biz days, about him and Buddy. He said they were big."

"That I can tell you is true," Savvie said. "Mitty and Buddy were huge in the business for a while. They played the Catskills and West Coast in the late thirties and forties, even into the fifties. They started in vaudeville, the resorts and lounges, did some gigs on early TV. They were hip. Chicks dug them, thought Buddy was cute. Everybody dug them. They were on Ed Sullivan four times!"

Braddock was flooded with relief.

"Mitty must have been some trainer. And some dog, that Buddy!"

Savvie looked puzzled. "Dog? Naw, Mitty never worked with no dog."

"But Buddy—"

"Was his dummy. Like Charlie McCarthy. Made outta wood. Sat on his lap. Mitty was a ventriloquist."

Braddock must have turned pale.

"Hey! You okay?" Savvie asked, his face screwed tight with concern.

"Yeah, sure," Braddock said. His voice sounded unnaturally high. He was having trouble breathing. Five thousand dollars! He had to get to a phone and try to stop payment on his check! But he knew it wouldn't do any good. The bank had been closed yesterday but open all morning. There had been plenty of time for Mitty to cash the check, pay Edgar his cut, then leave town.

Savvie glanced behind him at the beer advertisement clock. "I wish Edgar'd get here."

"He won't be coming in," Braddock said, laying a couple of bills on the bar for the coffee and a tip.

"How do you know? A little bird tell you? A breeze named Louise?"

"A little dog." Braddock got down off his stool and moved toward the door.

"You maybe oughta see a doctor, pally. You don't look so well."

"You're right," Braddock said in his new, high voice. "I feel arful."

THINGS DIDN'T GET any better for a long time for Braddock. He waited tables for several months in a restaurant where other show business hopefuls ate cheap meals and left meager tips and sad stories. Night after night Braddock would drive a junk Ford he'd been able to afford to an even cheaper apartment than the one he'd been evicted from after the talking dog affair.

Java still couldn't talk, but Braddock sure could. And what he asked himself aloud every few days was the simple and ageless question, "How could I have been so stupid?"

Braddock didn't know why he kept Java around. Maybe as a reminder of his own gullibility. Or maybe it was because he'd somehow gotten fond of the shy little dog, who, after all, wasn't a willing or even knowing party to the scam that had taken in Braddock. Java still occasionally wore that curious crooked smile that had so fooled Braddock into thinking there might be a glimmer of humanlike intelligence behind it. Of crude human ability. After all, if a dog could be embarrassed and actually had something like a sense of humor . . . But Braddock had to face facts. Java was merely a dog. And he, Braddock, was merely a dupe, another failure and Hollywood footnote so tiny and brief that no one would ever read it.

It depressed Braddock to distraction.

Then, inevitably, it angered him. He had to get even somehow, with somebody.

So it was that six months later, and with great care, he chose that somebody. A man who was a modest success in show business. Guilfoil was his name. Ernest Guilfoil of Guilfoil Associates, whose embossed, cream-colored business card had an old fashioned movie projector printed on it and read simply, GUILFOIL: WRITE, EDIT, PRODUCE.

"What have you produced?" Braddock asked him, in Guilfoil's reasonably plush Wilshire Boulevard office.

"Mostly European properties rather than home grown. There's richer soil to nourish greater success right now in Europe." Guilfoil, a short, plump, and seemingly completely hairless man whose smile was constant, smiled even wider as he spoke.

Braddock wasn't put off by this answer. He kept in mind the adage that you can't cheat an honest man, and noted that the furnishings of Guilfoil's office were fairly expensive. Deep enough pockets here, Braddock decided, but not so deep that if anything went wrong Guilfoil could afford top-notch Hollywood attorneys in a legal war of attrition.

"What I'm looking for," Braddock said, "is a promotional production featuring my grandfather's dog, Java, who has a very unique talent."

Guilfoil appeared politely interested. "Which is?"

Braddock couldn't quite yet bring himself to say. "Let me give you a little back story first." He reached for his briefcase that held the material given to him by Mitty, along with some freshly doctored photographs of "Buddy" the talking dog, in what appeared to be aged newspaper and billing images from two generations ago. Braddock had used a friend's computer to improve on what Mitty had shown him.

He watched while Guilfoil spread the material out on his desk and studied it.

After a while, Guilfoil looked up. If he'd had eyebrows, they would have been raised. "Are you kidding? A talking dog? Take a walk, kid."

Braddock was ready. "I'm willing to put up a thousand dollars of my own money toward this production." He laid a check on the desk, already made out to Guilfoil. "It isn't much, Mr. Guilfoil, but it will show my sincerity." Bait, borrowed from a loan shark in Central L.A. Braddock had been studying scams, and knew this was a necessary expense.

He watched Guilfoil stare at the check. "But this dog here, in what you've shown me, has gotta be dead."

"Buddy has passed," Braddock confirmed. "But let me tell you what my grandfather Mitty told me just before he, too, passed on. There are certain dogs of a certain breed and with palates of a certain type who . . ." And he spun the tale told by Mitty months ago in Savvie's bar.

Guilfoil didn't quite buy into it. Not yet. Braddock understood.

"I'm not asking anything other than a percentage of the gross in any further film appearances or personal, so to speak, bookings," Braddock said. "That's how confident I am."

"I know you're confident," Guilfoil said, "but are you sane?"

"I'll let you judge for yourself," Braddock said, standing up. Guilfoil drew back as if afraid, but Braddock merely walked to the door, opened it, and whistled softly.

There was the whisper of paws on the waxed tile floor, and a small figure entered the office and stood just inside the door.

"Mr. Guilfoil," Braddock said, beaming proudly, "meet Java!"

Guilfoil stood up. "Hello, Ja—" He caught himself. "And this is a direct descendent of Buddy of the Catskills?"

"Direct, and ready to demonstrate the fact."

Braddock walked back toward the desk, and Java followed to stand beside him, facing Guilfoil.

"I never saw a dog smile like that," Guilfoil said.

"Java, speak!" Braddock said.

Java simply smiled at Guilfoil.

Braddock knew it was time to bring into play the results of the other half of the money he'd borrowed from the loan shark. The part he used for his ventriloquism lessons.

"Well?" Guilfoil said.

Java said, "Arful!"

Everything went smoothly after that.

TWO WEEKS LATER, Braddock sprang the trap. He showed up at Guilfoil's office with Java and explained to Guilfoil that his mother in New Jersey needed heart surgery in a hurry, and asked Guilfoil for a loan against future earnings. Guilfoil, harder of heart and arteries than Braddock's nonexistent mother, refused with transparent reluctance.

"You don't leave me any choice, Mr. Guilfoil," Braddock said. "I can't stay here in L.A."

"We have a contract to do a promotional film and work up a talking dog act," Guilfoil reminded him. "I'm supposed to act as your agent."

"And I have to get to New Jersey, and fast."

"I'm not sure it's legal to take dogs across state lines without making a lot of arrangements weeks ahead," Guilfoil said, glancing at Java, who was seated near Braddock's left leg. Java returned his glance and smiled at him.

"You don't leave me any choice," Braddock said again, even more despondently. "I'm offering to sell you Java."

"*And* your end of the deal?"

"You mean Java's contract?"

"That's it, kid."

Java wasn't smiling now.

"Not for a million bucks!" Braddock said.

"I was thinking twenty thousand."

Java seemed to be listening carefully, glancing from one man to the other as they spoke.

"That isn't nearly enough!" Braddock cried.

"It's enough if it's the only offer you're going to get. And it is, since we've been keeping this dog act under wraps before springing it on the public."

Braddock hung his head. "Okay. Twenty thousand. Cash, so I can catch a plane for Newark tonight. But it's a lousy offer." He gazed mistily at Java. "It's a stinking damned world for people and dogs!"

"Show-biz, kid," Guilfoil said, reaching into a desk drawer for a contract form and cash box.

"Take care of Java," Braddock told him minutes later, trying not to break into a run as he went out the door.

HE SHOULD HAVE left town five minutes sooner. Braddock's suitcase was packed and he was hefting it down from the bed when there was a knock on his apartment door.

His landlady to check on the place and make sure all the lights and gas burners were off, he figured.

But when he opened the door, there was Guilfoil and Java. And a uniformed policeman. And a plainclothes cop who flashed an L.A.P.D detective's badge and said he was from the Bunko Squad.

Java couldn't meet Braddock's eyes. Guilfoil could. He looked furious. "You sold me ownership in a talking dog that doesn't talk!" he said.

"Maybe he just won't talk for you."

The detective looked dubiously at Braddock, shaking his head. "It appears that what you did was illegal, Mr. Braddock."

Braddock couldn't believe this. "Then I want to cross charges! Arrest this man!"

"What?" Guilfoil said. "Cross what?"

"This Guilfoil isn't any kind of producer, like his card says! He wasn't really going to do a film promo for me and Java."

"I never said I was," Guilfoil told him.

"That you were going to make a film?"

"That I was a producer. You just assumed."

"Your business card says you're a producer!" Braddock fished his wallet from his pocket, rooted through it, and pulled out Guilfoil's card. He handed it to the plainclothes detective. "It should say *con man*."

"It doesn't say *producer*," said the detective, "It only says *produce*."

"He writes, edits, and produces," Braddock said.

The cop stared at him. "*Produce,* as in fruits and vegetables. Produce is what Mr. Guilfoil sells. He has a produce stand near Malibu."

"About to open a second," Guilfoil said proudly. "With the all the money I'm going to have garnisheed from your future salary. We'll see now who's the con man!"

"And you can have your dog back," Guilfoil added, as Braddock was led away in handcuffs. "The kennel bill will be waiting for you."

BRADDOCK WAITED UNTIL after the arraignment, when he was out on bail, before finally admitting to himself that this had actually happened. His future was set, and it was bleak. As for his present, it was just as bleak. Here he was back in his crummy apartment with his dog that couldn't talk, unemployed and maybe going to prison. The best he would get was probation and a ruined reputation. Maybe house arrest, if he was lucky. Difficult to land a job when you're behind bars or wearing one of those electronic anklets.

The decision wasn't a hard one. Not in Braddock's state of mind. Before they put something around his ankle, he put a rope around his neck. He climbed up on a chair and tied the other end of the rope to a sturdily mounted ceiling fixture.

It's Hollywood, he thought. *Everybody's got an act, and mine wasn't good enough. I fooled nobody.*

Then he kicked the chair away.

He didn't fall very far, but far enough.

He changed his mind in an instant. Too late. As he was choking to death, tearing at the inexorably tightening noose with clutching, helpless fingers, thrashing his legs about for a nonexistent foothold, he heard a rough, throaty voice not his own:

"I'd help you loosen that knot if I could, but what can I do with these? I got no opposable thumbs, pal."

The last thing Braddock saw as the light faded was Java, sitting up on his haunches, holding out his paws.

Taking a bow? Smiling?

Blonde Moment

ELAINE VIETS

"KILLER," SAID JASON the producer, as he admired the blonde in the blue dress.

"Kill her," is what Evelyn Blent heard.

That's exactly what she wanted to do. Kill Tiffany Tyler Taylor.

It was Jason who gave Evelyn the idea to kill Tiffany. It was Evelyn's grandmother who showed her how to do it.

Tiffany. The little blonde was sitting at her new morning show set for the first time, but she looked like she'd been there forever. *Breakfast With Tiffany* the show was called, and the new set was created for her. It was all in shades of blue—sky blue and Dresden blue, peacock, azure, and sapphire—to set off Tiffany's rich buttery blondeness.

Blonde ambition, that's what Tiffany was. Five-feet-two inches of simpering, slithering ambition. Tiffany was after Evelyn's anchor slot. Evelyn knew it. There was only one reason why she'd get it. She was blonde.

Whenever Tiffany Tyler Taylor walked through station KQZX, every man looked at her like he'd been marooned for a decade on a desert island. From the station manager to the mail clerks, the men stared at Tiffany with dazed looks and sappy smiles. But Evelyn knew the station manager—Mighty Milt, as his toadies called him—was the real problem. In TV, mistakes started at the top. If Milt didn't treat Tiffany as his golden girl, that brown-noser Jason wouldn't fawn over her.

Jason was Evelyn's producer, too, but he had only perfunctory praise for Evelyn. "Nice job," he'd say. Or, "Thanks for covering that light plane crash. Nobody else would be on the scene at five A.M."

Certainly not Tiffany Tyler Taylor. She'd never trudge through a muddy field to get to the crash site. She'd mess up her little blue shoes.

But Jason never looked at Evelyn in that same dreamy way. Even Rick, a cynical, sarcastic cameraman, stared at Tiffany and said with a lovesick sigh, "God, she looks good."

"She's a poodle," snarled Evelyn. "An empty-headed little nothing. What is wrong with you, Rick? You've never fallen in love with the talent before."

Rick shrugged. "Blondes are easier to light," he said.

Evelyn almost believed him. When the harsh TV lights hit Tiffany, her blonde hair glowed like molten gold. She looked like a blue angel with Meg Ryan bangs.

Evelyn looked dark and a little angry on TV. Her brunette hair seemed to absorb light. Her olive skin created strange shadows. TV did odd things to her. If Evelyn gained a pound or two, the camera gave her a double chin and a pouchy stomach. That never happened to Tiffany Tyler Taylor. She always looked petite and perfect.

Tiffany couldn't get a scoop in an ice cream parlor. But St. Louis viewers were as dazzled as the fools at the station. In six months, Tiffany rose from feature reporter to morning show host. Now Evelyn was afraid that Tiffany would go after the ultimate prize—Evelyn's own hard-won spot as six o'clock anchor.

Already Tiffany had made two guest appearances on St. Louis' highest-rated news show. Co-anchor Dick Nickerson threw back his head and laughed so hard at Tiffany's mild (and scripted) joke about the weather that his comb-over flopped up like a pot lid. Dick got derisive letters from readers, calling him a drapehead. He didn't care. Dick adored Tiffany.

Nobody but Evelyn saw the hard little climber under that soft surface. Nobody but Evelyn heard Tiffany's catty remarks.

"Eeuww, are you really eating a bacon sandwich for lunch?" said Tiffany, pointing at Evelyn's BLT. "Bacon has nitrates and nitrites. And it's bad for your skin." Evelyn could feel the zits popping out on her face like dandelions after a rain.

"Bacon makes you fat," Tiffany said, staring at Evelyn's waistline until she felt her gut plop over her belt.

"That's why I stick to salads," she said, smugly. She tapped her green-heaped plate with her fork. Then Tiffany stuck her knife in Evelyn's back. "But I suppose a mature woman like yourself doesn't have to worry about her figure."

"Mature" was not a compliment in television. Tiffany had called her old and fat. No one else heard the insult.

Another time Tiffany suggested that Evelyn get some blonde highlights in her dark hair. "The lighter color around your face will make you look ten years younger," she said. "Go to Mr. John. He's the best colorist in the city. You'll look so natural."

No one heard that little dig, either.

Only Evelyn heard Tiffany on the phone to her stockbroker every afternoon before the markets closed. Only Evelyn seemed to catch Tiffany calling her agent. That's when Tiffany dropped all pretense of being the city's sweetheart.

"I don't know how I can live on a lousy two-hundred-fifty thousand a year," St. Louis's sweety pie hissed. Evelyn would love to have that quote on tape. She'd play it for all the Tiffany fans who said, "She's so down-to-earth."

Evelyn saw red when she heard how much green the gold-digging Goldilocks was trying to pry out of the station. Evelyn didn't make near that, and she'd been at the station ten years.

It was time to have a talk with her mentor, Margaret Smithson. Evelyn would demand to know why she was underpaid and underrated. Margaret would make things right.

Evelyn's anger boiled and seethed as she marched across the newsroom. It burst like a geyser when she opened Margaret's office door, and she spewed out a stream of hot words.

"Stop it!" Margaret said. "Evelyn, you must stop this stupid jealousy."

Evelyn felt like she'd been slapped. Margaret looked small and stern in her smart black suit. She weighed about ninety-five pounds, and most of that was her mop of dark hair. But Margaret was tough. Right now, she turned that toughness on Evelyn.

"Your petty jabs at Tiffany are getting back to the wrong people. I'm warning you. They'll come back and bite you in the ass."

"You're on her side, too," Evelyn said. She knew she sounded whiny.

"I am not," Margaret said. Even when she was angry, Margaret was striking. She had black hair, dark blue eyes, and pale skin. Evelyn often wondered why Margaret wasn't on camera. But Margaret preferred to be a special projects producer. Everything she touched turned to Emmy gold. The lustrous statues lined the shelves above her desk.

"I'm on your side, Evelyn. But you're making yourself look bad. It's contract renewal time, and I have to tell you: Milt is talking about making Tiffany the six o'clock anchor. I think I can head him off, but I don't know for how long if you keep undermining yourself. Milt wants team players."

"It isn't a team. It's a support system for Tiffany," said Evelyn, bitterly.

"See, that's what I mean," Margaret said. "How many times have I told you? Success in television is by the numbers. Right now, Tiffany has them. Viewers will tire of her professional cuteness. They always do. Then Milt will decide she's overpaid and dump her. She'll be gone soon. Sit tight and keep your mouth shut."

But the next morning, while Tiffany was doing a live remote in front of City Hall, a yellow blur of fur raced by her and ran into Market Street. The whole city saw Tiffany run after the dog and rescue it, just before it slipped under the wheels of a truck. In case anyone missed the dramatic rescue, it was shown on the six and ten o'clock news.

The following morning, Tiffany was on the set with the little yellow mutt. Saved and savior looked remarkably alike. Both were small and perky, with yellow hair and floppy bangs. Both oozed cuteness. The mutt licked Tiffany, and Tiffany smooched the dog. Evelyn couldn't decide which one she wanted to kick first.

Evelyn nearly choked on her breakfast eggs when Tiffany announced a contest to name the dog. She lost her appetite totally three days later when Tiffany said she'd received two thousand e-mails and faxes. Evidently, viewers also thought Tiffany looked like her dog. The winning name was Tiffany Too.

A week later, Milt sent out a memo that Tiffany and Tiffany Too would be featured at the Fair Saint Louis on the Fourth of July. Tiffany would be the dayside anchor, then do color commentary on the fireworks that night.

Every year, some two million people sweltered on the St. Louis Riverfront, under the Gateway Arch. The temperature and the humidity were in the nineties—if the city was lucky. Sometimes, it was a hundred degrees or more.

The staff complained about covering the three-day fair in the broiling St. Louis sun, but they knew it was a career showcase. For four years running, Evelyn had been the dayside anchor and nightside commentator. This year, Milt's memo demoted her to a lowly reporter. She'd be trudging through the almost liquid heat to interview boring people who said things like, "We're having a wonderful time. There's nothing like this in Festus."

Milt gave that sneaky, simpering blonde Evelyn's assignment at the fair. Soon she'd have Evelyn's anchor slot, too.

Evelyn told her mentor Margaret that she felt sick and wanted to go home. She wasn't lying. Her stomach heaved when she read Milt's memo. She barely made it to the restroom before she threw up.

Evelyn had to save her career before that fair-haired fathead took everything from her. She felt hot angry tears. This was dangerous. She couldn't be seen crying in the newsroom.

She ran to her BMW and started driving anywhere, nowhere. She didn't want to think. But Evelyn's driving was not aimless after all. She found herself on Christopher Drive, the road to Granny's house in the country. Granny was common sense itself. She'd help Evelyn.

Granny was the last real grandmother in America. No facelifts and hair dyes for her. Granny had a comfortable flour-sack figure and crinkly gray hair.

Granny's little white house had yellow plastic lawn ducks and red geraniums. It was surrounded by acres of Missouri woods. Across the street was a horse pasture. Subdivisions were creeping up the road, but you couldn't see them yet.

Granny had grown up on a farm in Tennessee, and she loved to talk about old-time remedies from her girlhood. As a teenager, Evelyn was disgusted when Granny told her that country people used to tie moldy bread to a bad cut to cure the infection.

Later on, Evelyn realized they were using a primitive form of penicillin.

Of course, not all of Granny's old-time remedies were useful. Evelyn didn't believe a pan of water under a bed would break a fever, but it did no harm.

Granny ran outside when she heard Evelyn's car and gave her a comforting hug. Evelyn breathed in her grandmother's old-fashioned violet sachet. Granny's kitchen was perfumed with the warm sweetness of fresh-baked blackberry pie.

"You're too thin," Granny said, which made Evelyn feel better. You could never be too thin on TV.

"And how's my other favorite TV girl?" said Granny.

"Who's that?" said Evelyn, as she felt her insides go dead. Had that tinselly Tiffany seduced her Granny?

"The little blonde who rescued that dog," Granny said. "She's got a good head on her shoulders."

"Too bad there's nothing in it," said Evelyn.

"Evelyn, is that the green-eyed monster I see in your eyes?" said Granny.

"No," Evelyn lied.

"Then have some homemade pie and tell me why you're dropping in on me in the middle of the day," Granny said.

"Because I haven't seen you in awhile," said Evelyn. She couldn't tell Granny the real reason. Not now. Not after she knew Granny was a Tiffany worshiper.

Granny cut a big slice from the blackberry pie cooling on the rack. Warm purple juice oozed out on the plate and dripped on the counter, but Granny ignored it. She was staring out the window.

"Those new people have their white horse in that pasture again on a sunny day," Granny said. "They know that field's full of rue plants. I've told them and told them, but they won't listen to me. Damn yuppies think I don't know anything. If that horse suffers, it's their fault."

"What's wrong with rue?" asked Evelyn.

"It's poisonous to white animals, especially in the sunshine," said Granny. "Grows right there." She pointed to some weedy-looking plants by the pasture fence.

"That doesn't make sense," Evelyn said. "Why would they poison only white animals?"

"Don't know, but they do," Granny said. "Poison white people, too."

"Come on, Granny, plants don't discriminate," said Evelyn. She wondered if age was eroding Granny's sharp mind.

"I mean really white people, like blondes. It won't hurt dark-haired types like you," Granny said. "And that's no old wives' tale. It's a scientific fact. If white animals eat rue, celery, and plants like that, then stand in bright sunlight, they can get real sick.

"But a chestnut horse can eat the same plants and nothing happens. Dark-haired animals and people don't get sick. The plants are only poisonous to very white people and white animals."

"What happens?" asked Evelyn.

Granny loved to describe symptoms. "Their face, throat, and eyelids swell up," she said gleefully. "They get dizzy and stagger around like they're drunk." Granny staggered around the kitchen, clutching the purple pie knife to her chest.

"Happened to your Aunt Virginia," she said solemnly.

Evelyn tried to picture her stout gray-haired aunt staggering. "When?"

"When Virginia was a young girl. At the Cedar Springs church picnic," Granny said. "I know you'll find it hard to believe, but Virginia was a little bit of a thing then, and had platinum-blonde hair down to her hips. Wild as a March hare, too. Some boy dared her to eat a plant in a field. Your Aunt Virginia saw a brown horse eating it and figured it was safe. But it was rue. Her throat swelled up terrible. That girl liked to died. Couldn't get Virginia to touch anything green again, not even a plain old lettuce salad."

Evelyn could see another little blonde eating a salad, then going out into the sweltering Fair Saint Louis sunshine. She could see her white throat swelling and closing up, and the blonde staggering and dying just before the paramedics arrived.

Then Evelyn saw herself taking back the fair assignment that was rightfully hers.

Granny had given her the solution to the Tiffany problem after all. In fact, she'd served it on a plate.

"What's this phenomenon called?" Evelyn asked.

"Photo . . . photo . . . photo-something," Granny said.

Photosensitization.

"A pathological sensitivity caused by eating certain plants that are not ordinarily poisonous," Evelyn's researches at the library revealed.

"A form of light dermatosis," said one old book that was a virtual manual for poisoners. Evelyn couldn't risk checking it out, so she stole it from the library, burying it in her briefcase. At home, she read the section on photosensitization over and over, gloating over each sentence.

"Its symptoms are an inflammatory swelling of the ears, face, and eyelids, with throat and lung disturbances, dizziness and a tendency to stagger," the book said. "When, in rare instances, death follows, it is due to mechanical asphyxia from the swelling of the nose and throat."

Death would be nice, Evelyn thought. But she would settle for seeing the golden girl swell up like a red balloon. Maybe she'd pop, right on camera.

Evelyn giggled, but it was not a cute Tiffany Tyler Taylor giggle.

Her researches only got better: Rue and celery, especially the green leafy parts of celery, were rich in furanocoumarins. The name alone was enough to make you turn red and swell.

Some people were supersensitive to them. They'd get a horrible sunburn-like reaction. The lighter-skinned you were, the more intense the reaction. Especially if you went out into the sun.

And if you were taking a drug like Coumadin, it further intensified the reaction, Evelyn read. Lots of people took the blood thinner Coumadin. It was also the main ingredient in rat poison.

All Evelyn had to do was make a nice salad with rue and celery, then spice it with a little rat poison. Not enough to make a brunette sick. Just enough to blow up a little blonde.

It was so easy.

Evelyn knew where to get the rue plants. The pasture near Granny's was filled with them.

Evelyn knew how she would serve them, too. She'd make a field greens salad, then add the rue. It was a field green, too. When people were chomping baby oak leaves and stuff that looked like it had been raked off a lawn, who'd notice some rue? Then she'd sprinkle on green celery leaves for color. Everyone used celery.

A cheese dressing would disguise any bitter taste. *I'll make raspberry vinaigrette with Gorgonzola,* she thought. *I'll add walnuts and dried cranberries to make it nice and healthy.*

For everyone but Tiffany.

For good measure, she'd Cuisinart a little rat poison and add it to the dressing. It would blend in with the herbs and spices. She'd calculate exactly the medicinal dose for a small woman—divided by three salad eaters. Sun, celery, rue—and rat poison. Tiffany would rue the day she went after anything of Evelyn's.

There was one problem. How would she get Tiffany to eat the salad? Everyone knew Evelyn hated the woman. She barely said hello to Tiffany in the newsroom. She had one month to make friends with her enemy: Evelyn would have to swallow her pride so Tiffany would swallow her salad.

Next morning, Evelyn walked into Margaret's office and said, "You're right. It's time I buried the hatchet."

"In Tiffany's forehead?" Margaret said, suspiciously.

"For real," Evelyn said. "Yesterday, I had some time to think about what you said. I'm only hurting myself. I want to take Tiffany to lunch. My treat. Would you come as referee?"

"Delighted," Margaret said, her pale face turning pink with pleasure. "I'm so happy you're taking my advice."

Tiffany was wary when Evelyn invited her, even when she explained that Margaret would be there, too. But she could not resist Evelyn's handsome apology. "I've behaved stupidly, Tiffany," she said. "I want this lunch to be a peace offering."

Tiffany looked flattered. She considered Evelyn's olive branch a tribute to her power. During a two-hundred-dollar lunch at a premier power spot, Tiffany prattled on about her favorite subject—herself.

"Tiffany Too and I are the marshals for the Hill Day parade," she said, while the worshipful waiter refilled Tiffany's water glass, and forgot Evelyn's.

The Hill was the Italian section of the city. "Your dog will love the fire hydrants," said Evelyn. "They're painted red, white, and green."

"Oh, no, she isn't allowed out of the parade marshal's convertible," Tiffany said seriously. "Not in those crowds."

Tiffany babbled on. Mentor Margaret smiled benignly. Evelyn cut her swordfish into smaller and smaller pieces until the waiter took her plate away. No one ordered dessert. The reconciliation lunch was over, and declared a success.

Evelyn suffered through two more Tiffany lunches with Margaret's approving company. Because she silently endured Tiffany's monologues, the beastly blonde now considered Evelyn her friend.

"I can talk to you," she said. "You're such a good listener."

Peace was declared. The nasty newsroom rumors ceased, and the gossip mongers went after the noonshow anchor, who was having an affair with the consumer reporter. The jokes about what she was consuming were relentless.

At their third lunch, Tiffany finally gave Evelyn the opening she needed.

"I'm not looking forward to covering the fair," Tiffany said, sighing dramatically. Evelyn knew Tiffany was dying for an excuse to talk about her big assignment. At least, Evelyn hoped the twit would be dying.

"It's going to be such a long day," Tiffany cooed. "Almost ten hours. The station is keeping Tiffany Too in the air-conditioned satellite truck. My little puppy will be cool, but I'll be out on the hot fairgrounds all day from eleven o'clock on."

Evelyn ground her teeth as she thought of Tiffany's taking over her assignment, but she forced herself to sound sympathetic. "That is a long day. What are you doing about lunch?"

Tiffany shuddered delicately. "I can either eat the station's food—tuna salad and ham sandwiches—all fat—or the fair food—hot dogs and buffalo burgers. Yuck."

Actually, the fair offered delicacies from chicken satay to, yes, buffalo burgers. But how would Tiffany know? She'd never covered the fair.

"I come in at noon," Evelyn said. "How about if I bring salads for you, me, and Margaret? I have this terrific recipe, with field greens, Gorgonzola, walnuts, and dried cranberries. A good healthy salad will get us through the day."

"Super!" said Tiffany. "You're a lifesaver!"

Yeah, thought Evelyn. *I'm saving my life. And my career.*

The night before the fair, Evelyn drove to the pasture near Granny's and climbed over the fence. Her pants were full of stickleburrs and her hands were scratched with brambles, but she picked the plants she needed by moonlight. The lights were off at her grandmother's house. Deep shadows along the pasture fence hid Evelyn. Even the night conspired to help her.

In the morning, she concocted the salad, adding the freshly picked rue to the store-bought field greens. She made her salad dressing with a carefully calibrated dose of rat poison. It was the exact dosage for one small healthy woman. Divided by three, of course. Because they'd all be sharing the salad.

She put the salad into a big disposable bowl. She would make sure everyone saw there was only one salad container. At lunch, she served the salad on paper plates, dividing the poisonous portions exactly in three.

"Delicious," Tiffany said, eating her salad greedily.

"Perfection!" said Margaret. Evelyn was too excited to eat. She forced herself to finish her salad.

After lunch, Evelyn gathered up the serving bowl, paper plates, and forks; even the napkins. After Margaret and Tiffany left, Evelyn threw the trash into an overflowing can at the far end of the fair. The incriminating remains would be taken away by the trash haulers long before Tiffany's first symptom.

All three women worked in the sweltering afternoon sun. Tiffany, with Margaret's award-winning assistance, was interviewing the big stars performing on the main stage. Evelyn went with Rick the cameraman for what he called "Bubba bites"—sound bites from dreary fairgoers.

After they interviewed a hefty woman from Herculaneum and a downright fat man from Florissant with two chubby children, Rick whispered to Evelyn, "Is there a weight requirement for this fair? Do you have to weigh at least two hundred pounds to get in the gate?"

Evelyn loved his misanthropic remarks. The sun was beating on her with almost physical blows. Sweat dripped off her nose. She knew on camera her face would look oily and her hair would look French-fried. She prayed that same sun was working on Tiffany's white skin.

When they heard sirens near the main stage, Rick said, "Maybe one of the fairgoers melted. Let's go see if there's some video."

More sirens screamed. Now police cars, fire trucks, and

an ambulance were heading toward the main stage. The music stopped abruptly.

"What happened?" Evelyn asked a woman running from the area, clutching her baby protectively.

"Some TV lady started staggering around and grabbing her throat," the woman said. "Her face swelled up something awful. Even her eyes were swollen shut. She looked horrible. I didn't want my Becky to see it."

Yes! thought Evelyn triumphantly, but she made concerned noises.

Rick was running surprisingly fast for someone with a heavy video camera. He loped past Evelyn. Other fairgoers were running after him, eager to see the tragedy. Evelyn felt a sharp elbow in her ribs. A small boy darted between her legs and she fell on the dry grass.

By the time Evelyn brushed herself off, the excitement was almost over. She saw the paramedics loading a stretcher with a small figure strapped to it. The figure was absolutely still, although the ambulance left with lights flashing and sirens howling.

Evelyn composed her face into a sorrowful mask to hide her glee. She didn't know if Tiffany was sick or dead, but she was definitely out of action. The fair was hers now. Evelyn would return to her rightful place on camera.

She went looking for Margaret. The satellite truck would be the logical choice. At least someone there could tell her where Margaret was. Evelyn was about to enter when the door opened slowly. Out stepped Tiffany. Her hated rival looked disgustingly healthy.

"How? What?" was all a stunned Evelyn could manage.

"Oh, Evelyn," said Tiffany, her blue eyes tearing artistically. "Margaret started gasping and choking and staggering around like she was having some kind of fit. Nobody knew what happened to her, and by the time the ambulance got there, she wasn't breathing at all. It was terrible. They don't think she's going to make it."

"Margaret?" Evelyn said. "Are you sure?"

What had gone wrong? Margaret was a brunette. If rue plants made blondes sick, why was Tiffany well and Margaret dying? Damn Granny and her crazy country remedies.

Blonde Tiffany had eaten no more salad than anyone. But brunette Margaret had the severe symptoms. Evelyn had eaten the greens, too, and they'd had no effect on her. They certainly weren't poisonous to one brunette—why another?

"I must see Margaret," Evelyn said.

But Jason, her producer, stopped her. "I'm sorry, Evelyn," he said. "You can't do anything for Margaret. We need you to carry on with the fair coverage."

But she couldn't. Evelyn couldn't concentrate. She missed her first cue for the live remote at the food booths. When she was finally on the air, she looked sweaty and disheveled. Several viewers called the station, asking if Evelyn was drunk. But it was shock, not booze, that slurred her speech.

Evelyn's "Bubba bites," the interviews with the boring fairgoers, were dropped to make room for the special report on the death of Emmy-award-winning producer Margaret Smithson.

Tiffany narrated that report. Everyone agreed that she did a splendid job, showing just the right amount of professional sympathy. Tiffany's story about sharing her salad with the deceased was especially touching.

Evelyn drifted in a fog, waiting for the autopsy results. Maybe the pathologist would find something that would exonerate her. Maybe Margaret had been stung by a bee and gone into shock. Maybe Evelyn didn't kill her mentor and best friend.

But when the report was released, Evelyn knew there would be no reprieve. Margaret had extensive swelling of the face, lips, and tongue. She'd suffocated. The details were too horrible to think about.

The pathologist said the severe symptoms were caused by an overdose of Coumadin. Margaret had been taking the blood thinner for her heart. The pathologist believed Margaret had mistakenly taken a double dose of Coumadin and died from it. Her death was an accident.

Only Evelyn knew it was no accident. Only Evelyn knew she'd killed her best friend. And she couldn't figure out how.

At the station, Evelyn stumbled through her standups, missed deadlines, flubbed her lines. She felt numb. She didn't care, not even when the station did not renew her contract. She knew Tiffany would take her anchor spot.

She didn't know why Margaret died, and that made her crazy.

Margaret had only had one-third of a normal dose of Coumadin. It shouldn't have killed her, even if she was already taking the blood thinner. The sun, celery, and rue might intensify the effect, but Margaret was a brunette. It should have been blonde Tiffany who swelled up from the sun exposure. It should have been Tiffany who died.

All Evelyn could do was ask herself, "What went wrong?"

She found out at Margaret's memorial service. Margaret's grieving family displayed photos of their daughter throughout her too-short life.

Evelyn saw the first-grade picture of a grinning gaptoothed Margaret. The little girl was blonde—and not just blonde, but so pale her hair was almost white. In high school, a teenage Margaret used too much eyebrow pencil and mascara to darken her pale brows and eyelashes.

By college, Margaret was a stunning platinum blonde. It was only after graduation, when she got her first job at a little station in Sedalia, Missouri, that Margaret had dark hair. She was a brunette in every photo after that.

"You were Margaret's best friend," said her mother, a

plump gray-haired woman in black. She took both of Evelyn's hands in hers.

"I didn't know she was a blonde," blurted Evelyn.

"Oh, yes," she said. "Margaret had lovely hair. Natural platinum. But Margaret said she couldn't take the 'dumb blonde' jokes at work. She said when she dyed her hair dark, her IQ went up 50 points."

That's where I went wrong, Evelyn thought.

Margaret was blonde. And Tiffany? She remembered why Dolly Parton said she wasn't offended by dumb blonde jokes. " . . . I know I'm not dumb. I also know that I'm not blonde."

Tiffany must have dyed her hair blonde. She recalled her nasty remarks about Mr. John being the city's finest colorist . . . "so natural." Of course. He certainly made Tiffany look natural. That's why the poison salad didn't bother her. She wasn't a real blonde.

It was the ultimate blonde joke on a dumb brunette. It never occurred to Evelyn that Tiffany was a bottle blonde. She should have known. Everything else about her was fake. And in TV, mistakes start at the top.

Evelyn realized Margaret's mother was still holding her hands and talking. "I told her, 'Margaret, it is a sin and a shame to cover up that beautiful platinum hair.' And you know what she said? 'Mother, I would rather die than be a blonde.'

"Evelyn? Are you okay? Why, you're white as a sheet, dear. Sit down here. It's not healthy to be that white . . . "

Lah Tee Dah

ANGELA ZEMAN

HERMIONE LISTENBERGER CONTEMPLATED her name as she plucked a slow riff of perfect, clear notes from her six-string acoustical Gibson (the three-quarter size model to better fit her small frame).

The ringing tones mellowed the acrid air with a leisurely sweetness she hoped would entice the West 50th Street subway patrons to slow their mad pace. In a few moments, after the number 9 train resumed its screaming rush downtown, she'd segue into her next tune.

Just this morning she'd re-strung the guitar with all steel strings, although this type of guitar was really created for nylon. As the train sat gathering its strength, she took advantage of the relative quiet to listen hard to the steel's sharper delineation of each note. As she had hoped, the sounds lingered longer, blending and reaching deeper into the tiled subway tunnel. The tunnel itself was her sound system.

Excellent.

Her attention returned to her name. Hermione possessed an orderly mind that trudged remorselessly down the path she had laid for herself. A new name was next on her agenda. Something memorable. Striking. Not for the first time, she marveled at her parents' choice. Did it reflect the stultified

Utica environment they adored? As soon as she had judged herself wise and strong enough to protect herself among strangers, she'd run to Manhattan with the desperation of a drowning man who knows only one place to find air. Hermione? Coupled with Listenberger it lost all hope of working as a stage name. For one thing, it was ugly. Now, ugly might have worked if it fit her musical image. However, she knew her music was strong. Also disturbing at times, an effect that delighted Hermione. But not ugly.

Also from long, detached inspections in bathroom mirrors she knew that she herself had beauty of a type. After careful consideration, she had eventually chosen to make her beauty an asset, to play it "up" onstage. Even though her current finances forced her to sluice her body as completely as possible in public facilities and to subsist mainly on juice and discarded sandwiches from overflowing trash barrels, her ivory skin was of such luminous softness that it seemed to invite touches from fascinated admirers. However, she allowed no touching. Her healthy abundant hair shimmered in any light, from bright brassy gold in the sun to a dusky red glimmer in the tunnels under fluorescent lights, even in subway air dusty with stressed steel and crumbling cement. In this July heat, tiny curls edged her peach-flushed face. In winter cold, she paled, her hair reddening by contrast, a flame in frost. Her figure had never had the leisure or the income to pad itself with baby fat. She had the lean litheness of an athlete.

Never mind. A name. Suddenly the edge of her consciousness registered that the train had left. After so many months, one learned to tune out the subway roar and thunder. So she quickly launched into a new song she'd written. With this one, she tasted success in its notes. Instinctively she knew this was going to be her signature, her door into the world of success. *The* song. It wasn't yet at its peak, but with practice she'd soon polish it into the perfect gem she'd heard in her head when she first thought of it.

She launched her voice, clear and high, with a fierce push on the highest notes, a rough drawl for the low ones: "Leave me now, I've moved on anyhow. Lah tee dah, down the MTA highway, the next stop will be better, lah tee dah . . . "

To her annoyance, a tall young man in vintage bell-bottom cords and a skin-tight tee shirt with the sleeves and neckband ripped out stopped short and stared at her in shocked recognition. She was used to this. Some of these guys were twice her size and sometimes nuts from drugs, or just plain nuts. Some were musicians who recognized her talent and wanted to use her to elevate themselves. Either way, she wished—oh how she wished—she had some means to keep him and those like him away, for there had been many.

This one was a musician. She read the thoughts crossing his face as if they were the moving electric letters on the Times Square news sign: He heard the work behind the melody, the breathing techniques that gave her voice the unearthly compelling quality that, although he probably didn't know it yet, was her trademark. He would want to hook up with her. They all did. It was a Manhattan thing, nearly half the population wanting to be a singer, an actor, an artist. A thousand competitors for each elusive "break."

Her eyes closed, not to submerge into the heat and thrum of the song, but in irritation. Yep, he was coming closer. She felt his intent stare through her closed eyelids. She opened her eyes and glared. Oblivious, he inched closer until rage, far too familiar by now, rose in her anew, choking the words in her throat. For a few lovely seconds an image of herself transformed into a she-wolf came to mind, bringing her visceral pleasure. With little effort her imagination gave her razor teeth with which to gnaw insanely at the muscular throats of these leeches, glorying in the taste of their ruined flesh. She dreamed how, covered with blood, she would lunge at horrified spectators, making them squeal, the spectacle a warning to others to leave her alone! Her frustration had reached a pitch where mere escape from their self-serving attentions would no longer satisfy.

But she was small and slight, and no fool. So she swallowed her fury yet again and only turned slightly to face another direction. Hoping the song and not her body had attracted him, she stopped playing to fuss with the tuning keys at the top of the guitar neck.

He howled like a wounded dog, "It's in perfect tune now, don't spoil it!"

"A stranger and the bastard's ordering me around! They're all the same," she thought.

She sighed and glanced at the huge round clock hanging near the stairs. Jeez, nearly twelve, and she hadn't come up with a good name yet. She'd wanted to get acquainted with her new name, live in its skin for a while, own that name before moving her act to a spot at street level she'd found near the Grand Central double doors on 42nd. Nobody there yet; she'd checked it out for several days. So in her mind it was already hers. But not Hermione Listenberger's, it was . . . she didn't know who yet.

She glanced again at the intruder. Not even one friggin' dollar in his hand to throw into her open guitar case that she'd seeded with a few crumpled bills as a hint to the listeners. She had a pretty steady following down here, made enough to keep her in juice and toothpaste, but was still sleeping in a secretly hollowed out refuge between some boulders in Central Park. She wanted, needed, more money. She faced him squarely, hating the creep not only for his intrusion, but for his cheapness too.

"What!"

Unfazed, he said, "We should join up."

As her head automatically began shaking side to side, he started singing her song, *her* song . . . "Leave me now, I've moved on anyhow . . . "

"Hey!" she roared.

"It's a great song! What's the rest of it?"

"Right, so you can steal the whole thing!"

"No, no, you misunderstand! I'm a singer too!"

"I work alone!"

He said with careful patience, "Just sing it with me and listen. I can counterpoint you. We'll do fantastic. It's really good, you realize that?"

"I work alone!"

"It's got elements of jazz and blues intermingled, and with us both—"

God, they never even hear me speak. It's like having breasts renders me insignificant. "Damn you to hell."

He shrugged, obviously unimpressed with her hostility. "Okay. Um, do 'Baby Jones' instead."

She thought a minute. It was already a favorite of the "underground entertainers," so no big deal. And if it would make him disappear faster . . . grudgingly she started. As promised, he leaped in, his voice alternating between falsetto and baritone, curling around hers. They sounded good. Great, in fact. Several people threw dollar bills and coins into her case. Some stood in rapt attention, wanting the whole song before moving on.

She had to admit when they finished, although her guts revolted, that he was an asset. She scooped up the bills, ignoring the coins, and split the take with him. He squatted and dipped into the coins. "All adds up," he grinned at her, holding up a fistful of quarters and dimes, roughly half; he didn't cheat.

Standing again, he towered over her by at least a foot, rail-thin but not wasted. If he had a monkey, it wasn't hurting his body or mind yet, at least visibly. He was blond, the bleached kind, with dark roots on a short but shaggy head. Doable.

"What's your name?" he asked, reminding her of her goal for the morning.

"What's yours," she countered, angry again. Damn him. Sure, money was good, but the right name would improve her future quicker. He'd slowed down her professional growth.

"Sody," he said. "Garrett."

Sody Garrett. Original, but not worth stealing, so he could keep it. With a resigned sigh she started strumming random chords again.

"Hey. I asked you your name."

"So?" She shrugged, again shifting slightly to face a new direction. A direction in which he wasn't the center of her line of vision.

"You come here every day?" he asked.

Not any more, she said silently. "Oh, yeah!" she replied, her smile almost too quick to catch. Polite, but not exerting herself. He wouldn't knife her. She knew what he wanted, and it had nothing to do with harming her. Another talent leech.

Sure enough. "I'll meet you here tomorrow, but earlier. I play bass guitar. Perfect with your tenor. Acoustics fab down here, the steel strings work perfect without amps. Smart!" She nodded. Duh. Why else would she replace nylon strings with steel. She returned to her immediate task, in her mind running through the names of all the movie stars she could think of. Willing him to disappear.

She started silently reciting a list of her high school class-mates' names. The popular ones.

"Don't forget," he added anxiously, interrupting her mus-ings.

She raked one hand through her hair in frustration. "You bet. Tomorrow!" Just leave, you maggot. Briefly she consid-ered the name "maggot." No. Wrong image.

She considered image. What image did she want to con-vey? Costuming came after picking a name, but both were totally related to the issue of image. Folk song shtick? She shook her head. Her stuff was more hard-edged but yet had a ballad structure. Deep in rumination she never noticed when Sody left. Besides, folksongs had died out in the seventies and RIP. Pop ballads. She did those sometimes, earned her big bills in the 42nd and Broadway area. All the Midwest tourists loved elevator music. She grimaced. Not ever.

She loved alternative, but couldn't do it well alone, on one guitar. Maybe with a synthesizer, but she couldn't play one if she had it, and she didn't have it. Hip hop wasn't her, either. Okay. Time to play again, the foot traffic had sped up, tired of her random chords.

"Leave me alone, or take me with you, I'm the woman you wanted all your life. Not a wife. Not a child, not a ruby on a pillow, a womaaaaaan . . ." They loved her songs. Edgy. Janis Joplin-ish . . . keep that in mind, she admonished herself. She could do worse for style.

Angrily she thought of Sody Garrett. Jesus, what a name. She ran through random names, still singing, but on autopilot. Auto. Ata. Atai. Alai. Alianna. Lianna. Well, think about that one.

She showed up the next day, having totally forgotten Sody Garrett's existence. She had her new name. Lian Logan. Since it had come to her late in the night, she'd decided to devote one more day at the familiar West 50th Street stop to "live" the name before moving to Grand Central. She wasn't Irish, but the Irish were famous for singing and writing and entertaining. Better than Listenberger. A Listenberger sounded like a manufacturer of pharmaceuticals. At best.

She considered picking up a slight Irish brogue. Clearing her throat she began, "Aye, 'tis so, me lad." Ick. She debated different ways to pick up a true Irish voice. Movies—too expensive. And what VCR would she use to play a video, even if she could pop for the three-dollar rental fee? Sometimes she stood and watched entire programs at the Wiz before being chased off. But some of those actors couldn't handle the brogue either without sounding like fake mish-mash. She put the thought aside for now.

The answer would come to her, like all the other answers. Luck shimmered in the air around her, it always had. She felt it. Ideas and songs—the assurance that all would come to her swam invisibly around her, nudging her in the right directions, bringing her whatever she needed. It was all there.

She started to strum, nudged her open case lid with one slender foot, moving the heavy molded-plastic case into the edges of the path of the crowd, not an obstacle, just a hint. Two crumpled dollar bills there already, her seed money. And then Sody walked up to her, shocking her into remembrance of yesterday's intrusion. She groaned to herself, wishing she'd gone to Grand Central after all.

On one thigh, he humped his big bass guitar in a black case. Duct tape patched several splits in the cheap cardboard, holding it together. It barely covered his guitar. She grimaced. You had to protect your instrument. His looked like he kicked it around on off days.

He greeted her with excitement. "Fantastic!" he exclaimed, not specifying just what was so fantastic. She lifted the edges of her mouth in a parody of welcome. And began to sing. An old tune, from Abba.

On the second stanza, he joined in, tuning his guitar as he strummed, swiftly catching up. She rolled from one style into another, one tempo into another. She couldn't faze him. They had to scoop up some of the money now and then and shove it out of sight, her case filled so fast. Never want the crowds to think you didn't need their dollars. After the third hour, suddenly she stopped, drained and unable to sing another note. He let his cords drift off into the tunnel and gazed fondly down at her. "Thought you'd never wear out. I been playin' on adrenalin the last hour. But we are so fuckin' good!"

"My name's Lian Logan," she said, trying it on him out loud. Her first foray into the great world of Irish balladeers.

"Yeah? Nice to meet you, Lian," he said, not looking at her. He was busy pulling out the dollars they'd hidden to dump them into her case. He crouched, then began making two meticulously neat piles. She watched, but he did the chore fair and honest.

He stretched as he stood. "Jeez, never did a three-hour gig straight through. I'm wrecked. How about you?"

She was, too, but ignored the question. "Listen, I play alone."

"Oh, c'mon! You never made that much money by yourself, don't tell me that."

She bristled. It was true. "I'm a lone act."

"Lian. Am I hustling you? Am I taking a bigger share, or all of it? And I could, a bitty thing like you, I'm twice your size. Don't you hear how great we sound together? We—we complement each other."

Lian scowled down at her case, now tenderly cradling her Gibson in its felt-lined bed, locked for safety. She swung the case up across her shoulders and back, the woven strap tight between her breasts.

"Tomorrow," he begged. "Just let me come tomorrow."

She looked off down the rails as if seeking the answer written in graffiti there. Feeling her success vibes, testing the idea on her surrounding luck. She stood motionless, waiting. Then, one last glance up at his pleading, handsome face, feeling the extra dollars in her pockets. "Ok. Tomorrow. Eleven." And she strode off toward the stairs to the streets above, melding into the crowd but alone in her thoughts.

The next day brought Sody and Lian together again, same place. Without consultation, she, leading off again, struck strongly into some vintage Dylan. He slammed into her path and, grinning, stayed with her all the way in a harmonic third, doing a fantastic job of it, too, she admitted grudgingly to herself. Then a bit of alternative that she'd picked up last week, not the whole song, but a change of pace and mood. Sody handled it well. Tall, slender, his blonde tipped hair shagged just right, he looked like a movie star. She thought about that as she watched him play. Talented, yes. And bringing in cash like a six-foot-tall ATM machine. She gazed off again down the empty track.

Maybe this was right for her at this stage of her career path. Maybe he'd been "sent" by those lucky airs that carried her to her golden goals. Suddenly she muted her voice, in effect offering him the lead. After a fleeting lift of eyebrows in surprise, he took off, letting her follow, making the decisions and taking the melody. He was excellent, she admitted. And he hadn't followed her home yesterday, so maybe he wasn't a creep. Finally, she nodded to herself and accepted him. This time at the end, she divided up the take and when handing over his share, looked up into his happy face and let herself really smile. "Welcome, Sody."

He heaved a deep sigh. "Thanks, Lian. You had me worried."

She shook her head as she wound the strap from her case around herself again. "Never worry, Sody. Bad for luck. See you tomorrow."

He lunged quickly into her path. "Want some dinner?"

She shut her eyes for a moment and silently cursed. Had she made a mistake after all? "No," she said shortly, then left.

The next day she and Sody were again at their post at the subway stop when a short dark young man stepped off the arriving train and walked directly toward them, the familiar stars in his determined eyes. Without pausing in her song, Lian screamed inwardly at her fate, enraged all over again. Was her life being wrenched from her control? Had she proven unworthy of her luck and had it abandoned her?

"Been hearing about you two topside, on the street.

Needing a keyboard?" he asked, and Lian gasped, forgetting her lyrics. Her hands dropped useless at her sides.

Sody let his bass chords die. He gazed coolly down at the short intruder and said, "You got one?"

Lian glanced at Sody. Normally she'd be furious at him for acting as leader, but now it didn't matter. Now she only strained to hear a distant voice come floating to her from down the presently empty track, telling her what to do.

The stranger was around five seven, a few inches taller than Lian, but his muscles strained his black jeans and tee nearly to bursting. A no-style no-neck, marveled Lian. Hadn't shaved for days, by the look of him, and not recently bathed by the smell, either. His dark hair, though, curved clean and smooth, the ruffled edges just hitting his shoulders, but unmarred by any purple or green dye, shit that Lian hated. He also lacked the endless body piercing Lian considered childish, although tattoos could make a statement—so long as the statement wasn't that you'd been somebody's "partner" in prison or membership in a drug gang. Losers, that lot.

She considered her last thought. Sounded a bit Irish. Excitement shivered through her for an instant. The lilt was coming. And to help it, this chunk of powerful Irish male had arrived. Again she threw her question down the tracks, asking her luck what to do with this keyboarder with muscles and the genuine brogue she'd longed to learn. No sign came. Or was the answer standing in front of her in the form of this new musician . . .

Just then Sody turned to her and said, "Let's give him a try, okay? If he sucks, I'll throw him back on the train." The young man glowered at that, as if his maleness had been challenged. Lian shrugged coolly, feeling anything but cool inside.

"Eleven tomorrow," she agreed. "Make an impression or Sody will help you fuck off."

The young man looked her over with black eyes melting

into black liquid. "Him? Small chance. Bugger you, more likely!"

She listened to this, lips parted and breathless. His voice slid like cream into her ears!

"What's your name?" she demanded.

"Joseph Francis Urban O'Rourke, then. Joe. And you?"

"Lian Logan," she said and his gaze changed. She saw the shrewdness in his lightning assessment of her. She knew he'd seen through her and out the other side. He knew it all. Her fake Irishness, her ambition, her dreams. Maybe even her luck. His eyes glittered but with a powerful maleness that Sody could never have summoned, despite his height. Lian doubted Sody would ever be able to throw this one onto a train. Or anywhere.

"Keyboard." She repeated stiffly, as if considering, and felt heat rise in her face.

She looked around for an electrical plug. As if he read her mind, he said, "I bring my own re-charge battery pack, if I need it, an' I usually do. Not a problem. Why ye got to sing b'neath God's good earth, though?" He looked around uneasily. "What's wrong with the open air?"

Lian's face hardened. "Not negotiable."

"Tomorrow then." They all nodded to each other and O'Rourke jumped down onto the track, and strolled along the narrow ledge where the trainmen usually walked to get to a needed repair down the line. Lian shivered to watch his carelessness of the massive trains and wondered if this was a stupid male display to impress her. It did.

In the coming days, O'Rourke became an asset, as Lian had guessed he would, since her luck must have summoned him to her. He seemed to live in an aura of confidence. He didn't know as many songs as Sody, but he could plug in spots as he caught on to the progression of chords and fill out the music until he quickly learned it.

Lian's voice soared like an angel borne up on the talents of these two, but she was careful to practice the song in private. Over the next weeks, they made a lot of money, enabling Lian to dress more and more to fit the image she had chosen, rather than to just cover her body. She sublet a closet of an apartment, one room with several doors, each of which opened to a murphy bed, the toilet, and a sink next to a two burner stove, so she finally had somewhere relatively clean—and safe—to sleep. And she carefully gave no hint of its location to Sody, Joe, or anyone.

Then it happened. Lian moved the trio to "her" place outside Grand Central's double doors on 42nd Street. Joe, relieved to leave the dank underground behind, bloomed in the bright sun and his performances sharpened, to Sody and Lian's delight. Within a week, a portly man dressed in all black stopped to hear not just one song, but several. He stood close by for nearly an hour, reminding Lian of a Catholic priest in his black three-button suit hanging open over the black silk mock-turtleneck tee. His head nodded to the beat of their music, obviously enjoying himself. Then a sudden realization caused Lian to drop out of the performance of "Baby Jones," too breathless to sing. It was *him!* Her "luck" had brought him!

Sody glanced at her in concern, but after a deep gasp for breath, she rejoined the chorus, her voice energized and full of new emotion.

At the finish, the man gave her his card, as she'd known he would. "I represent Krim Recordings. How about a meet tomorrow? Four-ish good for you? Bring your instruments." Lian nodded with as much coolness as she could muster. Sody and Joe gaped. As soon as the man turned the corner, disappearing from sight, Sody snatched the card from Lian's fingers.

"*Krim!* Omigod!"

"Aye! We got to—what do we got to do?" For the first time, Joe looked flummoxed.

Lian gazed at her partners in disgust. She thought Sody might cry, from the look on his face. "Well what did ye expect!" she shrieked at them both. Staying in her Irish persona was more important now than ever before. "What's the point of this if not to step up?"

Joe stared at her, blinking. "Oh, aye. Sure!"

Sody swallowed hard. "I can't sing anymore today. I can't."

Lian said, "And why should ye? We'll be superstars after tomorrow!"

Sody froze, absorbing that thought. After a long moment, he glanced at Lian and nodded. "Right." He packed his bass guitar into the battered case. "Go home, Joe. Get some rest. You too," he ordered Lian. "Go on." He gave them each a paternal wave, permission to leave. Joe, hugging his keyboard to his chest in excitement, nearly ran down 42nd street.

Lian didn't move. She gazed at Sody, her eyes interested.

"Go on, Lian," he repeated. "You need rest, too. See you tomorrow." He patted her shoulder, not noticing how she jerked her shoulder from beneath his hand. He jaywalked across the street to enter the small coffee shop he liked to frequent. Lian, still not moving, watched him through the shop window until he began giving his order to a waitress.

Then Lian turned and descended the stairs to the subways, took a train back to her old spot, the West 50th Street stop. When she got out, she opened her case again, seeded it with the two crumpled dollars, and began to sing alone: 'Leave me now, I've moved on anyhow. Lah tee dah, down the MTA highway, the next stop will be better, Lah tee dah . . . ' Her song. The song. Her voice lifted and the tunnel seized it to send it soaring. Passengers paused to hear the whole song before moving on.

And "Baby Jones." The two gits hadn't realized she'd written that song herself. It had caught on too fast to keep other street groups from stealing it, but it was hers. She'd registered that and the "Lah Tee Dah" song, and over twenty others she'd written, with the copyright office, the real one in Washington DC at the Library of Congress. She'd gotten a guy over at a Staples store to help her find and then fill out the papers. It had taken a few flattering lies, a few evenings of flirtation, but no sex, to get it done. Lian had no intention of sleeping her way to anywhere.

Her grandmother had taught her, *promise anything, but give them nothing.* Lian, a very young Hermione Listenberger at that time, had taken this advice to heart. Her bubbe was smart. She'd survived exceedingly well in a male-dominated world, with much worse circumstances to deal with back then, Lian knew. Bless you, thank you, Lian sent her gratitude floating through the air to her bubbe. Bubbe was her "luck." Her bubbe's was the voice she'd listened to all her life, her mother having proven to be of no help in any way—well, except to show the stupidity of trying to use sex to get ahead. Although Lian supposed that knowledge was useful, too.

All afternoon Lian sang only her own songs, no Abba, no Dylan, no anybody else but herself. And the crowds paused, entranced, and left dollar bills in their wake. After every song, Lian nodded her gratitude at her "luck," her beloved 'bubbe' watching over her from farther down the empty track. Then she went home.

The next day, she didn't show up at the Grand Central entrance doors. Like lost sheep, the two men split up to look for her, figuring she must be in trouble. She'd never missed a day, and certainly wouldn't miss today, their last rehearsal together to hone them for the afternoon meeting with the recording executive. They split up. Joe, by choice, set off to cruise the streets around Grand Central and Sody took the tunnels.

About an hour later, Joe reluctantly descended into the tunnels himself. They'd all three almost exclusively ridden the 9 train, so he anticipated finding both Sody and Lian with little trouble. At the 59th Street station, he heard an unusual commotion. Not that the tunnels weren't always echoing one racket or another, but this was different. These sounds were of terror, like animals trapped in a burning pen. As he threaded his way to the front of the crowd, Joe glimpsed a body being strapped onto a gurney in preparation to be lifted up the steep stairs to street level.

"What happened?" he asked a plump fiftyish Hispanic woman near him whose frozen expression reflected his own.

"He fell," she whispered, fear stark in her creamy brown eyes.

Just before the medic pulled the covering over the body's face, Joe recognized the corpse. He stifled a sharp cry and stumbled backward to nearly fall over the Hispanic woman, who hadn't moved.

"He—Madre de Dios, he fell!" she whispered again to herself. She shuddered, then suddenly retreated to huddle against the gate, far from the edge of the track platform and began mouthing words only she could hear.

Prayers, Joe guessed, and from a youthful habit, himself shakily began, "Holy Mary, Mother of God . . . "

Then Joe's mouth couldn't quite close and he suddenly felt claustrophobic in the tunnel. Grimy oil-slick stairs going down to lower, filthier tunnels, and more stairs to other dark exits and entrances taunted and closed in on him like living threats. He hoisted his keyboard in his arms like a long heavy baby and darted for the stairs to the street.

When he emerged, he raised his face to the sun and breathed until he could calm himself. A small hand touched his elbow, and he jumped, choking back a fearful cry. When his vision cleared he discovered Lian gazing at him in astonishment. "What's wrong?" she asked.

"Sody!" Joe's voice cracked. He coughed, then tried again. "It's Sody, lass. He's gone."

"Gone? What?" Lian suddenly huddled against his hard-muscled arm as if frightened. "You mean he's dead, don't you! How?" she demanded, but her voice was soft, trembling. "He was awfully tense about the audition. Did he . . . ?

Joe's testosterone kicked in and he straightened his shoulders. "Nay, lass," he began, "He had no reason to—the crowds . . . he fell. It was an accident." He shook his head. "He was looking for you. We both were. Where've ye been?"

Lian looked at him strangely. "Resting. For our audition today. Weren't you?"

"Nah. We came to play as always. Like a rehearsal. If ye wanted to rest today, why didn't ye say so yesterday? We worried! If we hadn't, then maybe Sody might still be . . . might not've . . ."

Lian shuddered. "You mean it's my fault, then? I'm sorr—"

"Nah. Didn't mean that. Forgive me. No fault to yersel'. He slipped, is all. It's so dark down there, and crowded, the floors coated with grease from the trains. I hate the tunnels, truth be known."

He put one arm around her and she leaned against him and they stood entwined in silence. "I'm scared, Joe," Lian finally said, her voice small. Joe's arm tightened around her and he let his keyboard slide to the sidewalk.

He kissed the top of her head and swallowed hard. "Lian, my angel, no reason to fear wi' me around. Ye must know how I've felt about ye since the first day . . . doesn't seem right to say so now with Sody gone . . . but . . . " He shook his head. "I'm here for ye, Lian. Always. I think ye know that, don't ye."

Lian lifted her head at that and sang softly to him, "Always, and forever, in darkness of night, in darkness of daytime, in darkness of sight . . . "

Joe's eyebrows lifted and he gazed tenderly at her soft mouth as it moved, digging words out of her brain, making a new song.

"Yer lovely, my Lian. A nightingale."

She backed away. "Joe, we have to go back down there right now."

"What! To the tunnels? Why?"

"It's my place. My luck. I must go! I can't let Sody's ghost keep me away. Joe, take me. Be with me. I need this, or I can't succeed at the audition! But I can't go down there alone!"

At the balky look on Joe's face, she said softly, "We'll pick a different station. A lighter one, cleaner. Where isn't important. It's that—I can't sing without my luck. And my luck lives in the tunnels. We have only an hour before our appointment with fame. Fame we deserve!"

Joe stared at her, then at his feet, then away. "Yer daft, lass. No good going down there again. Make your luck come up to you!"

She jerked herself away from him. "Forget it, then. No appointment."

Joe exhaled sharply as if she'd punched him in the stomach. "Audition alone? Me? I'm a keyboarder who can sing some, but not like you! Ye'd ruin me chances by leaving!"

"I have no choice. I can't go without my luck! And it's down there!"

Joe breathed heavily, lips pale.

Lian said, "Are you afraid of Sody's ghost? He loved us! He wouldn't hurt anybody, let alone you. I'm not afraid."

"Okay, okay!" Joe turned, then stopped. "Not here, for God's sake."

"I said so, didn't I? Our old place. 50th Street. Let's go there. And we'll walk, not take a train. Can you carry the keyboard that far?"

Joe nodded wordlessly and they walked side by side, Joe unhappy but unable to stop his Lian. "My Lian," he murmured to himself, as if comforting himself that she was "his" and so worth facing the tunnels. Worth facing the fright the tunnels had always held for him, but he'd kept concealed. As he walked on, gradually he relaxed and eased nearly all the way back into his normal cocky self.

AT FOUR, LIAN Logan appeared at Krim Recordings. When she stepped into the office of the man who'd worn all black when he'd first heard her sing, she saw that he was again dressed in all black. She idly wondered if he had four or five identical outfits like that.

Buoyed by this opportunity that her luck had brought, she stood straight and as tall as her small frame allowed. Krim Recordings was the top studio in Manhattan. Probably the Western Hemisphere, she speculated.

The man backhanded a flaccid wave at her in greeting, not rising from his black leather chair, rather leaning back and swiveling as he wordlessly examined her like a doctor preparing to give her a physical. She made a mental note that when she rose to the top she'd make sure every man in every room she entered would rise in respect. Soon.

"Where're your partners?" he asked.

"They weren't my partners. I work alone."

"And the music . . . ?"

"Twenty-seven of the songs are mine. I wrote them and own the copyrights to them all." Her assurance carried her through the long moment during which the man stared at her.

Suddenly she said, "Listen to my signature song. I don't believe you've heard it. It would be the showpiece of my first CD." And without permission, she lifted the Gibson from its case, slipped the strap over her shoulder and began, "Leave me now, I've moved on anyhow. Lah tee dah, down the MTA highway, the next stop will be better, lah tee dah . . . "

At the end, the man sighed. "Totally. Totally."

She nodded, taking the compliment as her due.

Then he rose from his chair, opened the heavy oak paneled door to his outer office, stuck his head through and shouted, "Get Bobby in here. And Frank—no, I don't care what they're in the middle of, get them now."

He shut the door again, smiled into her perplexed face and sat. "It'll only be a minute."

"What will—"

But just then the door opened and in strolled two young men. The blond one with very long hair had that emaciated, bad facial-skin look of chronic drug use, although his eyes were clear. Fresh from rehab, Lian guessed. The other looked like an ex–beach bum, sun-streaked curly mop of dark hair, dark tan, lean and muscled, his shirt unbuttoned to display sixpack abs and an outie belly-button ring. The ring had a large stone in it, all too obviously a cubic zirconium—if it had been a diamond, he'd have needed a body guard, she thought scornfully. The rings in his ears were too numerous to count, ending in one large stud in his right earlobe. Shmuck, thought Lian to herself. Both men gazed at her expectantly.

Then she got it. Lian exhaled deeply. She turned to the man in the chair. "They sing."

The man nodded enthusiastically. "You need partners. You three will blend like sons of bitches. And if not," he shrugged. "We have technology that will—"

"I work alone," said Lian, her voice deeper and clearly full of anger held in only tenuous check.

She repeated, in case he hadn't gotten the idea. "I work a—"

"You sing for us, we handle things the way we want. Only deal you'll get."

"And my songs?"

"Oh, you'll be the headliner, no question. Songs and all. We'll fix you up with some backup instruments."

Lian listened as the man in black outlined the next years of her life. The two "singers" bobbed their heads like plastic dogs in a back window of a vintage car. First Lian examined one, then the other. She nodded to herself, as if agreeing with a voice inside her head.

She turned her attention back to the black-clothed manager from Krim Recording Studios. He was digging in his drawer for a contract form. She read it over twice, crossed out one paragraph outlining a few rules about her so-called "band," then altered the three-year length of the agreement to one year. She raised her eyebrows to see if the man would object.

He waved away the rejected paragraph, but then looked up in disbelief. "One year? Most performers would give their mother's arm to increase their time with Krim!" He pronounced the agency name as if speaking of the pope.

"We'll see how you do," she only said.

He gave a short laugh, shrugged, initialed the changes, then signed and initialed three more copies. She did the same. He gave her a copy that she tucked into her deepest jeans pocket.

As he carefully recapped his burgundy Mont Blanc pen, she said, "I like to spend time underground."

The man's brow furrowed. "Under—"

"In the subway tunnels. The action there inspires my songs. I can't write them anywhere else."

The man waved a magnanimous hand at the two male "singers." "Hey! I understand art. You guys go with her, practice down there. You might even pick up her style better down there. Worth the effort."

The two men shrugged, obviously under total control of the man in black.

Lian placed her guitar carefully back into its case, hefted it up over her shoulders. She nodded at the two. "Bobbie?" she asked the ex-druggie.

He shook his head. "Frank. This here's Bobbie." He thumbed in the other singer's direction.

Lian ignored Frank's outthrust hand. "Meet me eleven A.M. tomorrow at . . ." she considered. "The East 34th Street entrance to the downtown tunnel. Right?" She felt she'd worn out the usefulness of the West 50th Street station.

The two nodded.

Just Another Hollywood Ending

DAVID BART

"IS SHE DEAD?"

It was a feminine voice, echoing through the hollow darkness in which Matt Corey lay; perhaps a faint glow from somewhere removed, he couldn't be sure.

A booming sound had preceded the unseen woman's question; something loud enough to have awakened him . . . though he must surely still be dreaming, suspended without sensation in this featureless void, a profound absence of feeling throughout his entire body . . . except maybe his face, seemed he could feel movement of air.

"I did the guy," the male voice said, followed by an ominous clicking sound.

Weird dream. Maybe one of those lucid kind where you—

—*another booming roar!*—*streak of fire pierced the blackness, briefly illuminating a . . .* hell, he couldn't be sure he'd glimpsed anything really.

"Never would have suspected she had a lover," the male voice declared over a papery sound; back of a hand scraping the edge of a lamp shade, groping for a switch.

The woman blurted, "What're you, *jealous?*"

The conversation seemed too linear for a dream; Corey's dreams were usually fragmented, jumping back and forth along the temporal line like a decaying quark, and he didn't really *hear* voices in other dreams, somehow just sensed them.

—incredibly harsh light flashed through Corey's eyes to the back of his brain! So phenomenally bright there should have been pain—which quickly faded into a dark-spotted glow, like flashbulbs discharging in your face, reminding Corey of the hoards of paparazzi at some promo tour or movie premier.

The male voice, exclaiming, "Wha—who in hell is this?"

The words were clear but also distant, like conversation skittering across a still lake at night, voices originating a half-mile away but so distinct it's as if the people stood next to you on the dock.

"I recognize *him,* I think, but that's not your wife!" the woman said.

Vague images began to congeal within the fuzzy glow before him, black spots fading . . . indistinct forms and surfaces grew ever-more defined, though his line of vision was along a single plane—couldn't move his eyes or even blink—staring fixedly upward at an angle.

The upper edge of a huge, Spanish-style armoire appeared in the gathering clarity, and a mirror, presumably attached to a dresser below . . . a closet, though all Corey could see were tops of louvered, white folding doors—above it was all black and empty, as though the periphery of tunnel vision. He was unable to move his line of sight downward, see if there were bodies to go with the voices.

Was there another form next to him? Another person? He sighed inwardly; if there were two of them, lying side-by-side, then this is definitely not a dream. This is getting caught in the act.

Corey felt a movement of air pass over his face, very cool but oddly abrasive, and he could suddenly *sense* that another form had moved next to the bed, standing there looking down on him—could make out a vague form at the edge of his view but could not move his eyes in order to define features.

"A *movie star* for Christ's sake," the male voice exclaimed. "Why the hell would someone famous be in my house?"

"They're naked, Vince," the female voice replied dryly, "it's obvious what they were doing—what I'd like to know is who's the woman, and why is she in *your* bedroom?"

LAST SUMMER . . .

Corey had removed a section of railing and was sitting on the elevated redwood deck of his Malibu home, legs dangling, gazing out over the frothy surf at the distant horizon of a startlingly blue Pacific—ignoring the giggling covey of string-bikinied starlets jogging by on the raked sand below, glancing up at him, unabashedly displaying their pendulous attributes, doing so with a great deal of enthusiasm.

All Matt Corey noticed was the emptiness he felt. He had always labored under the dense weight of some kind of indefinable angst, but lately the burden of this dark mood had grown intolerable . . . and now, when he sighed, it was as if it were his last breath.

Margo Aston lay behind him on a chaise longue, topless and gleaming under the afternoon sun—poster girl for tanning oil. "Whatsa matter, superstar?" she asked, using the term she knew he detested, trying to get him stirred up a little—even his explosive anger was better than this tiresome depression.

Making a point of looking around him, palms turned upward, Corey sighed yet again, asking, "This is *it*—all those movies and all the money, famous all over the planet, and this is all the better it feels?"

"You think too much, Matt," Margo said, raising eyebrows and causing mirror-glass shades to slip down onto the bridge of her nose.

He pulled up his legs and turned to look at her. Great body. Great personality. Average mind. "And *you* think too little," he replied, though of course that was bullshit; he knew she was always thinking, especially about whatever movie project she was producing—she just didn't cotton to philosophical musing.

Margo put a mirrored gaze on him, saying, "You work more than Hackman, never seen anybody work harder—you need to learn to play hard, too."

Corey smiled. "You complaining?"

"Not talking about sex, I'm talking about taking chances, living on the edge."

"You want I should rob a bank?" Pointing a cocked thumb and extended finger her way.

Shook her head, short red hair hardly moving. "Not anything illegal, just improper—course illegal would be better—but nothing with guns or where somebody gets hurt," Margo said, turning onto her flat stomach.

"You speaking from experience?"

Shrugged, resting her head on crossed hands. "When Jack and I were together we used to . . ." and she explained some adventures her former lover and she had gone on in Hawaii, Paris, São Paulo, and Morocco. "You could do things like that, too," she said, "nothing really dangerous, but risky in some way . . . gotta have an imminent deadline, clock ticking, a threat of being caught, something to lose."

Might work, Corey thought . . . then wondered what in hell was wrong with him; he was known by a couple billion people around the planet, richer'n Croesus, have any woman he wanted, and yet he was still not satisfied. Looking for some meaning to it all.

Course maybe it was true, you had to struggle to be genuinely happy . . . take a risk now and then, put something on the line—start out with a few break-ins, then maybe something riskier; he needed something to fan the flames, 'cause it sure seemed that getting there wasn't just half the fun, it was the whole enchilada.

*   *   *

. . . THIS IS DEFINITELY not a dream, it's a real bedroom.

Not *his* bedroom but something familiar about it.

Those roars must've been gunshots. Though if he'd been shot, why no pain? Was he in shock? Trauma-induced catatonia—like that horror flick he'd done early in his career about being buried alive? Or had a bullet severed his spine?

A sudden thought shied beneath him—the body next to him, who was it?

Margo? Yes, it had to be Margo. That was the second shot. Ah, damn . . . not Margo.

He tried to turn his head but couldn't move . . . after a few moments, various lines he'd memorized for doctor roles over the years began echoing through his mind: *I'm sorry, Mrs. Baker . . . no sensorimotor impulses emanating from your husband's brain . . . can't move a muscle.*

That fits . . . friggin' statue, stone cold and helpless.

Of course now something else has begun to happen— surroundings are growing darker, as though someone was slowly dimming a light switch; could still make out objects, top of the walls, but they seemed vague and indistinct. A grainy dense fog began to materialize in the air, dull and menacing . . .

Oh, Christ, he's losing even this limited vision . . .

—another part he'd played on daytime TV resonated inside his skull: *It appears certain, Ms. Moore, that your boyfriend is going blind, what we in the healing business call vision-dead . . . this is a condition caused by the fact that his primary visual cortex has nearly ceased functioning due to the extensive brain damage.*

Having recited that unwieldy line, the script had demanded even more from his character: *All that remains for your poor dear companion are the few moments left him before the rest of his brain dies,* he'd said.

The actress playing the girlfriend had cried out inappropriately, as though startled, emitting a strange, sustained shriek, sounding more like she'd been goosed than expressing anguish. Broke the whole crew up—even the asshole director had laughed.

Corey attempted a deep breath, though couldn't tell what was going on in his chest, thinking: *got no smell. Losing sight. Can't move. Margo dead. Christ, with all this crap there must be a pony in here some—*

"My God, lookit the blood," the female voice exclaimed.

Something about the exuberance in her voice made Corey want to scrunch up his nose and sneer . . . if only he could.

Because even spatial orientation was difficult, though he knew he was prone on a bed next to Margo—but it still felt like he was floating. A memory came to Corey as if it'd happened only yesterday . . . he'd been buoyed in a sensory deprivation tank on the set of a movie about regressive therapy; scene involved a portrayal of his character experiencing weird visions, archetypal images, and finally a kind of body-death, but with total consciousness. One line he'd had to recite: *"I can almost touch my soul."*

Corey hadn't wanted to say it but didn't have enough clout back then to refuse. Now he'd tell the biggest director in Hollywood to shove that line where the sun don't shine.

Complete darkness settled silently over him like a shroud of heavy ash . . . he was now totally blind—*where the sun don't shine.* Couldn't feel any movement in his chest, couldn't see, couldn't smell, didn't know if he could still hear or not . . . for all Corey knew, he was dead, his consciousness remaining behind like a child at the top of the stairs, not wanting to miss anything going on down below.

*   *   *

LATER THAT LAST summer . . .

"What if we get caught?" Corey whispered, his hand on Margo's shoulder as they both crouched in darkness next to the house, suddenly feeling he might have taken a wrong turn in his quest for meaning.

"That's the point, Gomer—things can go wrong—your crime could be reported in the tabloids, the cops would treat you like a felon, your career would be crippled by the notoriety . . . but you can't have the juice without the risk," Margo said.

She'd jimmied the door and turned off the alarm the way some ex-con crewman had shown her earlier that week at the sound stage. It was pretty dark in the foyer, though some faint light was coming from a distant room.

They made their way quickly up to the master bedroom, knowing they had less than an hour or so before the owner was to return to the house.

Making love was heightened by every tiny noise they heard, but it was as much the idea of trespassing that turned Corey on; brought up by an aunt and uncle who were fanatics about their privacy and respecting the privacy of others— step off the sidewalk onto somebody's lawn and you got a good smack on the back of the head. He'd learned to avoid the edge, not even walk along it.

After the lovemaking, they decided to not straighten the covers, Margo reciting from "The Three Bears": "Somebody's been sleeping in *my* bed," leaving washcloths and towels strewn about on the bathroom floor—then down to the kitchen where she made them sandwiches while Corey poured them stemmed glasses of wine, dribbling some on the counter.

They ate, drank, and talked until they heard the garage door go up—that would be Garry Howard, the former producer who owned the place returning home; this was a guy who hated Corey because he'd refused to do a couple projects and the industry rags had picked up on the rejection, ridiculing the executive, ultimately getting him demoted a few notches, assistant-assistant to someone or other.

Corey knew Howard would press charges if he caught them. Scream to the tabloids. Yeah, this little game was something of a risk—but they were both grinning at each other as they jumped to their feet, headed for the side door leaving the mess on the counter, laughing and giggling like teenagers.

DEAD.

An intense feeling of remorse flooded through Corey; he wanted so very badly to be able to look at Margo at least one more time—and in the wanting he could almost hear her breathing—no, that was the other woman, Vince's squeeze.

"What're we going to do?" the female voice asked anxiously, the sound of fingernails being nervously clicked together over and over.

"Jesus, why's some movie star in here anyway—my wife doesn't know anybody like that."

"You sure, hotshot? Maybe you got that wrong, too."

Corey heard a rustle of movement followed by a loud slap. The woman shrieked.

"I didn't get nothing wrong, bitch—dammit, we gotta figure our way out of this!" Vince said. His voice held panic, almost strident.

Silence.

Finally, the woman's voice. "Well, they don't belong here, if we just leave and let your wife find them she'll call the police and it'll look like somebody broke in and shot them—let her explain it," she said, adding, "when is she coming home?"

Vince snorted. "I didn't even know she'd be gone—thought that was her in bed with somebody."

"Well, why don't we just leave and let her find them—you're supposed to be in Seattle, right?" the woman said.

Corey could hear his own breathing, slow and shallow, hardly audible; like he'd been drugged or something.

Drugged?

—*hell, that was it!* Margo had told him that she knew the woman who lived here, heard she and her husband were not getting along and that he was out of town and the woman would be home at around—well, about now. So that was it; Margo had set it all up. They'd made love and afterward he'd dozed off like always—his ritual post-coital nap—and she'd injected him with something. The drug immobilized him, numbed him all over and temporarily shut down his vision. In fact, it was like a movie he'd refused to do for Garry Howard, the producer whose house they'd broken into—the plot was about a guy shot up with a drug that evoked catatonia. Too implausible, he'd told Howard.

Vince's voice interrupted Corey's musing. "I guess you're right . . . we'll take off and just let my wife find these bodies and call the cops."

—*empty wire hangers rattling, sound of something being taken from the closet—swishing sound.*

"What're you doing?" the female asked.

"Wiping for prints."

"You live here, dummy, your prints belong here."

Corey smiled inwardly. These people should get an Oscar for their performances. Very convincing. And how 'bout Margo's acting—lying over there so quietly he'd thought she was already dead, doing it all so he'd appreciate life more, being on the edge of death.

From downstairs came the sound of a door opening and closing, someone moving about.

Vince whispered, "Jesus, must be my wife."

Silence. Then more sounds of movement from downstairs. Humming.

The sound of a gun being cocked. "Vince, what're you doing?" the woman in the bedroom asked.

Dull footsteps on the carpeted stairs could be heard, another woman's voice calling up from below. "Vince, I saw the light—are you home?"

The woman in the room whispered harshly, "Watch that gun, dammit, it's cocked."

Vince whispering back, "I'm going to do her—make it look like she killed herself after a *ménage à trois* gone bad, killed them and then herself."

"Vince," the wife called again, "why can't you answer?" Sound of someone ascending the stairs.

Corey would have shook his head if possible—this little play was pretty involved. Next thing you know they'll be shooting every—

—*booming roar of a gun!*

Corey could hear a gurgling sound coming from the woman in the room, Vince gasping in alarm. "Noooo . . . it went off—the damn gun—"

"My god, Vince—was that a *gunshot?*" the wife shouted from the staircase, her voice tremulous.

Damn good acting, Corey thought—supposed to think Vince just accidentally shot his accomplice. If he could applaud he would. Now . . . how long before the drug wears off?

"SHE'S DUE WHEN?" Corey had asked as they entered the house.

"About an hour."

"Well, Margo, if you know her, where's the thrill?—she wouldn't turn you in."

A wry grin on her face, Margo had replied, "I fired her from a picture once and she hasn't worked in the industry since."

"Christ, she'll probably shoot both of us," Corey'd answered.

In the bedroom. "Nice armoire," Margo'd said, already undressed, just black bikini panties and a smile—a sight of which Corey never tired.

Shrugging out of his clothes, he'd asked, "So, she's divorcing her husband, huh?"

"Yeah, he comes from the hitters."

Corey'd nodded. "They say it's the violence in movies."

A HEAVY THUD!

Corey'd heard enough actors fall onto stages . . . that was the unmistakable sound a body makes hitting the floor.

"My God, my god, my god . . ."

And now comes ol' Vince, overacting after doing so well up to now. Corey felt a finger twitch. *Finally, the damn drug is wearing off.*

"Vince, please answer me, I'm scared!" The wife screeching now, calling up from a distance, probably the bottom of the stairs—must've gone back down after the shot, pretending fear. "Are you hurt, Vince . . . what happened?" her voice shaky.

From the foot of the bed comes the sound of hollow metal lightly clicking against teeth . . . the gun being cocked again. Low moan . . . .

Christ, more drama, Corey thought. A finger twitched again—felt something like a tickle at his wrist, a thickening in his throat and the sensation of wanting to swallow . . . still couldn't see.

Another booming roar!

Alright with the goddamn gunshots, Corey thought, wishing he could show his disdain for the tiresome little charade he'd been forced to hear. Goddamn day players.

—sound of yet another body crumpling to the floor . . . Corey was really sick of the whole thing by now.

From downstairs came the sound of movement as the wife apparently crossed the tile foyer, high heels clicking, front door being opened, hinges squawking, followed by the chirping sound of a cell phone being powered up. "Police?—I want to report an intruder in my house, there's been gunsho—"

Her words cut off—*sound of the slammed door dully reverberating throughout the house*—the noise caused a full-body involuntary spasm, the movement causing Corey's numbed head to loll to one side, vision partially clearing, but blotched with dark spots, bursting little stars before his eyes. But in that moment he could see . . .

Oh God, that looks like real blood!—could see in a tight close-up, staring at the gaping gunshot wound in—

It wasn't Margo! It was his costar, Jennifer Diaz!

"CUT!"

Sounds of people getting to their feet, a lot of sudden noises, the familiar sounds of a movie set. "Okay, people, that's a wrap—let's re-light for the overhead shots. Matt, you and Jenny can take a break but leave the bloody clothes on. And Jenny, try not to screw up the wound, please."

Corey recognized the director's voice. Young guy with the talent of a Spielberg—real comer. Shaven head, intense eyes. Smiled when he was pissed.

Thank God! This isn't real—they're just shooting a scene!

—a movement next to him in the bed caused his body to roll a little to his left from a sudden change in mattress support. Jennifer Diaz getting up.

So those sounds of footsteps on the stairs, the gunshots, door slamming—had all been effects.

—tsunami of memories flooded Corey's mind, apparently blocked until now by the drug. . . wait a minute, what drug? This was a

movie scene—but if he wasn't drugged, why had he forgotten about Margo's production?

—remembering now how Margo'd gotten the idea from them getting cheap thrills doing the break-ins and such; she'd put it into development and her staff came up with a movie treatment: about a disillusioned movie star taking small chances in order to feel alive, then everything going wrong—Adam Schaffer had penned a great screenplay, ended up with a high-concept thriller . . . and Corey remembered coming to the sound stage that morning, he and Jennifer doing the death scene on the bed . . .

—he'd noticed Garry Howard, the ruined producer, coming onto the set at about their seventh take, lot-pass hanging from his wrinkled suit coat pocket, smirking as he huddled in the shadows behind the floor lights; dumbass must've thought he was hidden. During a break Corey'd taken a nap in his trailer, woke up with an itching on his arm, thought it was a spider bite.

"Hey, superstar?" Margo said, voice coming out of darkness, the feeling of a hand on his shoulder . . . no, the pressure was just in his mind, still couldn't feel a thing. And it was dark again—his sight had faded.

"Matt?" Margo said, concern in her voice.

The spider bite?—had it actually been an injection, Howard creeping into the trailer while he napped, giving him a drug to put him in a coma and ultimately kill him?

"Something's wrong with Matt!" Margo shrieked.

Sounds of people rushing toward the bed. Voices urgent and scared—virtual chorus of screams, angry shouts and finally a few moans.

He could envision Howard standing back behind a set piece—maybe the demented ex-producer had found out about them breaking into his house last summer, thought Corey was mocking him—and the guy had *snapped,* little loose in the brain pan anyway from all reports—and so then the inevitable plot twist would have to be ol' Garry Howard deciding to kill the actor he blamed for ruining his career.

The set lights had been shut down; he could hear them ticking as they cooled—cast and crew had moved off to wait for the medical services team. He sensed a deep cold spreading through his body and he knew it was the last act. Final Curtain.

With imminent death comes a compensatory indifference, borne not of resignation but of humor . . . couldn't remember where he'd read that but it was true; his present circumstance seemed somehow funny. Even whimsical.

—and here's Margo, weeping, probably standing vigil next to him, his body still bloodied with that special goop the young director insists on—looks so real it turns your stomach—Corey imagined her there, head bowed, alone on the darkened set. Sobbing.

As for his killer, would justice prevail? Probably. Howard will more than likely brag about it, tell the story to some producer who'll drop a dime. Or the autopsy will reveal the lethal injection of drugs, cops'll get a list of enemies. Something . . .

Everyone knows you can't get away with murder in Hollywood.

The Search for Robert Rich

BOB SHAYNE

I'D COME FROM a land called Brooklyn where everybody was Jewish and poor. Now I was going to a land called Hollywood where everybody was Jewish and rich. Well, that might be a bit of an exaggeration on both ends, but it seemed that way.

It was 1957 and I was twenty-five. I may or may not have been the youngest licensed private detective in the New York phone book, but I was certainly the femalest. My name's Naomi Weinstein. The second syllable rhymes with the first.

We pulled into Los Angeles Union Station at 1:32 P.M. on a late April afternoon. I'd slept well and long to the rock and sway and the clicking wheels, and I was looking forward to seeing my dear friend David. He'd moved to Hollywood four years earlier, after a slight problem wherein he'd been charged with murder. I had a hand in getting him off, but then I'd had a hand in getting him accused, so it seemed only right.

"Naomi!" he shouted as I stepped off the train in the bowels of Union Station. We ran to each other and embraced. He picked me up and swung me around in a circle. I wriggled out of his arms to avoid throwing up on him, stepped back, and took a look.

He was just as tall and skinny as always, the ever-present gold modernistic mezuzah resting just under his Adam's apple, his long pointy nose angled slightly to the right, hazel eyes, enough of that thick, wavy, dirty-blond hair for two or three guys, and that great crooked smile that always made me smile to see.

He was studying me, too, all five foot three, fuzzy reddish-brown hair, and a few too many pounds of me. I stuck out my breasts and sucked in my tummy as his eyes passed various portions of my anatomy. If I could have added a few inches to my calves I would have done that, too.

"How was your trip?" he asked as he grabbed my bags and we walked toward the Moorish-Aztec style lobby. I doubt that the Moors ever met the Aztecs, but apparently the architect had.

David took me for lunch on a nearby block called Olvera Street. It's supposed to be a 150-year-old section of old Los Angeles, but it looked more like Coney Island to me. A block of souvenir shops and taco stands. (Okay, in Coney they'd be hotdogs stands instead.) I bought three things that were advertised as Mexican jumping beans. Later in my motel room I opened one; it turned out to be a soft capsule, and inside was a ball-bearing, so that when you dropped it the little bearing would roll to one end then the other making the capsule jump. How authentic can you get! I didn't know then it was the perfect metaphor for Hollywood.

We piled my stuff into David's spiffy aqua-and-white Chevy Bel Air convertible and he put the top down at my request. I'd never ridden in a convertible. (When I tried to untangle my Semitic curls that evening, I swore I'd never ride in one again.)

David asked me what my case was about, shouting over the wind as he drove up San Vicente, a wide street with trolley tracks down the middle, on our way to Hollywood. I told him it was to track down somebody named Robert Rich.

He laughed, saying that was the biggest mystery there was. It was all over the papers. The whole town wanted to know who Robert Rich was.

It seems Mr. Rich had won the Oscar a few weeks earlier for Best Original Story for the Screen, for a movie about a little boy and a bull called *The Brave One,* but nobody could find him. Or many people were claiming to be him. Or both. When the award was announced, Jesse Lasky Jr. of the Writers Guild stepped up to the microphone on national television and said, "I'll accept this on behalf of my close friend Robert Rich, who is at this moment at Santa Monica hospital where his wife is giving birth." But Hedda Hopper checked all the hospitals and no such baby had been born. A few days later when push came to shove Lasky admitted he had never met Robert Rich and hadn't a clue who he was.

You'd think the producers of the movie who bought the story would know who they'd bought it from, but it didn't seem that way. They were brothers named King. When a reporter noticed they had a nephew by the name Robert Rich, the nephew gave a statement saying, yes, he'd written the picture. But then his uncles denied it.

"Did the Kings hire you to find the guy?" David asked.

"No, the *L.A. Times* did," I shouted back over the hot wind—something David told me the locals call a Santa Ana. "Their reporters haven't been able to find him so they decided to try a private eye."

"Makes sense. But we have our own private eyes right here in Los Angeles. You know, like Philip Marlowe?"

"Yeah, but he's fictional. They wanted a factual one," I said. "I don't know why, maybe they're just prejudiced against fiction, being a newspaper and all."

"But why bring one in all the way from New York?"

I shrugged. "Not sure. I just know I got a call from some guy who said he worked there. Named Chandler."

David did a double take worthy of Oliver Hardy. "What first name?"

"Uh, Norman. Yeah, Norman."

"Norman Chandler doesn't work at the *L.A. Times,*" said David with a laugh. "He *owns* it."

"Oh," I replied snappily.

"How'd he happen to pick you?"

"You'll never guess."

David sat quietly for a moment, then said, "You're right. So tell me."

"A friend of his recommended me."

"Yes? Yes?"

"J. Edgar Hoover."

David broke out in laughter and said, "I should have guessed."

I'd had a sort of weird relationship with Mr. Hoover in the case that involved David. I wouldn't say I was exactly friends with the person who'd been called the most powerful man in America, but we had developed a kind of healthy respect for one another. Well, respect, anyway. Maybe "healthy" isn't the operative word.

I checked into the Hollywood Sands Motel at Sunset and Highland, across the street from Hollywood High. It was new and boxy and full of red and yellow plastic. Two single beds with bedspreads made of some chemical material that sucked the moisture from my fingers, drapes that stopped about an inch short of the bottom of the window, and prints of ducks in a swamp on the off-yellow walls. I liked it. No place ever felt less like the Morris and Sylvia Weinstein home in Canarsie, Brooklyn, New York. Not an antimacassar in sight.

After more sightseeing, David and I hit the Formosa Cafe on Santa Monica Boulevard for dinner, across the street from the Sam Goldwyn Studios. David called it a Hollywood dive.

The walls were full of pictures of movie stars you never heard of. And some you have. David warned me if the chow mein moved of its own accord, I probably shouldn't eat it. As far as I could tell, it was lying there fairly still when I tried to pick it up with chopsticks and get it all the way to my mouth before it fell back onto the plate and I started all over again. I'd never used chopsticks before. And I swore I'd never do so again. Back East we have things called forks. David said eating chow mein by this method was so much work it had minus two calories.

The following morning, I borrowed David's car and drove it to the Sunset Strip, past the Mocambo and Ciro's, those glamorous nightclubs I'd seen in movies all my life, the places where all the sophisticates go. Or used to. It all looked a little seedy now. The Mocambo had been "closed for alterations" for about three years, and Ciro's—where a few years before Dean Martin and Jerry Lewis and the Will Mastin Trio starring Sammy Davis Jr. had headlined—had replaced its floor show with an all-you-can-eat buffet.

A few blocks farther west was a small white stucco building with beveled corners, round deco windows, and black wood trim. The words KING BROTHERS PRODUCTIONS were embossed on a gold placard on the shiny black door.

It hit me that this could be an important case for me. I'd been thinking of moving to L.A. A lot of my work involved show business companies and they'd been moving west in droves. Getting on the good side of the *L.A. Times* would be a great way to build up a clientele.

I parked on the street and walked up and down the block thinking about how to play this. I knew there were three King brothers: Frank, Hymie, and Maury, and that their nephew—named Robert Rich, but allegedly not *the* Robert Rich—worked there, too. What could I say that would elicit more information than they'd already given out?

As I stood in front of the door, contemplating any options

I could think of, and finding none, the door opened right into my foot. "Ouch!" I said in response.

"Oh, sorry," said the young man who had pushed it into my big toe. His looks kind of reminded me of Anthony Perkins, who'd been nominated for an Oscar the year before for *Friendly Persuasion,* only this guy seemed a little crazier. He wore an alligator shirt and cotton pegs, and held several stamped letters in his hand. "Were you on your way in?"

"Uh . . ." Well, there was only one answer that made much sense. "Yes."

"Oh," he replied. It was a scintillating conversation.

He looked me over. I felt naked. "Are you the girl from the agency?"

Before I could weigh the consequences I said, "Yes."

"Good, good. Come in," he bid, holding the door open for me. I had the feeling he smelled my hair as I passed.

"What's your name?" he said, looking directly at my boobs.

I thought of answering, the left one's Zelda and the right Rebecca. Instead, I said, "Naomi. Naomi Weinstein." I'd learned when I first started out that staying as close to the truth as possible was usually best. That way I didn't have to spend so much time remembering which lie I'd told.

"Oh," he replied, letting the door close behind him. "They said the girl was named Carey something. McNally, I think."

My heart stopped while I searched for a reply. "Oh, yeah. Carey couldn't make it. She got called back to another job she was on last week. So they sent me." I only prayed that the agency in question was a secretarial agency, not a talent agency or an out-call brothel. The good part about being a lady private eye was that everybody always assumed I was a secretary. Or bank teller. Or school teacher. Or nurse. It made it awfully easy to pass. In fact, the one thing no one ever believed I was, when I told them, was a private eye.

"Well, good," he said. "Here."

He motioned to the reception desk facing the door. It was beige, like all the other furniture in the room. Everything had rounded edges and moderne designs. They must have picked it up at a going-out-of-style sale.

"Just answer the phones and take messages and I'll be back as soon as I mail these letters," he said, licking his lips repeatedly. There was something reptilian about him, like William Buckley.

I wished I could get a look at the letters before he deposited them in a mailbox. "Would you like me to mail those for you?" I asked.

"Naw. I'm gonna get a cuppa at Ben Frank's since you're here. Want me to bring you back one?" Well, he might appear dangerously psychotic, but he was certainly polite.

I said, "No thanks."

"By the way," he added, "the rest room is right though that door, the one next to my office, if you need to use it at any time. But tell me first so I can cover the phones for you."

I nodded, and shivered a little. I had a feeling he'd probably drilled a peephole in the wall between his office and the bathroom. Just then the phone rang. I picked up the receiver and pushed down the button that was flashing.

"Just say . . ." he was saying as I did.

"King Brothers Productions," I said into the phone.

"Good," he said with a cockeyed nod.

"Hello, this is Robert Rich," said a voice at the other end of the phone. I want to give you my address to send my Oscar."

"Hold on just a moment, Mr. Rich," I said, and put the line on hold.

"Did they say they were Robert Rich?" said the young man. He twisted his mouth into a grimace.

I nodded.

"That's funny, because *I'm* Robert Rich," he snapped.

I felt like I'd walked into the TV show *To Tell the Truth*. But where was Bud Collyer?

He picked up the phone on the other desk and pressed the blinking button. "Listen, you lying bastard, you just go jump in a lake." And he hung up.

"What was that all about?" I asked with the greatest of innocence. I may even have fluttered my eyelashes.

He snickered. "You know, our movie, *The Brave One*? It won the Oscar for Best Original Story. But no one knows who or where the writer is. My uncles, they used my name for the credit. They didn't know it was going to win an Oscar," he shrugged. "I tried to cover and tell the Academy I'd written it, but I sort of lost my nerve when they started questioning me. So my Uncle Frank told them it was actually another Robert Rich who he met in Germany some years ago."

"Was it?" I asked, even though he'd more or less confessed it wasn't.

"Oh, yeah. Of course," he said much too quickly. "They've been trying to locate him to give him the award."

"I see," I said, although I didn't see at all. "Any luck?"

"Naw."

I took a chance. "Then why did you hang up on the man on the phone?"

Robert Rich was startled. Perhaps he realized he'd dug himself a hole. "It . . . it was the wrong guy," he stuttered, and walked to his office as quickly as he could. He couldn't have known it was the wrong guy since he hadn't heard the guy's voice when he hung up on him. It could only have been the wrong guy if there was no other Robert Rich to be found. So I guess I had the answer to question number one: *The Brave One* was written by someone *not* named Robert Rich.

His departure gave me a moment to look over the outgoing mail he'd left on the desk. Phone bill payment. Electric bill payment. One to the Producers Guild. One to somebody named King in Glendale. And a letter to Blue Chip

Stamps. I'd noticed from the signs in gas stations and on grocery stores that that was a big premium company in L.A., like S & H Green Stamps back where I came from.

Robert Rich came back in with another envelope. I caught him looking at my boobs again as he gathered up the letters he'd left and headed for the door. "I'll be back in a few. My uncles are due to return this afternoon," he said, and left.

As the door closed behind him, I whirled around and started thumbing through the Rolodex on the side table. There was a Robert Rich in it, probably the one I'd just met. But I jotted down the address and phone number anyway. Before I finished, I was startled by the ringing phone.

"King Brothers Productions," I said into the receiver.

"Hello, is Frank there?"

"No, I'm sorry, he's not. May I take a message?"

"How about Maury?" said the somewhat high-pitched male voice.

"Afraid not."

"Hymie?"

"Sorry. They're all due back this afternoon."

"Okay, give me that little pipsqueak Rich."

"Sir, I'm afraid he's out as well. May I help you?"

The man sighed. "Okay, tell Frank to call . . ." He paused a moment. "U.N. Friendly."

"Could I have your number, Mr. Friendly?"

"Of course. It's Pleasant 6-5211."

"That's funny," I said. "Mr. Friendly has a Pleasant phone number."

"Yes, a laugh riot," he replied somewhat dryly. "Tell that son of a bitch Frank if he doesn't call me by this afternoon that I'm going to tell the *L. A. Times*."

Mr. Friendly didn't sound too friendly. I figured, what the hell. "What will you tell them, Mr. Friendly?"

He laughed. "I'll tell them they can renew my subscription. You just give Frank the message."

"Yes, sir."

"Good girl," he said, and hung up.

I added his admonition to the message and looked again at his name. Could it be a joke of some sort? I recalled in Agatha Christie's *Ten Little Indians* the host who invited all the guilty people to the island was "U.N. Owen," a homophone for "unknown." So "U.N. Friendly." Could it be as in the Unfriendly Ten? The ten Hollywood writers who were sent to prison for not cooperating with the House Un-American Activities Committee?

I looked through the Rolodex for the phone number Mr. Friendly had given me, and I found it when I got to the T's. It went with the name Dalton Trumbo. Yes! He was one of the Ten!

I wrote down the address in Highland Park, which I discovered, from a street atlas in the bookcase, was a suburb of Los Angeles between downtown L.A. and Pasadena. I rifled the filing cabinets, searching for any files marked Rich or Trumbo. Nothing.

There were two whole drawers of *Brave One* files, but before I could start searching through them the door opened and in walked a woman in her forties, a bit chubby, wearing glasses, her hair pulled back in a bun. "Sorry, I'm late," she said. "My car broke down."

Maybe she's someone with an appointment, I hoped.

She came up to me, stuck out her hand and said, "I'm Carey McNally."

I stood up and shook her hand as my knees knocked. What was I going to do?

"Uh, Carey," I said, being fast with witty repartee. "Uh, Carey, well, let's see." Finally it came to me. "How much do you get a day?"

"Twelve-fifty, but I seem to be starting two hours late, so I should get less for today."

I opened my purse and pulled out a twenty. "Here, take this for today, leave now, and come back tomorrow."

She stared at it in confusion. "I don't understand," she said.

"You don't have to. I'm paying you twenty dollars in cash for not working today. Come back tomorrow morning. But you have to go right now and not ask questions."

"I . . . but I don't understand," she repeated, not moving an inch.

I pulled another ten from my purse.

"If you'll leave immediately and not ask any more questions, I'll add this."

"I couldn't do that without calling the agency first. May I use your phone?"

I knew the jig was up. "Sure," I said, got up and motioned for her to take my seat behind the reception desk. While she made the call, I picked up my purse, put the thirty dollars back inside, and walked out the door, wondering what Robert Rich would think when he came back in and found her behind the desk instead of me.

I sat in the window of the cafe across the street, wearing my sunglasses, and watched the building. Soon Robert Rich entered. After half a minute, he stuck his head out the door and looked both ways, as if I'd still be on the block, having left ten minutes before. He shook his head and went back in.

An hour later a Chrysler with fins so big they could stab a pedestrian drove up and three middle-aged men got out. I assumed they were his uncles. I rushed across the street and climbed up the hill alongside the building hoping to hear the ensuing conversation through one of the small, high, open windows. A few loud words made their way to my ears. Like "Keee-rist!" and "Holy shit!" Of course, I didn't know if they were in response to my short presence there that morning or the phone message from Mr. Friendly.

A few minutes later, Robert Rich came out of the building holding a white business-size envelope and hopped into a beat-up, green 1949 Plymouth in a nearby parking lot. As he waited to make a left turn onto Sunset Boulevard, I jumped into David's Chevy and made a U-turn to get into position to follow.

The Plymouth drove east on Sunset and left onto Highland. It went through Cahuenga Pass to the San Fernando Valley, alongside the gigantic Forest Lawn cemetery, past NBC and the Warner Brothers and Disney Studios, and east on Riverside Drive next to a bridal path, to Figueroa, where it made a left. The sign said Highland Park. It turned out to be a rundown, blue-collar neighborhood that looked to have been built in the 1920s. A lot of the people and stores seemed to be Mexican.

The Plymouth pulled up in front of Fuentes Drugs, a neighborhood pharmacy. Robert Rich got out, envelope in hand, and walked into the store. I followed, keeping a shelf or two between us. I saw him give the white envelope to the white-haired Mexican pharmacist behind the tall prescription counter, and get a larger, nine-by-twelve manila envelope in return. I ducked behind the cosmetics counter as the pharmacist picked up a telephone and dialed and Rich walked past me up the next aisle.

Outside, I watched him drive off, knowing there was little reason to follow him any farther. I'd learned long ago at John Jay College of Police Science to follow the money. Well, in this case, it was more like "follow the envelope," but it looked like it contained money. A bribe, perhaps, for not telling the *L.A. Times*? But if so, what was in the larger envelope, the one the pharmacist gave to Mr. Rich?

It wasn't easy to kill time inside a fairly small drug store. I bought several items I didn't need. I'd heard of men being embarrassed to buy rubbers—not the kind for your feet—so they bought up a bunch of innocuous items, combs and toothpaste and such, to seem less conspicuous. But I bought only innocuous items; I had no need for rubbers, unfortunately. God, did they sell them to women? I'd never thought of that. In fact, it was hard to tell that drugstores sold them at all since they always kept them hidden behind the counter. Wouldn't want any children catching a glimpse of a box of prophylactics and asking their Mommy what they were. No, sirree. Of course, maybe there'd be fewer babies born out of wedlock if they had.

Speaking of children, a teenaged boy, maybe fourteen or so, passed me and went up to the pharmacist. They chatted a moment. The boy was Caucasian, unlike most of the customers. He wore glasses and looked like he'd be in the science and chess clubs at school, not the football team. The pharmacist handed him the white envelope he'd received from Mr. Rich, and said to give his parents his best; and the kid walked by me and out of the store.

I stepped out front and saw him climb onto a Schwinn and pedal away. I'd never followed a bike with a car before. Good thing I didn't have to jump into a cab and yell, "Follow that bike!" I learned it's not easy to go slow enough to follow a bike while cars are honking at you to go faster. Nevertheless I did my best Lamont Cranston imitation, trying to remain invisible to my prey.

Eventually he turned off Figueroa onto a side street of small cottages, and up a hill. He disappeared behind a fence of the house on the hill, a larger whitewash California bungalow not quite Craftsman style, overlooking the neighborhood. I parked where I could keep an eye on it and waited for something to happen. I'd been there half an hour and eaten all the candy bars and potato chips I'd bought in the drug store when something did.

A man in his fifties with a mustache, horn-rimmed glasses, and thinning, water-slicked hair came out of the house and walked down the hill toward my car. I pretended to read the paper while he passed. But he didn't. He opened the passenger door I apparently hadn't locked and slid right in beside me. He wasn't big and didn't look threatening. On the other hand, he did look like an accountant in an Alfred Hitchcock TV show. You know, the meek little man who murders his large, domineering wife and cuts up her body and carts it away in those cardboard cartons they call transfer files.

"Hello," he said.

I just stared at him in disbelief.

"You don't look like FBI," he continued. "Or HUAC. And you certainly don't look like a member of the I.A.T.S.E."

"What's that?" I asked.

"The International Alliance of Theater and Stage Employees," he said. "The watchdogs of the blacklist."

"Oh," I replied cleverly.

"So you must be a reporter."

"No, I'm not a reporter," I said. "I'm a private detective." I showed him my I.D.

He glanced at it. "From New York. Well, we're honored," he replied. He took a pack of Chesterfields from his inside jacket pocket and offered me one. I shook my head.

He lit up, coughed, and went on. "We get lots of FBI and police and HUAC investigators and reporters but very few private eyes," he said. "I think the city reserves this parking place for people staking out my house. It's a courtesy, like the green for fifteen minutes, yellow for deliveries, and this spot for watching Dalton Trumbo."

Oh. So that's who he was.

"So what were you doing following my son home from the drug store?"

I guess I'd failed at clouding his son's mind to make myself invisible to him.

"Trying to figure out what was in the envelope he picked up there. It looked like a bribe."

"Why did it look like a bribe? Why didn't it just look like an envelope?"

"Well, you've got a point there," I admitted. "It was the context that made it look like a bribe, Mr. Friendly."

"Ahh. I thought your voice was familiar. You really get around, Naomi. Would you like to come up for some tea?" I agreed, but I decided if we passed any transfer files on the way I'd make a run for it.

While it was 1957 outside Mr. Trumbo's house, inside it was 1940. He explained he'd stored all his old furniture when he moved to Mexico to try to make a living after he got out of prison, and reclaimed it all when that plan didn't work out. This was the furniture he'd bought back when he was the highest paid—and biggest spending—writer in Hollywood. I met his wife—she wasn't big or domineering but slender, younger, and pretty. He showed me some of her prize-winning photographs.

We had tea on the veranda overlooking the tree-filled valley and the San Gabriel Mountains beyond. "Who are you working for, Naomi?" asked Mr. Trumbo as he poured me a cup, catching the loose tea in a tiny strainer.

"I'm not at liberty to say," I said, feeling stupid considering I was hoping I could get him to answer that very question.

"Then answer this. What is it they want to know?"

"Whether you wrote *The Brave One*," I replied. I saw no reason to be cozy about that.

"Ah. Of course."

My heart raced. "Of course you wrote it?" I asked.

He laughed. "No, no. Of course, that's what they would want to know. It's the question of the moment." He picked up a pipe, fiddled with it but never lit it.

"So. Did you?"

"Well, I can't confirm that," he said. "But then I can't deny it either."

"Why is that?"

"Well, if I did write it, then the King Brothers must have hired me—or bought the story from me—despite the blacklist. Of course, the movie industry insists there is no blacklist. But on the other hand, the Academy of Motion Picture Arts and Sciences passed a new rule this year excluding blacklisted writers from winning Oscars. So if there were no blacklist, there'd be no reason for that rule. Of course, they did it only because my friend Michael Wilson was about to be nominated for writing *Friendly Persuasion* and Michael had already had the audacity to embarrass the Academy by winning the Oscar for *A Place in the Sun,* which he wrote before he was blacklisted."

"Have you won any Oscars since you've been blacklisted?" I asked.

He smiled. "I've been nominated once or twice, but I can't say if I've won. That would be telling. It's common practice for Hollywood companies, big and small, to hire blacklisted writers on the black market. It's an open secret that's received the blessings of the industry while at the same time the Academy is acting as policeman, beating up on weak victims, independent producers like the Kings. If *The Brave One* had been made by a major studio, I promise you the Academy would be looking the other way."

I asked, "Do you know who wrote *The Brave One?*"

He nodded. "I'd guess Michael Wilson. But what I know mostly is that it has no murders in it, no dope addiction, no gunfights, and no seduction of innocent girls. So now that I think about it, I don't know how it got onto the screen."

It hit me. The manila envelope probably contained script pages. He was writing another movie for the King Brothers. The money was for that. I tried my new theory on him.

He smiled and said, "Blacklist or no, it's impossible to stop a writer from writing. They murdered Thucydides, and beheaded Sir Thomas More, but all of the other writers who were thrown in jail continued to write, and so have I. Why just today I was writing a letter to the phone company. In fact, I was on my way to mail it when I stopped by to see you."

He pulled the envelope from his pocket. "They'd written me a very clever and charming missive about why they couldn't seem to make my phone lines work properly. Personally, I believe it has something to do with all the juice that's being drained off by the FBI tap, but they didn't mention that. They did say they had more pressing things to do than make the phones of a Communist work. So this is my reply."

He tore open the stamped envelope so that I could read his tome. It said in part, "When we Reds come into power we are going to shoot merchants in the following order: 1. those who are greedy, and 2. those who are witty. Since you fall into both categories it will be a sad story when we finally lay hands on it."

I looked up at him as he drained his tea. "You don't take this very seriously, do you?"

He put down the cup. "The Hollywood, or so-called Unfriendly Ten, including myself have had the worst press since Bruno Hauptman. I lost my livelihood, my house in the hills, my ranch in Ventura County, and all my savings. Well, I never had any savings. I didn't know I'd need them. I was imprisoned for a year. My passport was revoked. I've been audited chronically by the IRS. Since we moved here, my daughter was driven out of her elementary school by tormenting classmates, and tormenting parents of classmates. We had to put her into a different school where the parents are a little less red-blooded American. I have borrowed from all my friends and associates, not to mention lawyers, and struggle to pay them back. I will pay, every cent. I used to earn three thousand dollars a week. When I got out of prison, I was lucky to get three thousand for an entire script. I take it seriously." He shrugged his eyebrows and shoulders. I got the idea.

"How do you feel about the people who talked," I asked, "who named names to save their careers?"

"I used to look for villains, but I'm beginning to think there were no villains, or heroes or saints or devils; there were only victims. Some suffered less than others, some of us grew and some diminished, but in the final tally we were *all* victims."

He poured us both more tea. "Try Michael Wilson," he said again. "Maybe he'll tell you he wrote it."

I stopped at a payphone and called Michael Wilson at the San Fernando Valley number Mr. Trumbo had given me. He said he'd be happy to see me, especially after I told him who I'd just had tea with. We made an appointment for that evening at his house at 11662 Sunshine Terrace at nine. He asked me to give him a phone number to reach me just in case, and I did, both the motel's and David's.

David listened intently as I filled him in on my day over burgers at the Sunset Strip Hamburger Hamlet. It had a Southern plantation motif carried through to the point that the waitresses were all black and the customers were all white. I felt like Scarlet O'Hara sipping mint juleps with David Horvitz. Well, he didn't look much like Rhett.

David was a TV writer, working for a writer-producer named Roy Huggins on a new Western series at Warner Brothers that was supposed to premiere in the fall on ABC. He told me it was called "Maverick" and starred a guy named James Garner who David thought was going to be a big star. And, he said, the lead character wasn't a gunfighter, like on all the other Westerns, but a card sharp and confidence man who was basically a coward and ran from danger.

I laughed, thinking he was joking. When he made me

realize he wasn't, I said the American public would never stand for it. It didn't have a chance to succeed. He thanked me for my encouragement.

"But what would possess somebody to think up a hero who was a coward?" I persisted.

David said, "I have the feeling at some level, conscious or not, Roy patterned the Maverick character after himself."

I looked up, puzzled. He went on, "Roy named names to HUAC and saved his career. He says he's regretted it ever since."

I was dumbfounded. "But how could you work for someone who did that?" I said.

"The same reason he did what he did. In order to work."

When we got back to David's neo-Gothic apartment on Fountain Avenue, he raced in to answer the ringing phone and I followed. He surprised the hell out of me by saying, "It's for you." It was Michael Wilson begging off for tonight. He said something had come up, and asked if we could meet for breakfast tomorrow instead at Nate 'n Al's on Beverly Drive? I agreed. And hung up, puzzled. He'd sounded nervous. "What could have happened to make him cancel?" I said out loud.

David replied, "You're the detective."

He was right. I grabbed my purse and camera. "Can I borrow your car again?" He shook his head. "No. You can borrow me."

And we piled in, him at the wheel.

Twenty minutes and a trip over Laurel Canyon later we were coasting to a stop, lights off, on a winding road in the hills of Studio City overlooking the San Fernando Valley. We parked across the street from 11662 and waited. But not for long.

At nine, an old black Cadillac pulled out of the driveway. I couldn't make out the driver but we figured it was Michael Wilson. David followed, leaving a block between us and the

Caddy. "Funny, you wouldn't think a Communist would drive a Cadillac," I said.

"We don't know if he is or ever was a Communist," said David. "He just wouldn't tell the committee or name names, is all we know."

"I thought the Unfriendly Ten all took the Fifth Amendment."

"That wouldn't have made them guilty. But even so, they didn't. Ironically, if they had, they wouldn't have gone to prison. But they felt they weren't guilty of anything and therefore shouldn't hide behind it. They pled the First Amendment, believing that freedom of speech included the freedom not to speak, and that the committee had no right to force them."

"Is that a legal argument or wishful thinking?" I responded.

"Word has it that if two liberal Supreme Court justices hadn't died before the case got put in front of the Court, they would probably have won."

I whistled through my teeth at the vicissitudes of luck and history.

We followed Wilson's car back over Laurel Canyon to Beverly Hills. It pulled up in front of a large fur shop on Wilshire Boulevard just east of La Cienega. Flyer Furriers and Fur Storage said the neon sign. A moment later a Pontiac woody station wagon pulled up right behind, its Indian-head hood ornament aglow, then a Chevy panel truck. "Left-wing Jews don't buy Fords," David whispered. One man got out of each and they conferred quietly under a street light.

"Do any of them look familiar?" I asked David. He nodded. "Yes. They've all been in the paper. That is Wilson," he said, indicating the man we'd followed. He was tall, forties with prematurely white hair. "The others are Herbert Biberman and Paul Jarrico. Biberman's a director. Jarrico's a writer-producer. They're blacklisted, too." Biberman was barrel-chested and intense in his mannerisms. Jarrico was shorter, dumpy looking, and spectacled.

The men got back in their cars, turned the corner and into the parking lot behind the store. We waited a moment, then followed on foot.

By the time we got to the back of the building, a double door was open and the men were apparently inside. We crouched down in the dark. After a moment Jarrico came out carrying a cardboard carton, about twelve by eighteen inches. I swallowed hard and whispered to David, "Isn't that what they call a transfer file?" He nodded. "Yes, the studios use them to store scripts." It wasn't scripts I was worried about, but body parts.

Jarrico slid the box into the van. The others followed, each carrying another similarly shaped carton. I pictured three dead wives lying in pieces in the furrier's refrigerator. They loaded the boxes into the vehicles and went back inside the building, then came back again with more cartons and put them in the cars.

I decided I was being silly. Obviously they weren't body parts; they were fur coats. "Have we caught three black-listed Hollywood men robbing a fur store?" I whispered to David.

"Would furs be stored in cartons like that?"

"No, I guess not," I said. "What could they have in there?"

As if on cue, Biberman slipped, dropping the box he was holding, and several disc-shaped round cans, about an inch thick and twelve inches in diameter, rolled out of it and across the blacktop.

David stifled a laugh. "Those are film cans," he whispered. "They've been using the furrier's refrigerator to store their film."

"Why?" I asked, as the men finished loading their vehicles, and David and I, crouched down, ran back to his car.

"They made an independent movie," he whispered. "It's called *Salt of the Earth*. Wilson wrote it, Jarrico produced it, and Biberman directed. They all worked for free and raised the budget from private investors. It's a dramatized documentary about a union strike by poor Mexican-American mineworkers in New Mexico. I read the script. It's wonderful, sort of Italian neo-realism, like Vittorio de Sica's *Bicycle Thief*.

"The studios, and some congressmen, and Howard Hughes, all tried like mad to keep them from making it. There were demonstrations against the film. The cast and crew were thrown out of their hotel in New Mexico. Before they were finished shooting, the State Department deported their Mexican leading lady for no reason. And two of the buildings they were using were burned down."

I couldn't imagine such a thing.

"The union, the IATSE, tried to keep every crew person in Hollywood from working on it. And to keep every laboratory in the country from processing the film. They must have been hiding the work print in the furrier's refrigerator so it wouldn't get set afire by some patriotic citizen."

"Jesus," I sighed. "I thought this was America."

"Apparently it is except when it's under stress," he said with a sigh.

We followed the caravan at a safe distance to an old dilapidated bungalow on the outskirts of L.A., where they unloaded the cans. Through one of the small windows, we saw a five-foot-high Rube Goldberg–like apparatus full of wheels and levers, and a little four-by-six-inch screen. David told me was a Moviola, a film-editing machine. "This must be their secret editing room," David whispered.

Suddenly, I felt a presence behind me. I whirled around and saw the tall, white-haired man coming up the driveway, only two feet away, with a large flashlight in hand. He shined it in my eyes. "Who the hell are you?" he shouted. "What are you doing here?"

Oh, shit, I'd blown it. "Uh, hi," I said. "I'm Naomi Weinstein. I guess I'm a little early for breakfast at Nate 'n Al's."

"Oh, Christ," he sighed. "We've blown it," he shouted to the others, who were still inside.

"Shit," shouted Biberman. Jarrico threw up his hands.

"No, no," I said quickly. "I'm not going to tell anybody. And I'm sure my friend isn't either."

"Then why did you follow us here?" Wilson demanded.

"I was only hired to find out one thing."

"Yes?"

"Who wrote *The Brave One*? Who deserves the Academy Award?"

Wilson laughed. "And Trumbo sent you to me?"

I nodded.

He doubled over laughing some more. He told the others through the window and they laughed, too.

Finally it became quiet enough for me to ask, "Why is that funny?"

"Trumbo wrote *The Brave One*," said Wilson. "He's just trying to get extra publicity over it by confusing everyone."

"Are you sure?"

He shook his head. "I can't be sure. That's Trumbo's master plan. He's trying to shame Hollywood into ending the blacklist without exposing the people who buy our work."

I did have breakfast at Nate 'n Al's, the New York–style deli in the middle of Beverly Hills. But with David instead of Wilson. During which David pointed out to me that neither Wilson nor Trumbo was Jewish, so my theory about everyone in Hollywood being so must be wrong.

I wrote up my report on David's Smith-Corona standard— mentioning nothing about the Wilson-Jarrico-Biberman odyssey—and handed it to Norman Chandler in person in his palatial office at the *L.A. Times*. He was an imposing man, reminded me of Franklin Roosevelt. He read it. "There's not one actual admission in here. Trumbo says Wilson. Wilson says Trumbo. It's all a farce," he said.

"I think that was the idea," I added.

"That fucking Trumbo, pardon my French," he muttered, handing me a generous check for my services and expenses. Still, I had a feeling he wasn't about to give me a glowing reference.

David dropped me off at the train and kissed me goodbye almost as if he meant it.

I read two Agatha Christies and a Raymond Chandler as the train took me back across the country. I guess it hadn't been my shining hour. Or my country's.

Note

Except for Naomi's involvement, all of the events of the story are true, although I've tampered slightly with the timeline.

When *Salt of the Earth* was finally, against all odds, completed, it was blocked from distribution in the United States by the studios and the IATSE—which forbade all the union projectionists in every movie theater in the country from running it—while it went on to win the French equivalent of the Oscar as Best Motion Picture of the Year.

In 1958, the year after *The Brave One* debacle, another blacklisted writer, Ned Young, won the Oscar for *The Defiant Ones* under a pseudonym. In 1959 Kirk Douglas hired Dalton Trumbo under a pseudonym to write *Spartacus* for $50,000, and they let the story leak. Soon Otto Preminger hired Trumbo to write *Exodus* under his own name. And the blacklist was effectively over for Trumbo, Wilson, and the few other best known of the hundreds of writers, directors, actors, craftsmen and women who'd been drummed out of Hollywood. But the lesser known vast majority of them never worked in the motion picture industry again.

In 1973 Trumbo was finally given his Oscar for *The Brave One*. He was presented an Oscar for his earlier pseudonymous writing of *Roman Holiday* many years after his death.

The Writers Guild has spent the last twenty-six years trying to correct the credits on films made during the years of the blacklist.

The research and columns of Patrick Goldstein of the *L.A. Times* and recollections of Christopher Trumbo (the boy on the Schwinn) contributed immeasurably to this history.

Murder at the Heartbreak Hotel

MARK TERRY

WHEN FATE BLOWS open a shamus's office door, you can never tell who'll walk through. It could be a hot dame in a cool silk dress or a gun-packing gangster intent on harm.

It could even be Elvis.

I WAS CONTEMPLATING my checkbook when my office door swung open and Alicia Kingston stepped through. I dropped the black hole of my checkbook into the desk drawer where I kept the bottle and smiled pleasantly at the woman. "May I help you?"

"You're Jakob Hull, the private investigator?"

"Yes ma'am. Have a seat."

She plopped into one of my two office chairs, tucking a lock of her short, curly blond hair behind one ear. "You . . . you're confidential, right?"

"What you tell me will be private," I said.

She was maybe in her thirties, maybe in her forties. It was kind of hard to tell. She had the kind of voluptuous figure that was no longer fashionable—it disguised her age but didn't hurt her sex appeal. "I mean . . . really private," she said.

"Really private," I agreed.

"Really, *really* private?" She had a wispy voice, like a little girl's voice, and it went with her slightly plump body and vaguely innocent blue eyes.

"Yes ma'am," I said. "But maybe I'll know more when you tell me what you'd like me to do."

"Oh. Well . . ." She rummaged in her Nebraska-size purse and retrieved a large mailing envelope. "Do you . . . can you find people?"

"Yes," I said, once again back on firm ground. "Is there someone you'd like me to find?"

"Yes," she said.

I waited for her to tell me who she wanted me to find, but she was going to be one of those clients and it was going to be one of those days.

"Who is it you'd like me to find?" I finally asked.

"Elvis," she said.

I first shifted my gaze to the window, which offered no inspiration, then to my framed private investigator's license, which offered even less.

With a sigh, I said, "Elvis, uh, who?"

"Elvis Presley," she said, which was exactly what I was afraid she'd say.

I thought that over, debating responses. The first one that came to mind was: "Have you tried Graceland?"

The second one was along the lines of: "Get out of my office," with a colorful metaphor or two inserted somewhere in the middle of the sentence for emphasis.

Then I remembered my checking account balance and said, "Elvis Presley," which wasn't a question, merely a statement, and a repetitive one at that.

"Why yes," she said.

"*The* Elvis Presley," I said, cautiously narrowing it down.

"Of course," she said. "The King."

"That one," I said.

I thought of the checkbook. I thought of the bottle in the

bottom drawer of my desk. They were inherently related, these two thoughts.

Alicia Kingston reached into the envelope and retrieved a snapshot. "This is the man I want you to find."

I examined it gingerly. It sure looked like Elvis Presley. "Where did you get this?" I asked.

"In Detroit. At Cobo Hall. There was a convention of Elvises."

Ah-ha! A clue! My God! A clue! "So," I said. "This person is an Elvis impersonator."

"Oh no. He's the real thing. Elvis Presley. I saw his driver's license."

One step forward; two steps back.

"When, uh, did you see his driver's license?"

She faltered, her creamy complexion taking on a rosy tinge. "Well . . . I . . ."

Hmmm, I thought. There's a story here after all.

I made a wild guess, my particular specialty. "Did you sleep with him?"

She slowly nodded.

"Why," I said, "do you want me to find him?" And I hoped the answer wasn't: I'm carrying Elvis's love child.

She once again dipped into the mailing envelope and handed me the contents. There were a number of photographs of Alicia Kingston performing upon Elvis Presley what in some southern counties was referred to as an "unnatural act." Actually, it looked pretty natural in the photographs, but I'm just a private eye in a small northern Michigan resort town.

In addition to the photographs was a neatly typed letter demanding five thousand dollars or copies would be sent to Alicia's husband. She would be contacted and instructed on when and how to deliver the money.

I opened my top drawer and found a blank contract. I slid it across to Mrs. Kingston and handed her a pen. "I think I can help you," I said.

Once she was gone I retrieved the bottle from the bottom drawer. Maalox, it said on the side. I took a swig and toasted my P.I.'s license. "Here's to gainful employment."

MAURICE WINSTON HAD a head as smooth and hairless as a solar reflector, a thin humorless mouth, and the domineering arrogance of a first-class concierge. I stepped up to his desk at the Grand Bay Resort and handed him the snapshot. "I'm looking for this man," I said.

Maurice didn't smile, smirk, or snicker, but he couldn't control the gleam in his eyes. "Jakob," he said, "I believe Mr. Presley is dead."

"Come on. You've got the Elvis, uh—"

"The Amazing Elvis Extravaganza," he completed.

"Yeah. That's it. Starts tomorrow, right?"

"Correct. Will this gentleman be attending?"

"I hope so. Are there any reservations for Elvis Presley?"

Unblinking, Maurice said, "Several."

"Several?"

"There are seven."

"How do you plan on keeping them straight?" I asked.

I wouldn't have sworn to it, but I think Maurice smiled. Just a tiny bit. Then I got the room numbers of the seven Elvises. On my way out, Maurice said, "So this is your new career, Jakob?"

"Yes," I said. "I'm a licensed private investigator now."

"My niece says your class on the American detective novel at the university was the most enjoyable class she took."

"I'm much happier as a P.I.," I said.

"Perhaps Prozac would have been easier," Maurice said.

"WHY?" SHE DEMANDED of me, tears glistening on her cheeks. "Why is Elvis doing this to me?"

I patted her hand and said nothing. Elvis was doing this to her because she was a gullible flake, but I didn't think that would go over well. Her check hadn't bounced and we had a contract. Satisfying her delusions was all part of the service. In her mind Elvis was alive and well; he had not grown old and fat and addicted to over-the-counter medications. The reality of Elvis's ignominious death never registered on her in any way, not as an ode to the dark side of fame, not even as an advisory for the positive effects of a high-fiber diet. To her Elvis was alive and well and bopping her in a Motor City motel room.

I assured her I would do my best to locate Elvis Presley and retrieve the negatives. In the meantime, she was to sit tight and wait for him to contact her.

THE NEXT DAY I paid another call to the Resort, intending to knock on the seven Elvises' doors, looking for the man in the snapshot. I stepped into the lobby, all spacious atrium, soaring spaces, and glittering poshness. I stopped dead in my blue suede shoes. The lobby was jammed with about thirty men who were, well . . . Elvis. Some of them were dressed in rhinestone-studded jumpsuits, others in brown suits, jeans, and tee-shirts, you name it. But each and every one of them resembled, in some way, the man in the snapshot. Elvis had not left the building. Elvis had tripped and fallen on the Xerox machine.

I groaned. Out of the corner of my eye I saw Maurice laughing.

I fought my way through the Elvises, looking each of them closely in the face, trying to match one of them to the photograph. It was about as possible as looking fashionable in a white jumpsuit when you're a hundred pounds overweight. These men all had black pompadours, long sideburns, and fried grits accents. I eliminated a few, trained investigator that I am: too young (twelve), female (sex change?), and Japanese . . . (nah!) There were two who were very overweight, doing an Elvis-late-in-his-career routine, no doubt. Finally I made it to the front desk where Maurice was calmly waiting for me.

"Hello, Jakob," he said. "What can I do for you?"

I held up the photograph for him to re-examine. "Have you seen him?"

"Nearly a hundred times."

I sighed. "How many are there?"

He handed me the flyer for the Amazing Elvis Extravaganza. It advertised 101 Amazing Elvises. I was looking for an Elvis in an Elvis stack. "One hundred and one," I repeated in a stunned whisper.

"Yes," Maurice said. "And I understand the Grand Finale is a mass chorus singing 'Jailhouse Rock' *a capella*."

Before I could respond, Maurice patted my hand and suggested I go into his office and put my head between my knees. Instead, I went knocking on the doors of the performers who had registered under the name of Elvis Presley. The first two doors I knocked on didn't draw a response. The third door did—it swung open. An unlocked, open door to a private eye is like steak tartare to a pit bull. I glanced cautiously up the hallway, then down, then stepped into the room.

"Hello? Elvis? You in here?"

Elvis was not present. Alicia Kingston was. She was lying in the middle of the floor with a knife through her heart.

DETECTIVE RAY CHURCH glanced at me over his reading glasses. "Why are you here, Jakob?"

"I'm a big Elvis fan," I said.

"Let me rephrase that." Church paused long enough to

glance into the middle distance with his blue-gray eyes, then said, "Why are you here, Jakob?"

There was enough menace in the second version to count as re-phrasing, so I told him about my search for the Elvis who was blackmailing Alicia Kingston.

"Huh," Church said, using the edge of his notebook to scratch at the silver hair at his temples. Church was a big, powerful man in his mid-forties who looked like he spent a lot of time in a fishing boat with a rod and reel in his hand. As a matter of fact, he had retired from the St. Louis P.D. and moved to Grand Bay two years ago, hoping for just that. "Well, Jakob, I guess we'll have to round up the, uh, usual suspects."

"Usual?" I said.

"Work with me, Jakob," he said. "Work with me." He shook his head and muttered, "Show business."

IT WAS THE oddest lineup in history: six Elvis imitators leaning against a wall in an open conference room provided by Maurice Winston. It was like that old ad: short ones, fat ones, even ones with . . . well, no chicken pox, at least not as far as we could tell. The Elvises who had legally changed their names to Elvis Presley ranged in age from twenty-two to fifty-three and seemed to range in weight from a ninety-eight-pound weakling to a three-hundred-fifty-pounder who looked like a heart-attack-in-training. The seventh Elvis in the room was the guy who ran the Elvis Extravaganza, and his legal name was Myron Shalton. Everybody called him Big Elvis. Shalton was in his fifties and looked like what Elvis would have looked like if Elvis had lived, spent a couple months at Betty Ford, changed his diet, hooked up with a personal trainer, and aged gracefully.

"Where's the seventh?" Church growled.

Big Elvis said, "There are only six legally named Elvi with the show."

"Elvi?" I asked.

Big Elvis nodded.

Church turned to Maurice Winston, who was hovering like a panicky hummingbird. "There are seven registered," he said. "I gave the list to Jakob myself. Seven."

"Do you remember the seventh?"

Maurice eyed the six, uh, Elvi. "Yes, Detective. I checked the seventh Elvis in myself."

"What'd he look like? Can you describe him?"

Maurice turned to blast Church with an arctic glare. "Yes, Detective. He looked like Elvis Presley."

I thought I could hear Church's teeth grind for a moment before he turned to me. "Any ideas, Jakob?"

"One," I said. I withdrew the mailing envelope and its cargo of incriminating photographs, retrieved one and compared its likeness to the six men before me. I pointed at him. "You we'll keep. The rest, take a break—"

"But don't go too far," Church said.

Once Elvis Presley, Church, and I were alone in the room, I held up the photograph for him to see. His face grew red. "Who took that picture?" he blurted out.

"You didn't?" I asked.

"No sir. I did not."

"You're sure?"

"I was a, uh, little busy at the time," he said.

Church, meanwhile, was examining the mailing envelope. He tapped a finger on the cancelled stamps. "Mr. Presley, where were you six days ago?"

"The third?"

"Yes."

"Well, let's see. That would have been Indianapolis, I think. We're zigzagging across the country, more or less. Cleveland to Detroit to Cincinnati to Grand Rapids to Grand

Bay, then we're up to Marquette, then a long trip over to Green Bay. From there we've got an extended run in Branson, Missouri."

I took the mailing envelope from Church and examined the postage. The envelope, its photographs and blackmail note had been mailed from Grand Bay, Michigan, while our Elvis Presley was in Indianapolis, Indiana.

"Huh," I said.

"You can say that again," Church said. "Mr. Presley, you can go now."

Elvis nodded and left. Church said, "Any more bright ideas?"

I looked at the stamps on the mailing envelope. "Well, just one. But it's a good one."

RAY CHURCH AND I were watching the tide of visitors ebb and flow through the Kingston house, a neat colonial with robin's-egg blue vinyl siding and a beautiful crop of Kentucky blue for a lawn.

"I feel guilty," I said. "I should've noticed the stamp. Things might've been different."

Church shrugged. "You also told her to inform you when he contacted her and she didn't. She went and met him alone instead. If she'd listened to you in the first place—it's what she was paying you for—she'd be alive. Of course, it's possible you'd be dead. Frankly, I'd rather try to figure out who killed Alicia Kingston than try to figure out who killed you."

"I'm touched," I said.

"It's hard to find good fishing partners," he said.

"You say I talk too much and scare the fish."

He smirked. "You do. It's possible that's what makes you a good fishing partner."

We lapsed into silence. A couple people left the house, then another two cars arrived and a herd of people tramped to the front door and disappeared within.

Ray said, "Do other artists have imitators? I mean, are there Frank Sinatra imitators? Where's that imitation thing come from, anyway?"

I shrugged. "I always felt like Elvis was imitating himself, there toward the end. Maybe it was a natural progression."

"Huh. Sounds like a master's thesis."

"It probably already is," I said.

We watched three more cars arrive. Church said, "Ready?"

"Sure." I walked down the street and entered through the front door, mingling with this particular group of well-wishers. The Kingston house was crowded with mourners and family and friends. I nodded and shook hands, murmured my condolences, mingled, and kept my eyes open. John Kingston was tall and thin with broad shoulders and a narrow waist. To my mind he seemed to be handling the murder of his wife rather well. A number of attractive women were quick to drift his way whenever the weight of his grief threatened to overwhelm him, which it seemed to do at regularly timed intervals. Then his blue eyes would swell with tears and he would excuse himself, set his punch, juice, or coffee cup down and retreat to a back bedroom, the attractive ladyfriend following in his wake.

The third time this happened in the ninety minutes I was there I picked up his Styrofoam cup of juice and gracefully made an exit, walked down the street, and climbed into Ray Church's Ford Explorer.

"Got it?" he said.

"You make sure to keep me updated," I said.

"You bet."

RAY DID BETTER than that. He put me in the observation room when they brought John Kingston in. Kingston refused to talk without his attorney, but his attorney showed up in an hour. It was a small town, ultimately.

"Okay," said the attorney, a snowy-haired old smoothie who'd been practicing law ever since Clarence Darrow made his case against God. "Lay it out for us."

"Your client's being arrested in the murder of his wife," Church said. "He had a private investigator in Detroit follow her to the Amazing Elvis Extravaganza in Detroit and photographed her having sex with one of the Elvis impersonators. He then took the photographs, mailed them to his wife with a blackmail note in order to get her to go to a hotel room at the Resort to meet him. He registered under the name Elvis Presley and wore a wig, glasses, and sideburns so he would blend in with the one hundred and one other Elvis impersonators. When Alicia came into the room he stabbed her in the heart and left."

The attorney yawned, blinked, and said, "That's the most idiotic thing I've ever heard. You can't prove any of it."

"We'll see," Church said. "But I can prove he sent the blackmail letter. His house is being searched now and we'll be going through his accounts to track down the P.I."

Church then held up a sheet of paper that looked like a blotchy barcode. "This is a copy of Mr. Kingston's DNA fingerprint taken from a cup of juice he was drinking in his house." He held up another sheet of paper. "It's identical to this one. Which was taken off the postage stamps on the envelope the photographs came in." He shook his head. "Elvis stamps, no less. Should've used self-adhesive, Mr. Kingston. As you're aware, counselor, that's probable cause. I have warrants to search his house, his office, and draw blood for an official DNA sample. Do you have anything to say, Mr. Kingston?"

Kingston looked stunned. "Why would I do that? Why would I kill my wife?"

"Having sex with an Elvis impersonator isn't enough?" Church said.

"That's nuts! I'd just get a divorce. I wouldn't murder her."

Church leaned over and inspected something else in the file next to him. He held it out to John Kingston. "Just in case you were wondering if the only thing I had so far was the DNA samples, I've been busy. And we're only getting going, John. When we're done with you, your life is going to look like a large print easy-to-read edition. The truth is, I didn't think you'd murder her over her infidelities. But I do think you'd murder her over a half-million life insurance policy."

He leaned toward John Kingston. "Elvis is dead, John. And so are you."

Bring Me the Head of Osama bin Laden

A Hollywood Fable

GARY PHILLIPS

FADE IN.

ON SCREEN
[Sometime in the near past.]

INT. ALAN ROSS'S OFFICE—DAY

{ALAN ROSS is thirtysomething, a vp of development at Ten-Shun Productions. He is built like the runner he is, wears tortoiseshell glasses, and is in shirtsleeves and suspenders. Ross sits behind his stressed antique desk in his tastefully appointed office. Absently, he fools with one of his Mont Blanc pens as he listens to:}

{WALSH KAGEN, late fifties, sitting across from Ross. Kagen is craggy-faced, thick in the middle, the product of too many Scotches for lunch for too many years. He is a director-writer with a track record of cult features and cable movies.}

ROSS: I'm going to take a pass on the interstellar doctor transporting medicine for sick alien kids, Walsh. It's cute and touching, but not blue sky enough, you know? *Hardball,* how that was a heart-tugger and we could identify with those kinds of kids, their problems, what have you. See what I mean? (*beat; fools with pen*) What else?

{Kagen leans back in his chair, a satisfied smile spreading his cracked lips.}

KAGEN: *Bring Me the Head of Osama bin Laden.*

ROSS: Pardon?

KAGEN: You ever see that flick by Peckinpah?

ROSS: The old dead western guy?

KAGEN: Yeah, but he did other sorts of pictures, too. Though you could argue they all had western sensibilities. Anyway, this one, *Bring Me the Head of Alfredo Garcia,* was released in 1974.

{Ross says nothing, jiggling the pen in one hand. Kagen leans forward again.}

KAGEN (cont'd): Alfredo Garcia starred Warren Oates—

ROSS (interrupting): He was in that other movie of Peckinpah's, *The Wild Bunch.*

KAGEN: Right. Anyway, in this one I'm talking about, it's set in present day, and Oates is hired by this Mexican crime lord to bring back proof that the scum punk who seduced his daughter is dead.

ROSS: Wasn't this already re-made with Joe Pesci?

{Kagen swallows a caustic comeback, instead he says:}

KAGEN: Not really. That was *Eight Heads in a Duffle Bag,* and it was a comedy.

ROSS: Oh. I'm sorry, go ahead.

KAGEN: No sweat. Okay, in Sam's picture Oates goes through all manner of turmoil to get this Garcia's head. And his character arc is, each step of the way his psychological state deteriorates faster than the head he's bringing back.

{Ross says nothing. The pen is held motionless in his hand.}

KAGEN (cont'd): I mean, Oates at one point is talking to this head in this crummy stained canvas sack, flies whizzing all around it, as it sits on the seat next to him in his car.

ROSS: So in your picture, what, your protagonist is riding around in a jeep in the hills of Afghanistan yakking it up with the world's number-one terrorist's head next to him in a Trader Joe's shopping bag?

KAGEN: Not exactly. The idea here is a group of guys, men and women, who have failed at one thing or another, led by a disaffected vet, hunt bin Laden down, who has now fallen out of favor with his other Al Qaeda pals.

{Ross absorbs this.}

KAGEN (cont'd): Remember this guy has been called the "venture capitalist" of terrorism. He's got an extensive network and has been working out his strategies for a long time. He would have prepared for the contingency of capture.

ROSS: This is pretty, you know, out there, Walsh.

KAGEN: Jesus, Alan, the goddamn *Producers* is a fuckin' comedy about Hitler.

ROSS: We've had decades of distance, Walsh.

KAGEN: That won't bring back the millions who died in the camps or on the battlefields.

ROSS: So your point is?

KAGEN (enthused): It's a great story, it's got action and suspense, and a certifiable bad guy. See, the subtext is about how this isn't about Islam versus the world, because of course these terrorists subvert any religion they purport to advance. This is about how an extremist of any stripe is dangerous. Because they feel they can do anything in the name of God.

{Ross puts the pen down, leans forward on his elbows.}

ROSS: Mid-East politics is a very touchy subject, Walsh. *The Siege* and *Rules of Engagement* didn't exactly burn up the box office or make Arab-Americans all that slap happy either. We want heat, but not that kind of heat.

KAGEN: In this version of *Bring Me the Head,* the hunt for this bastard takes us to Paris, London, and out West.

{Ross taps his desk with his finger.}

ROSS: Here, too?

KAGEN: Yes, of course, this is where the third act will take place. And I see the lead as this semi-burned-out character who at first is hunting bin Laden for the money, the reward, you know. Then in the course of events, his arc is that his patriotism is reawakened. Not the stick-a-flag-on-my-car then put it away halfway into football season, kind, but real, tangible. (*beat*) Some of what was felt when we didi maued out of 'Nam. Even though by then, the grunts were disillusioned with our government and its policies

{Ross says nothing as Walsh shakes a faraway look from his face.}

KAGEN (cont'd): So here, try this. Our hero is a somewhat cynical, slightly burned-out veteran of Beirut or the Gulf War. This guy came home after doing his duty, wounded, you know, the whole bit. He's drifted from job to job, but now there's this opportunity within his grasp.

ROSS: Which is?

KAGEN: The twenty-five million dollar reward for bin Laden is reactivated when the rumors are confirmed that he isn't dead. Like Stalin and Saddam, I'm going to posit in the picture that bin Laden uses doubles to fool his enemies. One of them is killed and at first everyone thinks the sonabitch is dead.

{Ross scratches the side of his cheek.}

ROSS: But we find out different. How can the hero, ah, what's his name?

KAGEN: Flagg.

ROSS (nodding head): That's good. Who are you thinking about for the lead?

KAGEN: Not sure, maybe Cage, or even Snipes, who needs a hit.

ROSS: Yeah, yeah, I can see that.

KAGEN: Like I said, Flagg has been going from job to job, more bitter each time, more withdrawn. He comes to a town in rural Illinois. A friend from the service has sent him a letter, offering some kind of a vague opportunity.

ROSS: But this friend has been tied into some shady stuff, right? Cut-out kind of work for our intelligence agencies.

KAGEN: Exactly. He's a kind of NRA/soldier of fortune borderline nutzo.

ROSS: Bruce Willis? You know, he'll work for scale if he likes the project.

KAGEN: I had in mind someone like Ben Affleck, or maybe make him Latino or even an Arab-American. Get Tony Shaloub or that tall good-looking guy from *UnderCover,* what's his name? He was in the Mummy movies. This would show we're not out to beat up the Arab community. Anyway, the friend has these on-the-ground contacts and now has a line on where to get bin Laden.

{Ross holds up a hand.}

ROSS: Look, I get it, all right? I know you can do this, but I need to talk this over with . . . (*makes vague hand gesture*) the others.

(*smiles*)

KAGEN (**rueful smile**): How well I know.

{Ross rises, signaling an end to the meeting. Kagen gets up, too.}

ROSS: We'll noodle on it and I'll get back to you. I like it, enough to maybe talk about it further. But as you're well aware, it's going to be tough to do in this market.

KAGEN: Think on it, Alan. Without going out of our way this could be entertaining, but a subtle take on the meanings or rather, the dimensions of patriotism.

{Ross shakes Kagen's hand.}

ROSS: I will. I'll be in touch.

{Kagen exits, a noticeable limp to his gait. Ross sits back down and starts fooling with his Mont Blanc again. He then buzzes his assistant, JOSIE.}

ROSS (into phone intercom): Get me Eddie, will you, Josie?

JOSIE (over intercom): No problem.

{Ross leafs through that morning's Hollywood Journal, *the industry newspaper. He begins to read an article that catches his interest when Josie buzzes him again. Ross presses the intercom button.}*

JOSIE (over intercom): I have Eddie for you, Alan.

ROSS: Thanks. (*he picks up the handset*) Eddie? I just had a meeting with Walsh Kagen. (*He listens*) Yeah, yeah I know he hasn't made anything in a while, but he's got this crazy idea that, well, may be something.

DISSOLVE TO:

EXT. BILTMORE HOTEL, DOWNTOWN L.A., ESTABLISHING—NIGHT

ON SCREEN

{Three nights later.}

{Various limousines and trendy cars pull up to the valet parking at the swank hotel in L.A.'s downtown and disgorge smartly dressed men and women.}

INT. BILTMORE HOTEL, CRYSTAL BALLROOM

CU—SIGN

{Announcing the ninth annual Frontlines of Justice Dinner sponsored by the Legal Aid Council of Greater Los Angeles.}

{ WIDEN to reveal many well-dressed guests milling about drinking and talking in the large foyer of the ballroom, the curtain still drawn as the space is readied.}

ROSS

{—sips his drink and spots IVAN MONK, whom he has met before.}

MONK

{—is black, six-two, built like an aging linebacker, but solid, despite the fact that he's a private investigator who owns a donut shop. He's casual in a dark Bironi sport coat, open collar, and cuffed slacks. His shoulders say he's relaxed, but there's an energy to him that's notched in neutral.}

{Near Monk is a handsome Japanese-American woman with medium length brownish hair and alert eyes. She is JILL KODAMA, Monk's significant other and a superior court judge. She is smooth in her St. John ensemble. They are chatting as Ross walks up.}

{Ross sticks out his hand.}

ROSS: Hi, you remember we crossed paths when I was with Exchange Entertainment?

{Monk blinks, then:}

MONK: Right, Alan Ross.

{The two shake hands. Kodama looks on.}

ROSS: Exactly. We had some discussions with you about turning one of your cases that got some ink into a movie of the week.

MONK: This is my squeeze, I mean, this is Judge Jill Kodama.

KODAMA: *(to Monk)* Be cool. *(She and Kagen shake hands)* Good to meet you. I recall you wanted to make my character a Latina beer truck driver going to law school at night, because that would make Ivan more down, more like the working man.

KAGEN: The demographics you know.

MONK: What brings you here?

ROSS: We donate to the Legal Aid Council.

{Monk and Kodama look equally surprised.}

ROSS (cont'd): No, really. I'm at Ten-Shun now and we were developing a show a few months ago and their attorneys provided technical assistance to the project. My boss, Eddie Mast, took a liking to them and there you go.

{Ross has some of his drink.}

KODAMA: I'm glad you do, the LAC fills a necessary need.

{The two men nod in agreement. SANDI LOFTON, an aging beach bunny and reporter with the Hollywood Journal, *appears at Ross's elbow, butting in.}*

LOFTON (to Ross): Is it true you're considering doing a picture about bin Laden?

{Monk and Kodama perk up.}

ROSS (smiling): I shall demonstrate my usual blasé indifference to you, Sandi.

LOFTON: I heard this from our friends at the American Jewish Association. More than one of whom sits on your board, Alan. And it's not just Jews who will be upset if this project goes forward.

{She turns to Monk.}

LOFTON (cont'd): What do you think?

MONK: I'm not completely sure, but if other warped people and events aren't off limits, then why bin Laden?

Wasn't there a musical about the hijacking of that ship, the Achille Lauro?

LOFTON (jerks head at the sign): Figures a lawyer for this group of worn-out hippies and disillusioned revolutionaries with law degrees, that helps welfare cheats and renters duck their responsibilities would say that.

KODAMA (to Monk): Doggone dewy-eyed Taliban simp.

{Monk and Kodama exchange shit-eating grins. Lofton is unsure what to think while Ross looks bemused and tips his drink to someone else from the "industry."}

DISSOLVE TO:
EXT. ROSS'S LOS FELIZ HOME/ESCAPE ROOM BAR—NIGHT

INTERCUTTING

{Between Ross's house and Escape Room Bar that Kagen exits.}

{Later that evening, Ross pulls up and parks his late model BMW Z-3 roadster in the driveway of his restored two-story Tudor on a cul-de-sac street in the quiet neighborhood. He gets out and walks toward his home, fishing his keys out of his pocket. There is weak illumination from a nearby lone streetlight. He passes a high shrub.}

ROSS

{—turns toward the shrub at a Sound.}

ROSS: Who's there?

EXT. ESCAPE ROOM BAR, CULVER CITY—NIGHT

{Walsh exits the bar, arm-in-arm with a tipsy middle-aged dyed blonde with frizzy hair and a dress too short for her age. They are laughing and kissing as they meander toward his car.}

AN SUV

{—screeches around a corner.}

EXT. ROSS'S LOS FELIZ HOME

{The exec now has a anxious look on his face as an IN-TRUDER, indistinct in the dim light, emerges from the shadow of the shrub}

ROSS: What is this?

INTRUDER: Judgment.

ROSS: For what?

EXT. ESCAPE ROOM BAR

{Kagen and the woman kiss and grope each other but react to a voice yelling from inside the SUV zooming by.}

VOICE (in SUV): Charlatan.

{A Molotov Cocktail is tossed and breaks near Kagen, exploding into flame.}

KAGEN: Fuck.

{The woman SCREAMS as Kagen beats out the fire that has ig-nited his sleeve from a splash of lit gas.}

EXT. ROSS'S LOS FELIZ HOUSE

INTRUDER: You know, traitor.

{Ross regains his nerve and charges. The Intruder is startled as he throws his Molotov Cocktail. The bottle explodes on Ross and he's ablaze.}

ROSS: Oh God:

{Ross has enough presence of mind to drop and roll on the ground as the Intruder runs away.}

END INTERCUTTING

INT. KODAMA'S AND MONK'S HOUSE, BEDROOM, SILVERLAKE—DAY

{It's the next morning and the two are in bed under the covers making love in the tastefully appointed bedroom. Morning light creeps in beneath a partially drawn shade.}

CU

{—on one of the judge's oil paintings hanging over the bed. The work depicts denizens of Skid Row at dusk. Some wear Mardi Gras party masks. In the background, there's a building with a lit neon sign that reads: "Justice." The Sounds of the couple's passionate love-making can be heard.}

DISSOLVE TO:

INT. BEDROOM

{A little later and Monk exits the shower back into the bedroom. There's a towel wrapped around his waist and he's brushing his teeth. Kodama, in a slip, sits on the bed, using a blow dryer on her wet hair. The radio is on to the local NPR station.}

MONK: You meeting with the Asian Pacific Islander Caucus tonight aren't you?

KODAMA (wearily): Yes, as you well know.

MONK: I ain't player-hatin' baby. I'm all for you running for the State Senate.

{He rases the dripping toothbrush above his head and pumps his fist.}

MONK (cont'd): I'll door knock the 'hood till I've worn my shoes to my ankles for the one true Asian sister who'll stand up for all our rights.

{*Kodama makes a derisive sound as he re-enters the bathroom to finish his teeth-cleaning chore.*}

MONK (cont'd, from the bathroom): You said you wanted to do something different than adjudicate.

KODAMA: That doesn't mean—

{*The RINGING phone cuts her off. She leans over and plucks the handset up. Monk re-enters the room.*}

KODAMA (into handset): Hello?

{*She listens then:*}

KODAMA (cont'd): He's right here, Nona.

MONK: What's my mother want?

CUT TO:

EXT. MAGNOLIA AVENUE, SHERMAN OAKS—DAY

{*Monk and Walsh Kagen, his arm bandaged but not in a sling, walk along the thoroughfare in the San Fernando Valley. Monk has his hands in his pockets and Walsh puffs on a thin Parodi cigar.*}

KAGEN: Again, I'm sorry to have bothered your mother, but judges like cops have their addresses blocked by the phone company.

MONK: But they're aren't a whole lot of people with my last name.

KAGEN: Yeah, and Thelonious ain't with us anymore.

MONK: And you're willing to see if I can find out something about this attack on you and Ross the cops can't?

KAGEN: According to the piece in this morning's

Journal, you were one of the last people seen talking to him.

MONK: So was the waiter bringing the drinks.

{Kagen snickers.}

KAGEN: But you've got story potential, Ivan.

{Monk halts before a bookstore. On its green awning are the words: MYSTERIES, MURDER & MAYHEM. Through the window, the proprietor, a rugged individual with a red/browninsh beard, talks animatedly with a customer.}

MONK: So you want to make this into a screenplay? You follow me around while I look for whoever torched you and Ross? I got news for you, Walsh. He might be all doped up now from his third-degree burns, but in a day or two Ross is going to be able to talk and that will be the end of the mystery. His attacker got up close and personal.

KAGEN: But until then who knows what can happen. What if all he has is a vague description?

MONK: You mean of some Middle Eastern perp?

KAGEN: Middle Eastern doesn't necessarily mean an Arab or Muslim.

{Monk resumes walking and Kagen falls in step.}

MONK: Herv Renschel of the AJA gave you grief, too?

KAGEN: He hasn't been called the Jewish Farakhan for kicks. I got a few threatening calls the day after I saw Ross. Nobody I.D.'d themselves, but is it a coincidence that the day of the night of the attacks, the AJA ran a full page ad in the *Journal* denouncing Ten-Shun and the purported project?

MONK: Just to be broad-minded, what if it's one of the sleeper agents of the Al Qaeda that did the deed?

KAGEN: Okay.

MONK: Shit. I've already had somebody blow up my donut shop once.

KAGEN: Come on, Ivan, you got a rep as a man who goes at it until the job is done. This could be big.

MONK: Not to mention good press for you to get a deal.

KAGEN: I'll make you a producer if we roll film. Hey, I got enough to cover your nut for a week or so. If we get bupkis, no hard feelings.

MONK: I hope I don't regret this.

{Kagen beams, clapping Monk on the shoulder.}

EXT. SUPERIOR COURT BUILDINGS, DOWNTOWN L.A., ESTABLISHING—DAY

INT. JILL KODAMA'S COURTROOM

{A criminal trial is in progress. The defense counsel, MS. WIN-TERS, is about to talk but Kodama, from the bench, cuts her off. The defendant, MR. REESE, is white, twentysomething, dressed in jeans and a tee-shirt. He has an American flag tattooed on his tricep and slouches in his chair, seemingly disinterested in the proceedings.}

KODAMA: . . . hold on, Ms. Winters. (*to the defendant*) Mr. Reese, sit up.

MR. REESE

{—glares at Kodama then reluctantly obeys.}

RESUME

{—Kodama talking.}

KODAMA (cont'd): Mr. Reese, you and your friends are charged with a serious matter. You may think that because the man you chased and, by your own admission, fought, turned out to be Guatemalan and an undocumented worker, and not of Arab descent somehow mitigates the circumstances, but they do not in my courtroom, sir. So I suggest you make some effort to pay attention to what's going on, because I do take attitude into account should there be a sentencing. (*to the defense lawyer*) And counselor, do a better job of preparing your clients.

MR. REESE

{—looks at Ms. Winters, frowning.}

EXT. CONTINENTAL DONUTS, CRENSHAW DISTRICT, ESTABLISHING—DAY

{It's late afternoon at the donut shop—with a massive plaster donut anchored on the roof—on Vernon Avenue owned by Monk. The regulars are seen through the large picture windows sitting inside, talking, playing chess, and so forth.}

INT. CONTINENTAL DONUTS

{Monk selects a chocolate crueller from the case. ELROD, the six-foot-eight, muscled ex-con manager of the establishment looks on disdainfully.}

ELROD: You will have to do penance for that.

MONK: "Keep up appearances, there lies the test."

{Monk bites into the donut with relish.}

ELROD: You can quote Churchill all you like.

MONK

{ —is shocked that Elrod can place the quote.}

ELROD (cont'd): But that doesn't change the fact that you are backsliding, weak to the allure of butter and sugar.

MONK: Night school must agree with you.

{Monk walks into the back of the shop and then a right along a short hall. He unlocks a heavy screen door protecting an inner door.}

INT. MONK'S INNER SANCTUM

{Monk steps into the Spartanly furnished room. There's a cot, a small refrigerator, CD boom box, several old school file cabinets, a carburetor on top of one of the cabinets, a new model PC on a sturdy wooden table, and a comfortable swivel chair before it.}

{Monk turns on the boom box which is tuned to a jazz station. He sits down, finishes his snack, and fires up the computer.}

DISSOLVE TO:

INT. WILSHIRE OFFICE OF HERV RENSCHEL—DAY

{Monk stands at the window, looking out on the city. Kagen sits on a couch before a coffee table, a fine china coffee set before him.}

{HERV RENSCHEL, early sixties, lean and rangy, has a crew cut topping a lined face that bespeaks of his experiences from the Six Day War to being a political infighter. He prowls back and forth on the carpet before them.}

RENSCHEL: You guys crack me up.

MONK (turning): I try.

{Renschel stops and glares at the detective.}

RENSCHEL: I know about you, Monk, the black nationalist private eye.

MONK: I do my best to give everybody a fair shake, Renschel. I don't wear my race on my sleeve.

RENSCHEL: What, you leave your kafir in the trunk?

KAGEN: If we could stay on point, gentlemen.

{Renschel leans against his messy desk.}

RENSCHEL: Are you interrogating any Arab organizations in this quest for the attackers?

MONK: If that's where the case take us.

RENSCHEL: Somehow I doubt it will.

MONK: Doubt all you like. I know you were on a radio show the day the *Journal* leaked that Ten-Shun was considering the *Bring Me the Head* movie. You didn't parse your words too much when you said that a judgment should be levied against Ross and Kagen.

KAGEN: He said that?

RENSCHEL: I have a right to my opinion.

MONK: But did you put your words into action, Renschel? Like that time after the '92 riots when you and some of your more eager members jumped those kids coming out of Canter's on Fairfax?

RENSCHEL: There had been two gang shootings in that neighborhood in less than a week.

MONK: So any blacks would do, huh? Only these guys were UCLA basketball players and you got the shit sued out of you.

RENSCHEL: I'm a big enough man to admit my mistakes, Monk.

KAGEN (gesturing): We all want the same thing here, find the guilty party.

RENSCHEL: I can say without fear of contradiction, the AJA had nothing to do with these distasteful incidents. I suggest, as I did to the police, that you and your UPN Herculot Perot here could better use your time following up leads elsewhere.

MONK: Like with Josef Odeh?

RENSCHEL (nodding): I'll give you credit, Monk, you do your homework.

MONK: Like I said, I try.

EXT. WILSHIRE BOULEVARD—CONTINUOUS

{Kagen and Monk walk away from Renschel's office building and toward the latter's fully restored cobalt blue '64 Ford Galaxie parked at a meter.}

KAGEN: This Odeh I gather is a leader in the Arab Community?

MONK: Yeah, he's considered a moderate, particularly compared to your boy.

{Monk hooks a thumb in the direction of the AJA office.}

KAGEN: So why do we need to talk to him?

MONK: It's pretty fascinating what you can find online added to some old-fashioned working the phones, Walsh. One of the service organizations Odeh sat on the board of was caught up in the Justice Department net around the hawala method of money laundering to the Al Qaeda.

{Monk unlocks the car and the two get in.}

INT. '64 FORD GALAXIE

{Monk cranks the car to life and pulls away from the curb.}

KAGEN: So this charity was a front that skimmed off money to the terrorist network?

MONK: That seems to be unclear. But the point is that Odeh was tainted and did some back-peddling. He proclaimed he knew nothing of money transferring, etcetera. He wasn't arrested, but I bet he's been under watch.

KAGEN: But he could be jiving, and he really was part of some scheme to move funds.

MONK: Something like that.

KAGEN: You gonna be more objective this time?

{Monk lets some silence drag.}

MONK: You're right, Walsh, I was being unprofessional. I'll be on point.

{Kagen winks at him.}

EXT. '64 FORD GALAXIE: DAY

The car zooms along.

EXT. MASJID AL-FALAH ISLAMIC CENTER, INGLEWOOD: DAY

{Monk and Kagen walk up the steps of the Center and stop at a locked door where there's an intercom.}

CU

{intercom as Monk bends to it and pushes the button to speak.}

MONK (into intercom): Hi, I'm Ivan Monk with Walsh Kagen to see Jabari Hatoom. I had an appointment.

WIDEN

{Monk lets go of the button and the door BUZZES. Kagen opens the door.}

INT. MASJID AL-FALAH ISLAMIC CENTER— CONTINUOUS

{Monk and Kagen stand in a foyer. A twentysomething east Indian woman, SUNAR, in her hijab—head covered, long dress—comes out to greet them. As is the custom, she does not offer her hand.}

SUNAR: Gentlemen, this way.

{Monk and Kagen follow the young woman past a spacious worship area with a podium, classrooms, and into a spotless stainless steel kitchen off a well-lit hallway.}

INT. KITCHEN—DAY

{Monk and Kagen are ushered in by Sunar who departs. JABARI HATOOM is African American, tall, balding, early thirties, and dressed in slacks and a shirt with his sleeves rolled up. He has the garbage disposal unit out and on a table, working on it with a screwdriver. He smiles upon seeing Monk.}

HATOOM: Homeboy.

{Hatoom puts down his screwdriver and embraces the P.I.}

MONK: Glad you could see us.

{They disengage. Monk indicates Kagen.}

MONK (cont'd): This is Walsh Kagen.

HATOOM (shaking the director's hand): Man, what a pleasure. You don't know how many times I've seen *The Plunderers* and *One Deadly Night*.

KAGEN: That's flattering. And how is it you know Ivan?

HATOOM: He busted me.

{Kagen regards Monk.}

MONK: Long time ago, when I used to do bounty hunting.

KAGEN (to Hatoom): And you converted in prison?

HATOOM: Exactly.

MONK: Will you set up a meeting for us with Odeh?

{Hatoom is uncomfortable.}

HATOOM: I have not made the call.

MONK: I know it's hard, Jabari, but you know good and well it's the Muslim community that has to step up if there's an extremist running around.

HATOOM: Is that just another way to say we have to be good, shuffling handkerchief heads? Being a Muslim is not synonymous with being a terrorist, Ivan. And depending on the political winds, freedom fighters become rebels become evil-doers.

MONK: Odeh put himself in the mix, Jabari.

KAGEN: What am I missing here?

{Hatoom and Monk exchange a look.}

HATOOM: Odeh demanded and got a meeting with Alan Ross two days ago.

KAGEN: Does everybody read that *Journal* rag?

HATOOM: A possible movie about bin Laden that would invariably put our community in a bad light was bound to draw attention, especially in these times.

KAGEN: But that's the point; my idea is ultimately that the film is about tolerance. I'll admit I'm exploiting bin Laden because, well, frankly, like any out-size madman, he's great pulp material. I'm not a student of Sam Fuller and was an A.D. on a couple of Frankenheimer's films for nothing. Look guys, great villains and the horrors they commit make powerful statements about us. From King Leopold and the Congo to Pol Pot and his Khmer Rouge as depicted in *The Killing Fields* . . . that's show biz, fellas.

HATOOM: The meeting deteriorated, and Odeh, from what I understand, was removed by security.

KAGEN (to Monk): And you found this out by calling around?

{Monk shrugs.}

KAGEN (cont'd): Some Rolodex. Sam L. Jackson or Ving Rhames for sure, Monk. The best is what you deserve.

MONK: Lovely. Look, Jabari, you know damn well I'm not going to be part of an attempt to railroad Odeh or anybody else. But somebody tossed those hot totties.

HATOOM: And the Molotov is the Intifada favorite?

MONK: Maybe it's a set-up or it was done to send a message and a signature.

HATOOM: You've already made up your mind.

MONK: I'm suspicious by inclination, not vindictive, man. It comes down to this, you want it to be only the FBI that gets to talk to Odeh?

HATOOM: You drive a hard mule, Mr. Monk.

MONK: Make the call, will you, Jabari?

HATOOM: Okay. But I'm not promising anything.

MONK: Understood.

{The two shake hands again.}

CUT TO:

INT. '64 FORD GALAXIE—DAY

{Monk and Kagen drive away and Kagen's cell phone RINGS.}

KAGAN (clicking on phone): Hello? *(he listens, then:)* Thanks, Mina. We'll swing by there to see him.

{He clicks off the phone, and over this says to Monk:}

KAGEN: That was my assistant. She's got a friend over at Cedars. Alan is awake and lucid, and the cops don't know it yet.

EXT. '64 FORD GALAXIE

{The car picks up speed along the city streets.}

INT. BURN WARD, CEDARS SINAI
HOSPITAL—DAY

{Alan Ross is propped up in his hospital bed in the burn ward populated by several other patients, visitors, and hospital staff. His upper body is bandaged as is part of his face and head.}

{Numerous flower arrangements are spread out on the night stand and floor near his bed. Monk and Kagen stand on either side of his bed.}

MONK: That's it?

ROSS (soft voiced): 'Fraid so. He was young, about twenty-two or so, dressed in normal clothes (*beat*) you know, jeans and a sweatshirt.

MONK: Any logo on the sweat shirt?

ROSS: No, no it was plain.

KAGEN: And this kid was Arab?

{Ross hesitates.}

ROSS: He didn't have an accent, but he was, well, brown-skinned and dark-haired.

KAGEN (to Monk): All the more reason to get to Odeh.

MONK: But he called you traitor?

ROSS: That's right.

MONK: Are you of Arab extraction?

ROSS: No, nor am I Jewish.

{Monk says nothing, mulling over the information.}

DISSOLVE TO:

INT. KODAMA AND MONK'S HOUSE,
STUDY—NIGHT

{In the comfortable and book-lined study, Kodama is sketching with a charcoal pencil on a freshly stretched and guached canvas on a easel. Monk sits and sips on Scotch from a tumbler. His face is a barometer of his intense concentration.}

KODAMA: Even if the attacker was Arab, that doesn't mean he was operating on anybody's orders. There're plenty of people inflamed on all sides of this who are more than willing to act alone.

MONK: Sure, but the reality is I've got to talk to Odeh to satisfy myself.

KODAMA: What if he ducks you

MONK: Then how would you interpret that?

KODAMA: It doesn't mean he's guilty. It might mean despite Jabari vouching for you, he doesn't want to in any way further jeopardize his organization. He's doesn't know you to be the big, sweet, voodoo daddy I love.

{She laughs and he grins.}

KODAMA (cont'd): But you're right, you will have to have some face time with him.

{She continues working.}

MONK

{—is sullen then brightens.}

MONK: You got a sharp Number 2 pencil, baby?

KODAMA (stops sketching): What?

MONK (standing): Grab one and your sketch pad. We got a patient to see.

KODAMA (hand on hip): I am not your secretary.

{Monk has crossed to her, his arm around her waist.}

MONK: You're a Renaissance woman, you know that?

{He points at the canvas.}

MONK (cont'd): And bring your glasses, baby. I want those lines crisp in this next drawing.

KODAMA: Kiss my ass.

INT. BURN WARD, CEDARS SINAI HOSPITAL—NIGHT

{Kodama, wearing her glasses, sits next to Ross's bed, doing a sketch of the man who threw a Molotov at him. She stops and holds it up for the vp of development to see.}

KODAMA: How this?

ROSS: A little more shallowness in the cheeks and the eyes wider.

C.U. OF DRAWING

{Kodama resumes working on the drawing.}

ROSS (cont'd): (to Monk) This is the second time I've done this. I described this guy to the police sketch artist the detectives who interviewed me sent this afternoon. (*beat*) They've got a head start on you, Ivan. I heard the younger one tell the older one they were going to check the drawing against the Homeland Security database. And canvas several Arab hangouts in the San Gabriel Valley a sheriff's friend was hooking them up with.

MONK: When you hesitated this afternoon in describing this cat, that just wasn't about guessing at his ethnicity was it?

{Kodama stops sketching to look at Monk.}

ROSS

{—chews his lower lip.}

ROSS: It's just an impression.

MONK: Come on, share.

ROSS: As you know, I come into contact with a lot of actors. Not so much across my desk but at the hot spots, the watering holes that come and go on the A list one must frequent to keep up appearances.

MONK: And a starlet or two you might stumble over.

ROSS: Sure there's that.

KODAMA

{—*makes a face.*}

MONK: Are you saying you've seen this guy at one of those places?

ROSS: No, like I said, it's only a feeling. (*beat*) The way he, handled himself reminded me, well, like he was auditioning, you know?

{*Monk and Kodama exchange a look.*}

INT. TAYLOR'S STEAKHOUSE— NIGHT—CONTINUOUS

{*The steakhouse is an old school beef and booze joint with a dark interior and decor that hasn't been updated since the LBJ Administration. Under the din of the patrons, a basketball game plays on the TV at the end of the bar.*}

{*Monk and Kagen sit in a booth in the upstairs area, enjoying their heavy caloric intake.*}

MONK

{—*finishes chewing and swallows. He has a drink of water, then reaches over to extract a folded photograph out of his jacket's inner pocket hanging on a hook. He unfolds the photograph and places it on the table.*}

CU

{—of the photograph, an actor's headshot. His hair is longer in the shot, but it's the young man who tossed the Molotov at Ross. On the credit line of the photo it reads: ALEX TUCCO}

WIDEN

{—Kagen shows no reaction as he samples more of his whiskey.}

KAGEN: Good kid. He's got a kind of De Niro–Pacino thing going for him.

MONK: And I bet he's scared shitless, Walsh, wherever you got him stashed. I suppose your lawyer will argue in court that he never meant to set Ross afire. That like the other one you hired to chuck a Molotov at you, Tucco was supposed to miss. But Ross charged him when he was about to throw the Molotov and it shook him.

{Kagen calmly cuts a piece of his steak.}

KAGEN: That's good, I'll have to remember that.

{He eats.}

MONK: You like to gamble, Walsh, you once got a two picture deal in a poker game against a producer with a hand of trip kings.

KAGEN: I play the odds, Ivan.

MONK: Fake the attacks to build up interest in the property, and hire me to show you're still a player. But how the hell did you think engineering all this bullshit was going to get you a deal, Walsh? Nearly killing someone is a hell of a way to entice future prospects.

{Kagen has another piece of his steak and cleans his pallet with another swig of whiskey. He then clears his throat.}

KAGEN: Nobody was ever going to make *Bring Me the Head of Osama bin Laden,* Ivan.

MONK (pointing): But the attacks and the aftermath would generate coverage, you'd be the controversial writer-director on people's lips like you once were when you did *One Deadly Night.*

KAGEN (misty-eyed): How many times have you seen it, Ivan?

MONK: At least four. The scene where Hack has been beaten by the guards and pieces of glass ground into his face and he just grins and tells them, "The thieves and junkies will always be on my side." (*shakes his head*) Yeah, Walsh, you had it, man. (*beat*) Of course you've guessed when I got up to use the bathroom earlier, I placed a call to the cops.

{Walsh finishes his drink and dabs his mouth with his cloth napkin.}

MONK (cont'd): It wasn't the potential money you could make, was it, Walsh?

KAGEN: The magic, Ivan, I missed the magic.

Kagen places the napkin gently on the table.

KAGEN (cont'd): Let's have some dessert and coffee. The carrot cake's great here.

FADE OUT.

Line Reading

PARNELL HALL

FLETCHER GREENGRASS HANDED me the silver samovar and fell over dead.

I must say I resented it. That was the cue for my big speech, I'd been working on it all week, I was really looking forward to it, and I wanted to do it right.

Now, don't judge me too harshly. You gotta understand. I was nervous about my performance. For one thing, I hadn't acted in years. When I had it was in summer stock, at an Equity theater, where the actors got paid. I'd also appeared in movies, granted only fleetingly, but still enough to hold a Screen Actors Guild card. All of which made me a professional. And this was community theater. Amateur theater. And as a professional acting in amateur theater, I was *expected* to be good.

I had a lot to prove.

Which, if the truth be known, I probably wasn't capable of. Because if I'd been any good as an actor, I'd still be doing it, instead of working as a P.I.

I also didn't *know* he was dead. Because Fletcher Greengrass was one of the hammiest actors I'd ever met, and when he fell over on his face, I, like everyone else in the cast, assumed he was pulling another one of his outrageous stunts just to upstage me, and undercut my big speech. So I was justifiably pissed.

It was near the end of act two. I was alone on stage, awaiting the object of my affections, the virginal Emily, when young Mr. Greengrass emerged from her room instead.

"Surprised?" he inquired in an exaggerated mocking tone. "I don't know why. These thing happen, don't they? How do you like it? So I got to her first, what's the big deal?"

He put his hand on my shoulder. I brushed it off.

"Remember what you said? About women being like trophies?" He snatched up the samovar, held it out to me. "Here's the award for the world's worst ladies' man. I think this belongs to you."

His delivery was so over the top that when he proceeded to take a nose dive, I naturally figured he was clowning.

So did the director. A little man with no hair, except on his chin, he was given to histrionics, whether in an attempt to match Fletcher Greengrass's tone, or because he had seen a director portrayed that way on TV, I couldn't say. At any rate, he vaulted up onto the stage, which was at the far end of the Ridgewood High basketball court, to tell Fletcher Greengrass off.

"Fletcher," he declared. "That's the last straw. You cooperate, or you're out of the play. You think I can't replace you, well I can. I'll play the part myself, if I have to, rather than put up with this."

That was a brave boast. Fletcher Greengrass was our leading man, our young love interest, the one enamored of both Emily and Charlotte, the two young women in the piece. I say Emily and Charlotte—that's their stage names. Emily was actually a young housewife whose name I didn't know. Charlotte was Shirley something or other, a voluptuous young woman with auburn hair and a most remarkable collection of shirts, sweaters, and pullovers, none of which ever seemed to be hiding a bra.

But I digress.

Anyway, the director descended on the fallen body of Fletcher Greengrass like Washington marching on Richmond, (if that's where he marched; as I grow older, my American history fades with everything else).

"Get up and stop screwing around," he ordered.

Fletcher Greengrass had stopped screwing around, but he didn't get up. He just lay there, doing a marvelous impression of a dead man.

The aforementioned Emily and Charlotte crept out of the wings, where they had been waiting to enter after I had delivered my big speech. Also from the wings crept the other actor in the piece, whose name I couldn't remember, though his name in the play was Ralph.

The stage manager also poked his head out from behind the curtain. An elderly, often befuddled man, he inquired, "Where do you want to take it from?" a totally inappropriate comment, even if one of the actors hadn't been dead.

"Fletcher, get up now or you're replaced."

"Now, now, I want him in the show," Barnaby Farnsworth declared.

Mr. Farnsworth was the playwright, and I only knew his name because it appeared in huge letters on the front of every script. A balding, middle-aged man, with pudgy features and twinkling eyes, Barnaby Farnsworth was a bit of a joke to the actors in the cast. The joke was that his play, *Ride the Wild Elephant,* was largely autobiographical, and that the part of Brad, modeled after him, was the one played by young, handsome, studly Fletcher Greengrass.

Emily and Charlotte repressed giggles when Barnaby declared he wanted Fletcher in the play.

"Yes, I know you want him in the play," the director said. "But he can only *be* in the play if he stands up. I cannot direct an actor who takes naps in the middle of scenes."

The director placed his toe in Fletcher Greengrass's ribs. He pushed, not gently. His eyes widened.

I followed his gaze.

The director was staring at the white froth dribbling from the corner of Fletcher Greengrass's mouth.

I FELT SORRY for the cop. As the local chief of a small town in Westchester county, the poor man couldn't have had much experience with murders. Not to mention on-stage murders involving a full cast of characters and a silver samovar. While this was his jurisdiction, still I wondered how long it would be before a homicide sergeant arrived to relieve him.

"So," he said. "Who saw what happened?"

Everyone began talking at once. The actors, director, playwright, stage manager. Even the light man, who had climbed down from his booth when it was clear something was wrong.

The cop put up his hand. A large, overweight man, he was sweating profusely in his uniform. It was mid-July, and the gym was not air-conditioned. "One at a time, please. Who's in charge here?"

The stage manager attempted to assert his authority, but was quickly shouted down.

"I'm in charge," the director said.

"And you would be?"

"Morton Wainwright."

"Splendid. And where were you when it happened?'

"In the audience." He grimaced, shrugged. "I mean on the basketball court. Right here, watching the action on the stage."

Our eyes were drawn to the current action on the stage, which consisted of a doctor examining the body, while two EMS workers stood by with a gurney waiting to take it away. There was a crime scene ribbon up, and a police detective was searching the stage for evidence. Frankly, I had my doubts.

The cop cleared his throat for attention. "Who was on the stage at the time?"

"Just the two of them," the director said.

"The two of who?"

"Him and the other actor. Stanley Hastings."

The cop looked me over. I tried not to look guilty. Try that some time. It's like trying not to think of an elephant.

The cop didn't seem convinced. He grunted the police equivalent of *harumph,* and turned back to the director. "What were they doing?"

"They were playing a scene. They were doing okay. Not great, but okay. This was the first rehearsal off book—that means without scripts—and they had to be prompted a few times. No more than average, still it's hard to get any pace going when you keep blowing the lines."

"That's a fascinating inside look at theater," the cop said dryly. "But I have this dead body."

The director flushed. "Yes, of course. Anyway, they got to the point where Fletcher hands Stanley the silver samovar and he keeled over dead."

"You say he handed Stanley the whatjamacallit?"

"Samovar. Yes, sir."

"And that would be this gentleman here?" He fixed me with a steely gaze.

"That's right."

"Then you must have been rather close to him." He tried to say it casually, without insinuation.

"I was standing right next to him."

"And you two were the only ones on stage?" This time, the insinuation crept in.

"Were you thinking of fitting me for handcuffs?"

"This is no laughing matter, Mr. Hastings."

"Yes, I know." I tried to appear properly grave. Still, with the officer regarding me seriously as a suspect, it was all I could do to keep from giggling.

"Stanley wouldn't do anything like that," the actress playing Emily said. I found myself more favorably disposed toward her, wished I knew her name. The actress playing Charlotte, whose name I did know, said nothing. Emily was looking better, bra or no bra.

The author chimed in. "What's going to happen to my play?" he wailed.

I was pleased. It distracted the officer from me. He wheeled on the unfortunate man like an elephant about to crush a bug. "That remains to be seen," he said ominously.

THE COP COMMANDEERED the boys' locker room and proceeded to interrogate us one by one. First up was the playwright, probably, it occurred to me, just to teach him to keep his mouth shut.

As soon as the cop was gone, all of the actors huddled together, as no one had been assigned to ride herd over us.

"What do we do now? What do we do now?" Charlotte shrieked. I found my opinion of her plummeting, even though her agitated state was causing her chest to rise and fall in a most appealing manner.

"Yeah," the director put in. "You're the big P.I., aren't you? Why don't you tell us what to do?"

I found the big P.I. remark uncalled for. If I had mentioned casually during some rehearsal or other that I worked as a private investigator, I am sure it was only in response to some direct question by someone in the production, and not an attempt to influence anyone with the fact I had an interesting job.

It annoyed me that I had to keep making such self-assurances.

The stage manager, as he was wont to do, totally misunderstood the director's statement. "That's right," he said. "You're a professional actor. How does something like this affect the show?"

The question was greeted with audible groans. Luckily, I don't think the old boy's hearing was keen enough to notice.

Up on stage, the doctor finished with the corpse, and nodded to the EMS crew to wheel him out.

I excused myself from the actors, hurried across the basketball court, and caught up with the doctor.

I reached in my jacket pocket, pulled out my I.D., flipped it open. "One minute, doc. You got a preliminary cause of death?"

The medical examiner was a thin man with a trim moustache and a languid look. He regarded me with amused eyes. "Nice try. Is that a real I.D., or did you make it yourself?"

"Very funny." I pointed to the boys' locker room. "The chief's in there conducting interviews. It would probably help him a lot to know how the guy died."

"Thanks for the hint."

The doctor went out the gym door, following the gurney.

"So, what did you learn?" the director demanded as I rejoined the theater group.

I shook my head. "Doc's not talking."

"What does that mean?" Charlotte cried. She seemed particularly concerned.

"It means he doesn't feel we have a right to know." I shrugged. "In this assumption he is entirely correct."

"Oh, hell," the director sighed.

Charlotte was bouncing up and down in her pullover again. "What are the police gonna ask us? What do we have to say?"

I shrugged. "No big deal. Just tell the truth."

"About what?"

"Whatever they ask you. Most likely, what were you

doing when the guy dropped dead? Were you watching? What did you see?"

"Nothing personal?"

I frowned. "What do you mean?"

Charlotte had her face twisted up into a particularly unappealing knot. "I mean, like, you know. Relationships."

Oh.

I must say it should have occurred to me. That the studly what's-his-name and the curvacious Charlotte had been an item. I guess I'd chosen not to see it. Hadn't wanted to acknowledge the fact that Fletcher was still a ladies' man, while I was an old married fogey, a noncombatant, totally out of the running.

"If they ask you about relationships, tell them," I said. "Don't volunteer anything, but don't hold anything back. And, for goodness sakes, don't lie."

"Even about something like that?" Emily said. "What difference could it make?"

"Police mentality," I explained. "If they catch you in a lie, they'll think you committed the crime."

"Oh," Emily said. She didn't look pleased.

I blinked. Good lord. Emily, too? Wasn't she married? I was almost sure she was married.

At a rumble of voices off to my left, I turned to find the director and playwright arguing hotly. The bone of contention was obviously the play, though what the dispute was I couldn't imagine. It was, of course, recasting. The only reason I didn't think of it was I was so caught up in the homicide.

"Dean moves up," the director said.

"Not on your life," the playwright told him. "No way Dean plays that part."

"Well, who's gonna do it, you?"

"At least I know the lines."

"Yes, but you don't look that part."

"I beg your pardon?"

"Barnaby, give it a rest."

"I look the part as much as Dean does."

"I'll get someone."

"Who?"

"I'll get someone."

"Not without my approval."

"You approved Dean."

"Not for that part, I didn't."

My brain was having trouble catching up with the situation (which, as my wife could tell you, is a normal circumstance for me), but apparently while I was calming the fears of the two actresses, the playwright had returned from the locker room, and Dean, evidently the actor playing the part of Ralph, had been summoned to it. Which was why the two men felt free to disparage his acting talent so openly and bluntly. Besides having a very small part in the play, the actor Dean seemed by far the least likely murder suspect, but, hey, mine was not to reason why; if the police wanted him that was their business.

Dean was out about five minutes later and sent the director in.

The playwright immediately pounced on Dean, wanting to know what he'd been asked, what was going on, and whether the police seemed inclined to shut down the play.

Dean (I would say Mr. Dean, but I wasn't sure whether it was his first or last name), wasn't helpful. I saw at once why the playwright wouldn't want him in the part. He was a tall, shy, nerdy man, with a particularly nasal voice. Dean hadn't really established his presence in the few short lines his character had been given, but his vocal quality was certainly apparent now.

I had to sympathize with the playwright. Dean was

younger, taller, thinner, and had hair, but throw in the voice, and Barnaby Farnsworth was an Adonis compared to Dean.

"Geesh, so many questions," Dean whined. "You're worse than he is."

"What did he want?" the playwright insisted.

Dean let out a horsey-toothed guffaw, which further cemented the fact he would have been totally inappropriate for Fletcher's part.

"The murder, of course. He asked me about the murder."

"Did he call it a murder?"

Dean frowned. "Dunno. Can't remember. Did he call it a murder when he talked to you?"

"If he *had,* I wouldn't be *asking,*" the playwright said witheringly.

"Oh. Then I guess he didn't."

"So what did he want to know?" Charlotte said. "Did he ask you about me?"

"Or me?" Emily chimed in.

"He asked about everybody."

"And what did you tell him?" Charlotte demanded.

"That he was a goofy guy, but everybody seemed to like him."

Charlotte and Emily moaned in mutual distress.

"Did he ask you where you were when he died?" I said.

"Of course he did."

"What did you tell him?"

"I was in the wings like everybody else."

"I was in the light booth," the light man said.

"He didn't ask about you."

"Oh." The light man seemed somewhat miffed at being passed over as a murder suspect.

Next up was Charlotte. Her mouth fell open in disbelief when the director came back and told her. One might have thought he'd just accused her of the crime. *"Me?"* she said. "He wants to see *me?"*

"He wants to see everybody," the director said. "It's just your turn."

"Did he ask for me, or did he just tell you to send someone?"

"He asked for you. But it doesn't mean anything."

"What do you mean it doesn't mean anything? How can it not mean anything? What did you tell him about me?"

"I didn't tell him anything."

"Then how did he know to ask for me?" Charlotte wailed.

"Relax," I said. "It's simple police procedure. He's just taking all our statements. Trust me. The order doesn't matter."

I WAS LEFT for last. I knew what that meant. I was the chief suspect, and the cop was gathering all the evidence he could before he questioned me.

The boy's locker room had water and towels on the floor and smelled of sweat, and reminded me of my days on the high school basketball team, so many years ago.

The cop was straddling a wooden bench in front of a row of metal lockers. His notebook was open in front of him. He gestured to me to sit opposite him. I wasn't sure whether to straddle the bench, as he was, or sit sideways. I wondered what the women had done. I opted to straddle.

"Mr. Hastings, is it?" the cop said.

"That's right."

"You're Stanley Hastings, you're a private investigator from New York City?"

"Yes. How did you know?"

"It's been mentioned."

I bet it had. What with my relative position to the corpse when he took a dive, the others must have been invoking my name every chance they got.

"Yeah, I'm a P.I. But nothing glamorous. I work for a negligence lawyer in Manhattan."

"So what are you doing here?"

"My wife's aunt retired after twenty-five years of civil service, took a trip abroad. Gonna be gone all summer. She needed someone to housesit, water the plants. Alice thought it would be a free vacation."

"Alice is your wife?"

"That's right."

"How's it going?"

"So far we've run out of bottled gas, repaired the central air conditioning, had the plumber in twice, rewired the kitchen, and retiled the bathroom ceiling where the cat fell through."

"That's very interesting, Mr. Hastings, but I have this murder."

"You asked the question."

"That I did. Anyway, you're here for the summer and you tried out for an amateur play?"

"I always wanted to be an actor. I just never got much work."

"So this meant a lot to you?"

"I was hoping to enjoy it. Not much chance of that now."

"Or then?"

I blinked. "Huh?"

The cop flipped through his notebook. "According to the other cast members, Mr. Greengrass gave you a pretty hard time. Kidded you, needled you, made fun of your age, your experience, your talent, or lack of it."

I winced. "They said that?"

"Hey, this is not a review of your performance. They said *Fletcher* said that. That he was the type that was always trying to build himself up by tearing others down. I assure you, none of them had any illusions about Fletcher Greengrass."

"Well, that's a relief."

"Still, they pictured you as his chief rival."

"Oh, for goodness sakes."

"You take exception to that?"

"I take exception to the suggestion I might have killed him."

"But you were his chief rival, and you were alone with him on stage."

"And just how did I kill him, might I ask?"

"I have no idea. I was hoping you could tell me."

I stared at him. "You're expecting a confession?"

He shrugged. "Well, it's so much neater. And it saves on detective work."

"I'm sorry to disappoint you, but I didn't kill the gentleman."

He shook his head. "Ah, the flat denial. I hate the flat denial."

There was a knock on the locker room door and the detective stuck his head in. "Excuse me, sir. I found something."

"What is it?"

"In front of the suspect, sir?"

"Absolutely. Confront him with it."

The detective brought his hand out from under his coat, held up a plastic evidence bag. It appeared empty.

The cop squinted at it. "What's that?"

"It's a pin, sir. A straight pin, like a seamstress would use to pin clothes."

"Well, it's a theater. You'd expect the costumes to be pinned."

"Yes, but no one's in costume, sir."

"Where'd you find it?"

"On stage. Right near where the body was."

"What makes you think it's important?"

"Point's discolored, sir. Discolored twice. Black and red. It's been dipped in something black, goes nearly halfway up the pin. There's red on the point, looks fresh, could be blood."

The cop nodded approvingly. "Run it down to the lab. If it's blood, have it analyzed, try to match it up to the victim.

Have the other substance analyzed, and alert the doctor to check for poisons."

"I'm sure he is, sir. He's the one who told me to look for a sharp object that could have pierced the skin."

The detective left on his mission.

The cop turned back to me. "You were asking how you could have killed him."

"I stuck him with a pin?"

"You were close enough to do it."

"So was everyone else. These poisons are not instantaneous. He was offstage with the other actors. Someone could have stuck him before he went on, the poison could have hit him just about then."

"I suppose it's possible."

I sighed. Good lord. Here I was, trapped with a small town hick from the sticks who hadn't got a clue, who had done nothing but listen to people tell stories about me all day, and who was going to arrest me for the crime, just because he was incapable of imagining it the work of anybody else. "Pardon me," I said, "but since I seem to be your favorite suspect, would it be impolite to inquire if you have any others?"

The cop flipped the pages of his notebook. "The playwright, Barnaby Farnsworth. Forty-two-year-old bathtub enclosure salesman, fancies himself a man of letters. (That is the right term, isn't it—it's been so long since college). Considers himself an intellectual, finds his job beneath him. He was entirely less concerned with the young man's death than how it will affect his play. He didn't like the young man much in the role, but preferred him greatly to the actor, Dean.

"Dean Stanhope, assistant manager at Burger King, resented the decedent, thought he was an arrogant showoff. Jealous of his success with women, particularly the actresses in the play." He looked at me. "That's your motive, also. At least the jealousy bit. Anyway, that's him. Would probably be considered too ineffectual to do it, were it not for the cliché serial-killer profile of quiet, unassuming, kept to himself.

"The director, Morton Wainwright, resented the decedent because he eroded his authority by refusing to take direction and humiliated the poor soul whenever possible. You probably noticed that first hand."

"I have. I can't see killing him over it."

"Me either. But it's something to be considered." He referred to his notes. "Morton Wainwright is thirty-seven, he's a high school English teacher, married, two children, been active in community theater for the last two years, this is his third play.

"Then there's Becky Coleman."

"Who?"

"The actress playing Emily."

"Oh."

"You didn't know that?"

"No, I didn't."

"No wonder Mr. Greengrass had more luck with the ladies."

"I'm a married man."

"She's a married woman. She's thirty-two, been married five years. Has two kids. That didn't stop her from finding Mr. Greengrass most attractive. Unlucky for her, the man was a bit of a jerk, wasn't at all discreet, practically everybody knew—except you, I guess—and she was quite concerned he might spill the beans to her husband unless she found some way to silence him first."

"You've gotta be kidding."

The cop shrugged. "I thought you didn't want to be the only one with a motive. Anyway, that's hers. As for the other actress . . . "

"Shirley?"

"Ah, you know *her* name. So you're not impervious to

feminine charm. You at least notice women without under-garments. Perhaps you would have cause to eliminate a rival."

"I thought we were discussing other people's motives."

"We were, we were. Miss Shirley Goodhue. Single, twenty-eight, hairdresser. Rumored to be the first of the two to be involved with the decedent. When I say *rumored,* that's because these witness statements are so inaccurate. The women themselves are reticent, the observations of their peers are deficient, and the result is hopelessly inadequate."

"May I ask what you majored in in college?"

"What, a cop can't be literate? I read a lot, in between homicides. Luckily, there aren't that many."

"You don't think a little experience might be of help?"

"Oh. Irony. I am cut to the quick. I may have to arrest you after all."

"You were saying about Charlotte."

"Charlotte?"

"Sorry. That's her stage name. I mean Shirley."

"Ah, yes. The lovely Shirley Goodhue. Apparently the first of the decedent's affections. Which is significant in that if she felt herself replaced, so rudely and abruptly, by a married woman no less, perhaps to rub it in her face that she was nothing more than a brief dalliance . . . " He shrugged. "Well, a woman scorned. She would have every reason to hate young Mr. Greengrass. Wouldn't you say she made a dandy suspect?"

"I prefer her to me."

"How ungallant of you. Anyway, those are your chief suspects. You also have Sam Dobson, a harmless old coot of a stage manager. Seventy-seven, retired postman, living on a pension. Some men his age are sharp as a tack; Sam isn't. Even with all the stories you hear about postal workers snapping, I bet you a nickel he didn't do it.

"An even longer shot is the light man, Randy Haines,

thirty-five, certified public accountant. He was in the light booth when it happened and didn't see a thing."

"And he resents it bitterly. I agree, he's most unlikely."

"So who did it? I gotta arrest somebody. Otherwise the people will feel I'm not doing my job. If you were me, who would you arrest?"

"I don't think you have the evidence to arrest anyone."

"Is that wishful thinking?"

"No. I just happen to have the advantage over you in knowing I didn't do it."

"You have any idea who did?"

"Not really."

"Too bad."

"Yes. But it occurs to me, there might be a way to find out."

"Oh? And just what might that be?"

"Re-enact the crime."

THE SUSPECTS WERE all seated in the audience. Actually, they were seated in the gym on folding chairs, right under one of the basketball hoops, which in theory would be cranked up out of sight for performances, but was left down for rehearsals. The suspects consisted of the playwright, the director, the stage manager, the light man, and the three remaining actors.

I didn't count myself as a suspect. If that's unfair, sue me.

Also on hand were the cop and the detective, back from dropping the pin off at the lab.

The cop stood on the stage. "Ladies and gentlemen, I'm sorry to hold you here. But we must clear up this crime. Because it is a crime, without doubt. Fletcher Greengrass did not die of a heart attack, or stroke, or any such natural cause. He was killed by a lethal poison injected into the skin. The implement was a small straight pin. It is being analyzed now. I have no doubt it will prove to contain a fast acting poison of some type. It remains for us to prove who injected Mr. Greengrass, and why. In order to do so, we are going to go over the movements leading up to his death.

"I am going to ask you all to take your positions. Randy Haines is in the light booth. Sam Dobson is at the stage manager stand, backstage next to the curtain. As to the actors, Becky Coleman and Dean Stanhope, you're both behind the left doorway, are you not?

"The right doorway," the director corrected.

"I beg your pardon?"

"Stage directions refer to the *actor's* left or right. Assuming the actor is facing the audience. So that would be the stage *right* doorway."

"Fine. You two are there. Shirley Goodhue, you're over there in the doorway that I've just learned is stage left.

"Mr. Hastings is on stage alone, about to be joined by the decedent, who will be entering by . . . that doorway there . . . now you've got me confused."

"Upstage right."

"Yes. Upstage right. Where Miss Coleman and Mr. Stanhope are.

"Mr. Wainwright, you're on your feet, directing this action. Mr. Farnsworth, you are sitting here watching.

"All right, that's everybody."

"Except Mr. Greengrass. Unfortunately, he is incapable of reprising his role.

"Mr. Farnsworth, you were sitting in the audience the whole time. We don't really need you to re-enact that. Why don't you come up here and play the role?"

"Thought you'd never ask," the playwright said. He got to his feet, picked up his script.

"Don't you know the lines?" the director said ironically.

"I'm familiar with them. I haven't memorized them. Or the blocking."

The playwright scampered up the steps on the side of the stage, took his place with the other actors.

"All right, Mr. Hastings. What are you doing?"

"I'm alone on stage, waiting for Emily to enter."

The cop hopped down from the stage, turned to the director, said, "It's all yours."

The director seemed slightly disconcerted to find himself running the show. I guess he'd assumed the cop was going to do it. But after a moment he said, "All right. Let's treat this as a real rehearsal. We can certainly use it. Stanley, Charlotte has just exited stage left, you watch her go out, and . . . "

I watched her go out, whistled to myself, then strolled over to the mantlepiece and adjusted the trophies on it. This being nowhere near the dress rehearsal, the mantle and trophies were yet to come. I pantomimed them, then turned at the sound of footsteps, expecting to see Emily.

Instead it was the playwright, with his script, reading the Fletcher Greengrass part.

"Surprised? You shouldn't be. Things come full cycle. More often than not. Or so it seems. And what's she to you but a casual fling."

He put his hand on my shoulder. I brushed it off.

"Do you recall those words?" he went on. "Uttered many times, I'm sure. On many occasions, about many different women. Like those trophies you were perusing. Chalk up one more."

He snatched the samovar, our one lone prop, from the downstage table. "And the award for the most ignominious, self-serving, egotistical, manipulative matinee idol, goes to . . . "

He turned and handed me the silver samovar.

It was time for my big speech. The one the dead Fletcher Greengrass had dorked me out of. The one I'd feared I'd never get a chance to play.

I was getting another crack at it now.

I didn't take it.

"Hold on," I said. "That's not what happened."

The cop turned to the director. "Is that true?"

"It's basically what happened." The director looked up at me. "What are you getting at?"

"Yeah, what do you mean?" the cop asked.

"That's not when he gave me the samovar. It's not the same line."

"It's the line in the script," the director said. "Did you give it to him on, 'manipulative matinee idol goes to . . . '?" he asked the playwright.

"Yes, I did."

"Yes, you did," I said. "But Fletcher Greengrass didn't. He said something else entirely."

"Right," the playwright said. "He was paraphrasing his lines because he wasn't using his script."

I shook my head. "He was paraphrasing his lines, all right. But it had nothing to do with his script. He'd been paraphrasing them from the first day of rehearsal. Even when he was *using* his script. What he said today was a lot closer to what he'd been saying in rehearsal than to what you just read.

"Which had to be very frustrating. You finally get your first play produced. It's only community theater with amateur actors, but even so. People will see it. People will hear your words.

"Only they won't. Because all those nice verbal constructions, that must have been a labor of love, that had to be the reason you wrote the play in the first place, they're never gonna be heard. Because Fletcher Greengrass is gonna say any damn thing he feels like right up to and including performance.

"The director can't do anything. He won't take direction. He's a loose cannon, wrecking your play.

"He must be stopped.

"Lucky for you, Fletcher Greengrass is the type of man people hate. He's involved with the two women in the production, he's belittling my acting ability, you can bet he dumped on Dean. So if you can just kill him onstage during rehearsal, in the midst of all those actors, while you're out in the audience, it would be the perfect crime.

"So, how'd you do it?

"Easy.

"Fletcher Greengrass was stuck with a poison pin. Where'd the pin stick him? According to the doc, right in the hand. Yes, where I could have easily done it during the scene, but I didn't. Nor was he stuck by anyone backstage before he came on.

"No, he delivered his line and grabbed the samovar. The pin was wedged in the handle, sticking out. He pricked himself with the poison, handed the samovar to me, and fell over dead. The pin fell to the floor, where it was discovered later by the detective processing the crime scene."

I shook my head pityingly at the playwright. "You're going down for murder. But if it's any consolation, you got to play your scene. Just now, in front of all of us. And you were good. You did a good reading. With all the right lines. The way it should be done."

The playwright stood there, on stage, tears streaming down his cheeks. He offered no resistance when the detective handcuffed him and led him away.

"YOU MIGHT HAVE told me it was him," the cop complained.

"I didn't know for sure until we ran the scene."

"How'd you know then?"

"Easy. He may not look the part, but his line reading was right on the money. Those were the words he wanted said, in the manner he wanted to say them. I'd never heard them before, and I never would while Fletcher Greengrass played the part."

"He really killed him for a bad performance?"

"Basically. I'm sure Fletcher being an arrogant creep didn't hurt."

"I suppose it made it easier." The cop grimaced. "Even so, I'm going to have trouble selling this to the prosecutor. Some motive. I'm mean, killing a guy for changing the lines he wrote. Can you imagine someone doing that?"

I chuckled ironically. I've done some writing myself, and I once had a screenplay produced. So I had no problem answering the question.

"Oh, yeah."

Arrangements

SUSANNE SHAPHREN

I WILL BURY Cameron at the top of the hill. Under his favorite elm tree. Solid bronze hardware on a casket that costs almost as much as the candy-apple-red Jaguar he lusted over before settling for the Volvo and the minivan.

His partners will litigate right up till the moment the service starts over who should deliver the eulogy. Agonize over the script until the words achieve perfection.

Hardly a secret what the winner dares not mention. Not a whisper of how Cameron slept with each and every partner's wife except Henrietta. Not even her very own husband did that except maybe once. The boy looks exactly like him.

There won't be bragging about how Cameron racked up more billable hours than the rest of the partners combined and still managed to play golf three afternoons a week. Not a word about the late nights and nearly dawn sessions trying to keep the firm's most famous clients out of the headlines. Cameron was a master at cleaning up, covering up, making sure witnesses never dared sell their stories to the tabloids.

The *Entertainment Tonight* crew will walk away without the prize soundbites. Not a word about Cameron's collection of conquests. No mention of the aging beauty queen with the face of a twenty-year-old whose body made Cameron laugh as he tortured me with details of their weekend together. The tiny blonde with braces is perfectly safe. She can go right on playing the innocent teen on her weekly series. Nobody will ever know what she and all the cookie-cutter starlets like her did with Cameron. Nobody but me.

Will the triumphant partner say Cameron was a good husband, a loving father? Lie with words as well as silence?

All of the partners will want to be pallbearers. Who else? Cameron's favorite cousin. The firm's highest-grossing rock star if he's vertical. One of the movie stars if he's sober. Papa of course. Ramrod straight with no trace of a limp to tell the world about the fiberglass leg he brought home from Vietnam along with a Purple Heart and enough nightmares to last a lifetime.

No. Not Papa. After all these years, you'd think I could remember that Papa screamed through his last nightmare three months after he walked me down the aisle and gave me away to Cameron.

Papa woke up sweating, shaking and alone in a stinking motel room two states from home. Scrawled a few bits of gibberish in the Gideon Bible on the night stand. Reached for his gun and redecorated the drab room with his splattered brain. Finished the job started in Nam long before I was born. Bequeathed his father's chain of sinfully successful auto dealerships and his very own beloved daughter to Cameron.

So many arrangements. Should I hire a caterer or just pick up a few things at the supermarket? Hope it's not just an outdated custom that nobody would dream of ringing the doorbell unless they're juggling a tuna casserole and a coconut cake, a standing rib roast and a peach pie, or chocolate chip cookies and a honey-baked ham.

Perhaps I should call my mother to help. She's not dead like Papa . . . or is she? How strange that his presence is so strong after so many years of being cold in the ground and it's like my mother never existed at all.

We never had a maid or a nanny so all those soft clean

clothes must have been her handiwork. Just like the freshly baked cookies still warm from the oven that were on the kitchen table to help with all that homework. She must have mixed the meatloaf with her fingers, mashed the potatoes, peeled the carrots. I can't remember exactly what she looked like or what she wore. All I remember is a shadow in front of the TV laughing at what seemed to be the same six *I Love Lucy* reruns again and again.

That's how I got my name, Lucie, just like Lucille Ball's daughter.

The rumpled detective at the door wears a shabby raincoat just like Columbo's, a hat identical to Ricky Ricardo. He sounds like Ricky Ricardo, too. "You got some 'splaining to do, Lucie!"

"I didn't do anything, detective. It was the cancer." Such a long and painful way to die. All those operations. All that radiation. The chemo. Even the alternative medicine therapies we tried. So much time for Cameron to reflect on a lifetime of sins that might merit such divine retribution.

I try to explain to the detective with Columbo's raincoat and Ricky Ricardo's hat that the real crime is that Cameron never found a moment to say how much he loved me, how sorry he was for sleeping with anything in a skirt that glanced his way. Never once apologized for shattering our carefully crafted arrangement.

We agreed that I would postpone college, slave at any kind of minimum wage job I could find to put him through law school. Then, it would be my turn. No matter what.

We made love in those hectic first years. Passionate love worthy of big screen exposure that somehow faded into dutiful sex with three wonderful exceptions. Two nights of passion that followed Cameron's almost never spoken "I'm sorry."

We celebrated Cameron's law school graduation with a bottle of decent champagne. I proudly showed him my application and tentative class schedule.

"I'm sorry, Lucie. That will just have to wait a bit longer. This is a once-in-a-lifetime opportunity for me. I've been offered a full partnership in the largest firm in town. We have to buy a sinfully expensive house suitable for entertaining clients, put on an impressive show." Cameron kept pouring champagne, kept trying to convince me everything would work out fine.

Tyler arrived precisely eight months and three weeks later. Just a few short months ago, Cameron said "I'm sorry" again. I hadn't told him about the new baby yet. One magical night in between, Cameron said "I love you" for the first and only time during all our years of marriage.

In all those years, would it have killed Cameron to mumble a simple apology for all those nights he abandoned me in a sea of strangers without so much as a kind word or a strong arm to lean on? Treading murky water to stay afloat. Praying for a scriptwriter's magic to give me something to say that wouldn't make me sound stupid, make Cameron look bad.

Wishing I could magically make myself disappear on that nightmare evening when I finally realized how impossible it was for me to successfully play the role of glamorous wife. Wasting more on having my hair done than I usually spent on a week's worth of groceries and raiding Sasha's college fund to acquire a lavender silk cloud to match my newly frosted nails hadn't transformed me into one of the perfect trophy wives proudly displayed on their husbands' Italian-suited arms.

Sasha! My night-of-passion-I-love-you baby is wide awake in her soggy crib. She whimpers like an abandoned orphan when I lift her. By the time we get to the changing table, her cheeks are fire engine red and her screams could easily drown out the most powerful of sirens.

I imagine her angelic face on one of those missing children milk cartons, force myself to wonder what it would be like to spend my days staring at progressively older strangers and mentally adding years to what baby Sasha looks like. She could be gone in an instant, snatched away forever. So help-less. So precious that I could never ever consider hitting her just because she won't stop crying.

Finally. Her stiff stubborn body softens as we rock with her love-tattered teddy bear. She's almost asleep when the car door slams, starting the screaming even louder than before.

Cameron fills the nursery doorway with his pinstriped bulk. "Can't you keep that child quiet? I had a really lousy day at the office!"

I make his martini just the way he likes, shaken not stirred, with two olives and an onion. Push the salty chips and salsa where he can reach them without effort. Grill him a steak big enough to clog the cleanest of arteries. Butter, real sour cream, and bacon bits on the baked potato. Asparagus with fresh Hollandaise.

I will bury Cameron at the top of the hill. The prevailing partner will drone on and on about Cameron's big good heart, tell the Central Casting crowd how it just stopped without any warning. Cameron's cardiologist will put his strong comforting arms around me and assure me there was nothing more either of us could have done.

"Lucie, you were the perfect wife. Making sure he gave up alcohol. Cooking with no fat and very little salt. You mustn't blame yourself."

"Earth to Lucie. Come in please." Cameron saws off a huge piece of steak, lets it bleed all over the snow-white tablecloth as he dangles it as if to capture my attention. "There will be sixty for dinner on Saturday. Hire a caterer if you like. The last one was adequate."

Adequate my foot! At least a dozen of your guests in-cluding the movie icon and the television idol wannabe tried to hire the caterer out from under me. If only they knew. If only you knew!

I was the caterer. I shopped the Farmer's Market and the discount warehouse store. Peeled and chopped, baked and broiled, froze and thawed. Produced a veritable garden of radish roses and carrot curls to decorate tray after tray of hors d'oeuvres. Designed a gourmet dinner that Julia Child would have been proud to serve. Baked a picture-perfect dessert buffet that tasted as heavenly as it looked.

Paid the babysitter's older brothers to rent tuxes and serve. Stashed the difference between what I spent and what it would have cost to hire a caterer in my secret bank account along with the profits from the newspaper route.

Four hundred houses each and every morning when Cameron thinks I've driven Sasha and the ritzy jogging stroller to the park. Over the years, I've perfected the routine and learned how to avoid complaints by doubling back to deliver a spare paper to the houses where neighbors snatch the first delivery. A spotless record earns generous tips added to the regular fee without any face-to-face contact with customers. No chance of being recognized.

By the time Tyler and Sasha and the new baby are in school, I might actually have enough to pay for my tuition. Just like Cameron promised he would do.

If the balance were larger, maybe I could afford to leave. No! I'd be lucky to walk away with the clothes on my back. This isn't a community property state. No-fault divorce means Cameron's adultery doesn't count. He'd pull every string in the book to win custody of children he never bothers to pay attention to. There's only one way to be free. I will bury Cameron at the top of the hill. Someday.

The flowing black dress is perfect for Saturday. Smocked at the top with tiny pink rosebuds. Big enough to hide the first bulge of pregnancy just in case I change my mind. Maybe that's why I haven't said anything to Cameron yet. No! Even though I marched my quota of miles and then some, carried my share of signs proclaiming a woman's right to choose, there is only one choice for me.

Matthew . . . this has to be another boy like Tyler. He's

already heavy and demanding in my womb, nothing at all like Sasha. Matthew will be born in exactly seven months and one week if he's as punctual as his older siblings.

The dress looks like crushed velvet, but it's really washable polyester just in case there's a kitchen disaster to contend with while I'm expertly playing the role of carefree hostess. If I cut off the tiny rosebuds, the dress will be perfect to wear to Cameron's funeral.

I will bury Cameron at the top of the hill, try to ease my grief by volunteering to speak at those anti-drunk-driver rallies. Only a matter of time before Cameron's luck runs out. All those late hours spent at the office or wherever he really strays when he should be here helping with baths and bedtime stories . . . surely it's only a matter of time before some drunk driver proves the Volvo isn't really safe after all.

The party comes off without a hitch. My mother would be proud. Is proud? I can't quite force myself to use the speed dialer and find out once and for all if she answers or if the number's been disconnected.

My "caterer" would be an instant success if only I could figure out a way to hide that sideline as easily and efficiently as I do the paper route.

Cameron disappears into the study the instant the last of the guests departs. No need to try to hide the cleanup. The babysitter and her brothers are thrilled with their pay, thrilled enough to stick around and help.

My internal alarm clock goes off precisely as Grandma's clock chimes four times in the living room. I'm not in the master bedroom or the guestroom where I wake up most mornings. The kitchen chair is hardly a comfortable resting place. There's an icy mug on the table with the hardened remnants of what was once hot chocolate. A half-eaten bag of mini-marshmallows and crumbs of carefully crafted pastries from the party complete the scene. Didn't I ever go to bed last night? I can't quite remember.

Tyler will want bananas sliced on his favorite sugary cereal with just enough nutrition hidden in it to make it acceptable to me. Instant oatmeal and strained peaches for Sasha. Bacon, eggs, and hash browns for Cameron, or maybe a nice four-egg omelet oozing with cheddar cheese and ham. I'll ask him what he prefers as soon as the shower turns off.

Something's wrong. I don't hear the shower. The master bedroom is dark. I tiptoe to the edge of the cavernous bed that seems so small and suffocating on those rare occasions when I still bother to go though the motions of playing loving wife to Cameron. Dear God, there's so much blood. I should pick up the phone and dial 911, but it's obviously far too late for that. I should call the police. No. I'm beginning to remember why that would be a bad idea, a very bad idea.

I will tell the children Daddy is already working in the study, mustn't be disturbed, feed them breakfast. Never skip a beat of the normal routine. Tyler will help with the newspaper inserts, then curl up in the minivan for a bit more sleep as I fly through the paper route in record time. He won't tolerate a kiss when I drop him off at preschool, but he might grudgingly accept a hug.

Just another morning. No reason to panic. Deep breaths. Play the role of the perfect wife. Once more with feeling.

Cameron's Volvo will pull out of the garage at exactly the same time as any other morning. By the time his partners realize he didn't get to work, I will have taken care of all the messy little details.

Just this once, I will give thanks that I'm not a perfect size two. Better to have the bulk and the strength to do what must be done.

I will bury Cameron at the top of the hill. Maybe under a tree. Maybe not. Wherever the soil is soft enough to dig and wherever there's enough loose brush to cover up my handiwork. No lie of a eulogy. No mourners. Just me, and Sasha sleeping soundly in her baby seat. I will be ever so careful to leave traces of Cameron's blood in the trunk of the Volvo. Maybe I'll even leave the sheets and buy new ones in the kind of ritzy linen emporium worthy of a prominent attorney's wife. Nobody would ever suspect the K-Mart sheets and blankets belonged to us.

No need to wipe fingerprints from the Volvo. Everybody knows Cameron insists that I drive it at least once a week so he can do God knows what with the minivan. I will wear gloves when I drive the Volvo one last time so there will be smudges on the steering wheel.

Just in case Cameron was wrong about how close crime is sneaking up on us. Just in case nobody steals the Volvo after I park it at the bottom of the hill on the far side from home, leaving the keys in the ignition.

Sasha isn't that heavy yet. We'll be home long before anybody misses us or Cameron.

Even if they discover Cameron's body, nobody would dream of suspecting his grieving widow. Loyal wife. Mother of his three beautiful children. So brave to sleep alone in the cavernous bed in the big house so far away from any neighbors, so courageous to pick up the pieces and move on.

If there's ever a knock at the door, ever a detective with Columbo's raincoat and Ricky Ricardo's hat, Lucie will have some 'splaining to do. I will tell him what I remember, tell him how Cameron pushed me over the edge by admitting our Hollywood happily-ever-after marriage was nothing more than an icy business arrangement, carefully crafted with Papa.

Cameron told me more than I ever wanted to know, repeating Papa's opinion that it would be a waste of time and money for me to go to college. "She's a headstrong filly who needs a firm hand."

After all the questions, surely the detective will come to understand who's really responsible.

I will bury Cameron at the top of the hill.

A Berlin Story

LIBBY FISCHER HELLMANN

HERR HESSE SHOULD never have stayed for the last number. Indeed, some expressed shock he was there at all. A physics professor at the University of Berlin. Well-dressed, a touch of gray in his hair. Why would Friedrich Hesse visit *Der Flammen,* a seedy cabaret tucked away on a side street?

It came out later that Ilse had asked him to stay. Ilse— the star performer at *Der Flammen*. Ilse—with the sad brown eyes and short blonde hair and a black sequined costume that stopped at the top of her thighs.

He sat in the audience that night, a glass of schnapps in his hand. Elbow to elbow with the riffraff, all of them vying to be decadent. The life of the genteel Prussian had vanished, replaced by the ennui of the jaded. No one pretended to innocence in the Berlin of Thirty-two. What counted most was scandal. It masked the pain and despair.

He suffered through buxom women in skimpy costumes and the men pretending to be. He turned away from the animal parade. But when the orchestra sounded a drum roll, he twisted back toward the stage. And when Ilse appeared in the wavering beam of the spotlight, he brightened like a man glimpsing salvation.

In her first number she flounced across stage as a mountain girl, long braids pinned to her head. She wore a leather vest laced tight across her breasts, but not much else. It wasn't until the shepherd boy unlaced it and forced her to ride the goat that Hesse looked away.

Next she marched onstage in an Imperial Regimental jacket, a rifle slung over her chest. She sang and crawled and shot and saluted her superior officer, who relieved her of her jacket and threw it into the wings. The randy shouts of the audience drowned out the last verse of her song. Through it all, the professor politely sipped his schnapps, as if Ilse were reciting poetry in a salon.

In the finale, she sang a sad ballad, wearing black sequins, fishnet stockings, and stiletto heels. A stray lock of hair fell across her face, throwing her profile in shadow. As her final note hung in the smoky air, the professor rose, put on his hat, and walked out. Skirting the bank of snow on the street, he cut through a narrow alley and knocked at the stage door.

The janitor found his body the next morning, half-hidden behind the stage in a corner. A pool of blood, now congealed, had seeped across the floor. The police found entry wounds in his chest and bullet casings that had come from a Luger.

ILSE SLOUCHED AT the manager's desk wearing a silk robe with oriental pretensions. The smoke from her cigarette floated above her head like a halo.

"When did you meet him?" The burly detective asked. His weary eyes said there was nothing more that could shock him.

"Several months ago. At a cafe on the Kurfürstendamm." She smiled prettily. "We were both having tea."

"He was alone?"

"Not then. But he returned the next day. Alone."

The detective took off his coat and slipped it over a chair. He knew her type. Arrogant. Smug. Confident in her charm. "What happened when he came into your dressing room?"

Crossing one leg over the other, she dangled her foot in front of him. "He paid me a visit."

"And what was the nature of this visit, Fraulein?"

"Must I be so indiscreet, Herr Inspektor?"

The detective shifted. The office wasn't much bigger than a closet. He felt too big for the room. "You knew, of course, that he was married?"

"Aren't they all?"

"What did he give you in return for your—favors?"

"What I expect from all my lovers. Kindness. Passion. A gentle touch."

"And perhaps a few thousand marks, conveniently wrapped in a white linen handkerchief?"

She fluffed her hair. A whiff of cheap perfume drifted his way. "You presume, *mein lieber*."

"When did he leave?"

"When we were finished."

"And you made sure your friends were waiting for him, yes? Ready to roll him for his cash. What was your cut, Fraulein?"

"Inspektor. You are unkind."

"But he put up a fight, didn't he? Your friends didn't count on that. He struggled, and things spun out of control."

She drew herself up and tossed her hair. Even in the dim light of the office it gleamed. "I do not know what happened when he left my room. I had nothing to do with his death."

FRAU HESSE POURED tea from a Chinese teapot on a cloisonné tray. A small, birdlike woman with brown hair swept back in a bun, she sat primly on a flowered sofa, flanked by two men who she said were colleagues of her husband.

The detective sat on a silk-covered chair, his bulk spilling over the seat. He would have preferred to question her alone, but she was the wife of an important man. Fumbling his teacup, he was loath to ask the key question, and was taken aback when she preempted him.

"I knew Friedrich was unfaithful," she said, her face bland and composed. "I've known for years. But you must understand. He was an excellent provider, and in these times, when inflation bleeds the value out of everything, I was grateful."

Hoping his face didn't reveal his surprise, he asked about Hesse's work.

"He was a professor at the Chemical Institute. He was experimenting with radioactive elements."

He frowned. "Radioactive elements?"

"Uranium."

His frown deepened. "It is what—this uranium?"

Frau Hesse and the men exchanged glances. "He studied neutrons, protons, and electrons." Frau Hesse said. "Subatomic particles."

He shrugged. He was a police officer. Not an educated man.

Patches of red flared on her cheeks. "They are tiny particles. The elements of all matter. Together they form atoms. My husband theorized that under bombardment by neutrons, an atom of uranium would split in half. Much of his time was spent stripping protons from neutrons in an attempt to verify his hypothesis."

"And did he?"

Again the wife and the men exchanged glances. "He was close," the wife said. She bowed her head.

The detective made another note. "You seem very knowledgeable about his work."

"We met at the University years ago. I am a scientist as well." A tiny shrug fanned her shoulders. "But there was only room for one in the family. I was content to be his wife and the mother of his children. He is—was—a brilliant man."

He set his teacup down.

Clear blue eyes gazed at him. "Indeed, he *was* a man.

With a man's flaws. Yet, he always came home to me. I loved him beyond description." She looked away, then, and her jaw tightened, as if she was struggling to control her grief.

One of the men laid his arm around her delicate shoulders. "If that is all, Inspector . . ."

"Of course." The detective took the names of the colleagues and rose from his chair. "Auf Weidersehen," he said with a slight bow.

As he stepped outside, he noted the mezuzah on the door frame.

TWO DAYS LATER the Inspector stamped his feet, shaking the snow off his boots. The manager of *Der Flammen* led him into the office. A little man with a sparse mustache, the sour smell of fear rose from his skin.

"She's gone," he moaned, wringing his hands. "She was due here an hour ago. I sent a boy around to her apartment near the Nollendorfplatz, but she was not there, and all of her things are gone. The show begins in thirty minutes. What shall I do?"

A bevy of women, their cheeks rouged, eyelids darkened with kohl, filed past the open door. "It would seem you have replacements," the detective said.

"*Nein.*" The manager threw his hands in the air. "You do not understand. They demand her. If they do not see her, they will hold me responsible. They are not patient men."

"What men are these, Herr manager?"

"You know of whom I speak. They come in their brown shirts and boots. Almost every night, now."

"Were they here the night Hesse was killed?"

"I do not know."

The detective scratched his cheek. "Herr manager, I hear rumors about *Der Flammen*. Many rumors. I am sure you do not want trouble with your license."

"You would not. You could not."

The manager hesitated, then took a step back, seeming to shrivel against the wall. "Yes," he said reluctantly. His face grew pinched. "Yes. They were here that night."

IT WAS NOT difficult to find her. A street urchin in need of a meal, a hundred marks exchanged; it was done. Entering a dark, shabby building, he mounted rickety steps. The stench of urine hung in the air. A yellow cat hissed.

On the third floor, a woman answered the door. Her eyes, suspicious and hard, widened when he showed her his badge. She was wearing Ilse's oriental robe. "Ilse, you have a guest."

Ilse came to the door, dressed in a tattered robe and slippers. Her hair was lank, her face haggard.

The detective wasted few words. "Fraulein, did you know Professor Hesse was a Jew?"

Ilse looked at the floor.

"I do not hear you."

She looked up, her brown eyes rimmed in dark circles. "Yes, I knew."

"So that is why they killed him."

"Who?"

"The men who have been visiting you at *Der Flammen*. The ones in the brown shirts and boots.

"Why do you wince?" The detective went on. "You did your part. Lured the dirty Jew into a trap. Softened him up with your favors. Made him weak and defenseless. He was no match for them."

"No. You are wrong." Her hands flew to her face.

"How much did they give you to set him up?" She turned away. "How much, Fraulein?" She shook her head. "You are aware that I can make your life most unpleasant. A charge of lewd behavior or accessory to murder will not sit well. Even in Berlin."

"You do not understand, Inspektor. If I tell you, I sign my death warrant."

"And if you do not, you go to jail." He circled a chair, letting the weight of his words sink in. "But you see, Ilse, you have another problem. You see, these men—these Brown Shirts—they will never believe you did not confess. So when you leave jail, as you eventually will, they will find you."

She stared at him, her eyes vacant and dull. "So I am *fickt*. No matter what I do."

He shrugged. She pulled her robe tight and started to pace. He waited. It wasn't long.

"They wanted to know what Friedrich was doing at the University."

"And what did you tell them?"

"The truth. I did not know. We did not talk about his work. We had—other matters to discuss."

He folded his arms.

"They didn't believe me either. They—they forced me to service them. One at a time. Like dogs in heat." She spat on the floor. "They said they would kill me if they found out I lied."

He studied her. Not just a whore. A pathetic, used-up whore. "And so they killed him because he was a rich, powerful Jew."

"No. They did not like him, but they did not kill him."

"How do you know?"

Her sad eyes burned with a curious light. "They did not come until the night after he died."

"The night after?" The inspector stiffened. "You are lying, Fraulein. The manager said—"

She snorted. "He will say whatever you want him to."

"Perhaps you are mistaken. The stage lights are harsh and blinding. Perhaps they were there. But you didn't see them. They hid at the back of the theater until he left your room."

Her eyes tracked him up and down. "No. I told you.

They came the night after. Demanding to know if he was the Jew who worked at the University."

The detective leaned his hands on the back of the chair.

"Please, Herr Inspektor. I beg you. Do not tell them I told you. They will surely kill me." She covered her face with her hands.

ILSE NEVER CAME back to *Der Flammen*. For weeks the detective sifted through the reports of bodies that washed up from the river, or were found in the alleys, but none matched her description. He went back to the woman Ilse had stayed with, the cabaret manager, even the urchin he found on the street, but no one knew where she was.

He read up on uranium at the library, then, late one afternoon, met with a Berlin physicist. Afterwards, he took a walk. An icy wind slicing through him, he trudged down the Nollendorfplatz, ignoring a come-on from a young boy with eyes as heavily kohled as a woman's. On the Kurfürstendamm he gazed at a church as if its gothic spires might tell him what to do. And on his wintry hike, he thought about the professor, his wife, his colleagues. The Brown Shirts and what they were doing. His own job, his family, his country. By morning he had made his decision.

He arrested the Brown Shirts and prepared to bring them to trial. Of course, there were heated denials. Even some threats on his life. His case, nonetheless, was solid: he had the manager's story and Ilse's friend's. He also had the casings from the Luger, which everyone knew was their weapon of choice. He ignored Ilse's claim that they came to *Der Flammen* the night after. She was a whore; she had fled. Dead or alive, her word would be suspect at best.

By the time it came to trial a year later, though, everything had changed. Hitler was in power, and the Brown Shirts were acquitted. The next day the detective told his wife to pack. They would go to Switzerland or Holland. Perhaps, if they were lucky, New York.

A LIGHT DUSTING of snow coated the streets. Hobbling on a cane, the former detective let his grandchildren drag him towards the skating rink. It had opened in Thirty-six, just after they came to New York. Now, twenty years later, it was a family tradition. Every December, he and his wife brought the children, and now the grandchildren, into the city to take in the tree, the glow of lights, the holiday glitter.

The children chattered excitedly, their cheeks red from the cold. They watched the skaters circle the ice, dipping and gliding to the music. His attention was drawn to a tall, graceful girl, whose helmet of bright hair gleamed as she twirled.

Shadows chased the sun away, and dusk settled over the rink. The skaters cut sharp silhouettes against the pale ice. But it wasn't until the lights snapped on that he noticed the group at the next table. A tiny woman wrapped in a fur coat, her hair pulled back in a bun, surrounded by children and two adults.

"*Oma.*" A little girl squealed in delight. "You must taste the chocolate. Like Lindt's, but hot."

"You taste it for me."

Steam rose from the cup. The little girl sipped and smacked her lips. Chocolate rimmed her mouth. Her smile revealing a deeply lined face, the old woman brushed her hand across the girl's hair. Then, as if aware she was being watched, she turned toward the detective.

The old man blinked. He knew this small, birdlike woman. The steady gaze. The clear blue eyes that, after a moment's appraisal, deepened in recognition as well.

"Herr Inspektor." Her voice was serene and pleasant. "How delightful to see you again."

His forehead wrinkled. "Madame, I apologize, but—"

"I am Frau Hesse, Herr Inspektor." She smiled. "Wife of Friedrich Hesse."

Her name burrowed into his memory, and the long ago case sprang into his mind. He rose and slowly made his way to her table.

"It is good to see you on this side of the ocean." Her smile made it seem she'd been expecting him.

"We came from Holland."

She nodded. "I came after the trial."

He remembered the trial. He leaned his hand on his cane. "My one regret was that I did not bring them to justice, Frau Hesse. In failing them, I failed you. And your family."

She looked at him for a long moment. "No. You did everything you could." The thin smile on her face made him frown. This woman had the ability to surprise him, he remembered. Anticipate him. Say the unexpected.

"You see, Herr Inspektor, justice *was* served. The men who were tried, they were not guilty. They did not kill my husband."

He chose his words with care. "Madame, please do not spare my feelings. We are both too old for that."

"Deanna, take the children. I will follow."

The young woman collected the children and walked them to the ice. She tapped the chair next to her. The detective sank into it.

"Do you remember what my husband was working on at the University?"

"Radiation, was it not?"

"Not quite," she said, the teacher correcting a student. "Radioactive elements. Subatomic elements that could be isolated in uranium." Her expression softened. "What neither I nor my colleagues told you was how far his work had taken him."

The detective held up his hand. "No Madame. You are mistaken. It was not radioactive isotopes—uranium or otherwise. It was simple radiation."

"Inspektor, do not presume to tell me about my work. I was a physicist, too, if you recall."

"Yes, Frau Hesse. I remember. It was radiation. Not the other."

She frowned, the lines at the side of her mouth tightening. "Perhaps you should tell me what it is you remember."

He cleared his throat. "What I remember is that a group of Nazi thugs ambushed your husband. He was set up by a prostitute in a cabaret. Unfortunately, those type of incidents were all too common back then."

She tapped her spoon against her cup. "But Inspektor, that was only part—"

He rode over her words. "No, Madame. You are wrong. You see, if it were any other way, if it were radioactive uranium your husband and his colleagues were experimenting with, I might have deduced something quite different." She studied her tea cup. "I might have suspected they were trying to create nuclear fission."

She jerked her head up.

"Which would mean they would soon be able to build a nuclear bomb."

Her eyebrows arched. "Indeed."

"I might also have suspected that word leaked out, as it always does in these matters, and that the Nazis demanded he turn over his work. Your husband would have refused, but it would have only been a matter of time. They would have blackmailed him, exposed his "activities," perhaps even tortured him. And not just him. His colleagues, too. Your Friedrich would have—"

"We couldn't allow that to happen," she said quietly. "In the end, we had no choice. We had to protect the work. You must understand." She drew in a long, shuddering breath. "It was decided I should come here."

"Where you met with scientists who would later work on the Manhattan Project."

She nodded.

"And let the Brown Shirts take the blame for his death."

"So we hoped." She shrugged her delicate shoulders. "Indeed, our biggest fear was you, Inspektor."

"Me?"

"We were certain you knew. Or would discover it soon enough. You made us hasten my departure. Later, we were surprised by your silence. We decided you were a friend." She paused. "And so you were." She leaned back in her chair. "But how? How did you know?"

He hesitated. "His mistress confessed that the Brown Shirts came to the cabaret the night after he was killed. The rest was not difficult." He stared at the skaters. The tall blonde was now partnered with a dark young man. Arms entwined, they skimmed the surface of the ice, skating in perfect synchrony. "But my dear Frau Hesse, I have a question for you. How could you do it?"

Swallowing, she stared at her teacup for so long he wondered if she would reply. Then, she looked up and waved a hand towards the children. "There is your answer, Inspektor."

He twisted toward the children, his and hers. Their eager young faces sparkling as they followed the skaters. Bright new stars shooting across a cold, dark heaven. He looked back at Frau Hesse. Her eyes filled.

"You see?" Blinking hard, she smiled her tears away. The gentle smile of a friend. "Perhaps you will join me for a schnapps, Herr Inspektor? It was my husband's favorite."

Goin' West

CHARLES ARDAI

I

Arthur French, a man whose bearing and expression were not so much boyish as they were a failed attempt to appear so, looked down at the avenue outside his office and wished he had the guts to open his window and throw himself out of it.

But he hadn't, so after a few minutes of staring at the traffic below while a cigarette burned itself to ash between his fingers, Arthur returned to his desk. The portfolio he had been going through when he had been overcome with his sudden attack of self-revulsion lay open on his blotter. Arthur stubbed out his cigarette and went back to work.

He had already discarded twenty-three women, turning the pages that held their hopeful eight-by-tens without so much as a stirring of interest. He had only pulled two photos from their plastic sleeves: Lisa Brennan, a striking blonde who'd have to look over her shoulder to see thirty, much less the twenty-seven she claimed, and Angela Meyer, a homely brunette—that nose!—whose bikini shot had nevertheless caught Arthur's eye. He'd covered her face with his hand. Maybe she'd do for some body doubling, or for the shower scene establishing shot where they'd need extras. Nobody would have to see her face. Arthur had pulled the picture and dropped it face down next to his telephone.

Angela's credits, listed on the back, read like a young actress's dream: Cordelia in *King Lear,* the baker's wife in *Into The Woods.* But that's probably all they were—a dream. What she'd left out was that *King Lear* had been a showcase in someone's apartment on the Upper West Side and that *Into The Woods* had been summer-stock in Connecticut. Or vice versa. Hell, Arthur told himself, a woman who wants to do Cordelia doesn't send her agent around with a photo that shouts "playmate of the month" at the top of its lungs.

Brennan's credits had sounded more realistic: bit parts on a couple of soaps, some commercials, guest spots on two short-lived sitcoms. Plus one feature a few years back where she'd played Goldie Hawn's sister, a two-line part that had gotten her into SAG. At least she wasn't as likely to embarrass herself in front of the camera.

Arthur flipped through the rest of the portfolio, his interest waning from minimal to zip. Bunch of hungry little tramps who'd push each other in front of a train for a line of their own in the end credits, especially as a character with a name instead of something like "Woman In Cab."

Hell, they'd kill for "Woman In Cab," too.

He closed the book and zipped it up, then slipped the two photos he'd selected into his project folder. Two appointments for Rose to set up, two distant, distant, *distant* possibilities for *Goin' West,* and one less agent to deal with on the project. He stuck the portfolio in its mailer and started it on its way back to Jennifer Stein, the madam who had pulled this Kodacolor harem together and dropped it on his desk.

He fingered his lead-crystal ashtray, overflowing with Camel butts, then pulled a new cigarette from his pack and lit it. Somewhere halfway through the pack, Freddie Prinze's agent blew Arthur off, followed by Jason Biggs's and James van der Beek's. Never mind Ashton Kutcher's—it wasn't worth the phone call. Not for a project that would get a five-week theatrical release, if that, on its way to video stores across the U.S. of A. James *van der Beek* was too big for this project, for God's sake.

Arthur ran his hand through his hair, permanently damp from a steady diet of Grecian Formula and Nexus, then slid the project file into its pendaflex folder and left it for Rose to file. The women would be easy to cast—no star or even B-lister needed. The male lead and his buddies, on the other hand, had to be names that meant something to teenage boys.

If all else failed, he'd go after Corey Dunn or Jon Farrell. William Fitch, their agent, owed Arthur favors that had major price tags hanging all over them. Shame to call them in for a dog like *Goin' West,* though.

He made one more phone call before cutting out early. Then he took the elevator down the thirty floors to street level, a slower method than the one he'd contemplated earlier, but at least you didn't end up a stain on the concrete. He picked up his Audi in the building's garage, spent a good half-hour in Manhattan traffic (a lousy half-hour, actually, city driving was always lousy), fought a traffic jam all the way out to Bronxville, and parked in front of his townhouse. Sandy was waiting for him when he got home and he got up a smile for her when he walked through the door. That was the most he could get up, though, and they went to sleep apologizing to each other.

All night Arthur dreamt about going through with his suicide, opening his office window and smashing to a jelly on the pavement. In a strange way, the dream didn't feel like a nightmare. In it, he left a note to his wife saying, "It's not you, honey, I can't stand this stinking business." Which was his dream's way of making him feel better, because in his waking moments he knew it was her, as much as it was anything.

Sandy would never let him forget that "East Coast casting director" was a contradiction in terms, especially when it came to features. You had to be in California to really be in the business, unless you were Juliet Taylor and did the casting for Woody's pictures, but he wasn't, and he didn't, and he never would come close.

Arthur French was a peripheral figure in the industry, a name people half remembered in connection with films they would just as soon have forgotten. He'd given up, years before, his original ambition to do work he was proud of and had become a whore for the mid-budget studios who were still willing to use him. Sandy would ask him from time to time why he'd pissed away such talent as he'd had when she'd met him—as though he knew the answer himself. Over the past few weeks Sandy had also started asking him about other women, stopping just short of accusing him of having an affair. Then she was surprised when he flopped worse than *Waterworld* in bed?

It didn't help the situation that Arthur couldn't divorce her, mainly because his townhouse was really Sandy's townhouse and *Goin' West* wouldn't pay for a replacement. Twenty years of films like *Goin' West* hadn't, and twenty more wouldn't.

Arthur sat up in bed next to where Sandy lay, blowsy and paunchy and forty-eight, and dragged on his first Camel of the morning, thinking about divorce and thinking about suicide. Suicide seemed simpler and less painful.

He tried to go back to sleep, but he found he couldn't keep his eyes closed. He went to work instead.

ARTHUR MADE SOME more calls before the girls started filling Rose's office, touching up their makeup and hiding their bra straps. The calls didn't go well, but why should they? The script for *Goin' West* had made the rounds and every agent Arthur called knew it was garbage. No agent would let his actors appear in the film. If Kreuger had been willing to cut the scenes on the beach, maybe, but the bastard had been stubborn. How can you fight a writer-director-producer who's making his own film? On the other hand, how do you get any actor who's got a sense of self-preservation to go in front of the camera and play the sort of scenes Kreuger wrote? He made the Farrellys look like Noel Coward.

Arthur ran his fingers through his hair, wiped his hand, threw the tissue out, smoked halfway through a cigarette, and buzzed Rose to start sending the girls in.

The female roles were interchangeable. Arthur kept a checklist and marked off character names one by one. Kreuger would have to approve his choices, of course, but that's what callbacks were for. Arthur picked two women for each part, jotting down information on the Polaroids Rose had taken while the girls were waiting in the front office.

Angela Meyer showed up at eleven, uglier in person and less talented even than Arthur had expected. She did have a good body, though, and Arthur wrote her down for extra work: the shower scene, the skinny-dipping scene, wherever they needed background T&A. Angela's face fell when Arthur told her this was all she could get, but what could he do? Ugly is ugly.

Lisa Brennan appeared after lunch, when the crowd had thinned out. Arthur was already numbed from the morning's parade of spandex-and-silicone hopefuls, and he didn't stand up when Lisa came in. He was tired of standing up. Lisa sat opposite him and handed him another copy of her headshot. Arthur dropped it on his desk and stared at her.

You could see the desperation in her face, and with thirty-plus showing around her eyes, Arthur wasn't surprised. Her hands were twisted around one another in her lap. He glanced at Lisa's credits again and noted that her last project was half a year old—which meant she hadn't worked for the better part of a year, and that in turn was why she was in his office trying to get a part in a teen sex comedy.

Arthur launched into his spiel. "We're casting a new film by Daniel Kreuger called *Goin' West*. There are several parts for young women . . ." The words poured out of him on automatic, along with pauses during which he waited for Lisa to answer the standard questions. She answered them. The answers were standard, too. Arthur started to feel his stomach.

When Arthur told Lisa to undress, she stood, pulled her sweatshirt over her head, and undid the knot on her hip that held her wrap in place. Under it she wore an orange two-piece swimsuit. She turned in a circle, then bent to pick her wrap off the floor.

Arthur made a gesture with his hand. The gesture wasn't any gesture in particular, just a tired wave of the hand that wasn't holding his cigarette, but Lisa knew what it meant and she forced a smile as she unclasped her top in back and slipped it off her shoulders.

Lisa had a nice body, but that smile . . . smiles like that gave Arthur ulcers. He forced himself to smile back, but he knew it came out wrong, a pained, cut-the-crap expression that he quickly wiped off his face.

Lisa stopped smiling, too. Arthur waited, but she just stood there, not smiling.

The ones who stripped naked without being asked were bad enough, the ones who thought that seeing another naked, young body could be any sort of bribe at all for Arthur. The ones Arthur had to ask were worse. But it was his job and he did it.

Arthur made his gesture again, knowing already that he wouldn't use Lisa, knowing that Kreuger would laugh if he sent him any woman who didn't have the body of a teenager. Laugh, hell, Kreuger would find another casting director.

But Arthur made his gesture and waited for Lisa to pull down her swimsuit, let him see what he'd be casting if he'd cast her, which he wouldn't. Though he'd have liked to, Arthur realized suddenly, since personally he found her more attractive than the twenty-year-olds who had been in and out of his office all morning.

Lisa hesitated. "Do I have to? If you think it's likely that I'll get the role, fine, but if not I'd rather not." She had her thumbs hooked under the straps at her hips.

Arthur's stomach burned. "You don't have to do it," he said. "I don't care. You don't have to do anything you don't want to do. You don't have to be in the movie. No one's going to force you." Lisa stood uncertainly while Arthur stared at her.

Here's a woman who's done commercials and soaps, Arthur said to himself, and she's dying inside but she's letting you get away with this because she's desperate for a break, which you're not going to give her anyway. For God's sake, let her go.

"Listen—" Arthur started, but Lisa had made her mind up and was bending over, stepping out of her bikini, standing up naked in a stranger's office to get a role where she'd have to do more or less the same thing in front of a million moviegoers.

"Get dressed," Arthur said, disgusted with himself.

Lisa stared at him. "Is something wrong?"

"Please."

"Is there something wrong with me?"

"Just get dressed." She was frozen. "Christ, there's no part for you, okay?"

She didn't say anything, just picked up her wrap from the arm of the chair, wound it around her waist, tied it, and quickly pulled the sweatshirt over her head. She grabbed her photo and her bikini.

He turned his chair to face the window and heard the door slam.

The next girl he saw was a nineteen-year-old from Toronto, a bottle blonde whose headshot mentioned parts in *Hollywood Hookers* and *Hollywood Hookers in Bermuda.* He stopped her before she could unbutton her shirt and told her she had the part and asked her to leave. She blushed tremendously and thanked him.

Bill Fitch didn't return his calls all afternoon.

ARTHUR TOOK LISA'S headshot home with him, hidden between two pages of budget projections for *Goin' West.* Some time after midnight, he got out of bed and carried his briefcase into the living room. He turned on the lamp next to the TV set and angled its shade so that no light shone toward the bedroom. Then he took Lisa's photograph out and looked at it for a long time. He lit a cigarette, but it burned most of the way down untouched on the rim of the ashtray.

He had no idea whether Lisa Brennan had talent. But hell, what was talent anyway? Didn't plenty of successful movie actresses come up short in the talent department?

Arthur dug through his briefcase until he found his Filofax, and through his Filofax until he found Bill Fitch's home number. Bill had written it in there himself, back when he was still taking Arthur's calls. Next to the number, Bill had written, "Call any time."

A groggy voice answered the phone on the fourth ring.

"Bill? Arthur. Arthur French."

There was silence on the other end, for perhaps half a minute. "Hey, Art. Sorry I didn't get a chance to call you back. I was in meetings most of the day."

"That's what I figured," Arthur said. But to himself he said: Sure you were, you lying son of a bitch. You knew I was trying to land someone for *Goin' West* and you didn't have the balls to tell me no to my face.

"What can I do for you?"

"Listen, I've got a—"

"Hold on one second. Sorry to interrupt. Just hold on." Arthur held on. He heard Bill put the phone down, get out of bed, pad softly away. In the distance, a little while later, a toilet flushed. The footsteps returned. "I'm back. Sorry about that. Twice a night these days, rain or shine. Shoot."

"What I wanted to say is, I saw a girl today. Her name's Lisa Brennan. She was in *Telling Lies,* you remember that one?"

"No."

"With Goldie Hawn . . . ?"

"No. I don't. But I'll take your word for it."

"It was out, I don't know, four years ago. She was Goldie's sister."

"Okay, fine. Go on."

"She's also done soaps, small things here and there, nothing big since *Telling Lies.*"

"And?"

"She's good. She's really good, Bill. I saw her today—" I saw her today, made her take her clothes off, told her I wasn't going to hire her, and then she left. "I saw her and I had her read, and I'm telling you, this girl has got it. She could be— oh, I don't know. Hillary Swank. Cate Blanchett. Any part they do, this girl could do. But she's good looking, too, so it's the best of both worlds." Then, because there was only silence on the line, enough silence for Arthur to start asking himself, "Why are you doing this?" he added, "You've got to see her. I'm telling you, she'll be a star. With you or with someone else, she'll be a star. I'd rather it was you, Bill. You wait too long, she'll be with CAA or ICM, making the fat cats fatter."

"Who is she with now?"

"Jennifer Stein."

More silence, and lots of it.

Finally: "You screwing her, Arthur?"

"I'm not screwing her. I never even touched her."

"So what's the real story?"

"I told you the real story."

"Jennifer Stein rents bimbos out to Italian directors who want to remake *Caligula,* Arthur. Jennifer Stein supplied the cast for *Caged Women.* Don't tell me Jennifer Stein has found herself a real actress. Jennifer Stein couldn't sign a real actress to save her life."

"You're right, you're right," Arthur said. "Did I say you're wrong? No, you're right. I agree completely—nine times out of ten."

"Please—"

"Maybe ninety-nine out of a hundred. But this is the one time, Bill. I'm telling you this based on thirty years in the business: She's got it like no one else I've ever seen."

"Come on. You're calling me at two in the morning to tell me about some girl you saw once in your life? Give me a break, Arthur."

"Trust me," Arthur said. "Write down her number. Give her a call. See her. You're going to thank me."

"I can't believe you called me up in the middle of the night just to tell me about some girl."

"Would I—tell me this, Bill, I'm serious—would I call you in the middle of the night if she were just some girl? Don't I have better things to do in the middle of the night? I couldn't sleep."

"You couldn't sleep."

"Please. Write down her number."

"Okay, fine," Bill said. "Give me her number."

Arthur heard a pencil scratching against paper as he read off Lisa's phone number.

"Arthur, are you using her in *Goin' West?*"

"No," Arthur said. Then: "She's too good for *Goin' West.*"

"Well, listen," Bill said. "If she's as good as you say she is, which I still don't believe, but *if,* I'll see what I can do about getting Corey to do the film for you."

"That'd be great, Bill."

"I'm not making any promises."

"That's fine," Arthur said. "I know you'll do your best. That's all I can ask for."

When Bill had hung up, Arthur dialed the number written on the back of Lisa's headshot. An answering machine clicked on, spieled, and beeped.

"This is Arthur French calling," Arthur said. He paused. "I'm sorry about what happened today. I passed your headshot to William Fitch at ASC and I think you'll hear from him soon." He paused again. "I told him I had you read for me today and that I was very impressed. So if he asks, go along with it." This time he took a deep breath before proceeding. "If I could have cast you in *Goin' West,* I want you to know I would have. But I'm just a hired hand. I have to do what they tell me."

As an afterthought, Arthur left his phone number. "In case you need to reach me," he said.

"THAT WAS BILL," Arthur said as he replaced the receiver in its cradle. "He says hello."

"Did he say if he's made a decision?"

"It's only been a week."

"I know." Lisa stood up, walked a lap around the office, and fell into the chair again. "I'm just anxious."

"You should be anxious. Fitch is a dealmaker. If he decides that you're going to be in a movie, you're in it."

"Do you think he will?"

"Yes," Arthur said.

"*Pale Moon?*"

"I'd put money on it. If not *Pale Moon,* it'll be something else. He's already said he'll handle you. It's just a question of which project he places you in first."

Lisa turned her chair, back and forth, back and forth.

"You want to know what I said to myself the last time I walked out that door?" she said.

"Probably not."

"I said to myself, 'If that little prick ever calls again, I'll hang up in his face, I don't care who he is.'"

"Well, I deserved that," Arthur said.

She stopped turning. "Then you called. I was lying in bed listening to my machine, and when you said your name, I started crying."

"Sorry."

"No, you don't understand. I was crying because in that instant I thought, 'He's calling to give you the part after all,' and I was so goddamned grateful. And I hated myself for feeling that way. I hated you for making me feel that way. I wanted to kill myself. I didn't even hear the rest of your message until later, when I played it back. I almost didn't hear it at all. I almost pulled the tape out and threw it in the garbage."

"Good thing you didn't."

Lisa paused. "I still don't understand why you did this for me."

"You mean, what's in it for me? No, that's a fair question." Arthur took a file from the stack on his desk and from the file retrieved a photo of Corey Dunn. "He's going to do *Goin' West,* ninety-nine percent certain. Why? Because I sent you over to Bill Fitch and he liked you."

"But you sent me over without knowing if I was any good. You sent me over blind."

"So? What did I have to lose? Dunn wasn't doing the picture. Fitch wasn't returning my calls. So you go over there and bomb. Dunn's still not doing the picture and Fitch still isn't taking my calls. What could I have lost?"

"You told him I was good. You could have lost your credibility."

"Don't make me into a white knight," Arthur said, thinking to himself, credibility? What credibility? "I took a shot and it paid off. If it hadn't, I'd have tried something else."

"You could have taken a different shot. The fact is, first you were a real asshole to me, and then later the same day you helped me out when you didn't have to."

Arthur shrugged. "I felt I owed you a good turn."

"You're a tough guy to figure," Lisa said.

"It's part of my charm."

"Why me?" Lisa said. "No offense, but I'm sure you're an asshole to lots of women."

Arthur thought about it. Why? Because she looked like she needed help more than those other girls. Or maybe like she deserved it more than they did. Or maybe it was just that she was the first woman he'd seen that day who wasn't young enough to be his daughter. "I don't know," Arthur said. "It was a feeling I had about you. And I had seen you in *Telling Lies*. I knew you were good."

"I only had two lines in *Telling Lies*," Lisa said.

Only one of which I've heard, Arthur said to himself, seeing as how I only caught the second half of the movie last night on HBO. "They were good lines," he said. "A person knows talent when he sees it."

"You're such a liar."

"Yes," Arthur said, "I am. Want some lunch?"

She faced him dead on, arms crossed over her chest. "Let's get one thing straight, okay? This feeling you had about me? No, listen to me. I don't care what you did for me or why you did it, I'm not going to sleep with you."

"What did I say?" Arthur said. "I said, 'Want some lunch?' I did not say, 'Want to sleep with me?' Lisa, I'm a married man, and though my wife wouldn't believe it if I slapped my hand on a pile of Bibles and sang it soprano, I haven't had sex with another woman since a few weeks before November 5, 1976, which is the day she and I got married. You've got nothing to worry about."

"Because that was the only thing I could figure," Lisa said, going on as if he hadn't said anything. "That you'd thought about me some more and decided you wanted to get me into bed. The only other thing I could figure was that you felt sorry for me, which would be even worse."

Arthur took his coat off the hook on the back of the door and slung it over his arm. Why had he done it? Why had he taken her picture home and called Fitch and put himself on the line for her? He wasn't sure. Lots of reasons. No reason. Oh, hell, what could he tell this woman that would make her understand?

"Totally honest?" he said, and she nodded. "Maybe I did feel a little sorry for you. Jesus, who wouldn't? And maybe I wanted to get you into bed, too, just for a minute. I don't any more, believe me."

"Which?"

"What?"

"Feel sorry for me or want to get me into bed? Which don't you any more?"

"Either," Arthur said. "Listen, you say you felt like you wanted to kill yourself when I called. I don't know if you meant that or not. But I could have said the same thing that very morning, and I would have meant it, every word of it. I was standing at that window—" he pointed "—and I was this close, *this close,* to opening it and saying sayonara to the whole goddamn shooting match.

"Why? You're asking yourself why. Here's a man, corner office on the thirtieth floor, casting for major Hollywood blockbusters, has beautiful women in his office at all hours showing him their tits, bigshot agents call him all day long begging him to let their stars be in his pictures, why would a man who's got all this want to do a double gainer from his office window?" He ran his hand through his hair. His fingers itched for a cigarette.

"That's what you're asking yourself. Well. All I can say is, the agents aren't calling, the stars aren't begging, the thirtieth floor stinks as much as the third in this lousy city, my business is all on the West Coast, my wife's sure I'm shtupping every girl who walks in here, and the girls—yourself excluded, God bless you—all look like they got inflated with the same bicycle pump. I walk out of here at five o'clock, I don't want to see another pair of breasts as long as I live.

"Then you walk in here, deserving better than me, deserving better than this whole lousy business, and I treat you the same as the rest of them. And you let me do it to you." Arthur shook his head. "I had to call you back. That, or come back here, open the window, and get it over with once and for all."

II

The descent into LAX had left her with a headache, and though normally she could cure her headaches by promptly applying chocolate, the Snickers bar she'd bought from a vending machine by the escalator was doing no good. It wasn't hunger that had given her the headache this time, it was reading on the plane. It always did. But she had scenes to do in twelve hours—no, less, ten and a half—and, my God, this dialogue was not the sort to stick in your head on first reading.

Why couldn't it have been *Pale Moon*? She'd really loved that script, not because it would make such a good movie, but because the part she'd have had was just a great part. Melanie Lyons had lots of screen time and a great arc—from docile wife to heroic rescuer of her family to drained and bitter widow after her plans went all to hell. She'd have gotten to play opposite Michael Keaton, who may not have had much of a career lately but had always struck Lisa as a generous actor, judging by his films. But now it was Michelle Glassberg playing the wife (Michelle *Glassberg?* What was she, *fifteen?*) and Lisa was struggling to learn page after page of pseudo-scientific gibberish.

Why did they even bother with dialogue? No one would come to the theater curious about the combination of tachyons and muons and pi-mesons it took to make a man invisible, they just wanted to see the results. They might as well hang a sign around her neck labeled "exposition" and let her keep her mouth shut. She'd get to carry a syringe, wear a lab coat over surgical greens, restrain the hero on a gurney, and explain breathlessly to Jon Farrell what had gone wrong. She couldn't imagine a more generic part. Even the character's name was generic: Carol Brown. *Doctor* Carol Brown, but so what? You want to talk invisible, you don't need to mess with tachyons and muons, just name someone Carol Brown, stick her in a lab coat, give her a clipboard and a stethoscope, put her in a hospital hallway, and you've just made an invisible woman right there.

Checking in at the hotel was mercifully quick. Lisa dropped her suitcase heavily on one of the room's twin beds and stretched out diagonally across the other. She couldn't read, the words were swimming before her eyes as it was. The radio was on, playing classical music that was obviously supposed to relax her, but she turned it off as soon as she was able to locate the switch. Rest. That's what she needed. Tomorrow she'd be a trooper: show up on time, know her lines, hit her marks, demonstrate that she was a pro. A job was a job, and she was glad to have it. God willing, there would be other jobs after this one. Sharon Stone got started in that horrible Wes Craven movie, after all, and Jamie Lee Curtis screamed her way through *Halloween.* Careers survived.

Although it probably helped if you got your screaming roles out of the way while you were in your twenties.

Lisa had one foot in the shower when the phone rang. Who knew she was here? The studio, she supposed, since they were footing the bill for the room. The director, presumably—he had to know where his cast was. The entire production staff. But who would call at midnight?

She picked up on the third ring.

"Hey, Lee. It's Bill. Get in okay?"

"I got in fine." She belted her robe. "I've got a bit of a headache, but it's nothing that won't go away with a little sleep." Then, belatedly: "I want to thank you again. I appreciate your getting me the part."

"Look, we both know it's not the one you wanted. But this is just the beginning. I want you to remember that."

"Thanks."

"Listen, mind if I stop by?"

"Stop by? Where are you?"

"Right outside the hotel. I just parked."

"Bill, it's late, I need to sleep." Lisa stepped to the window and looked out, but the room faced the rear courtyard. She let the curtain fall. "I figured we'd have dinner tomorrow, after the shoot."

"You think you're tired today," Bill said, "just wait till tomorrow after the shoot. It really takes it out of you. You wouldn't think so, all that sitting around, but when you're done, you just want to hit the sack."

"Bill, I've been on a movie set before."

"Yeah, but you've never had to shoulder this many scenes. Trust me."

"It's midnight, Bill—no, it's one A.M. I'm tired, I need a shower, I need sleep. I don't mean to snap at you, but really, I need—"

"Come on," Bill said. "I'm already here. I'm getting out

of the elevator. Let's just sit down for ten minutes, then you can go to sleep."

"It's one in the morning!"

"Ten minutes." She heard his steps outside the door, then his knock: shave-and-a-haircut. Jesus. Did he think he was being cute?

Lisa opened the door, wedged it against her shoulder, and looked out at Bill through the opening. He still had his cell phone at his ear. He shut it. "It's great to see you," he said.

"It's good to see you, too, Bill. It's nice that you came by. But I really do need to sleep."

"Don't tell me I come all the way here and you're going to turn me away at the door. At least let me use your bathroom, for Christ's sake."

Lisa couldn't think of a way to refuse that. She stood back and waved him inside, then shut the door after him and belted her robe tighter while he stepped into the bathroom and pissed noisily. He came out wiping his hands on a washcloth.

"The bathrooms here are unbelievable. Bet you never had anything like this back in New York. Bet you could fit your whole apartment in there."

She gave him the smile he was fishing for but couldn't keep it aloft for long. "What do you want, Bill?"

"I want to talk about you." Bill was bigger than Arthur French, but had something of the same quality about him: the forced boyishness, as though by dressing young and putting gel in your hair you could convince the world you hadn't hit fifty yet, or maybe convince yourself. She'd only met him in person twice before this, but both times he'd impressed her as someone with more energy than was good for him, as though he were running too hard, pushing too hard, straining too much. It showed around his eyes, it showed in his hands. Also, the man couldn't sit still.

"When I say this is the beginning, I'm talking about a fast ride to the top. This picture, forget it. It's just a way to get your face in front of the audience. What I'm thinking is, what's going to be Lisa Brennan's star vehicle? What's the picture that will put you front and center? And this morning I got it." He paced back and forth in front of the window. "I want to plant the idea in your head, get your subconscious working on it, see what you think."

"What is it?"

He spread his hands, palms toward her. *"Corner of State and Main.* Celia. The younger daughter, the one who got married at sixteen and comes back when her husband goes into the army. You've read the book, right?"

She had. Who hadn't? Once every few years a book hits on all cylinders—*Midnight in the Garden of Good and Evil, Bridges of Madison County, The Da Vinci Code*—and suddenly everyone you know has read it, or at least bought a copy. Then there's a film version, and sometimes it's a hit, sometimes it isn't. Mostly it isn't, but still, these are prestige projects and appearing in a leading role in a movie like that . . . it was miles away from the sort of thing she'd be doing tomorrow. (Today, she corrected herself with a glance at the clock.)

"Sure," she said. "I'd love to be in that movie. So would Helen Hunt. What makes you think I can get the part?"

"They picked a director. It's Michael Haber. We went to school together."

"School?"

"We go way back," Bill said. "He owes me plenty."

Was it really possible, Lisa wondered, that Bill believed his old school ties would trump studio demands on a picture this big? Or that he thought she would believe it? Or was it just possible that he was right, that he had an in she could use and this could be her break? No: that wasn't possible. It just wasn't. And even if it was, why the hell did he have to lay this on her at one in the morning?

"Bill, I am really grateful for everything you've done for me, you know that, and if you think you can pull this off, well, God bless you and I hope you're right. But right now I've got seven hours before I have to be on the set of *Transparent* and I don't think they want Dr. Brown to have big bags under her eyes. So I'm going to say good night to you and go to sleep, and not get my hopes up, and go to work tomorrow, and do a good job because that's what I'm being paid to do—and if you can get me a better part next time, that's great, but tonight what I need is sleep."

"Oh, you're good," Bill said, gripping her chin between his thumb and forefinger. "Such honesty. Such openness. Just show some of that when you're in front of the camera, and I'll get you any part you want." He leaned in and kissed her— briefly, but it startled her, and she pulled the lapels of her robe together when he leaned back. She wanted to ask him what he thought he was doing or tell him not to do it again, but by then he was already halfway to the door, and hell, this was no time to start a fight. She closed the door behind him.

Honesty. Openness. These weren't what her experience told her made for success in Hollywood. But they'd gotten her agent out of her bedroom, so maybe they were good for something after all.

WHEN SHOOTING WRAPPED, she sat by the catering table nursing her third cup of coffee. Grips were busy dollying cameras and lights back to the storage pen. In the operating theater set, the stunt coordinator was pointing at a balcony that had been fitted out with a breakaway section while his chief construction engineer was trying to explain why it hadn't broken properly on the first take. Lisa felt her eyelids drop in spite of the caffeine. Bill was right, of course: even if she'd had enough sleep the night before she'd be tired now, and as it was she just wanted to crash.

But she'd promised Bill a dinner, and there was no reason to think she'd be less tired tomorrow. Besides, she'd hustled him out of her room a little brusquely last night and though he'd deserved it, this was still someone she didn't want to piss off needlessly. She owed him this job, and while today's shooting had been roughly as bad as she'd expected, it was better than ushering Off-Broadway for thirty-five dollars a night or waitressing at the Union Square Coffee Shop, both of which she'd done not too long ago.

There was a phone in a cabinet under the stairs, next to the water fountain and the door to the men's room. She called Bill's office number, but judging by the background noise reached him in his car.

"You're done already? It's not even nine o'clock."

"They still have work to do, but they told me I'm not needed again till tomorrow. Just position shooting for the computer animation."

"Who's doing the effects, ILM? Digital Domain?"

"I don't know, Bill. They probably told me, but I've forgotten."

"I bet it's Digital. Listen, are we still on for tonight?"

"Sure. As long as it's some place quiet, and not too far away."

"Why don't I pick you up where you are, I'm just a few miles away, and I'll take you some place nice."

"Not too nice."

"You got it."

She stepped into the women's wardrobe room and changed back into her street clothes. No dressing room with a star on the door for her. Not yet.

Bill was waiting for her when she made her way out to the street. He reached across the passenger seat and opened the door for her. When she slid in, he gave the back of her neck a quick massage.

She tensed. Was everyone in Hollywood this touchy-feely? As a born-and-bred New Yorker, Lisa was suspicious of people who kissed and patted and touched too freely. On the other hand, when in Rome.

"So, where are we going?"

Bill pulled off onto the road. "I have someone I want you to meet."

"Oh, not tonight, Bill, I won't make a good impression—"

"Not tonight, not tonight—then when? Don't worry. You look great."

"I can't keep my eyes open."

"You'll keep them open."

"Who is it?"

He turned to her, and waited till she said, "Well?"

"My old friend, Michael Haber."

"Jesus, that's too important, I can't see him tonight—"

"That's where you're wrong. You can't not see him tonight. Now is when he's thinking about who he wants in *State and Main,* and you want to meet him before he starts thinking about someone else for your part."

"I—" Lisa put her forehead in her hands and rubbed her temples. "Okay."

"Damn right, okay." He flipped open his cell phone and dialed one-handed. "Mike, you there? Goddamn, I can't hear a thing. Hold on." He rolled up the car's windows. "Let's meet at Santiago's. Yes, she's right here. She's dying to meet you. You want to say hello? Hang on." He handed her the phone. "Say hello."

"Hi, this is Lisa." He said something, but she didn't catch it. "What's that? Yes, it'll be nice to meet you, too."

Bill took the phone back. "We'll be there in ten minutes. Meet us in the cigar room."

Michael Haber met them, hand extended, as they came in. She didn't recognize him at first—he'd shaved the beard he'd had the last time she'd seen him on "Access Hollywood" and he wasn't wearing the baseball cap he seemed to have on in every photograph ever taken of him. What the cap would have covered was a high forehead and very little in the way of hair. He looked a little like Ron Howard, Lisa thought.

"Lisa? I'm Michael. I understand you're working on a picture out here?"

She nodded. "It's called *Transparent*. Science fiction. We just finished for the night, and I didn't even get into L.A. until one this morning, so if I seem a bit groggy, that's why."

"Don't worry about it. Bill warned me." He guided her to a corner table with a hand at the small of her back. "We'll go easy on you tonight."

The meal was a blur. She didn't fall asleep in the soup, but by the time the waiter brought coffee with dessert, she grabbed at it like a life preserver. The conversation veered in her direction every so often and she answered questions about herself—Had she always lived in New York? What had she done for the stage?—with as much energy as she could muster. Bill spent the evening fidgeting in his chair and got up twice to take calls on his cell phone. The second time, Michael put his hand on Lisa's and said, "You look tired. Let me get the check and we'll take you home." By the time Bill returned, Michael was helping her on with her jacket.

The topic of the new movie hadn't come up during dinner. Lisa was relieved when Michael stopped her in the parking lot and said, "Let's talk about *State and Main*."

"Okay," she said.

"Bill tells me he sees you as Celia, but I have to say, Celia is supposed to be what, twenty-three, maybe twenty-four, and very plain, real salt-of-the-earth, and I don't know, forget the age, that just doesn't seem like your type."

"I understand."

"Margo, on the other hand, twice married, working on her third, snaring men like flies, cosmopolitan, chafing at having to endure small-town life again—I could see you as a great Margo."

Had he said what she thought she'd heard? A great Margo? She couldn't remember the last time she'd literally felt her heart beating in her chest like this. She felt like she couldn't speak, like one wrong word could shatter the fragile opportunity and leave her with nothing.

"Obviously, I need to bring you in to read for the producers, but we've worked together before and I'm confident they'll leave the casting decisions up to me. Except for Mitch, of course, since they've already got Russell Crowe lined up."

She found her voice. "Michael, I'm very flattered. I really— I don't know what to say."

"Let me send you a copy of the script, so you can read through it."

"She can have the copy you sent me," Bill said. "I have it at home. We can pick it up on the way back to her hotel."

Michael nodded. "Sure. Sooner the better." He shook Lisa's hand, held it between both of his. "I like you. I'm glad Bill introduced us. I hope this works out."

BILL STEERED HER back to the car and drove off in the direction of his house. "What did I tell you? Did I say he'd like you?"

"This is wonderful, Bill. You were right."

"So the next time I tell you I know someone you'll believe me?"

"I believed you knew him, I just didn't think—oh, what difference does it make? You were right, you were right, you were right, I'll say it till you're satisfied."

"I'm never satisfied."

"Do you really think they'll let him cast someone like me as Margo?"

"Absolutely. They'd be idiots not to let him. You're going to make this picture for them."

They drove for a while in silence. Lisa felt herself drifting into and out of sleep, lulled by the motion of the car and the lights streaming rhythmically by on the side of the highway. She felt full: a long day's work, a good dinner, and for dessert, a job offer that could make her career. No, she corrected herself, not an offer, not yet. But an opportunity, and what an opportunity!

She woke up when the engine stopped. Bill led her up a half-flight of stairs to his front door and she stood in his foyer while he rummaged around for the script in a pile of papers. "Hold on, I know where it is." He headed into the kitchen, then on to a room beyond. "Why don't you make a drink for us, we can celebrate."

"It's too soon to celebrate. I don't have the part yet."

"So celebrate making a good first impression."

She opened the refrigerator, passed up some bottles of beer and a re-corked bottle of white wine—they still had driving ahead of them—and went for a carton of lemonade instead. She carried two glasses into the other room, which turned out to be a den set up as a sort of miniature screening room: large leather recliners flanking a matching couch, chrome cup holders mounted on the arms, grapefruit-size surround-sound speakers balanced on pedestals behind the pillows, a sixty-inch TV on the far wall.

Lisa swapped one of the glasses for the script Bill was holding out. He reached over to clink his glass against hers and took a sip.

"Lemonade! My God, you're adorable. Come on, sit down, we can look it over."

She sat next to him on the couch and spread the script open on her knees. Margo was in the first scene—in fact, the voiceover that opened the movie was hers. " 'They say you can't go home again,' " she read, " 'but what I've never understood is why you would want to.' I still can't believe I've got a shot at this part."

He snaked an arm across her shoulders and pulled her

close. "You've got more than a shot, Lee. You've got me."

She went on reading, not oblivious to the gentle pressure of his arm or the fact that he was shifting closer to her on the couch, but not focused on it, either. And when she did focus, she forced herself not to flinch away. So he was a toucher—she'd found that out last night, hadn't she? There were worse back in New York, God knows, and most were people with a lot less to offer her than Bill Fitch had. Anyway, a peck on the lips and a pat on the back she could deal with, even if she didn't much care for it.

But she dreaded what might be coming next. And when it came, when his hand started slowly, casually to descend, she wanted to scream. Why? Why did everything good always have to be tainted in this business? Why couldn't he be satisfied with what looked likely to be a real success for both of them? Why ruin it? She lifted his hand from her side, prepared to pretend it hadn't happened and praying he had the good sense to do the same.

But he didn't: Two pages later, his hand was back, this time resting on her leg, kneading her thigh.

"Bill, don't." She moved his hand away, turned to face him, and found him leaning toward her, his face only a few inches from hers. "Please."

"Lee, I've got to confess something, I'm crazy about you."

"Come on, Bill. We're both excited about what happened tonight and we're both tired, and it's got you confused. Don't turn this into something romantic."

"It's too late. You've got me hooked."

"What, in one day?"

"I'm not joking."

"You're my agent, Bill. Let's leave it at that, okay?"

"I can't," he said. "You're so goddamn gorgeous I can't get you out of my head. I can't tell you how badly I wanted to give you a real kiss last night."

"Okay, we're going to stop this right now." His hands

had started to wander again. She batted them down and tried to stand, but he pulled her back with an arm around her waist.

"What? I'm not allowed to leave? You're going to keep me here by force?" She meant for it to sound like banter—self-possessed, annoyed, imperturbable—but she could hear the tears in her voice, the sound of frustration and fatigue and disappointment. He had relaxed his grip, but his arm was still around her, his fist bouncing impatiently against her thigh, and he was shaking his head. "I'm going to go now," she said. "You understand? I'll drive myself. You can pick up the car tomorrow. We'll both get some sleep, and tomorrow we'll forget this happened, okay?"

He didn't move his arm. "I want you to stay with me tonight, Lee."

"It's not going to happen."

"You want the part in Michael's movie," he said. "You deserve it. Why throw it away?"

"I don't want it this way."

"Now you're being silly. You screwed Arthur, and what did he ever give you? Except my phone number, so maybe he did deserve it." He pulled her toward him and shifted his weight, and suddenly she was looking up at the ceiling and he was on top of her. She pushed at his shoulders, but only succeeded in sinking further into the couch. She could smell his breath—he wasn't drunk, he didn't even have that excuse—and she could feel his erection pressing against her belly through their clothing. In this moment, her anger and frustration gave way to fear, the simple, physical fear that she wouldn't be able to fight him off.

"Oh, Lee, Lee, we have so much to give each other."

"What's wrong with you? Get off me!" She groped around the back of the couch for something to grab onto, something she could use to lever herself back to a sitting position. A different thought sparked when her questing hand hit one of the speakers. She couldn't see it and didn't know what it was, but it fit in her hand and, though it was heavy, she was able to lift it off its stand. "Get off me this instant!" She swung the speaker as hard as she could, hoping to bring it down squarely on his back.

But, feeling the movement of her arm, he raised his head, pushed her shoulders down, and started turning to look. The speaker caught him, hard, in the side of the head. He rolled off her with the force of the blow, landing face down on the wall-to-wall carpet at the base of the couch. When she looked down, she thought she saw his head move, but it was just an optical illusion caused by the steady flow of blood from his temple.

III

Arthur put the phone down and turned off his desk lamp. He could still see by the light from other buildings coming through his window, but there was nothing much he wanted to look at. Not the headlines, certainly—he'd already thrown the papers away, crushed them down at the bottom of the garbage along with the cigarette butts and used tissues.

Sandy had been the first to notice the story, and she'd hit him with it when he'd come home two days ago. "Have you heard what happened to Bill Fitch?" And: "Did you ever hear of this actress, this Lisa Brennan?" No, he'd said. Never heard of her.

He'd shut the door to his home office on the second floor and gone to one of the industry sites on the Internet to learn more. The coverage appeared under "Breaking News" first, then later under "Today's News," then under "Updates," and finally under "Obituaries."

Lisa left him out of it when she told her story, or at least the papers left him out of it when they reported it. He didn't have any illusions that this was because either Lisa or the writers wanted to protect him. His name wouldn't sell any more papers, and as for Lisa, how much had he really had to do with what had happened? He'd made an introduction. It's what people did, that's how the business worked. He was just doing her a good turn.

At least that had been the idea. She'd have been better off cast in *Goin' West,* stripped naked for a shower scene like Angela Meyer, nobody ever seeing her face. Oh, she had fame now, everyone knew who she was, and given the story she was telling, he supposed she probably wouldn't go to jail. But there was no chance anyone would ever hire her again. When they made the movie-of-the-week of her story, they'd cast someone else to play her. Maybe Michelle Glassberg.

Arthur carried his cigarette to the window, dragged deeply on it and watched the pinpoint of red reflected in the glass. The note he'd left pinned under his tape dispenser fluttered when he opened the window. *It's not you, honey. I can't stand this stinking business.*

He'd finished the casting for *Goin' West*. Corey Dunn was doing the picture, and on the phone just now Kreuger had been ecstatic to hear it. "You're the best, Arthur," he'd said. "What would I do without you?"

Arthur tossed the butt and watched it trail away into the night.

"Oh, you'd get by," he'd said. "You'd get by."

All Said and Done

GREGG HURWITZ

HE WOKE UP with sweat washing over his body in tight chilly shimmers and the paddles of the fan whirring above him like a copter. He jerked out of bed and ran both hands over his face, top to bottom, then down around the back of his neck. They slid on the moistness of his skin, and he felt something less than human. Reptilian.

Crossing the tiny square that passed for his bedroom, he pulled the metal folding chair away from the stack of empty fruit crates. He sank into the chair and faced the small Smith Corona typewriter that sat on a slight angle atop the highest box. BURSTIN' ORANGE. FLORIDA'S BEST! the crate proclaimed.

He laid the pads of his fingers gently on top of the keys and slid them in the rounded grooves. It was "a laying on of hands," as his father used to say when he spoke of New Testament tales when there still had been a New Testament or an Old. He felt the power contained in his eight little fingers perched on the starting blocks of eight little keys. A big door. It had always been. Trouble was you couldn't control what flew out when you opened it. The moon slid into view in the edge of the window as the earth continued its tedious rotation, and the straw-colored light fell patterned across his bare mattress. A big fucking door. He opened it.

*It was the summer of the year and every year and yet there
were no seasons, just time awash with a blend of the four. It
was sometime in the sixties but then time never held when
you were really alive or really dead and for the sixteen
months of my tour I was both.*

He stopped. "I am Janson Tanker," he said softly to the four
walls that he could all but touch from his seat at the makeshift
desk. He looked around the room, noticing the spill of the
moonlight turned metallic as it passed through the small window splattered with rain and neon. He had New York on his
windows, and the rain couldn't wash them clean of it any more
than he could wash the New York from his body with the
small sink in the corner.

Do I really want to do this? he thought. *It's not much. God
knows it's not much, but at least it's familiar.* He raised the heel
of his hand to his eye and rubbed, his eyelid pulling down
in a droop.

*We came over in units, but one by one, and we left all to-
gether. We left in a big mess—a human meat pie—with the
leftovers of all our lives molded together until we could no
longer separate whose limbs were whose. They always said
that you come out a man, and I supposed that was true, but
I never anticipated coming out as bits and pieces of a bunch of
men which may or may not have added up to one of whatever
I was before. You heard echoes and voices of all the men and
you remembered them so clearly you couldn't distinguish their
stories from your memories. And Tom from Minnesota with
the girl he'd asked to marry dressed up like Santa Claus
("me not her") and Jimmie Jankens from Baltimore who had
a burn mark on the side of his face from a car engine exploding in tenth-grade shop ("already had a tour once, I told
'em, first when I walk in, and their mouths all drop not
knowing my tour was through the shit engine block of a*

'62 Chevy") and Jessie who used to bite the skin off his
knuckles when we'd wait in the leaves and you could barely
hear his teeth clicking underneath the hammering rain. And
which were their lives, their voices, their clicking teeth in the
dark and which your own? Couldn't really tell then, let alone
now.

And so I went into the jungle in a season of a year, and I
left in a season of another year.

Janson paused for a minute, his fingers straining at the bit.
Then the warm, warm rain brought back Henry Wilder
running through the wet, and Janson's head dropped to the
edge of the crate. He could close the door if he strained with
all his might, if he bent all his energy to ignoring the searing pain it sent through his back. But it was a heavy door in
a strong wind; once it opened, even a crack, everything outside fought and clawed to invade the warmth on the other
side. And there wasn't much warmth to spare.

He had let the first breath of air get through, he had let in
Jimmie Jankens from Baltimore and the long, ebbless tide of
the hours and days, and he knew he couldn't go on. They
were pooling at his feet and rising to his knees, and there was
even less space in his mind than in the room. Slowly, he felt
the panic gripping his heart with iron fingers again and
again, like those decades spent on evening lookouts that still
came to him in harsh whispers and the whirring, the inces-
sant whirring of the blades of the helicopter as it moved
ahead and out of the world.

He felt the tears pressing beneath the line of his cheek-
bones and his nose, and then he felt them spill over and
down his cheek, but he couldn't feel the crying, only the
moisture. He still wasn't used to the crying—he had not
cried, not once, for the entire sixteen months of his tour or
the empty box of the eleven years to follow, but after that he
had started and then he didn't know what it was, much less

how to stop it. And so, with the flashing beer signs outside illuminating his room like blinks of a neon eye, with the slow rotation of the haunting fan above, with his forehead pressed tightly to the top of a BURSTIN' ORANGE fruit crate, Janson Tanker cried more tears of penance for the years when he could not.

"I'M TELLING YOU, we got him. This guy's fucking unbelievable—he's like from a time warp," Adam Diamond said, as he slid back from his large glass desk and clicked the fourth red button in from the left.

He tucked the phone against his neck, covering the mouthpiece momentarily. "Janice. Double cap, dry—and I mean fucking dry. If I wanted a latte I'd order one."

With a deft movement of his shoulder, Adam brought the phone back up and against his ear. "Stable, not stable, who gives a fuck? He's brilliant. No, of course I haven't read him. Scott checked him out. Said he's like Faulkner and—I know, I know. So Faulkner was a failed screenwriter, but Scott's Ivy. What do you expect? It's his way of saying he thinks he's good."

Adam listened for a while, working a set of jade duo balls back and forth in the palm of his right hand. They clicked now and again, but rarely touched, even when he rested his elbow on the table and raised them in his hand up next to his ear. His eyes didn't flicker when Janice came in and left his cappuccino on the desk next to a stack of phone messages.

"I'm not talking David Rabe. David Rabe was shit—for Christ's sake, who the fuck casts Michael J. Fox as a lead? I know . . . I know, Harvey. No one wants to see another Vietnam film, but I'm telling you I've got a longer line of thumbs up than a San Francisco bathhouse. We're talking *Platoon* here, Harvey. Okay, I know. But we'll check him out, get some raw material, see where we can run with it. *Rules of*

Engagement used Vietnam . . . Yes, yes it did. I don't care if it wasn't the primary line, it was in there and what'd that gross?" He whistled. "Holy fuck. And we're just talking domestic.

"Where'd we get him? We found him, Harvey. We found him. One of Scott's friends from his New Haven days runs a soup kitchen lower West Side. Regular guy comes in, always asks for a couple sheets of paper towel from the kitchen. Turns out—this is beautiful, Harvey—turns out he's been writing on them. Both sides, ink bleeding through and all.

"Scott's friend's a warm-hearted liberal from an Upper East Side family, so he goes and buys this guy a shit second-hand typewriter and some paper. Month and a half later, the guy shows up with four sheets, typed. No, no I'm not joking. Month and a half later, only four sheets. So Scott's buddy reads 'em—What? I don't know why he brought them in to him. Anyway, so Scott's buddy reads them and they're absolute crap, right? Some science fiction shit about a world taken over by machines or something. We're talking the first *Terminator.* So he sends the guy on his way and doesn't think twice about it. One week later, the guy shows up and hands him a sheaf, a fucking sheaf of paper. I don't know, like sixty, seventy pages. Scott's friend reads them, goes nuts and calls Scott and Scott drives down—I know, I know. In his cherry-red Z3 to a fuckin' soup kitchen."

Adam broke off laughing. "He's dedicated, Scott. Phi Beta Kappa from Yale, when it's all said and done he drives down to that soup kitchen if he thinks it'll yield.

"So Scott gets them, these, however many pages, and they're gold. No, not gold. Platinum. They're fucking platinum. Best thing he's ever read, and keep in mind he's our novel guy. So I tell him to run it through the loop. All tolled, five reads, all give him four stars on style and writing. Wanted to wait for the big men to make the call on story, just because it *is* Vietnam. So it's up to you and me.

"Of course I'm waiting. Don't worry, no one else even knows where to find this guy. He's completely ours—he couldn't find his way to an editor if we left him in the lobby of S&S. We're waiting until we get the second half. It's a short novel, only gonna be about two hundred pages, all said and done. We'll wait on him, then we'll talk. We'll talk."

Adam Diamond hung up the phone. It left his ear for the first time since 8:30 that morning, and it was well after 2:00. His lunch meetings often slid late, but this was late even for him, and he could feel his stomach complaining about last night's Scotch and this morning's caffeine.

He leaned over and hit the red button. Fourth one in from the left. "Get Cathy on the line, let her know it's still Baldoria, but it's gonna have to be three, not two thirty. You can reach her in the car if she's already left."

Adam Diamond was remarkably good-looking for a forty-five-year-old man. His dark brown hair lacked even a hint of gray—"distinguished my ass, I want be dead and gone before they call me distinguished"—and it fell in short wavy ringlets over his smooth forehead. He had a cruel face, but it was a learned cruelty. The anger did not flower naturally from beneath the skin, but sat across it, etched in the wrinkles he did not have.

He switched the jade balls from hand to hand, turning his left hand over on top of the right as if to clap. Adam Diamond rarely clapped, however, and when he did, it was to punctuate a command, not to display appreciation. "Clapping is for fools," his father used to say. "Take what you can from a show and run." His father was a famous agent, almost a living legend in New York, a city with a lot of names. Then he died, and was just a legend.

IT HURT, IT hurt like excising a cancerous growth, but once he started, he was steeped in blood too far to return, and so he continued. He entered them all, entered the voices one by one, and felt their words as the breath in his throat. Janson Tanker felt as if there were steam running through his insides, but he still had several nights of burning to do before he was spent. He only hoped that the stack of paper, which was shrinking like water leaving a tub, would last until the words ran out.

He had written them, written them one and all—his fallen comrades whom he loved and hated as he did his own flesh. He supposed he was trying to exorcise them or purify them, not that there was much of a difference anymore. He had reassembled them, brought them back from their homes in Heads Creek, Louisiana, and Culver, Texas, from Little Rock, Arkansas, and Detroit, Michigan. Using no discretion (for the war had not either), he plucked them from their homes like babes from a tit and sent them all back to the jungle.

Yet the scariest part was pulling the nails from the coffins and prying open the lids. Was watching the skeletons grow flesh and rise. And Janson resurrected them so precisely, adding even the optimistic shine of their smiles, only to kill them again. And he wished he had only to kill them with bullets.

He went to bed when he faded from his chair to the bare mattress. He wasn't really sure when that was, just as he wasn't really sure when his crying crossed from waking to sleeping hours. But somehow he always fell asleep because he always awoke with his mouth shut and his body screaming under the whirring paddles of the fan. The sweat was awful, so awful he didn't even bother to try to clean his pillow in the little sink anymore because he knew it would be doused again the next night or the next sleep, whichever came first.

Sleep evaded and stalked him. It would slip away, fleeing through a tangled jungle path at night and drawing him inexorably along with it, through a waking hell. And then, just when he got his feet under him and adjusted to the rhythm of his footsteps, it would turn and pounce.

He had come to fear the typewriter. The 1951 Smith Corona typewriter on the stack of crates. He would stare at it, sometimes for hours, with hints of sleep glazing his eyes. Even when he turned away, he always knew it remained, always knew where it was. But after they routed Mai Teng, he knew it wasn't the typewriter, that he would finish even if he had to write the rest on the walls in his own blood. He wondered what Barry's friend would think of the skewed type on the sheets that he passed along.

He had a meeting in the morning, somewhere across the city, and his check had run out so he didn't have money for a bus. He'd have to leave at 10:30 to make sure he got there by noon. He didn't know what exactly it meant, but Barry said he had a friend who might give him money for his story, and he needed money right now more than almost anything. Barry said he'd pay for lunch if it was a lunch meeting, and Janson would have walked an hour and a half across town just for a decent meal.

He had written up to the very end. He didn't know how many more pages, but he could feel the door closing. He didn't think about it consciously, but he knew somewhere inside that he'd have to get through Henry Wilder to put it down, to put it all down. But for now, he couldn't face the typewriter, so he concentrated on washing his pants and shirt in the sink so he wouldn't smell at the meeting. He would try to tape the hole in the knee from the inside so it wouldn't hang open.

He had given Barry the latest segments—the total was now one hundred seventeen pages and two paragraphs on the one hundred eighteenth. The pages were not numbered and he did not consciously count them, but each fresh sheet tolled, somehow, inside his head. Although he turned over the new pages the day before yesterday, he remembered just how he had written the storm, and could still feel it rattling inside him.

> *The thunder was still there, and it was all light that didn't fade and shrapnel still in flight. I waited for the trees to stop shaking—what world what ungodly world where even the trees shake and the soil flies at you and folds under you— and for the rain to stop whipping my cheeks, but I had waited days or months already to no avail. When the ground eats its own progeny, then we've all come to judgment day, but I'd seen it all, seen the very ground spread its jaws and pull my struggling comrades down into tunnels and unimaginable torments, seen bodies waist deep in soil jerking with the movement of hands gripping them beneath the ground. And yanked down in a flash of foreign tongue moving vertically even in sound and then a scurrying of footsteps beneath. Always beneath and below. Footsteps in the cellar of my mind, even then in the rain with the shock of the blast still settling over and throughout me.*
>
> *And the skies opened only with rain.*

He knew that he was almost there; he had even allowed one of Wilder's hands to creep over the edge of the coffin, but he slammed the lid on it. It would have to wait until after his meeting if he was going to get through it.

"I'M TELLING YOU, you would've died if you saw him. I know, I know—the suit. Last year Armani. Well he's a prick. He was a prick when I knew him at Doubleday. That's right, that's exactly right. Can't talk foreign, I want him off my fuckin' Rolodex."

Adam Diamond leaned forward and hit the fourth red button in from the left. "Janice. Richard Dawkins. Off the fuckin' Rolodex, out of the computer. Done."

"Yes, just like that, Harvey. I trust your judgment, especially when it coincides with mine. Hey—and guess who I've got coming in in about . . ." Adam flicked his Movado out from beneath a cuff. ". . . five minutes? The guy—the bum guy I told you about. Jaston Tanker. I'll—"

The green light flashed on his desk, and a female voice crackled through. "We have a security problem, Adam. A homeless man in the lobby won't leave, says he has an appointment with you, but I have you with Janson Tanker for your twelve o'clock and Michael Weaver for your twelve thirty."

"Goddamnit Janice," Adam roared. His voice dropped with the second half of the same breath. "Harvey, I'll call you back." He slammed down the phone and stood up, leaning over his desk toward the intercom. "That probably *is* Jaston Tanker."

The intercom was silent for a minute. "You mean *Janson* Tanker, Adam?"

Adam was silent for a long time as he tried to control his breathing. Finally, he spoke, his voice wavering with rage. "Just you push me, you cunt. You push me about an inch further and you'll be rolling calls the rest of your *fucking* life. Now get him in here."

He sighed, and raised the jade duo balls from their box, a blue case with a flowing Asian design. He sat down and rolled his black leather chair to his enormous glass desk.

After a few seconds, there was an uncomfortable knock on the door, and then Janson entered the room. Adam could see how security had mistaken him for a bum; his shirt was so washed out that it had faded to a greenish gray, the color all clothes turned to once they were old enough.

Janson crossed the room, a walking shadow. He hadn't shaved, but the stubble was as much a part of his face as anything else.

He was probably the kind of guy who grew scruff within

seconds after shaving, just to cover his face a little, Adam thought. Not just to make him look tough, but to keep something in. He had the hardest green eyes Adam had ever seen. They reminded him of his father's.

"Please. Sit." Adam beckoned Janson forward, indicating the smaller seat on the far side of the desk.

"Tha—" Janson cleared his throat. "Thank you," he said, and sat down. His voice was rich and deep; it had a full rainbow of colors in it. Adam found himself instantly charmed.

"I like you," he said.

"Excuse me?" Janson replied. He didn't look shocked (Adam bet it took a hell of a lot more than that to shock a guy like Janson), just perplexed. And more than a little out of his element. Adam tried again.

"I like you. I like your writing. I haven't read it all, but I took home the first half of your book as a weekend read and I like your style. Reminds me of . . ." Adam stopped for a minute, studying the Lichtenstein hanging behind Janson's head. "Reminds me of Faulkner. I'm intrigued. I want to read more, I want to know more. You've got a rough style that's not meant to be polished. I like that. I like the . . . animal feel. Where'd you get it?"

Janson frowned, biting his lip and pulling it to the side. Adam could see something moving in him like wind through a chime. Discomfort, maybe. "My mother was a schoolteacher," Janson finally said. "Had me reading early and typing by high school. I had a year of junior college before the war." He was proud of that. Proud, yet not asking for approval.

"I have always thought," Adam replied, "that formal schooling is vastly overrated."

Janson flicked his head back slightly in response, and Adam could detect a slight edge in his eyes. Suddenly he didn't like him quite so much.

"You want me to cut the bullshit and tell you why you're here, don't you?" Adam asked.

"Yes."

"Do you know what I do?"

"No."

"I'm not really an agent like you'd think of an agent. More of a packager. I put deals together. Books. Movies. People. I like your style, I like your writing. I already told you that. I need the end of your book, then I need to run it through a circuit of editors and producers."

Janson watched Adam attentively, chewing on the skin underneath one of his fingernails.

"Now, here's what I can do for you," Adam continued. "I can run this story through my circuit, and if it goes, it goes. Not small time. I'm talking book deal, publishing, hard and soft cover—I don't work with anything without a hard release. I'm talking film rights, and we can negotiate for screenwriting credit. It depends what you come up with, how much the studios like it and you, and if you can give them what they want. A publishing deal can get you from twenty-five thousand to a quarter of a million. That used to be more than you could expect for a first-time writer, but first-time writers are hot. Unless you're John Grisham or Jane Austin, established writers are having a tough time at the movies right now. They're looking for hot young writers. You're not exactly young, but you're new and that's the biggest word from LA to New York. Film rights go, they can go seven figures."

Adam watched Janson's eyes widen. *I have him,* he thought. *He's mine and only mine until I decide if I'm using him.* He continued, tasting the words as they rolled from his tongue. "Now *I* deal mostly with film rights, but if those go, you can expect a publishing deal. What publisher isn't going to want to get a book if we get you on line with a big

studio? None. More money for you, more money for them."
He paused and let the thoughts sink in, fumes settling over
a softly lit meadow.

Adam cleared his throat once. Sharply. "Now before you
go picking out the color of your new BMW, I'm telling you
now that none of this could go. When it's all said and done,
I'm making you no promises, no guarantees. But I will tell
you this." He leaned forward in his chair. "I want the end of
the book, I want you to release the whole thing so I can have
people 'officially' read it and so I can move it around my office
and through my contacts. I want you to sign this—customary
procedure. Leaves you with the rights to all profit, the ability
to decide your own contract with us or with anyone else. It
just gives us the right to read it and says you're aware we may
have other properties with similar themes."

Janson leaned forward and signed.

You idiot, Adam thought. *I could be taking your house right
now and you wouldn't know the fucking difference.*

In fact, Adam was moving through proper legal channels
just as he'd claimed. He was too far along in his career to
risk "borrowing" material, but the simple scrawl of Janson's
signature on the form infuriated him. The trust in simply
giving up his name like that, in relinquishing it.

But he had him now, and had him just where he wanted
him. He had the full story (and the only copy from the appearance of the first two-thirds of it), and all the time in the
world to decide if he wanted to make it hot.

Adam took the form back across his huge desk. "Great,"
he said, forcing a smile, though he didn't feel much like
smiling at all. "We'll be in touch. I'll have Scott pick up the
end of your manuscript from your buddy at your . . . dinner
place. Any questions?"

Janson studied a dirty fingernail. "Yeah." His eyes were
glazed, distant. He raised them. "Are we having lunch?"

"No. Sorry. I have a lunch meeting later. I'm afraid you'll have to pick something up on your way back," Adam said. He smiled handsomely and his eyes flashed to the door.

HIS FEET ACHED from walking by the time he got home, but he was good at ignoring pain, and he thudded heavily up the stairs to his tiny room. The meeting hadn't gone too badly. He remembered the manic nausea that had washed over him when Adam introduced those numbers, that money, so casually. Twenty-five thousand dollars to a quarter of a million. Janson couldn't think in numbers that big, couldn't quite get a handle around them and put them somewhere that showed what they were. He didn't even try.

The lowest number was more than his father had saved in his entire life, let alone earned in a single year. But a lifetime of blue bruises that turned a sickly black was enough to wash some of the green from the dollars floating through his head.

Just one thousand dollars, he thought. *That's not much, not much given the numbers these men talked. Could get me far and away from here and put me up for a few nights in a new town—a town, not a city—until I found work. Somewhere I could see the sky, not just a translucent gray fog, and trees glancing from pools of water standing as still as sleeping shadows. And cool nights with stars laid out like holes clear through to heaven.*

He closed his eyes and thought for a minute, his mind catching the image of a wood fire burning in the country somewhere, of smoke moving through the night air along lines as soft as the curves of a woman.

There were things he could still do. Not many, not skills, but there were things, and a check with four digits on it could get him to a place where he could show just what those things were. Once he didn't have to bend his back to keeping the door shut, he could bend it to other tasks. And leave the city with its one check a month, its stamps for meals, its pitiful offering of a lifeline which did not include a life.

He swung the door open to find the typewriter staring at him, a metal eye in the middle of the stark room. The odor of his sweat drifted to him as the draft sucked the stale air past him into the hallway. The typewriter watched him expectantly. Not yet, he told it with his eyes. Not yet. He fell on his mattress, exhausted, and watched the rotating fan overhead.

Janson couldn't write for several days and nights, until he was convinced that it would never come, and that he had lost it all. He had lost the check with four figures on it, the town that was not a city, and worst of all, the demons would forever stay their perch inside him. He watched the fan spin for nights and nights and then, at last, it lulled him to the edge of a cliff where sleep was waiting.

He had no idea when he woke up, but he woke up typing, and there was night all in his room and in his head. He was drenched in sweat, and it took him great effort to pull his clinging undershirt off. His fingers were running, running away from something, and they hammered on the metal keys until they ached with a dull throbbing pain. The ragged skin on the side of one of his fingernails finally gave way. He winced as he typed on. Droplets of blood made their way down under the key and flew up with the key's release, faintly spraying the sheet. The paper was almost out, and he prayed to a God he no longer believed in that it would hold just that much longer, just until it was out of him.

The wind picked up the rain on its bosom and bore it to my face. It was no longer liquid, but a thick, solid paste smearing my brow and eyes. I was all feet and knees high-pumping and knocking my gear, but I had Henry's footsteps to pull me through the mud and the brush. The one face from before the war, the one laugh I knew from a time when all laughs weren't merely crackings of the soul to push the fear out. Again I thought of his footsteps when he blocked for me against Allston and I was the county sweetheart. A two-hundred-eighteen-yard game, and all two hundred and eighteen had been my feet in his footsteps just as they were now, but that was back when boys would be boys and when we loved rather than feared the thickness of soil and turf. I watched his feet sink in the mud ahead of me and pressed my own into the messy mounds they left.

The copter was there just like they'd sent word on the radio, but then they sent all codes and numbers over the radio and all we usually got was fire and brimstone. They were behind us still as they always seemed to be and we could see the spinning blades lowering in the clearing ahead, and suddenly our whole lives narrowed to a single gem-like point. Three hundred yards from the jungle to the clearing. I could feel my soul moving to the clearing with the might of a boulder on a downhill roll. It pushed toward the opening with euphoric longing, with a desire to escape that was red tinged pink around the edges and lit like a forest fire underneath my moving body.

That was when the ground gave and I saw Henry's knees where his feet had been and then his shoulders and he dangled above the tunnel, the roaring rain crashing on him even through the leaves. The whirring of the helicopter tormented our ears with the full glory of our world just in reach and leaving without us. The ground yawned around him and a furrow opened up and I saw his legs still moving like they were running. One of them appeared beneath him in the tunnel with his gun trained up on us. On his ridiculously kicking legs and my head framed in the light above the tunnel, and with our guns somewhere back in the blast behind us, dropped in tangles of brush and churning soil when we first heard the full promise of the metal bird which would carry us like babies to our re-

birth. And it called to us still, deep-throated from the clearing ahead, the only sweet-voiced bird I heard in sixteen months spent in a bird's habitat.

He stared at me from below, all cruelty in the smallness of his eyes, and jerked once with his gun to indicate my movement, that he wanted me to drop to them, to fall into the earth of my own volition after willing myself to life with a will like steel doubled over. And it called, hovering gently, that it was leaving without us and we had been so close, Henry Wilder and I, to going back shoulder to shoulder and starting to drink away the memories together but alone. We had been strides away that I counted in my mind as I gazed ahead and saw the line of the blades through the bend of the trees and the mist, and Henry was already lost, his legs within their reach and no hope of pulling up and out and free.

I flooded with instinct; it moved through my body like water washing across my grave, and I kicked him, just once, a shove of my boot on his shoulder and I was running before he fell. I didn't see his face—no, I did not, or even the few hours of sleep that I now steal would be lost—just the surprised face of the underground rat below as Henry's living body hurtled toward him blocking out the sun and his arms raised momentarily above his face as he stepped back in surprise to avoid the falling man and missing, sweetly missing, me as I fled on fairy's wings to my bird.

I swear to God, though by then I was all but through to the clearing with footsteps between us that had never turned over faster, I swear to God that even above the angry wind and the cry of the copter I heard his body hit the ground. I heard it then, and I've heard it every night since. It comes to me, all echoes in hallways and rapping knuckles against wooden doors. The sound of Henry Wilder's living body hitting beneath the earth in a jungle that carried the licks of Hell's little flames on every leaf.

Janson was sobbing now, sobbing so thickly he barely noticed when the "d" went out. The underside of the key was soaked with blood from his split finger, and it stuck. He had to type a "c" next to an "l," to make a "d." He had come this far sprinting underwater through blood, and a single damned key wasn't going to stop him. He saw he was at the bottom of the last sheet of paper, and the words had slowed from a torrent to a trickle, but still they came relentlessly.

They hoistecl me up with strong arms onto my metal bircl, the angel of heaven which woulcl commancl me through the wincls ancl the rains ancl bear me home. Bear me home to the smell of hospitals with forever walls of white ancl to my mother's kitchen ancl the full breastecl sobs ancl vicarious embrace of Wencly Wilcler, a woman grayecl past the age which she sharecl with my mother to the clawn of a new sunset. Ancl they bore me on, these strong arms, to a forgotten hero's welcome, ancl to half paracles where they clressecl me in recl, white ancl blue. Because that's what I was. A

The paper ran out. The stack, the whole stack was out and gone, and with all the tears gone from his eyes, all the sobs racked from his chest, Janson had a word, a single word, left stuck in his throat. He yelled once, a hoarse, frightened choke, and pushed back from the typewriter, sending it and the crates crashing to the floor. Stumbling into the hallway, he found what he was looking for, a crumpled-up page from a newspaper that was lodged in the wall beneath some pipes to keep the cold air at bay. He pulled it out and smoothed it flat on the wall. There was an advertisement on the back side with some blank space at the top, and he ripped out a small segment of the grayish-white paper and returned to his room.

He sank to his haunches and righted the typewriter, noticing, as if for the first time, the blood sprayed through it. Turning the small blank piece of newspaper to meet the keys, he typed his final word.

The weight, a weight he had been living with for so long that he felt it as a part of himself, lifted slowly from his aching shoulders. He left the word in the jaws of the typewriter and fell to his back on the mattress, the rotating paddles of the fan breaking up the neon flickers into dove-like featherings across his face and bare chest. He cried a different cry this time, a softer cry. The tears were just as resonant with pain, but they cleansed him. They fell like a late autumn snow, blanketing Janson Tanker as he fell into an exhausted sleep.

HIS FEET HURT like hell by the time he got there, but he felt better overall. Lighter, somehow. It had been weeks since the exorcism, and although he didn't have his story (manuscript), he knew that his demons were laid out on paper, and contained in words and sentences.

He grimaced when he saw the security cop, a large mustached man with neat hair flipped back at the front. He felt a wave of disgust as he recalled his "escort" to the street, the cop's meaty hand closing on his forearm. The humiliation had left a red stain on his cheeks, and the blush returned as he entered the building. He skulked past the cop, both of them pretending they did not recognize each other.

Please let him give me something for the book, he prayed. *Anything, even an option fee for the rights like Barry explained. Just don't let him give me nothing.*

The receptionist was much nicer this time, and then he was up and up and being buzzed through, once again, to the office of Adam Diamond.

He was on the phone. "I need the writing samples. Damn right I'm getting aggravated—his new script's in every office and I don't have a fucking file on him? Find them. Make it." Adam hung up the phone, shook his head, and raised his eyes to Janson's. His left hand twitched around on the desk, searching for the duo balls. "Hello, Janson. Now I'd imagine you're pretty tense so I'll cut the bullshit and let you know where you're at. When I first read your manuscript, I was a little hesitant. We have two rules right now about material: no Vietnam, no AIDS. Now your manuscript was good—I'm not saying it's not good, I'm not saying you're not a talented writer. You just have to understand that when it's all said and done, nobody wants to see another Vietnam movie right now. It's the material, it's not you."

Adam's last sentence struck Janson like a blow. Realization settled in, fluttering like a black sheet over his expectations. *It's the material, it's not you.* It echoed until it pounded in his ears. When he could finally hear again, he was not surprised to find that Adam had not stopped speaking.

"—and a more likable protagonist. I mean, are we supposed to like this guy? It's tough to sympathize with someone who kicks an old friend to the wolves, you know what I'm saying? We need more of a stud for the hero. When it's all said and done, every guy who reads this book's gotta want to be him, every chick's gotta want to fuck him. Stupid? Of course. But that's how this industry runs. It's a stupid industry because it caters to a stupid populace.

"Now don't be discouraged. This went a long way—what with it being (I assume) your first piece, and you having no professional editor. Everyone likes your style, likes your writing, just not the material." Adam leaned forward and recited, again, the phrase that he had uttered across his desk to countless writers. "It's the material, not you they don't like." It had an aged quality, the phrase, as if it had been stored in oak wine barrels, only brought out to be savored from time to time. Adam hoped it didn't sound as rehearsed to Janson as it did to himself. As trite with repetition. His fingers dug the jade balls out of their intricate case, and the chimes sang to him quietly as he spun them in his hand.

Janson was quiet. *And cool nights with stars laid out like holes clear through to heaven.* It slipped away, it all slowly slipped away like sand through an hourglass and suddenly he was pale and thin and so, so tired. His mind filled as if with the rust-tinged water from the sink in the corner of his room, and he saw his years unfold slowly before him, a series of small checks on the first Wednesday of every month, checks that stretched about three weeks wide. The town that was not a city was whisked away by the short deft movements of Adam's hands. Whisked away. And yet the city remained.

Adam saw Janson's green eyes go dull and he worried, for a moment, that he would have a crier on his hands. He shifted in his large leather chair, rolling to his left side, and casually checked the clock on his desk. It was 12:57. He had a one o'clock.

He tried to soften his voice, but it sounded effeminate even to his ears. "When it's all said and done, we think you're talented, Jaston. I will personally read anything you write. I just think you need to shift your subject matter around a little. Vietnam is out, it's old. Nobody wants to see another Vietnam film, read another Vietnam book. You know what's huge right now?"

He leaned forward, imparting a precious jewel of knowledge, a stock market tip, the secret password. Even the air seemed to wait on him as the clock on his desk moved silently to one o'clock. "Women's road movies." Adam was quiet, letting the magnitude of his pronouncement settle around the room. "They're selling left and right this year. I think if you work in that direction, with your talent, we could really go somewhere."

There was a moment of awkward silence that stretched an eternity in the distance between the two men. Janson waited for the watch to flick out from its cover. It did. Adam cleared his throat. "I'm really sorry, I've got another meeting right now." Another silence.

The bastard's going to make this difficult for me, Adam thought. "Any questions I can answer, anything I can help you with before you leave?"

"Yes," Janson said. "My name is Janson, not Jaston." He rose to his feet, running a hand up the scruff on his neck and along the ridge of his jaw. He leaned over the desk and plucked his tattered story from the other papers. A memo floated loose from atop the stack and fluttered down like a feather to Adam's desk, but neither man turned his eyes to the distraction. They kept them locked, until Adam felt that his would bruise on the hardness of Janson's. Janson squinted slightly, and Adam felt him looking over and through him before he turned.

"Oh yeah. I forgot to tell you. There's a part missing at the end of the manuscript. Maybe even just a word."

"Yeah," Janson said. "There is."

The door clicked softly behind him as he exited, and Adam's breath left him in a rush of relief. He felt better with the door between them.

JANSON WALKED OUT onto the crowded New York streets and filled his lungs with the moist New York air. Clutching his story tightly under his arm, he turned into the crowd, losing himself in the bustling sea of elbows and shoulders. It was a long walk to his apartment and an even longer walk home, and his feet ached with each touch of the concrete. The buildings rose in firm spires about him, and as his feet pattered on the sidewalk, somewhere, miles and mountains away in a lost town, a wisp of smoke curled from a country fireplace and made its way sleepily up the chimney to the darkened sky above.

Fred Menace, Commie for Hire

STEVE HOCKENSMITH

IT WAS JULY in Los Angeles, and my little one-room office was hotter than the glowing steel foundries of Minsk that were busy pouring out the molten foundation of a worldwide workers' state. A woman walked through the door, and things got even hotter.

She was dressed plainly in a brown shirt and matching slacks, with a mannish jacket wrapped around her broad shoulders. Steel-toed boots covered the sturdy feet at the end of her stout legs. Her dark hair was cut severely, barely reaching her thick neck. But most enticing of all were her hands. They were big and calloused, the hands of a woman who wasn't afraid she was going to break a nail when she wrestled the controls of production from the withered claws of the bourgeoisie.

I was in love.

"Are you Fred Menace?" she said, and she didn't purr like those soft, dime-a-dozen starlets who pop up in a P.I.'s office every ten minutes. Her voice was hard and strong, yet still unmistakably feminine. She was all business, so to speak, but all woman, too.

"I ain't Joe McCarthy," I drawled back at her.

I instantly regretted it. Cynicism is a decadent pose, a

facade of apathetic ennui that's antithetical to the committed idealism of the true internationalist. But when you're a private eye, it sort of gets to be a habit.

"Yes, I'm Fred Menace," I said, dropping the hard-boiled routine. "Please have a seat, Miss . . . ?"

She sat in one of my rickety old office chairs and locked eyes with me across my desk. She regarded me coolly for a moment before speaking.

"Smith. Mary Smith," she said. "My brother is missing, and I want you to find him. His name is John Smith. He's a screenwriter. He's been gone for four days."

No flirting, no innuendo, just the facts. I liked that. I like that a lot. I knew immediately that I was going to take the case, whether she could pay or not.

"My fee is thirty dollars a day, plus expenses," I said anyway, just as a formality.

She nodded brusquely. "Fine. That seems reasonable."

It was reasonable. Maybe too reasonable, but what could be done about it? I'd tried to organize the other private investigators in Los Angeles into a collective so that we could create a sliding scale tied to the means of our clients and the needs of each individual dick. Unfortunately, I hadn't gotten very far with the idea. The other P.I.s in L.A. don't talk to me anymore.

"Do you have some reason to suspect foul play?"

"Foul play?" Mary raised a thick black eyebrow. "I don't know. I just know that my brother has disappeared."

"Did he have any reason to skip town in a hurry?"

"Yes, I suppose so," she said, still icy cool. "But that's not John's way. He's a very brave, committed man. He wouldn't just run away."

"He wouldn't just run away from what, Miss Smith?"

That finally warmed her up a degree or two. "The House Committee on Un-American Activities," she said, spitting the words out as if they were a mouthful of rotten borscht. "John's been subpoenaed. He was supposed to testify yesterday. He never appeared."

I leaned back in my chair, my mind spinning back to the years before the war. John Smith. Screenwriter. Pinko. Sure, I remembered him now. I'd met him through the Hollywood Anti-Nazi League. He was a squirrelly little knobby-kneed guy with all the sheer animal magnetism of a paper cup. His sister had fifteen pounds on him, easy.

I hadn't seen him since 1945—six years ago. Like so many Tinseltown Communists, his passion for revolution cooled once Hitler was out and Red-baiting was in.

"I know what you're thinking, Mr. Menace," Mary said, and her voice was softer now, almost pleading. "Everybody in town knows about you. You're a proud Marxist through and through. When it comes to the fight against bourgeois capitalism, you won't back down an inch."

I knew she was stroking my ego, but what the hey, I liked it. The way her lips caressed the words "Marxist" and "bourgeois" was enough to get Lenin up out of his tomb.

"You got that right, sister," I said.

"My brother . . . he was a true believer, really he was. But he couldn't just throw away his career. He had to make a living."

"I thought you said he was a brave, committed man."

Her expression turned cagey. "Keep waving the flag of the proletariat from the mountaintops, Mr. Menace," she said, the vulnerability gone from her voice. "But don't think that it's the only way to serve the cause."

"What do you mean?"

"My brother planned on confronting the Committee. He wasn't going to name names. He was going to throw their fascist grandstanding back in their fat faces."

"That's what a lot of these weekend revolutionaries say.

Fifteen minutes under the spotlights and they're coughing up names like a talking telephone directory."

Mary reached into the pocket of her slacks—she didn't carry a purse—and pulled out a small wad of bills. "Believe what you like, Mr. Menace," she said as she counted out three tens. She held them out across my desk. "Just find my brother."

I looked at the money. Sometimes it really eats me up that I run a business. But until the day an American workers' state nationalizes private investigation services, what can I do? Like the lady said, a guy's gotta make a living.

I took the money.

THESE DAYS, YOU'RE not a real American—which is to say a member in good standing of the dominant consumer culture—unless you own a car. So I don't. That can be a little tough on a guy in my racket. Tailing somebody without being seen is rough enough. Tailing them when you're relying on the Los Angeles public transit system is next to impossible. But I manage.

After picking up a bus from Wilshire to Culver City, I hitched a ride with a fruit truck and a moving van before hoofing it the last twelve blocks or so to 545 Venice Boulevard—the home of John Smith, screenwriter. It only took me three hours to get there.

Some Hollywood types go in for shabby chic—homes where a little peeling paint and crumbling stucco add a touch of faux bohemian ambiance. But the rotting wood and weed-choked yard of Smith's little bungalow weren't there for show. His place was just plain shabby.

I let myself in with the key Mary had given me—her stubby, muscular fingers brushing my tingling palm all too briefly—and headed straight for the refrigerator. I didn't hope to find any clues there. I was drenched with sweat and

I needed a cold beer. And I found one. Property being theft and all, I felt free to help myself.

Beer in hand, I gave the place the once-over. It wasn't exactly neat—dirty plates were piled up in the sink, clothes were scattered across the floor, the sheets on the pull-down bed looked like they hadn't been made since the Battle of Stalingrad. But I didn't see any signs of a struggle. A plain, wooden dining table was wedged into one of the bungalow's dark corners. A typewriter sat on it next to a stack of white paper and a dictionary. I sat down at the desk and tried to put myself in the mind of John Smith, hack. I stared at the typewriter, searching for inspiration. I didn't have to search long.

The typewriter wasn't empty. A small wedge of white was still wrapped around the cylinder. I pulled it out. It was about a third of a sheet of typing paper, ripped. Somebody had been in a hurry to pull the page out of the typewriter— too much of a hurry. I read what was on the paper.

D'ARTAGNAN
Thou hast erred, fiend! At this moment, Athos nears!

CARDINAL RICHELIEU
Ahhh, ridiculous rubbish, I vow!

Zontak strikes Richelieu with the butt of his ray gun, sending him to the floor.

ZONTAK
Earth scum!

CARDINAL RICHELIEU
(cowering)
A terrible mistake, I declare!

ZONTAK

No, I g

That was it. For a second there, I considered dropping the case. A writer this bad needed to stay lost for the good of mankind. Then I remembered his sister. And her thirty bucks. And my rent. I slipped the scrap of paper into my jacket pocket and got back to work.

Somebody had nabbed Smith's screenplay, but they hadn't done a very thorough job. Maybe they'd left even more behind. I leaned over Smith's typewriter and pushed down the shift key.

Bingo. The typewriter ribbon was still there. I carefully removed it and put it in my other pocket. Then I turned, ready to nose around some more.

I didn't get far. Before I'd taken two steps, I heard voices outside. Someone was walking up to the front door.

"So this guy was some kinda pinko?" voice number one said.

"Not a pinko—a Red to the core," voice number two replied gruffly.

Voice number one I didn't recognize. Voice number two I did. I started looking for a place to hide.

I threw myself on the floor and slid under the bed just as the front door opened.

"Not locked," said voice number one.

Voice number two—a.k.a. FBI special agent Mike Sickles—just grunted.

The two men stepped inside.

I began sweating worse than Henry Ford at a union rally. Sickles and I have a little arrangement: If he doesn't see me, he doesn't shoot me.

I was anxious to keep my end of the bargain. But if Sickles or his flunky looked under the bed, this comrade would be headed to the big workers' paradise in the sky.

"Pretty lousy dive, ain't it?" said the first FBI agent.

"I dunno," Sickles replied absently. I could see his big feet moving slowly toward the sink, then to Smith's desk.

He needed new shoes. "Makes my place look like the Ritz."

The other agent moved over to the desk next to Sickles. "Say, what's that?"

They stood side by side for a moment, silent.

"Nothing," Sickles finally pronounced. His feet moved in my direction, then suddenly swiveled.

I braced myself. His weight came down on the flimsy bed frame like the Battleship Potemkin. The mattress sagged under him, pinning me to the floor. A bed spring poked my back. Somehow I stayed quiet.

"You think he skipped town? Maybe the country?" Sickles' partner asked.

"Could be," Sickles mumbled. "Dirty Reds. Turn on the lights and they scatter like roaches."

"So what's our next move?"

"Well, there's that producer he was working for—Dominic Van Dine. We should lean on him a little, see if he knows anything." Sickles leaned back and sighed. The spring gouged my back like a shiv. "Tomorrow."

"Tomorrow? Why tomorrow?"

Suddenly the crushing weight on my back was gone. I could breathe again. Sickles' scuffed shoes shuffled away from the bed toward the door.

"Because I've got an itch to play the ponies today, knucklehead," Sickles said. "And Dominic Van Dine's not going anywhere."

The other agent followed Sickles out the door like the loyal lapdog he was. I waited a minute, just in case Sickles was toying with me. There's not much to do when you're stretched out underneath a bed, so naturally my eyes started to wander. Having a rat's-eye-view of the place gave me a whole new perspective.

I caught sight of a bright yellow ball on the floor under Smith's desk. I slid out from my hiding place and groped under the desk for it.

It was another piece of paper, balled up tight. I flattened it out.

It was notebook paper from an oversized steno pad. Covering it top to bottom, back and front, was a list of scribbled words. It started with "t" words: tacky, tantalizing, tardy, tedious, tempting, tender, terrible, tiresome, etc. Then the list switched to "m" words, then "i" words, "d" words, "n" words and finally a few "g" words.

I folded the list and stuck it in my pocket. There would be plenty of time to puzzle over it later. Right now, I had to get moving.

So Sickles was going to visit Smith's producer tomorrow. Good. That meant I could drop in for a chat today. But first I wanted to pay a call on an old acquaintance of mine—a safecracker known as Barney the Bat. He had good fingers and tight lips and bad habits. He owed me a favor.

I left Smith's bungalow and started looking for a ride.

ABOUT FOUR HOURS later, I was standing in front of Dominic Van Dine's house in West Hollywood. I'm using the term "house" a little loosely here. It was actually something halfway between a house and a mansion. It was big alright, but it had the wide, flat roof and squat, squashed look of those ultra-modern boxes they've been throwing up all over Southern California since the war. I figured at least three families could live in there comfortably. And after the Revolution, they would.

I rang the doorbell. It played the first five notes of "We're in the Money." That would have to change, too. Maybe it could be set up to play the Internationale.

The door opened just enough for a head to poke out. It was a good head, if you go in for long, golden locks of purest sunshine and big, blue eyes like two bottomless lagoons and soft, sensuous lips just waiting to be kissed and kissed hard.

Me, I don't cotton to blonde bombshells. The only bomb-shells that strike my fancy are the ones that will free the proletariat from the shackles of wage slavery.

Her baby blues devoured me. "Yes?" she said, caressing the word, making it sound more like an invitation than a question.

"I'd like to speak with Mr. Van Dine," I replied flatly.

"He's not home today. But I'll tell him you dropped by, Mr . . . ?"

"Menace," I said. "Fred Menace, P.I. I have a feeling Mr. Van Dine *is* home today. And I have a feeling he *will* speak with me once you scoot your pampered caboose in-side and tell him a private dick's nosing around asking questions about John Smith and the House Committee on Un-American Activities."

She didn't bat an eyelash—which was a good thing, since her eyelashes were so long and heavy batting one around would probably hurt somebody. "Wait here, Mr. Menace," she said.

Her head disappeared. The door closed. I waited.

A minute later, the door opened again. "Come inside," Blonde and Beautiful said, holding the door just wide enough for me to slip into the house. I had to brush against her lightly as I stepped inside. B and B smiled. "Follow me." She turned and walked across the foyer toward what looked like a study.

I followed. I had an unobstructed view of B and B as she moved. I could have charged admission for a view like that. She had curves, lots of them, just the way a pencil doesn't.

But such decadent sensuality couldn't hold my eye. I was more interested in the dimestore opulence of Van Dine's home. Glass chandelier and scuffed tile in the foyer, a faded Diego Rivera print on the wall, imitation mahogany desk and shelves in the study, row after row of dust-covered books that had never been read and never would. Van Dine was making a stab at class that wouldn't fool a poodle. Everything was fake. I took another look at Miss B and B, wondering how much of her was real.

"Please make yourself comfortable," she purred. "Mr. Van Dine will be with you shortly."

She left the study, closing the door behind her. It's every working man's right to do a little freelance redistribution of wealth, so I took her advice, pouring myself a cognac and lighting up a cigar I found in a box on the desk. I was just leaning back in one of the room's ridiculously overstuffed chairs when the door opened and a middle-aged man greeted me with the kind of welcoming smile hungry spiders flash at fat flies.

"Ahhhh, I'm glad to see you're making yourself at home," he said. He closed the door behind him and walked over and offered his hand. "I'm Dominic Van Dine."

I shook his hand without bothering to rise. "Fred Menace."

"Yes, yes. I've heard of you, Mr. Menace," he said as he slipped behind his desk and took a seat. The chair he sat in was about four inches taller than any of the other chairs in the room, making him seem a bit like a kid in a high chair. Except this kid was fifty-something years old, had a Vandyke, and was wearing a red silk smoking jacket. He looked like Leon Trotsky pretending to be a debauched playboy. "People call you 'the Red detective,' correct?"

"Some do."

"You know, I've always thought there was a movie in that. *The Red Detective.* It would make a good title, don't you think? Communist sympathizer, private eye. Explosive. Ripped from today's headlines. It would be perfect for Brian Dunleavy."

He was a producer all right. Nobody in Hollywood would put a plug nickel in a picture like that. But he thought he could snow me with visions of movie stars and royalty checks. I blew a big cloud of cigar smoke up over my head. "Sounds boffo, Mr. Van Dine," I said. "But I'm only interested if you get Paul Robeson to play me. And I want a Russian director. Is Sergei Eisenstein still alive?"

Rigor mortis set in on Van Dine's smile. "So you're looking for John Smith," he said, his tone suddenly brittle.

"Why, yes, I am. How did you know he's missing?"

"Because I've been trying to find him myself. He's working on a script for me. Production's set to begin in three weeks. If he's left the country because of this witch-hunt in Congress, I need to know."

"This script Smith's working on—it wouldn't be a Three Musketeers picture, would it?"

Van Dine's eyes bulged out so far I thought they were going to hop out of his face and slap me. "Yes. *The Three Musketeers Versus the Moon Men.*" He blinked, and a curtain of false calm dropped over his features. "Have you seen it?"

"I haven't just seen it, I've read it," I replied nonchalantly. "Well, not all of it. It's not done yet. But enough to know that it stinks."

I was trying to shake things up a bit, and it worked. I shook up a bona fide earthquake.

"I don't care if it stinks," Van Dine said. "A man in my position can't afford to care. I've got actors signed, costumes and sets being made, a studio that wants this picture in theaters by Thanksgiving. 'Stinks' or 'doesn't stink' doesn't enter into it." He smiled his spider smile at me again. "I would be very interested in knowing how you got your hands on a copy of that screenplay, Mr. Menace."

The fly smiled back at the spider. "It was handed to me wrapped up in a ribbon."

A moment of silence passed before Van Dine realized that was all he was going to get. He chuckled and reached toward the cigar box. "Despite your reputation as a revolutionary, I see you're really just a businessman like the rest of us," he said. He stuck a cigar between his curled lips and lit it with a gaudy, faux crystal lighter. "You expect to be compensated for your efforts. Of course. I can make it worth your while to bring me the script."

I took a big puff on my own cigar and tried to blow a smoke ring toward Van Dine. All I got was a misshapen cloud that fanned out over his desk. It turns out I'm not as good at blowing smoke as I thought.

"You've got the basic idea," I said. "Except I don't want money. I want your help. You use your industry connections to open some doors for me, help me find Smith, and you'll get your script."

Van Dine nodded. "I understand." He pushed a button on an intercom set on his desk. "Miss Shapely, send Mr. Grey in, please. I'd like him to have a word with our guest." Van Dine leaned back in his chair and blew a smoke ring of his own. It was a perfect circle that floated up toward my head like a dirty halo. "My assistant Mr. Grey will get you started. He's the last one of us to have seen John Smith."

As he was talking, the door opened behind me. Before I could turn to see who'd entered, a sudden, crunching bolt of pain shot through my skull. I came to my feet clutching my head and spun around to see a hulking man in a dark suit that could barely stretch itself around his massive body. He was standing behind my chair with a blackjack in his hand and a look of surprise on his broad face.

"I'm not your usual soft-headed gumshoe," I spat at him. "I've got a head harder than Siberian granite. It's going to take a lot more than a love tap from a blackjack to—"

Another explosion of pain echoed through my head. I looked over my shoulder. Van Dine stood behind me, the crystal lighter in his hand. It was smeared with blood. My blood. I laughed bitterly.

"Careful there, Van Dine. You're going to break your

pretty bauble trying to use it as a nutcracker. Next time, try a—"

A heavy weight crashed into my back, sending me spinning to the ground. Mr. Grey had smacked me with a chair.

This time I shut up and stayed down.

I passed out, too.

LAUGHTER ECHOED THROUGH my mind. It was John Smith, giggling maniacally.

"Smart boy, aintcha?" he said. "A real smart boy."

His head tilted back as he let out another roar of laughter, and suddenly his face was frozen, the mouth open wide. Lightbulbs twinkled in his hair, and a neon sign flashed on and off on his forehead. FUNHOUSE, the sign said. The wind began to howl, and I was pulled screaming into Smith's huge, oval mouth. The wind stopped, replaced by the clanking of chains and gears. I found myself strapped in a cart, jerking through the darkness one tug at a time. A spotlight stabbed through the gloom to my right, pinning Dominic Van Dine and his apelike lackey Mr. Grey in a harsh cone of light. They stared at me with huge, multifaceted eyes that sparkled in the light like diamonds. Poison glistened on their fangs. Another spotlight snapped on to my left, revealing Mary Smith dancing the tango with a black bear. A third light broke the dark directly in front of me. In its glare, I could see Sigmund Freud juggling monkeys. He was dressed up like Carmen Miranda, with a tight skirt and fruit piled high on his eggy head. "Talk, smart boy," Freud sang to me. "Wake up and talk."

"Wake up," I sang back dumbly. "Talk."

"That's right. Wake up and talk, Mr. Menace."

Something about hearing my name caressed so obscenely swept the visions out of my mind. I blinked hard and shook my head. A wave of nausea washed over me, but when it passed I could see where I was.

I didn't like it. I was in the center of a small, dank, dungeon-like room, sitting in a chair, my feet strapped to the legs, my hands tied behind me. A single lightbulb hung a few feet above my head, blinding me with its bright, un-filtered light.

Dominic Van Dine and Mr. Grey stood a few feet away, watching me. Van Dine leaned in close and smiled. "So you're back among the living at last. Let's see how long that lasts. Mr. Grey."

Van Dine moved back, and his gorilla stepped forward. I heard a sharp cracking sound, and my head jerked to the side. Pain knocked on the door of my addled brain. It forced its way inside and made itself at home.

I'd been slugged on the jaw. Hard.

"I hope ya' like them apples, smart boy," Grey said in a wheezy, high-pitched voice. "Cuz I got me a bushelful."

There was another crack, and my head jerked again. The pain in my brain had company.

"Alright, alright! Enough with the rough stuff," I barked with as much force as I could muster—which wasn't much considering the blood in my mouth and the ringing in my ears. "Why don't you ask me some questions already?"

Grey glanced over his shoulder at Van Dine, who looked thoughtful for a moment before nodding his head. Grey moved away, rubbing his knuckles.

"Very well, Mr. Menace. Let's see if any more 'rough stuff' is necessary," Van Dine said. "Tell me where your copy of the script is."

A new sensation joined the party in my skull. It was hope. If there's one thing a guy needs when he's been tied to a chair by people of less-than-sterling virtues, it's leverage. Or a free hand and a .45. I was happy to have the leverage.

"Why are you so desperate to get your hands on that script?"

"Mr. Grey," Van Dine said blandly.

Grey stepped toward me, a smirk on his heavy, simian face.

"Hold on there, King Kong. You don't have to bother," I said to Grey before he could belt me. I looked past him at Van Dine. "You were going to remind me that you're the one asking the questions here."

"Exactly. How did you know what I was going to say?"

I tried to shrug. "I've been to the movies."

At this point, Monkey Man got tired of all the talk and slugged me anyway.

"Buddy," I said to Grey after my head stopped spinning on my neck like a top, "I realize that you're just a humble working man trying to survive in this dehumanizing Darwinian jungle we call the capitalist system. But one day you're going to find those knuckles of yours jammed down your thick throat."

Grey turned to Van Dine. "He just threatened me, right?"

Van Dine nodded. "That's right."

"That's what I thought."

Grey raised his fist. It was time to use that leverage, but fast.

"I'll give you the script."

"Wait!" Van Dine snapped.

Grey unclenched his fist and backed off. He looked disappointed.

"I'm glad you've decided to be reasonable, Mr. Menace," Van Dine said. "Now tell me—where is it?"

I licked my lips. I was about to see how much leverage I had. "I'll do better than tell you. I'll show you. If you untie me and let me out of this rat-hole."

That got a good chuckle out of Van Dine. "What kind of

fool do you take me for? I don't even know for certain that you really have a copy of the script and I'm supposed to let you walk out of here and stir up who knows what kind of trouble? I think not."

"I think so. I'm guessing you sent your primate playmate here over to Smith's bungalow to grab the script. But Mighty Joe Young didn't get the job done. He left a copy of Smith's script behind."

"Awww, applesauce!" Grey broke in. "There wasn't no other copy. I looked all over."

I graced Grey with a pitying smile. "But you didn't look in the right place, Cheetah. This copy wasn't sitting around, nice and neat, double-spaced on white paper. It was inside the typewriter."

"Phooey!" Grey spat. "This is a buncha bunk."

"Shut up, you oaf," Van Dine snapped. His oily confidence was dripping away before my eyes. "You're talking about the ribbon," he said to me.

I nodded. "That's right. Everything John Smith has typed for the last week or two or even three, who knows? It all hit that ribbon. And it's still there, just waiting for someone with the time and the patience to get it. In fact, I've got a friend—a friend with very bad eyes and very, very sensitive fingers—who's going over that ribbon right now. I gave it to him just before I came here. I'll bet he's half-way through the script by now."

Van Dine stared at me. Or, more accurately, he stared through me. I could practically see the wheels in his mind turning, spinning faster and faster like pinwheels. And then they stopped.

"You have failed me, Mr. Grey."

"What? Don't tell me you believe this two-bit gumshoe," Grey protested, crooking a thumb at me.

"You know the penalty for failure," Van Dine replied

coldly. His left hand slipped down toward one of the big silk pockets of his smoking jacket.

Fear twisted the thick flesh of Grey's face. "No! Don't!" he cried. "Please!"

"I'm afraid you leave me no choice."

Van Dine pulled out his hand slowly. In it was a slip of thick paper.

"No screening pass for you this weekend," he said. "If you want to see—" He glanced at the paper, then began tearing it up. "—*Bedtime for Bonzo,* you'll just have to wait a month and pay your fifty cents like the rest of the little people."

Grey's whimper turned to a snarl as he whipped around to face me. "This is your fault, shamus! I'm gonna—"

"Untie him," Van Dine broke in.

"But—"

"I said untie him!"

Grey glared at Van Dine for a moment before moving his bulky body behind me and fumbling with the ropes. My hands came free first. Within seconds, they were stinging with the pain of a thousand needlepricks as the bloodflow returned. A moment later, my feet felt the same way.

"Smart move, Van Dine," I said, buying time while my hands and feet recovered. "You're playing this the right way."

"If he double-crosses us, kill him," Van Dine said to Grey.

Grey leaned in close to my ear. "With pleasure," he said.

But the pleasure was all mine. Grey was a sloppy man. He'd done a sloppy job searching Smith's bungalow, and now he'd done a sloppy job untying me. He'd merely loosened the rope around my hands without bothering to take it away. And when he stuck his big ape head next to mine, it was simplicity itself to take that rope and wrap it around his neck.

It took all my strength to stand and take three steps forward, dragging Grey behind me. He toppled over the back of the chair. The chair pitched forward, and Grey came with it. The chair came down with a crash. Grey came down with a snap. His body went limp.

I turned my attention to Van Dine—but he was gone. For the first time, I got a good look at the room around me. Several black monoliths loomed in the darkness. At first, I thought they were bookshelves. But as my eyes adjusted to the gloom, I could see that they were loaded with bottles, not books. I was in Van Dine's wine cellar.

I heard a quick shuffle-step behind me. I whirled around just in time to see Van Dine rushing me, a champagne bottle clutched in his hand.

I wanted to meet him on equal terms, but there was no time to go looking for a bottle of vodka. So I ducked. The champagne bottle cut through the air just above my head. Van Dine's momentum carried him forward, and I gave him a good shove as he moved past. He stumbled, off balance, and slammed into the nearest wine rack. He hit the ground amid a shower of mid-range cabernets.

"Defeated by the trappings of your own decadence," I said, shaking my head. "Clifford Odets would pay me twenty bucks for a metaphor like this."

Van Dine groaned from beneath the pile of bottles. I gave him a moment to reflect on his predicament before I grabbed a foot and gave it a twist. Van Dine's groans turned into a yowl. I pulled the foot—and the rest of the body it was attached to—out to the center of the tiny room.

"I want to thank you, Mr. Van Dine. You've given me the perfect set-up."

I twisted the foot again. Van Dine howled again and kicked at me feebly. I twisted harder, then let go.

"I've been tied up. Beaten. Tortured. I've got the wounds to prove it." I walked around Van Dine's cowering form until I was just a step from his head. I placed the heel of one shoe on his face and gave it just a little bit of pressure. "So anything that happens now is purely self-defense. Because I'll be the only one left to tell the story. Get me?"

Van Dine was panting so hard I could barely make out his words.

"What was that?"

"I said, 'I get you,'" he rasped.

"Good. Now I want you to tell me what happened to John Smith." I put just a little more pressure on Van Dine's face. I could feel the cartilage of his nose bending almost to the snapping point. "And I don't want any fibs."

Van Dine talked. When he was through, I slipped the rope from around Son of Kong's throat. I left Van Dine lying face down, his hands tied behind him, in a puddle of cabernet and champagne. That wasn't very nice, I know. But if he got depressed waiting for the police to arrive, he could always slurp his cares away. Anyway, I could've left him in a puddle of blood.

Upstairs, I ran into Miss Shapely. She gaped at me, stunned, from a sofa. A copy of *Film World Exposé* slipped through her suddenly slack fingers. I didn't have to be Criswell the Mind-Reader to know what thoughts were flying through her platinum-plated skull.

"Yeah, that's right, honey. All that screaming and yelling was your boss, not me."

"I . . . I . . . I didn't . . ."

"Save the smooth talk for the cops, glamour-puss." I went to the nearest phone—one of those old-fashioned gold-leaf and pearl jobs you always see Bette Davis gabbing on in the pictures—and asked the operator to give me police headquarters. Some lucky desk jockey was about to get the anonymous tip of a lifetime.

While I was waiting for the connection to go through, Miss Shapely jumped off the couch and made a beeline for the front door. I took mercy on a poor working girl and let her go.

IT WAS DARK by the time I got back to my office. That was fine. It fit my mood.

I'd been settled behind my desk all of five minutes when my client came through the door. My heart went pitter-pat. My head told my heart to get lost.

She sat down across from me.

"Have you found my brother?"

Oh, that voice. It didn't purr like a kitten. It didn't caress me like a silk glove. It chipped away at me like a jackhammer. It was a husky, no-nonsense, "¡Viva la revolucion!" kind of voice. I loved her even more.

But . . . There's always a but when you're a private dick. And my but was as big as they come.

"I've found John Smith," I said. "Up until this evening, he was in a flower bed at the home of a movie producer named Dominic Van Dine." I glanced at my watch. "By now, I'd bet he's on his way to the Los Angeles County morgue."

I watched her for a reaction. She didn't disappointment me. She didn't have one. No false hysterics. No crocodile tears. Just a cocked eyebrow and a single word.

"Explain."

I obliged.

"Van Dine knew about Smith's ties to the Communist Party. That's why he hired him to work on a script. Not because Van Dine's some kind of sympathizer. He's just greedy. Smith's past made him vulnerable: It meant he'd work cheap. But when the House Committee on Un-American Activities started tossing around subpoenas, Van Dine got nervous. If it came out that he'd knowingly hired a Red, he'd be finished in this town. So he sent a musclebound messenger boy out to collect Smith and his script. Smith told Van

Dine he *wanted* to appear before the committee. He wanted to . . . how did you put it this morning? 'Throw their fascist grandstanding back in their fat faces'? But Van Dine couldn't have that. He's not one of those studio producers. He's an independent. He has to finance his projects himself. He already had a small bundle tied up in his next picture, and a small bundle's more than a guy like that can afford to lose. So he convinced Smith not to testify—convinced him with a piece of rope wrapped around his neck."

My client's grey eyes didn't fill with tears. Sobs didn't erupt from her thin, colorless lips. Such displays would be beneath her—beneath *us*. Because we were both players on the same team. Maybe you've heard of us. The Los Angeles Reds.

"And the script?" she said.

I nodded. "Yes. The script. That's what you're really interested in, isn't it, comrade? Smith wasn't your brother. He was your stooge. And you need to get that script back to cover your tracks."

I finally saw her smile. It broke up the marble smoothness of her face, revealing the animal cunning beneath. "Yes, comrade. You recovered the copy from Van Dine's residence?"

I nodded again. "I had time to do a little nosing around before the cops showed up. I found it."

"Good. Give it to me and our work will be done."

No more nodding for me. I shook my head. "I don't think so. Not until I get an explanation."

Her face turned to stone again. "If you are a true revolutionary, you will give the script to me."

"Why don't you let me decide that? Now tell me— what's in that script that's so important?"

She shrugged with a nonchalance so transparent you'd have to call it outright chalance. "Nothing. As you said, I'm just trying to tie up loose ends."

I grunted unhappily. I don't like being lied to, even by

women I'd like to run off and make little proles with. "Then why is it written in code?"

"I don't know what you're talking about."

A deep, sad sigh rose and fell in my chest. "Nobody in this town writes dialogue that bad on purpose—not unless they've got a hidden agenda. Or maybe a contract with Universal. I spent quite a few hours on buses today, so I had plenty of time to work out Smith's system. Take the first letter of each word of dialogue, add them together and voila, it's Western Union time. But I still don't know what it all means. 'Rosenberg says no.' 'The fluoridation is working.' 'The Roswell prisoners are ill.' It's all Greek to me."

As Spymaster Mary listened to my little speech, the smile I'd seen earlier started to return. I was hoping it would be a warmer smile, a more human smile, a throw-herself-into-my-arms-and-declare-her-undying-love kind of smile. But it was none of the above. It was a smug smile.

"And it will stay Greek, for the good of the cause," she told me. "All I can tell you is this: That screenplay is the key to America's greatest secrets. It represents the accumulated work of our entire spy network here. How fitting it would have been to deliver it to our comrades overseas in the form of a Hollywood film—the ultimate symbol of Western foolishness. That can't happen now. But the script can still be smuggled abroad. With the information it holds, the Soviet Union will finally crush the United States like an insect."

Under different circumstances, I would have swooned. Mary Smith—real name Maria Smithostovovich or some such thing—really knew how to get a red-blooded Red worked into a lather. But I'm not just Red. I hate to admit it, but under the surface I'm white and blue, too.

"Since you put it like that, it's no dice, sister." I wanted to bite my tongue off with every word. Somehow I managed to keep going. "I'm a traitor to my class, but not my country. I'm not giving you that script."

I didn't even get a raised eyebrow out of her, let alone a wistful tear. She simply pulled a revolver from her jacket and leveled it at me. My heart was broken. And in a second, it was going to be filled with hot lead.

"Now hold on. We can still talk this out, comrade."

"You are no comrade of mine," she hissed back at me. "You call yourself a Communist, yet you let nationalist loyalties come between you and your duty to the revolution. I should shoot you down like a dog."

"But then you wouldn't get the other copy of the script."

"Other copy?" The barrel of the gun wavered just a bit—from my heart to my gut. It wasn't much of an improvement, but I wasn't in a position to be choosy.

"When a typewriter key hits the ribbon, it leaves an impression. And I've got the ribbon from John Smith's typewriter. Or, to be more exact, a friend of mine has the ribbon. A blind friend. I gave it to him this afternoon after I left Smith's bungalow. He's had plenty of time to go over it. I'm sure he's got the whole script transcribed by now."

It looked like my little visit to Barney the Bat was going to pay off for the second time today. Looked like that for about two seconds, that is.

"But as you pointed out, it's written in code. He won't know what it means or who to take it to—if you're dead."

What could I say? "Good point"?

She cocked her revolver. "Now give me Van Dine's copy of the script."

"Like I said, no dice. And if you shoot me, you'll never find it. Looks like we've got us a stalemate."

She waved the gun at a corner of my desk. "But isn't that the script sitting right there?" She sounded amused. At last, I'd gotten a little warmth out of her. It didn't help me feel any better.

"Well, I guess that was the dumbest bluff I ever tried to put over."

"I'll have to take your word on that, Mr. Menace." The barrel moved again. Now it was pointed squarely at my forehead. *"Das vedanya."*

I sighed again. "Yeah, O.K. So long, sister. Tell the boys in the Kremlin I said—"

A shot rang out before I could finish. I thought that was pretty rude. Not only does she kill me, but she's got to interrupt me, too. Some people ain't got no manners.

Then an amazing thing happened: The woman who just killed me toppled off her chair. The back of her head looked like a lasagna. Even more shocking—I was alive.

"Boy, am I gonna regret that in the mornin'," a familiar voice said.

FBI special agent Mike Sickles was standing in the doorway of my office, his gun in his hand. He was shaking his big, bald head.

"If I'd just waited two more seconds—*bang*. You'd have been out of my hair forever, Menace."

I wanted to say something like "What hair, cueball?" But I wasn't about to push my luck. He could still change his mind and let her shoot me retroactively. It was just a matter of how he wanted to write it up in his report.

Sickles stepped into the room and bent down over Mary Smith. He was followed quickly by the lackey I'd seen him with earlier in the day. At least it looked like the same guy from the shins down.

"She dead, Mike?" Sickles' partner asked.

"Nah, she's just hibernatin'. Now call the meatwagon, knucklehead."

Knucklehead scooped up the phone off my desk and asked the operator for the coroner's office.

Sickles waved his meaty hand back and forth before my eyes. "Hey, anybody home? Snap out of it, Menace. She scare you to death or somethin'?"

I blinked, maybe for the first time in a good minute. "Thanks," I said.

Sickles grimaced. "Don't thank me. I handed you a break because you wouldn't give the broad the script. Next time I might not feel so merciful."

"How long were you there in the doorway?"

"Not long. I only moseyed over when things started to heat up."

"Moseyed over?"

"Sure. Knucklehead and me, we were next door listening to the whole conversation. It was mighty entertainin', too. Like *The Bickersons* and *Suspense* rolled into one."

"You've got my place bugged?"

Sickles cocked his head and gave me a don't-ask-stupid-questions frown. "Course not. We had tin cans pressed up against the wall."

I didn't push it. Besides, I had other questions on my mind. I nodded at Mary Smith's body without letting my eyes move that way.

"So what's her real name, anyway?"

Sickles ran his hands over his smooth, sweaty skull. He was obviously trying to decide whether or not to tell me the truth. The truth won out. What a day for sworn enemies. Around the world, cats and dogs stopped fighting and kissed each other on both cheeks.

"Beats me, Menace," Sickles said. "I didn't even know she existed until she walked in here and started gabbin' with you."

He saw my confusion and went on. "You were the one we were following. Ever since we walked in on you at John Smith's place." He cracked a cock-eyed smile. "You were hidden O.K., but that beer you were guzzling wasn't. It was still cold when we came in. All the windows were closed and bolted, so I knew somebody was still in there somewhere.

I dropped a little hint about Dominic Van Dine—the next stop on my hunt for Smith—then stepped back to see what happened."

I grunted with grudging admiration. "You amaze me, Sickles. You played this one better than Machiavelli himself."

Sickles glared at me. "He some kinda Commie?"

I shook my head.

He allowed himself a half-smile. "Yeah, well, maybe. Only if I'm so smart, how come I've got boils on my butt the size of grapefruit from all the hours I spent sittin' in the car today? I tell ya', Menace, tailin' you is like getting in a high-speed chase with a three-legged turtle."

What a charming development. Sickles and I were so thoroughly bonded now he felt free to tell me about his carbuncles. I stifled a sigh.

My eyes drifted back to the body of Miss X, the Unknown Communist. I hadn't killed her, but I hadn't helped her, either.

What kind of revolutionary was I? What kind of detective was I? What kind of man was I?

"All that is solid melts into air," Marx wrote. That was me alright. Fred Menace, the Red Detective, had melted. I'm just vapor now, part of the smog that chokes L.A.

I still charge thirty dollars a day plus expenses, though. Even vapor's gotta make a living.

The Dying Artist

SHELLEY FREYDONT

EVERYONE LOVED WATCHING George MacCready die. His dying was unparalleled. No one could clutch at his throat quite like George MacCready. No one's knees buckled with the gusto of George MacCready's. Nor could they sprawl on their backs, legs quivering ever so slightly, as they gasped their final breath. Only for him would the ermine trim of a velvet tunic kiss the floor as he fell, then twine about his outstretched legs like fingers of a foggy night.

No one could die quite like George MacCready. And no one enjoyed watching him die more than I.

For you see, George MacCready learned how to die from life. Not his life, for that would have been pointless—to die in order to perfect the business of dying. George MacCready learned by watching others die.

The first time I saw him watching death was after a performance of *Macbeth*. I left my seat in the stalls and hurried outside to wait for the great expirer at the stage door. MacCready had just exited the theatre when a cry rose up from the street behind us. MacCready lifted his head, listening. Then he strode down the alley, brushing away his admirers as if they were mere coal dust. I joined the others who followed in his wake.

When next I spotted him, he was standing among a

crowd that had gathered to watch two constables pull a boy from beneath a hansom's wheels. His body was mangled and crushed. A strange gurgling sound arose from within him. His head rolled and spurted blood with equal abandon. But his legs. Ah. His legs hopped around much in the same manner of that other great expirer, Edwin Forrest.

It seems only fitting that EF would pattern his death scenes after the snuffing out of a lower class soul. EF was all blast and bombast in his dying. His whole body would spasm and his arms shoot heavenward. Then he would fall and roll along the floor, his legs kicking out with as much grace as that poor urchin who lay in the street. EF didn't understand finesse in dying.

I watched MacCready study that poor boy—draw closer and peer over him until the constable eased him aside. And all the while, I watched him watching. I could tell the moment when he dismissed the boy's demise as beneath his study.

After a time, he sauntered away and I sauntered after him. Watched him walk along the cobbled street, opening and closing his fist just as the boy had done.

He stopped outside the Three Bells Oyster Bar and lifted his hand to the gaslight. Slowly, he contracted his fingers and spread them out again. He shook his head once, dropped his hand and went inside to dine.

I followed him. Studying the man who studied the dying. I leaned against the wall nursing a mug of flat beer while MacCready sat at a table for one, and a plate of oysters was placed before him. I watched him lift the corner of the napkin, shake it, and fold it into his shirt collar. Then his hand made a graceful arc toward the plate. In one deft movement, his fingers closed around a shell, while MacCready stared into the oyster's face.

Slowly he brought it to his lips, all the while his fingers throttling the shell. My own throat closed against the beer I had been drinking, and I had to spit out the mouthful onto the floor.

Later that night in my rooms above the Majestic Theatre, I practiced bringing my hand to the light, clenched and unclenched my fingers as MacCready had done. When finally I put out the lamp and went to bed, I was filled with a sense of purpose that I had never known before.

Every night, I watched him from the stalls; *Lear, Hamlet, Richard III, Othello.* It didn't matter, though I liked his Hamlet best. Afterwards, I would wait with the crowd at the stage door until the great man appeared. Sometimes he would catch my eye, and a thrill would shoot through me. I felt his kindred spirit. And I was sure he must have felt mine.

I took a job with the theater company as a bit actor just to be near him. To witness the discovery of some new detail— the tiniest nuance that could be incorporated into his death scenes. I, too, learned to die—as a Roman soldier, a Capulet, a Nubian slave. Even when I wasn't dying, I stood on stage watching MacCready take his final breath. Night after night, I watched him as a lover might watch his beloved. I stayed in the wings after my exits, went early for my entrances, practicing his gestures as he performed them on stage.

During the breaks at rehearsals, I engaged him in conversation on his method of acting, staying away from the manner of his deaths, lest he become wary of my interest.

On our days off, we would find ourselves at separate tables at the oyster bar. It wasn't so unusual. The oyster bar was a few doors away from the theatre entrance. I didn't care much for oysters. I was always waiting for a grain of sand to crunch between my teeth, sending a shiver down my spine. But I ate oysters, platefuls of them, just to be near my mentor.

Sometimes, we would meet by chance in the street. Then he might invite me for a pint and I would take my place at the bar next to him, soaking up his presence. We would part with a hearty handshake and go our separate ways.

Only my way was his way, though he never knew it. I would follow, unseen, behind him, down the streets of the town, marking his unending quest for the perfect death scene that would enhance his own.

We witnessed (separately, for he never knew I was there) several deaths during that time, but none out of the ordinary, everyday kind of expiration. A rather amusing tumble down a flight of steps by an old washerwoman, unmentionables flying out in all directions as she bounced and squealed to the bottom. Nothing that could be used. A straightforward heart failure at the entrance of the Mercantile Bank. It was over before it began. Disappointing, since the fellow looked to have some promise about him.

Once we stumbled onto a woman that was hemorrhaging on the stoop of a tenement building. MacCready stopped to watch. I wanted to run to him. Tell him not to waste his time on so paltry a dying. He should witness the death of great men of wealth and intelligence and make them his own. But before I could budge from my hiding place in a doorway across the street, MacCready had moved on.

Every night I followed MacCready through the streets, stopping when he stopped, taking up his pace again. And while MacCready searched for death, I was perfecting my own dying. Not that it was noticed. I was only one of many bodies, roiling about the stage beneath the clang of metal swords and the clop of horses' hooves made by the beating of a spoon against a wooden barrel just off stage left.

I don't remember when I first began to formulate my plan to aid MacCready in his search for the perfect death. Winter was coming on, and the nights were damp, with the wind cutting like a knife around the corners of buildings. I didn't mind being uncomfortable, but I could see that MacCready did. His wanderings became shorter. The stops into pubs more frequent. The stay longer. I waited outside, stamping my feet and hugging my hands beneath my armpits to keep warm. Impossible for me to join him in the pub, and I was afraid that if I went into another, I would miss his exit.

And then one night, a Saturday I think it was (we had just finished *Twelfth Night,* a dreary play as it had no commendable death scene in it). MacCready wandered in the direction of a derelict section of town. Prostitutes huddled in doorways and opened their cloaks just long enough for a man to catch a glimpse of their wares, then wrapped up tight again. Drunks lay on pillows of hoarfrost, neither alive nor dead. Windows were shuttered tight, only an occasional wink of light escaping through the chinks. I couldn't understand why MacCready had chosen this section of town to look for death.

I found myself wishing he would go home. There was no one here that was worthy of the great MacCready's talent.

A carriage pulled to a stop ahead of MacCready. He slowed his pace. I slowed mine and watched. The carriage door opened and a man in evening dress virtually fell from the top step.

And suddenly I knew what MacCready was about. Clever MacCready. A gentleman might die comfortably, undramatically at home, eased into death by a scented handkerchief dabbed at his brow, his fluxes and vomitings carried discreetly away. But here in the streets, where no one knew him, he must enter death with the kicking and squirming of lesser men.

The man tossed coins toward the driver then wove toward a door in one of the nondescript brownstones that lined the street. After a moment, the door opened and light and noise spilled into the night air. The man entered and the door closed behind him leaving the street once again dark and silent.

I have to admit that I was a little irritated at my idol. I thought I knew what he was hoping for, but it would be a long cold winter before we might stumble across a robbery or murder if a man insisted on alighting from his carriage at the very door of his assignation.

The carriage pulled away and, like a great curtain, revealed a quartet of men coming our way. They were a gay bunch, drunk and singing and lumbering toward me like a giant multi-headed beast. MacCready was intent on the closed door of the brownstone and didn't see when they knocked me into the gutter.

It was soon after that night that I began to carry a metal pipe beneath my coat as I followed MacCready through the murky streets.

Several weeks passed and winter was full upon us. Snow fell by the bucketfuls on the stage and in the streets, turning to frozen sheets at the least hint of thaw. The audiences were sparse and there was talk of closing the theater until the weather broke. Everyone was at sixes and sevens trying to prepare for unemployment. MacCready alone seemed to be unconcerned about the possible closing. He needn't be. One week of his salary could pay the rest of us for a month.

I was already stretched as far as I could be stretched and could ill afford to lose even a week of work. I loathed the thought of giving up my cozy rooms, humble though they were. Not that I spent much time in them being in the theater all day and wandering the streets with MacCready at night. But what I feared most was the loss of MacCready if the theater were to close.

One evening as I lay dying during the second act of an undistinguished melodrama, I felt eyes upon me. Somehow I knew they were MacCready's. I fought the urge to exalt in that supernumerary death, but I forced my attention inward and died with great subtlety. I was very pleased with how it went. As soon as the curtain rang down and the slain cleared the stage at a run, I made sure that I would pass by MacCready who was, indeed, standing in the wings.

The briefest tip of his chin as I passed sent me into raptures. I had been good, really good, and MacCready had acknowledged my performance. And in the glow of that euphoric mood, I determined to do something to show my gratitude.

The snow was drifting down as we left the theater that night. The sky was clear above the roofs of town; the stars twinkling like diamonds on a black velvet drop. Once again MacCready went to the lowest neighborhood. I stayed farther behind than usual, for I had a twofold purpose.

He led me to a dismal street, the lamps of the streetlights broken into jagged icicles, the gas turned off to prevent an explosion. But the moon was high, casting a magical light over the whole. The night wore on and I was suppressing a yawn when I saw my purpose weaving down the street toward the square. A fine, tall man, with top hat, walking stick, and an opera cloak that swirled about his ankles. A young nob out slumming, alone. It was perfect.

The man stopped and looked about him, then peered up and down the street as if looking for someone. I felt my stomach clench. God, that he should be meeting his friends on this corner. I wanted to shake my fist at the heavens, Lear-style. My blood raced with impatience; the metal pipe weighted down my chest. At last, he took up his perambulation again, and he drew slowly nearer.

MacCready was nearly a block ahead of me now. If this drunken sot didn't hurry, it would be too late. I pressed into the shadows, my back feeling the impressions of a wrought iron gate that led into the square. I could hear the fellow muttering to himself.

My gloved hand closed around the pipe and drew it ever so gently from my coat. Poised, calm, fully into the part I was about to play, I lifted the pipe over my head. His shadow passed in front of me, and the pipe crashed into his head. His top hat flew to the ground. He staggered and tried to turn, the blood spraying in all directions. I repeated the blow to his back, knocking out his wind, making it impossible for him to cry for help.

There was no time to observe my handiwork, but I was almost certain that he had received a mortal blow, and there was no time to give another. I backed through the gate into darkness and cried out, "Murder, murder by the square." I only paused long enough to see that I had aroused the attention of several passersby who further sounded the alarm. I raced through the square and exited on the far side, then made my way back to where a crowd had already formed around the fallen man.

And yes, there was MacCready. I could see him well. I could not see the dying man, but I watched MacCready's hand clutch the air as he followed the man's progress toward darkness, and my hand followed his. His shoulder twitched, and I knew he was internalizing every detail, and so did I.

A constable came and pushed everyone aside. I was very nearly caught out because I had lingered until the last moment so as not to miss one tiny part of MacCready's mesmerizing performance. He turned suddenly and I fairly threw myself into the entrance of an ale house to avoid his gaze.

I was sweating beneath my overcoat, and I was covered with blood. I dared not stay where I could be seen, though I craved an audience. I skulked away into the night, assaulted in turns by fear and exaltation.

That was the first of three studies in dying that I arranged for MacCready. And while he was watching death, I was watching him. Breathed as he breathed, lolled my head as he lolled his, sighed just as he sighed.

Over the weeks, his death scenes became more powerful and so did mine.

I had never been adept at learning parts. A line here and there I could manage, but more than a few together left me stammering and sweating with confusion. Ah, but my dying was exquisite. Even the little ballet girls surrounded me with their fluttery eyes and hands and layers and layers of tulle, tittering over the beauty of my recurring death.

And so what are words? Hardly anyone can remember a speech heard the night before. But long after the words are forgotten, the memory of the twisting, writhing, agony of death remains.

I have studied diligently, learned everything I could. Endured cold, hunger, and impatience to perfect my craft. I think I've got it right now, the precise amount of quiver at the lower extremities, the languid droop of the hand as it slips from the breast or sword. The little ballet girls agree that my dying is quite as good as MacCready's.

And so I have invited MacCready for a dinner of oysters in my rooms. And he has accepted. I am so very honoured. I've bought a special Madeira wine for the occasion and have popped the cork this very minute. I pour it out and hand a glass to MacCready. He holds it to the light, smiles his appreciation, and takes a sip.

I offer him my best armchair and he sits down. We discuss the theater, and I pour more wine. I'm careful not to drink too much. A host must keep his wits about him.

There's a knock at the door and I go to open it. It's the boy from the oyster bar with a platter piled high with oysters. He places it on the center of the table I have pulled away from the wall.

Now here's the tricky part. The piece of stage management upon which everything hangs. I finger the little packet of powder in my waistcoat pocket. It will take a mere second, if MacCready will only turn his back.

I ask if he would mind fetching the wine bottle from the side table behind me. I only need the briefest moment. But my hand turns stiff and MacCready is back with the bottle before I can extract the packet from my pocket.

My hands are sweating just as they do when I have a speech to deliver. I have lost my chance, there may not be another. And yet, here is MacCready asking where he might relieve himself. I point to the screen which conceals the commode.

He nods his thanks and carries his wine glass with him. I cannot believe my good fortune. My fingers are suddenly nimble as if released from a spell. A mere tap of the paper onto the largest oyster, and I place it directly in front of the place where I intend MacCready to sit. I refold the paper and push it back into my waistcoat just as MacCready returns.

I offer him a chair. He sits. I go to the other side of the table and pull out my own chair, and MacCready realizes he has left his wine glass on the window sill next to the convenience. Would I be so kind as to retrieve it for him.

Of course, I say. Anything for my dear MacCready.

When I return, he has already tucked into the oysters, the shells are piling up on the tablecloth. I sit down and reach for one of my own, my eyes on MacCready. I watch his side of the plate of oysters disappear as I eat. I don't want to miss a moment of the great man's death scene.

And then it begins. His hand goes to his throat, his eyes bulge. I feel my own eyes bulge in response. He begins to shake and I shake with him. His eyes are on me now, and mine on his. His body convulses, racked with spasms. I feel his pain. I clutch at my stomach. MacCready is a blur across the table, writhing. We move together, my rhythm, his rhythm. Locked together in a synthesis of the inevitable. It is glorious, this searing, horrible joining. We cry out and our voices commingle over the table.

He pushes to his feet. His chair crashes to the floor. I try to stand, but the pain is too intense. I grope for the table, but my fingers are frozen claws that will not move. He leans forward, peering into my face. He is swaying over me. But no, it is I who am swaying, not MacCready. I whose entrails are on fire.

I see my hand rise in the air, the fingers grasping. MacCready's fingers grasp the air across the table, mimicking mine.

My hand clutches my throat. MacCready clutches his. My throat is an oyster shell, being ground and crushed and seared with flame. I can not think. I fall back in my chair, watch my legs jerk and twitch beneath me. Fire engulfs me. I hear the rattle of someone choking. I try to scream but my throat closes on the sound. My arms flail outward, then fall limp at my sides. I search for MacCready, my eyes darting about as if controlled by another. At last they latch onto his solid figure and I understand.

Across the table, MacCready is watching . . .

On the Bubble

ROBERT LOPRESTI

THE PHONE RANG and Mitch Renadine jumped a foot. Running across his living room—how had the phone gotten way over *there?*—he felt as if he were moving in slow motion.

It was his mother calling. "I can't talk long, Ma. I'm on the bubble."

"On the bubble? And what does that mean?"

Mitch sighed, not in the mood for a long explanation. "The network is setting up its fall schedule. Some shows have been cancelled. Some have been renewed. But they haven't decided on *Muldoon* yet. We're waiting to hear, one way or the other. Out here that's called being on the bubble."

She was outraged. "But your show is in the top twenty, Mickey! How could they think of canceling it?"

Good old Mom. She was the only person in the world who still called him Mickey. Also, the only person who thought *Muldoon* was a hit.

Yes, the show reached the top twenty—sometimes. But it followed a program that usually made the top ten. That meant millions of people hit the remote control as soon as they saw Mitch's smiling face. The network assumed that *Muldoon* was doing as well as it was only because of the strength of its lead-in.

"I love you, Mom. I'll call you as soon as I hear anything." He hung up and checked for messages. No one else had called. Damn.

Mitch stepped out onto the deck and took a deep breath. There was a beautiful view and he had paid dearly for it. Maybe he shouldn't have spent so much on a house up here in the hills above Laurel Canyon, living like he was already an established star, instead of a near-unknown fronting a rookie TV show.

But damn it, he had paid his dues. He had parked cars, painted houses, done a thousand auditions for a thousand bit parts. And now that he had a starring role—as a tough but caring police lieutenant—why shouldn't he *live* like a star?

Like Lou Garlyle, for instance. Mitch looked down the mountain at his neighbor's estate. Lou lived down the hill, yes, but *his* home had a pool. And Lou had a live-in servant.

They were stars on the same network, but at opposite ends of their careers. Lou had come to TV after twenty years as a movie star when a string of high-budget bombs left his career flailing. For Mitch, TV was a first chance, for Lou it was a last one.

Now they were both on the bubble, waiting to see if their shows would be renewed. Who would sink when the bubble burst, and who would float.

He wondered where Lou was now. Most days when his neighbor wasn't working he sat by his pool, drinking.

"I'm so glad these little fellas are back in style," he had told Mitch one night as he poured another martini. It was the tail-end of one of Lou's many parties and they were sitting beside the pool. "A few years ago if you ordered anything but wine or spring water in this town they pegged you for a drunk."

Lou *was* a drunk, of course, getting smashed almost every night. But to his credit, it had never affected his work.

Some critics suggested that that had to do with the quality of his work at the best of times, but you couldn't argue with good box office and Lou had always had it. Always, that was, until a few years ago, and then he had flawlessly made the jump to television.

"That's the thing about styles, Mitch," he had continued. "They can change overnight. Take you and me, for instance."

"What about us?"

"We're actors of a certain style." Lou waved a hand. "I don't mean a school of acting or anything fancy like that. I mean that you and I are both born to play action heroes. Nobody is ever going to ask jokers who look like us to play Hamlet." He bent over and picked up a big knife, one of at least a dozen of the ugly things he kept lying around his house.

Lou's show was called *Cutting Edge* and he played a body-guard whose favorite weapon was a throwing knife. He swore he kept them around the house for practice, to look more natural in front of the camera, but Mitch thought it was mostly a publicity gimmick. The photographers loved to show him sitting by the pool, flashing that famous smile and dangling one of those lethal-looking blades like a toy. Mitch had also noticed that at the end of the evening when Lou wanted his guests to leave he could always start tossing blades around.

"How does that relate to style?" Mitch had asked.

"Sometimes action heroes are fashionable. Sometimes sensitive weepy guys are more popular. Four years ago my show went on the air and caught the tail end of the last macho revival. Now your show is fighting against the tide."

Lou had sipped at his drink. "The big trend today is the so-called reality programming—quiz shows, talk shows, lock-ten-people-in-a-room-and-see-who-cracks shows. That's what we're up against, Mitch. You have to know your enemy. And know who your friends are, too."

"Who has friends?" Mitch retorted. "This is Holly-wood."

The older man laughed. "Touché. Let's say, at least, that you can have allies. People who share a common goal." He tossed his knife casually in the air and it came down a few inches from Mitch's sandaled foot. Mitch made a point of not moving his leg. "Damn. Sorry."

If we're such good allies, Mitch thought, *why don't you retire and get the hell out of my way?*

THAT HAD BEEN back in December, not long after *Muldoon* was picked up for the second half of the season. Now it was April and Mitch was still waiting to hear if the show would be stay on for another year. And Lou was in the same boat.

His agent called to announce every new blip on the radar. "They cancelled *Lucky Day,* Mitch."

"That's great, Si."

"Maybe. Not if they're gonna reshuffle the whole Monday schedule. And they renewed *Puppet Wars.*"

"That's bad."

"Not necessarily. It's an 8 P.M. show, so it's not likely to push us out of our slot."

Slots. Twenty-two hours of prime time. The most expensive real estate on the planet. *Muldoon* owned one hour of Monday night on one network—if they could hold on to it. A show like his employed almost one hundred people. Not just the actors the audience saw, but the writers, the producers, and hell, even the caterers and floorsweepers had a reason to want this show to keep going.

But nobody needed it more than Mitch. When the network stars you in a drama they are resting a million bucks or so on your shoulders. If you drop it down the tubes you needn't hold your breath waiting for them to offer a second chance.

The next day Si called back. "They renewed *Brain Trust,* and *Money for Nothing.* And they're moving *Ike and Alice* to Wednesday."

"My head is swimming. Who's left on the bubble?"

"A couple of comedies, plus *Muldoon* and *Cutting Edge.* I gotta tell you, Mitch, I think there's only one slot left for a drama."

Mitch stood on his mortgaged deck and looked down the mountain at his neighbor. A washed-up movie star, floating around his pool without a care in the world.

"The Veep says we'll hear by the end of the week. You hang in there, Mitch. It ain't over yet."

AND NOW IT was the end of the week and Mitch was still hanging in there, waiting to hear whether he was going to spend the next year collecting paychecks or unemployment. Driving his Lexus or driving a taxi. He thought about calling Lou to see if he had heard anything, but something made him hesitate.

And suddenly he could see Lou, back from wherever he had been. He was out by the pool in his swimming trunks, shouting instructions to Marta, his maid. Mitch watched as Lou stood at the shallow end of the pool, carefully settling himself into his float—not a raft so much as a blow-up chair, complete with indented spaces for a cell phone and a shaker of martinis—and paddling out into the center of the pool to bask in the sun.

What did his neighbor have to look so cheerful about?

The cell phone rang. Mitch yanked it to his ear and heard a familiar Latino accent. "Mr. Renadine? This is Marta. Mr. Garlyle wanted me to invite you to a party tomorrow night."

Mitch felt a cold fist cramping his guts. But, in spite of what some of the critics said, he was an actor. His voice came out as cheerful as a talk-show host. "Terrific, Maria. What's the occasion?"

"The network just renewed his show for another year. Isn't that wonderful?"

"Wonderful," Mitch agreed. "I'll be there. Tell him to have plenty of champagne."

Then he hung up and began to plan a murder.

WHEN MITCH WAS a kid he had always felt he was destined for something. Not being a TV star necessarily, but something that would take him out of suburban New Jersey. When they studied *Julius Caesar* in high school and the teacher talked about the concept of fate he felt as if he was at last being introduced properly to someone he had known for years.

Fate, yes. The destiny that shapes our ends.

Until that phone call from Marta homicide had never crossed his mind. He was certain that was true. And yet he had prepared himself for it so perfectly. Or had fate done the preparing?

Mitch was not what Hollywood called a spiritual person but, hell, when ten thousand handsome faces apply for the same acting job there must be someone or something spinning the wheel and deciding who wins and who loses. And that force had given him the tools he needed to win now.

Look at what he needed to know—and *did* know. That Lou would be drunk and probably asleep on his float all afternoon. That Marta would be preparing dinner. That she couldn't see the pool from the kitchen.

And if you argued that he only knew these things because, at some level, he had been preparing for a murder all these months, well, what about buying this house in the first place? Surely that had been fate, preparing him for this day, when he had to climb off the bubble before it burst.

Mitch opened the cabinet under his sink and pulled out a box of disposable latex gloves. He had worn them several times on the show when Lieutenant Muldoon was investigating a crime scene and, having seen how useful they were, he had brought home a box for cleaning up messes.

Was that preparation again? Or fate? He wondered about that as he tucked a pair into his jacket.

The trail through the brush between his yard and Lou's had been worn long before he moved in. Mitch had taken it a dozen times when his neighbor invited him for a drink, so he knew that no one could see him as he moved through the thick brush. At the bottom of the hill he carefully pushed the vines out of his way and looked out at the pool.

Lou was lying on the big red float, his head tilted a little to the side. He snored softly. The martini shaker was in place but the cell phone was not. That was perfectly reasonable. After all, he had already *gotten* the phone call he cared about, the call Mitch had waited for in vain.

The inflatable float drifted slowly clockwise. Soon Lou would be facing away from him.

Mitch knew that no one could see the pool from the neighbor's houses. Except from his, of course. He put on the disposable gloves.

It was easy to open the gate in the fence and step quickly onto the cement surface around the pool. The pool skimmer—a long pole with a hoop and net on the end—hung on the fence not far away.

Mitch was a strong man, built to play an action hero, as Lou had pointed out. It only took a moment for him to pick up the pole, bend over, and tuck the hoop end under the edge of the float and drag it slowly toward the edge of the pool.

Good ol' Lou didn't even stop snoring.

When the back of the float was almost against the edge of the pool, Mitch put the skimmer back in its place on the fence. A knife lay on the nearest table; one of the throwing knives Lou so loved to show off with.

Mitch picked it up in a gloved hand. He took one last look around and saw only the beautifully cared-for estate and the back of Lou's house. No one in sight.

The idea was simple: make it look as if Lou had thrown the knife in the air and it had landed in the float. What was so odd if a drunk, known for tossing knives around, and not a good swimmer, sank his own float and drowned?

Sure, it might have raised a few eyebrows back in Plainfield, New Jersey, where Mitch grew up. But this was Los Angeles where the coroner heard stranger stories practically every day, most of them having to do with the show biz crowd.

Detective Carl Chaney, the cop who served as technical adviser on *Muldoon,* had told Mitch they even had a name for it: HRD—Hollywood-Related Death.

Mitch studied the float carefully. A knife coming down from the air would only make one cut, so he had to get it right the first time.

Kneeling at the pool's edge Mitch took a deep breath. *My career or your life,* he thought. It was an easy choice. He raised his arm and brought it down hard, cutting through the fabric near the left edge of the float.

His one fear had been that the float might burst, making enough noise to wake Lou, but the fabric tore instead, letting water slide in gently. The float had several compartments so it would take a while to sink, but sink it would.

Mitch smiled and dropped the knife. It slipped, shimmering, to the bottom tiles. He gave the back of the float a gentle push, nudging it toward the deepest part of the pool.

Moving quickly now, he slipped back through the gate and up into the brush. When he reached his own property he risked a look behind him. The big red float was in the middle of the pool, listing badly to the left.

Mitch walked over to the compost bin at the far end of

his yard. A few months ago the president of his studio had gotten a bee in her bonnet about organic food and suddenly everyone who worked for the studio had to install one of these damned smelly rat hotels on their property. Now this one was finally earning back its cost. He reached in, still wearing his lab gloves, and shifted the organic muck around.

If by any chance the police suspected him of being involved in Lou's death they would look for evidence that he had taken the trail down to Lou's property. And that brought up something else Detective Chaney had told him about: The Law of Contact.

The Law of Contact was the basic rule of crime-scene technicians. You go somewhere, you leave something behind. You touch something, you take part of it with you. If the techies started looking for signs of him beside Lou's pool they might find them, but could they prove they were from today and not from his last visit, a week ago? Mitch didn't think so.

And if the found Mitch's lab gloves in his own trash, well, the compost easily explained their use, and he figured the organic waste would make it harder to find a trace of chlorine. As a bonus, turning the compost over would explain any vegetation from the trail that stuck to his clothes.

A year of playing Lieutenant Muldoon had taught him well. *Prepared* him well.

Once he had disposed of the gloves, Mitch went back into the house. He forced himself to walk at his usual pace, acting the part of a man without a care in the world.

Only after he poured himself a Scotch did he walk out onto the deck and casually glance down toward his neighbor's property. The float had upended and he saw Lou's arm come out of the water, flailing. He was trying to hold onto the float, but the thing was slippery and unstable and Lou was far too drunk to control it.

Goodbye, old man. You should have retired.

He strolled back into the house. The message light was

blinking on the answering machine. No doubt it would be Si calling with the bad news. Well, the network was going to have to rethink their schedule now, wouldn't they? All of a sudden they had a big hole to fill. He touched a button.

"Hey, Mitch baby, this is Si. I just met with the network guys. Most amazing thing. Turns out we calculated wrong. They had decided to cancel *Muldoon* and *Cutting Edge.* That's right, *both* of them. Make more room for those damned reality shows.

"But hold onto your hat, kid. Your neighbor changed their minds. He convinced them that what they needed to do was run the shows together. He said you're a better lead-in for him than that doctor show they have on now. The network decided he might be right. They're gonna move *Muldoon* to Saturday night, run it between *Private License* and *Cutting Edge.* Call it "Men of Action Night." Maybe do some crossover episodes.

"You better buy ol' Lou some champagne. He's keeping your show alive. Bye bye, babe. We'll talk later."

Mitch could hear something down the hill. He knew it must be the wail of a distant siren, but to him it sounded more like the bursting of an enormous bubble.

Slap

MAT COWARD

I USED TO rob women, which is how I got into acting. I don't do it any more because it is morally indefensible (I'm talking about robbing women), but it was a good living for a while. I could easily make five hundred pounds in a day, if it was a good day.

Women in the UK spend twelve million pounds a year on anti-cellulite treatments. There is no such thing as an anti-cellulite treatment, it is a scientific impossibility, but British women spend twelve million quid a year on them. And that is only the tip of the icebird. If you factor in the billions spent on women's magazines, makeup, slimming pills, and so on, you begin to get a picture. I'm not saying all women are stupid, but enough are stupid that robbing them is never hard.

For my targets, I would choose women who were not attractive. I didn't choose out-and-out hounds, because they have nothing to lose—no dignity, no delusions—and so they might possess confidence. I chose women who were *just* sufficiently the right side of ugly so that they'd spend every minute of their lives in a preoccupying torment of hope. I picked them up on the pavements outside busy shops in the West End. I knew the location of every CCTV camera in Oxford Street, believe me.

I would approach them smiling. This in itself is confusing.

Do they know me? I'm a good-looking young man, quite tall, slim . . . I'm smiling at them, but if they knew someone like me surely they'd remember? I'd walk right up to them, my smile not crazy, just confident, and then when I got up close enough to smell their breath, still smiling, I'd slap them across the face with my open hand. Right hand. Big swing. Exactly the way a woman slaps a man when he tries to kiss her in an old film.

Her hands go to her face. Naturally—instinct. She can't help it. If she's carrying anything, she drops it. If her bag is still on her arm, I take hold of her wrist and slide the bag off. Then I run, and I can run fast. Along the way I dump the bag; I only ever take cash. Cash is safest.

A woman of that sort—even once she's recovered from the astonishing shock of being slapped like that, almost certainly for the first time in her adult life, and by a handsome young man who was smiling at her—it's going to take her several seconds before she can bring herself to react. To raise her voice, scream, say something, tell someone. Get her breath back. Five seconds, maybe more.

And in five seconds, believe me, I'm in a different borough.

ONE SATURDAY AFTERNOON during this period of my life I was in a pub in Fitzrovia, having finished work for the day, and the old potman was telling me about some mate of his who'd died the previous day during an operation to remove a brain tumour. "Well, that's the thing about brain tumours," I said. "You can't live with 'em and you can't live without 'em."

The potman laughed and said, "I don't know, son, the things you come out with!" Then he went back to collecting pots and I went back to reading the international news in the paper.

I was reading about an attempt by lawmakers in Arkansas to force teachers to declare atheism or agnosticism along with previous criminal convictions on job application forms, when a female voice said in my ear: "Five hundred quid. Half now, half after, and more to come." Of course, I looked up and smiled.

She had one of those chafed faces, as if her midwife had buffed it up the middle with a sander. It was pink, with invisible eyelashes, a bent-back tip to the nose, and a moist, quivering chin which was trying to hide behind her Adam's apple. She didn't look like the kind of woman who would have the confidence to say the sort of thing she'd just said, to a handsome young stranger. She was about forty and rather thin. No man had ever looked at this woman lustfully, unless it was her own father. Still, though stereotyping can be a useful tool it makes an unreliable master.

"Have a seat," I said, standing up and touching her elbow. "Gin and tonic, is it?"

"Thank you," she said. "No ice."

I fetched the G&T for her and a particular beer for me. There are great beers from around the globe available easily in London, if you care enough to look for them.

"Do you," she said, "ever watch daytime TV?"

"My life has never yet been that empty of purpose," I admitted.

She sipped her drink. "Fair enough. Well, in that case, you won't have seen a cable show called *Libby's Place.* It's presented by a young woman, a very forceful young woman, named Libby Priest, and it takes the form of an audience-participation discussion show, centred around a number of invited guests."

"Not really my sort of thing. I prefer history shows."

"Really?" She looked at me over her glass. "Any particular period?"

"All periods," I said. "There is only one period."

"The past, you mean?"

"The present," I said. "From then to now, it's always the present when it happens."

She nodded. She wasn't that interested. "Well. *Libby's Place* can, itself, be quite educational. The invited guests that I mentioned just now, they aren't experts or celebrities—they're ordinary members of the public. Extraordinary ordinary members of the public. People to whom things have happened, or people who have done things, and they tell Libby about those things, and then the audience—"

"Rips them apart?"

"Discusses what has been shared."

I finished my beer, and she went to fetch another round. I watched her at the bar, and noticed that not one man looked at her for more than a second, not even the barman. When she returned, I said: "You work on this show?"

"I'm an assistant producer. Specifically, I source guests."

"You *source* them?"

"Yes."

"And you wish to *source* me?"

"Yes."

"And you'll pay me?"

"Yes."

"And there's a hell of a lot more to it than that?"

She smiled. When she smiled, her face looked like something her worst enemy had done to her and then said, *"What's the matter, can't you take a joke?"*

"Yes," she said. "There is more to it than that."

And that's how I got into acting.

SHE TOOK ME out to dinner, to a Thai place, and at the table she showed me her business card and her building pass because she didn't want me to have any doubt about her genuineness. Her name was given on both documents as

Annabelle Inwood. She didn't ask for my name. It was Jez Becker, but she didn't ask for it.

"The trouble is," said Annabelle, as I ate my curry and she poked at hers with a fork, "there aren't enough genuine weirdoes to go around. This isn't America. In California—I worked there for a while—all you've got to do is open the office door, grab the first half dozen people you see, and you can rely on at least four of them being completely eccentric and perfectly telegenic."

"But not over here."

She shook her head. The motion failed to dislodge the piece of rice which was stuck to her chin. "We are handicapped in this country by an archaic belief that personal grief should be kept private. We're getting over it, slowly, but in the meantime—well, there are a lot of shows like mine to be filled."

"A lot of guests to be sourced."

"Exactly."

"I don't think five hundred pounds is very much."

"Ah," said Annabelle. "But, like I said, more to come."

"I don't see how," I said. "Surely, once I've been on the show once . . ."

"You'd be surprised. Provided we handle things subtly, and make good use of lighting, makeup and so on, it's perfectly possible for one guest to appear on many shows, over a period of time."

"And nobody notices?"

She put down her fork. "Look, this kind of program—people don't exactly give it their full attention, you see what I mean? It's something you watch while you're doing the ironing, or feeding the baby."

"Or applying wrinkle cream."

She snorted, and the piece of rice finally fell from her chin. "Yes, sure, whatever. So, if a guy called Joe comes on the show and says he's just got engaged to his sister, and then six weeks later a guy called Phil, who looks *maybe* vaguely like Joe, only without the mustache and with darker hair, says he was born a man but he had an operation to become a woman, only now he's had an operation to turn him back into a man because he dreams of being a professional footballer—well, who's to notice? Who's to care?"

I ate the rest of my meal, even though it wasn't very good, because it is morally indefensible to waste food, and then I said: "What happens when you get caught?"

"We don't get caught."

"But if you did?"

She shrugged. "Slap on the wrist from the regulators. It's not exactly genocide, is it? It's just showbiz."

We ordered coffee. "For five hundred pounds, who would I be?"

She got her personal organiser out, and flipped through it to find her place. "Okay, if you're available on Monday, it'd be a choice between 'Youth Detention Center Turned Me Gay,' or 'I Oppose Legalising Drugs Cos It'd Put Me Out Of Work.'"

I stirred my coffee. "I wouldn't like to be a drug dealer. It might cause complications."

"All right then, you're a queer ex-con. Shall I pencil you in?"

"You have the money with you?"

"Half the money, like I said. Got it right here." She tapped her trouser pocket. "I never keep money in my bag."

"Very wise."

"I know," she said. She smiled.

I smiled back. "I might be available on Monday."

"Good."

"Sure. I think I might be." I called the waiter over and ordered a brandy. "But I'd like to know why you chose me."

She shrugged. "Spur of the moment. I saw you in the pub

and thought you looked like the right kind of guy for the job."

"What kind of guy is that?"

"Guy like you. You see, what we're looking for are people who are convincing, imaginative, talented—and reliable."

"You could tell all that from looking at me in the pub?"

She picked up the bill, glanced at it, put it back in its saucer and laid her credit card on top of it. "I've watched you working," she said. "You're a good actor. The way you smile at them."

I felt like someone had slapped my face.

I DID THE Monday gig. Annabelle gave me a basic script—more of an outline, really—around which I improvised. That's what it's called, in acting, when you make stuff up: improvisation. Elsewhere, it's just called making stuff up.

The whole thing took maybe two hours. I met Annabelle at a cafe around the corner from the studio, she took me in through a back way, and a makeup woman dusted my face with powder and gave me a shirt to wear. My own shirt wasn't in character. The shirt she gave me was pink and had sweat stains under the arms, though it smelled fresh enough.

I was the first performer (or "guest," as they say) on the show. I sat on a tubular steel chair and told Libby Priest my sad story. Once or twice she asked a question which I might have known the answer to, but didn't, so when that happened I just cried and said I didn't want to go there. The sad story had a happy ending ("I've learned to accept myself for who I am, and to be my own best friend"), which pleased everyone. The audience offered me various pieces of advice, all of them flatulent. I didn't see anything of Libby Priest before or after my performance, which suited me. I don't care for artificial women.

My work was clearly judged a success, as Annabelle

sourced me for several other roles over the next couple of months. I appeared, under various guises, not only on *Libby's Place* but also on a spin-off program named *Libby's Out,* in which the studio audience ruled the set in Libby's absence (a far superior format, in my view).

I wore spectacles of various types, and disposable coloured contact lenses during all my performances. Sometimes the makeup woman, or some other functionary, would ask me to take them off, saying they weren't in character, but I always refused. I am no more immune to vanity than anyone else in showbusiness, but I'm not stupid. When you slap a woman's face and take her handbag she will remember your eyes, if nothing else. She may be wrong about your height, build, beard, or clothing—and casual witnesses, by-standers, will be even less accurate—but she will remember the eyes, for sure. And the smile, of course.

It was a decent living; not as rich as robbing had been, but good enough and much easier. I had no regrets about leaving my old line of business. The work came naturally to me. In essence, all I needed to know was when to smile and when to slap. Indeed, life in general can be reduced to this formula, as any study of history will quickly prove.

The TV life is an enjoyable one; drugs, food, and alcohol (sex, too, no doubt, if that is one's preference) are all freely available, and available free. I indulged carefully. It's always best to be careful.

Every now and then—and constantly, at the back of my mind—I wondered what Annabelle might have meant when she said she'd seen me working. I didn't ask her. If she didn't want to say, I wasn't going to ask. You have to know when to smile.

I was confident she couldn't have been one of my victims; she was quite the wrong sort for me. Besides, I have a good memory for faces. I can remember them all. Not the features, as such, but there was a particular look I used to scan for when I was working as a robber, something of the woman's spirit displayed on her face, and that look always stayed in my mind.

She could've been a witness, it was possible, but if so how had she tracked me down? I am a fast worker, and a fast mover. Just chance, maybe—she remembered me, and then saw me again some time when I wasn't working. Possible. London's a big city, but the West End is a small town. It could be coincidence. Or doggedness, or professional assistance.

At one point, after we had been working together for a few weeks, Annabelle asked me if I was still working. I pretended not to know what she meant, and tried to change the subject. We were in the studio canteen, speaking quietly.

"Doesn't bother me if you are," she said. "As long as it doesn't interfere with the show."

The way she spoke it seemed almost as if she was encouraging me to continue in my old trade. I thought that perhaps she found the idea of it exciting, in an indecent way. There are such women.

ONE BRIGHT DAY, the traces of makeup sticky on my face, I was exiting the studios in the direction of the Underground— my work as a Bus Conductor Who Converses with Dead Passengers done for the day—when I felt an unsought and unwelcome female touch on my elbow.

"George? Or whatever your name is. Can I have a word? It's about money."

I turned, to greet an ordinary-looking young woman of the sort who makes a great effort with herself which doesn't quite come off. I was about to smile at her, when I realised that I knew her face. I frowned. I had to hope that a frown, and the sunglasses, would be enough to save me.

"I'm in a hurry," I said. "I have another appointment."

"OK, sure, I'll make it fast. My name's Miranda—hi."
She put her hand out for shaking. I didn't take it. She took a
few nervous breaths and stuck her snubbed paw in her back
pocket. "You're in a hurry, I know. Sorry. Here it is: I admire
your work, and I—"

"My work?"

"You *own* the screen. I'm not kidding. And at the same
time, you're so versatile that a casual viewer wouldn't recognise you from one part to another. I, obviously, am not a casual viewer."

How much could I trust the sunglasses? How much
would the frown protect me? "I have to go."

She scrabbled at her handbag—a small thing, chic or
childish depending on your viewpoint, its strap looped sensi-
bly over her right shoulder and under her left armpit—and
pulled out a business card. "Give me a call. Okay? I think we
could do good business together. But don't tell Annabelle,
whatever you do! She'll kill me—probably kill you, too."

She got in her car and drove off, and had hardly vanished
around the corner before Annabelle was upon me. Her face
was blotched red and white, her teeth were exposed, and her
hair frizzed as if before a storm.

"What the hell were you doing talking to that bitch?"

"*She* approached *me*," I said, my voice considerably qui-
eter than Annabelle's. "Apparently she knows you."

"You're telling me you didn't know who she was?"

I shrugged. "Miranda something, that's all I know."

"Miranda something! Miranda *Denny*. She's one of the best
known talent spotters in TV. Or used to be. She's been off sick
for the last year, with depression or something. You're saying
you didn't recognise her?"

"I swear to you I have never seen her before in my life." I
crossed my heart and kept my face straight.

"Well, all right." Annabelle seemed calmer now. "Fair
enough. What did she want?"

"I think she wants to employ me."

"Oh, does she?" Annabelle put her hands on her hips. She stared through me, and bit repeatedly at her bottom lip. "Does she, the bitch? I'll bet she does! Oh yes, that's Miranda's style, right enough. The *bitch*."

"Well, you don't have to worry, I'm not—"

"Do you know what I think I'll do?" She stopped fidgeting, looked right into my face, her eyes glowing. "I think I'll get you to kill her."

I was aware that people in show business take their rivalries as seriously as Mafiosi take theirs, but even so I was somewhat taken aback. "Really?"

She nodded. "Yes. Yes, I think I will."

"Oh, really?"

"Yes," she said. "My mind is made up. You're to kill her, Jez."

I took off my sunglasses and wiped the sweat from my eyes. "Why would I do such a thing? Annabelle, our relationship is based on business, not friendship. I owe you no favors, I am not under any obligation to you. What makes you think I would do you such an extraordinary service?"

Annabelle smiled. "Due to blackmail. If you don't do it, I'll tell the police what you do for a living."

Did for a living, I thought, but didn't say. "Any crime I may or may not have committed in the past has certainly been a lot further down the scale than murder. Even supposing you had something to blackmail me about, and even supposing you told the police, I would sooner be given community service for a lamb, than jailed for life for a sheep."

"Do this for me, and you won't have to do either."

"I'm not a killer," I said. "I've never killed, I never will kill."

"We'll see," she said over her shoulder, as she left me standing alone by the back door.

"We *won't*," I called after her. And I meant it.

On the other hand, and there was no gain in denying this to myself, Miranda's death would be convenient and reassuring, should it happen suddenly and soon. She hadn't recognised me today, I was sure of that, but if she saw me in the unadorned flesh for any length of time she certainly would. If she saw my eyes, and my smile.

I had no direct evidence to support my fear. I had never actually been recognised, on a tube train or in a pub, by a shop assistant or a tourist, but I was convinced I was right: Surely, no woman I had robbed could easily forget the slap, or the smile. Or really, I mean, the both of them together.

Even now, perhaps, Miranda's memory was tickling her, whistling at her, trying to attract her attention. If so, eventually she would turn me in. If not, then she would pursue me, for professional reasons, and *then* she would remember me . . . and turn me in. And if she didn't, it seemed now, Annabelle was quite willing to do so, the moment she feared she was losing control of me. Really—ideally—I could do with being rid of both of them. I felt it was time for me to move on, in any case. I was already thinking of sidestepping from people shows into, maybe, commercials. An actor must constantly seek to stretch his craft.

I couldn't kill, though. Killing people is morally indefensible. Still, if Annabelle hated Miranda so much, perhaps I wouldn't have to.

"I'LL DO IT. But I'm going to need two things. First— money. A lot of money."

"That's no problem," said Annabelle. "Say, five thousand?"

"Say ten." I sipped my beer. She hadn't touched her G&T. If the tonic was as flat as the beer, I didn't blame her. The pub we were in was a filthy dump, not the sort of place either of us would normally frequent. Which was why we'd chosen it, of course. "In advance."

"Ten. Okay. Sure, I can go to ten."

"And the other thing," I said. "The other thing I need. You've got to come with me. When I do it, I want you there."

She grinned. "What, the big, brave ladykiller needs Mummy to hold his hand?"

I wondered again what she knew about me, and how. "I need *Mummy* to be in it with me. In as deep as I am. I'm being frank with you here, Annabelle. When this is done, we'll never meet again, and whatever it is you think you have over me will be cancelled out by what we'll *both* have over each other. You understand?"

She picked up her glass, fished out the slimy slice of lemon and put it in an ashtray. She put the glass down again. "I understand. That's no problem, either. In fact— yes, in fact, that'll be fine."

More than fine, by her tone. "What is it?" I said. "What is it, that makes you so keen to see Miranda die?"

With her finger, she pushed the piece of lemon around the ashtray, as if cleaning it. "We used to be close friends." She looked up at me. "Very close friends."

"I see." Such matters, though disgusting, were none of my business. "So you know where she lives."

"Better than that. I have a key."

"All right." I finished my beer, unappetising though it was. "How are we going to do this, have you thought about that? Fire, maybe?"

Annabelle shuddered. "God, no!"

I thought of making a joke about old flames, but decided it might be considered tasteless. "I understand, you don't want her to suffer. That's admirable."

"*Admirable?*" She laughed, in an unattractive manner.

"What do you have in mind, then?"

"A gun," she said.

"I see. Do you have a gun?"

"No. But I suppose *you* can get one, easily enough."

I thought about that. Yes, I probably could. Easily enough, and safely enough. "All right," I said, and it was decided.

Less than a week later, we sat in Annabelle's car outside the Bloomsbury mansion block which contained Miranda's flat. The gun was in the pocket of Annabelle's raincoat. She'd suggested that she keep hold of it until we were inside, in case I needed both hands free to prevent Miranda from fleeing. I'd agreed to that—though only after what I hoped was a convincing show of reluctance.

I was confident that once the action was underway, Annabelle herself would do the shooting—and do it with pleasure. Whenever she spoke to me of Miranda, her ugly face burned with anger. Despite what she'd said in the pub, it was clear to me that *she* was the one who needed the reassurance of company on this outing.

I had told her that I had plans for disposing of the body which it would be better for her not to know about. In fact, the thing being done, I planned to leave the scene with all the considerable speed I could muster. Afterwards, Annabelle either would or wouldn't be arrested. An ex-lover would, no doubt, be an obvious suspect. If she was, she wouldn't tell the police about my part in the business since that could only serve to upgrade a case of manslaughter between lovers to one of conspiracy to commit murder. To be on the safe side, I would disappear for a while, until it seemed prudent to emerge, during which time I thought I might indulge in a little plastic surgery. Nothing major, a small nose job, which I hoped would enhance my employability as well as my anonymity.

If she wasn't arrested, then so much the better. I'd still be free of her, since I could in theory turn her in at any time. Either way, I'd be free of Miranda.

We paused on the landing outside Miranda's door. Annabelle handed me a large envelope containing my money. I checked it quickly, and nodded my acceptance. She inserted the key in the lock, more noisily than I had hoped. Before turning it, she said: "Here goes. Give us a smile for luck, Jez."

Miranda Denny stood before us, in the center of her hallway, completely naked.

"Grab her!" said Annabelle, closing the door behind us.

I did so, overcoming my natural revulsion. She didn't struggle. I heard Annabelle breathing heavily as she came up the hallway towards us. "Get ready," I said, and I threw Miranda away from me with all my force, so that she bounced off a closed door and slumped onto the carpet.

I saw a flash of light in front of me, and then a nauseous pain colonised the back of my head and everything I had ever held to be true gushed out of my nose and down my shirt and onto the floor.

"YOU GAINED ACCESS to the flat by means of a door key which you had stolen from Ms. Inwood's handbag when you visited her office earlier in the day," said the detective chief inspector sitting opposite me in the little interview room. "Surprising the two occupants of the flat in bed, you became irate and irrational, ranting and saying that you were in love with Ms. Denny." He put a finger on his notebook to mark his place, and glanced up at me. "Do you deny any of this, Mr. Becker?"

I said nothing. I had said nothing since waking up in the hospital, two days previously.

"They tried to reason with you, and were able to persuade you to retreat as far as the hall. But then you pulled out a handgun and said that if you couldn't have Miranda, then no one could. You raised the gun and made as if to fire it at Ms. Denny. At this point, however, the lady's partner, Ms. Inwood, hit you over the head with a Chinese dog."

"With a *what?*"

He checked his notes. "Sorry, a *china* dog. An ornament, which had stood on a side table. So, you have got a tongue after all?"

I regretted my involuntary outburst, and said nothing more. There was very little I could say. Perhaps forensic evidence would have assisted me, but the police would only look for it if they had reason to—and I could not afford to give them that reason. The truth was useless to me, not only because it wouldn't have been believed, but because, if it *was* believed, it would only place me in a deeper hole than the one I was already in. I did not wish to face charges of robbery and conspiracy, in addition to those already proffered against me.

"The gun went off as you fell," said the policeman, "causing a single round of ammunition to enter the wall of the hallway at about head height. No one was hurt as a result of the shooting."

I didn't listen to the rest of what he had to say. I used the time instead to ponder upon the disgraceful nature of the events which had overtaken me. It was a mortal outrage that I should face time in prison for attempted murder, when I had never in my life attempted to murder anyone, and for firearms offenses, when I had never in my life handled a firearm of any sort (except very briefly, and then only as an intermediary). It was a mortal outrage that an ugly woman and a plain one should conspire to take such disproportionate revenge on a man whose own crimes were minor—and who had, in any case, renounced his former trade, and reformed of his own free will.

My life ruined in exchange for a purse full of cash: Yes, I would call that disproportionate. I would call that a mortal outrage. I would call that a slap in the face of justice.

Break a Leg

STUART M. KAMINSKY

KENNY KILLED THE wrong poodle, but it really didn't matter.

You see Kenny wanted to kill Pinky of Ben Burke and His Amazing Poodles. Pinky was the star. Pinky was also getting old which was one reason Kenny didn't feel so bad about poisoning Pinky's food bowl. Actually, there were signs of arthritis or something in Pinky. Kenny was doing the dog, and himself, a favor. At least he would have been had Pinky eaten the food instead of Puddles. A mistake. But it was enough to cancel Ben Burke and His Amazing Poodles from the show which moved Kenny up a notch on the bill.

He still had a long way to go. Ben Burke would be replaced. That couldn't be helped, but given Goobernick's budget and the dwindling number of vaudeville houses and smaller audiences, the replacement would be someone cheap, a whistler, an alcoholic comic with a big tie, a juggler.

It was 1924. Movies were taking over the vaudeville houses. First the movies were an act like the seals and the dancing Bronte Sisters, but now the movies were taking over and the old acts were becoming filler for Valentino, Keaton, and Garbo.

Kenny was an optimist. Vaudeville wouldn't die completely. People would get tired of mimes in black and white on a flat screen. There'd always be room for a few good acts like Kenny Poole the Dancing Fool. Actually, Kenny's real name was Pemerhoven. But except for Sid Scrimberger and his Musical Seals no one Kenny knew in the business had kept their real names. Of course the Scrimberger name had been associated with seal acts for who knows how the hell many years but that didn't really matter to anyone anymore. Besides, if things went right, the Scrimberger seals wouldn't be belching or playing their horns or balancing their balls or clapping their fins much longer. The two of them would be dead. There had once, not long ago, been three Scrimberger seals. Old Betsy, who was temperamental and fat but the smartest of the trio, had swallowed a light bulb and died.

The problem was simple. Goobernick had told the eight acts on the traveling bill that three of them were going to have to be cut and soon. It didn't take The Amazing Weller, the World's Greatest Mind Reader, to figure out that it was the last three acts on the bill that would go. Even having moved up one with the death of the poodle, Kenny was still only one act up from the bottom. For him to survive, three of the top five had to meet with accidents.

They were in Chicago, the Rialto on State Street. Winter. Blizzard. Small houses. Almost not worth selling the tickets, but the show goes on, the girls stripped. Strippers didn't belong. Burlesque was taking over. Burlesque and moving pictures. Vaudeville was talent, real talent like Kenny's or even the dogs and seals and those cousin contortionists and people like Callahan the World's Greatest Irish Tenor who, when sober, could hit a note Caruso would envy.

Kenny sat in the diner across from the Rialto. Cars went by. The snow was blowing at an angle. Getting heavier. Cold out there. Mug of coffee and the sinker felt good.

Kenny had bills to pay. No relatives he could turn to. If he didn't take care of himself, who would? Nobody, that's who. Like Bert Williams sang, "Nobody." Kenny liked to dance to that song, self-taught, making it all up. Now Bert Williams's songs were too slow for the audiences. Kenny was so far down the bill that by the time they got to him, the people on the other side of the lights were looking at their watches. Kenny had to dance fast, smile, do tricks like the once over with a double click. He had to use taps. Make noise. Eccentric dancing wasn't enough anymore. Kenny could only do the one-legged rollover to his right, but nobody knew or noticed.

Kenny got older. He had to dance faster. Smile more. That was okay. What the hell, but if he were higher on the bill, he could hang on, at least through the season which was just starting. No way Kenny could work in a diner like the one he was sitting in. He'd rather die. Well, not really. But he would rather kill.

It was best if it was just animals. He hadn't killed a human yet. Tonight would be the first time. He'd get backstage early so he'd be there when Vogel, the World's Strongest Human, dropped dead on stage. He'd be there so when Alf the stage manager with no teeth panicked, Kenny could say, "I'm here. I can go on."

By the way, Kenny knew that Vogel was not the World's Strongest Human. Lots of men on the circuit and in circuses and side shows and lifting logs somewhere in the woods in Norway or wherever were probably a lot stronger than Vogel. Hell, Kenny even knew two women who were stronger than Vogel.

Helga Katz who was retired now but could still hold up a platform on which sat five girls, an anvil and a fat man in a chair smoking a cigar and pretending to read a newspaper. The other woman was Marge Corsat, who Kenny preferred not to dwell on because Marge had once punched him in the chest when she thought he was getting fresh with her. That was a long time ago. Maybe Kenny was getting a little fresh wondering what it would be like to be with a woman as big and strong as Marge.

Vogel had a gut. He didn't deserve billing above The Dancing Fool. Vogel didn't do anything original except maybe for bending the two-inch pipe over his head, which he did with much grunting. Kenny knew if he examined that pipe he'd find Vogel had done something to it. Besides, where did Vogel get a new two-inch pipe two shows a day? Pipe cost money. He had to be using the same piece of pipe over and over. It had probably gone soft in the middle five years ago.

Kenny checked the clock on the wall. Time to get back. He had put the rat poison in the egg salad sandwich on Vogel's dressing table. Vogel ate an egg salad sandwich every night before he went on. Vogel had great faith in eggs. Four acts including Kenny shared the dressing room. The women had another room. The animal acts were downstairs.

Kenny had to get back to get rid of the sandwich remnants if there were any. He hoped Vogel didn't die till he got on stage. The good thing about killing Vogel was that Kenny really didn't like him. Nobody liked him. He was a grunter, a loner. He read books in German. The U.S. of A. had goddamn just a year ago beat the crap out of the Huns and here was one of them taking money from people like Kenny, good Americans. Vogel had probably been a Hun soldier, maybe even killed Americans. Kenny was performing a patriotic act. Maybe. At least he was helping one American named Kenny Poole.

He finished his coffee, dropped a quarter on the counter near the cash register, pulled his coat collar up, and went out on State Street. It was damn cold. He had seen worse. Buffalo, just last year. Snow up to your neck almost. Cold as an icebox. Colder. Six people in the audience. Where the hell had they come from? Buffalo. Kenny crossed the street almost slipping, avoiding the cars, hearing the elevated train rumble above him half a block away above Wells Street.

In the stage door. Old guy at the door sitting with a pipe

barely looked up. Kenny didn't want to be one of those old guys who everybody called Pop, old guys whose name no one ever remembered, who wore sweaters and sat at stage doors and went home to a small one-room walk-up to open a can of beans and maybe listen to Amos and Andy on the radio.

The dressing room was empty. The sandwich was gone. So was Vogel which meant he hadn't died right away. Kenny put on his costume, smoothed out the wrinkles in his trousers with his palm, adjusted his tie in the mirror, checked the taps on his shoes, spit on a rag, and rubbed the toes and heels. He was ready.

The Bronte Sisters were on. He could hear their music, *Together in a Corner, Juntos en el Rincon,* their signature final number. Kenny clicked down the dozen metal steps from the dressing rooms and moved toward Vogel waiting to get on. Vogel was not doing his usual preparatory muscle flexing. Alf the stage manager, little Alfie who always looked as if he were about to cry, looked at Kenny and whispered,

"What the hell are you doing here? You've got a forchrissake half hour for chrissake."

Kenny shrugged.

"Staying warm," he said flexing his shoulders. "Being ready. Never know, do you?"

"You always know," said Alf turning to Vogel and asking, "What's wrong with you?"

"Shtomack," said Vogel, hand to his gut. Vogel wore blue tights with a black sash. His black dyed hair was parted in the middle. He had once had a mustache, but had shaved it last year. No one knew why. Vogel didn't say.

The Bronte Sisters danced off the stage right past Vogel and Kenny. Their huge smiles ended. The applause behind them wasn't bad, especially for a frozen night in Chicago.

Vogel rubbed his stomach, made a face, and watched the curtain come down. Then he wheeled his low, flat cart full of weights onto the stage and nodded at Alf. Alf waved at the stagehand who lifted the curtain.

Kenny stood watching, waiting for Vogel to die on stage, ready to dance in to save the show. But Vogel didn't die. He lifted bars, bent pipe over his head, held a reluctant volunteer from the audience over his head with his right hand and then moved the terrified man to his left hand. Applause. Vogel bowed in dignified silence. The curtain came down.

One of the Bronte sisters, probably Lizzy, screamed from the women's dressing room upstairs,

"Alfie, somethin's wrong with Corrine. Get up here."

"Corrine's on now," Alf said. "Tell her. She's on. Chrissake."

Kenny looked toward stairs. Lizzy was standing at the top.

"She's not movin'," Lizzy said.

Corrine was a ventriloquist, the World's Greatest Female Ventriloquist, but they didn't put that in the program. There were already too many "Greatests" in the show and besides, anyone who saw Corrine's act could tell that she was far from the greatest. She was the bottom of the bill, below Kenny. Corrine's dummy was Fifi. Fifi was supposed to have a French accent, but when Corrine had been drinking, she forgot the accent or used an Italian or Spanish one instead. When Corrine had been drinking, which was frequent, she also sometimes forgot to move Fifi's mouth when Fifi spoke. Corrine was over seventy, and her false teeth clacked. She forgot most of her punch lines. She wasn't a bad sort, but she wasn't much of a mingler.

"I'll go see," said Alf. "Kenny, you go on. You're ready. You go on. Tell Al and Spitzer in the pit."

Al was the piano player. Spitzer played clarinet, trumpet, sax, whatever was called for. Spitzer of all trades. Versatility and mediocrity combined to make one perfect inexpensive musician.

Kenny moved past Vogel and asked,

"How's your stomach?"

"Not good. Couldn't even eat my sandwich."

"You gave it to Corrine didn't you?" Kenny asked.

Vogel nodded seeing nothing meaningful in the question.

Kenny stuck his head through the curtain and signaled to Al and Spitzer that he was going on next. They both shrugged. Made no difference to them.

They started his music. *Chinatown*. The Dancing Fool came tapping out. No applause. He didn't expect any. Not yet. If he were lucky, the few dozen people out there would clap out of sync when he finished. Kenny was determined to wow 'em. He doubled the tempo. Al and Spitzer had a hard time keeping up with him. Al frowned. Kenny Poole danced like a fool trying not to think about Corrine. There was no point killing Corrine. It wouldn't move him up in the bill. First he kills the wrong poodle and now the wrong person. But maybe she wasn't dead.

Kenny sweated through three fast-paced numbers and then did his special, hands-in-the-pocket slow dance to *Silver Threads Among the Gold*. The trick was, the skill was, not to tap, to defy the metal cleats. It took work, practice. Only the pros knew how hard it was. Audience's almost never got it. Once in Rochester a woman had applauded wildly after he did the slow dance. He had tried to get a good look at her, but she was in the back of the house. That was five, maybe eight years ago.

He ended the act with the lean-forward kick and double back arm swing to the slightly flat rendition of *Stars and Stripes Forever*. You had to be unpatriotic not to applaud, especially when Kenny stopped dancing and pulled the flag out of his jacket pocket.

He tapped offstage, smiling over his shoulder, exhausted, tucked the flag in his pocket, and wiped the sweat from his forehead. He'd have to get the soaked costume cleaned. Two bits, maybe half a buck. Cost of doing this kind of business. The seals were sitting there already barking, being fed fish from a bucket.

"Corrine's dead," Lizzy Bronte greeted him, tears in her eyes.

The seals and Sandy Scrimberger moved onstage to the pit duo playing *The Battle Hymn of the Republic* that they played because Sandy was dressed in a Union uniform and the seals were going to play the song on their horns.

Scrimberger and the seals were number five on the list. Few would mourn a pair of deal seals.

Kenny allowed himself to stand panting and comforting Liz Bronte.

"It's the drink what did it," she wept. "We tried to tell her. Doctors tried to tell her. Would she listen?"

"No," said Kenny.

Alf came down the stairs shaking his head.

"Doctor's coming," he said. "But she's gone."

Liz Bronte ran up the stairs where her sister stood at the top. They hugged.

"Between you and me and Charlie Chaplin," Alf said. "Corrine's breath smelled like she'd been drinking some thousand proof."

Alf hurried off behind the flat of a Civil War battlefield.

If the doc said Corrine had a heart attack, he couldn't kill Vogel and make it look like a heart attack. There are coincidences and coincidences, but . . . Kenny got an idea.

No Bronte sister act with only one Bronte sister. One Bronte sister with a broken leg and no act. Show business tradition. "Break a leg, girls," someone would say when the house was good and they remembered.

Kenny would find a way to break a Bronte leg, probably Charlotte's. Charlotte was stronger. She'd recover faster. Not fast enough to get back in the season. And Kenny wouldn't have to kill her. So, get rid of the seals and one Bronte and Kenny would make the cut.

When? The sooner the better. Why not now?

Risky, but look at it this way: Corrine's dead. Charlotte's distraught. She comes down the steps crying her eyes out. She trips, with a little help from Kenny hiding under the stairs. It shouldn't kill her. With luck, a broken leg, especially if he hits the leg hard when he trips her. Hit the leg, duck into the janitor's closet under the stairs, go through the window, close it, back around fast to the stage entrance, to the sound of people screaming about the double tragedy. Get a chance to feel Liz leaning against him again. Bonus.

He moved under the stairs, hid in the shadows, picked up a broom leaning against the wall.

The seals on stage were blowing their horns. He could hear the Brontes coming, comforting each other.

"Maybe one of us should stay with her," Liz said.

"Go on," Charlotte said. "I'll be right up."

Perfect. Liz was heading back to the women's dressing room. Charlotte was already coming down the stairs. He heard her at the top step. Then the second. Saw her ankle. Nice ankle. She was moving slowly. Kenny was sweating even more now. Life or death. Kill or be killed, but he wasn't going to kill her.

He thrust the broom handle between the steps and swung it hard against Charlotte's ankle. Charlotte screamed, maybe she reached for the metal railing. She tripped and tumbled down the last nine stairs, but Kenny had already put the broom back and was closing the closet door behind him.

He went through the window. Cold out there. Sudden shocking chill. His sweat froze. He felt dizzy. Had to move fast. Around the corner, stepping through a thin layer of ice into a puddle of icy water. Hurrying, taps sliding on ice under snow.

Inside, Liz heard her sister, ran down the stairs screaming. The two-man pit band got louder to cover whatever the hell was going on backstage. Alf appeared, shouting "Chrissake, what now?"

Charlotte lay at the bottom of the steps, her eyes closed, her sister cradling her head.

"Oh God, Char. Oh God."

The old man who guarded the stage door shuffled over, tucking his pipe in his pocket. Vogel came down the stairs quickly and knelt at the fallen dancer's side. He touched her forehead, cheek, put his ear to her chest.

"Water," he commanded.

Alf ran for water.

Charlotte opened her eyes.

"What son-of-a-bitch tripped me?" she demanded, woozily sitting up.

"You fell down the stairs," Vogel said gently.

"You were upset about Corrine," said Liz.

"Someone tripped me," Charlotte said. "Help me up."

Vogel lifted her as if she were a raggedy doll.

"My ankle hurts like hell," she said leaning over to look at the purple and red welt.

She tested it.

"For chrissake, who are you?" asked Alf looking at a lean, white-haired man in an overcoat and muffler who had apparently come in the stage door while they were busy with Charlotte.

"I've come at a bad time," the man said.

"It could be worse," said Alf. "The roof could collapse."

"Happened in the Fairfax in New Haven four years ago," said the stranger. "I was there. No one was killed but . . ."

Charlotte was limping around now.

The white-haired man turned not toward the stage door but the door that led into the theater.

"No," said Alf. "You're here for chrissake. What do you want? You a cop? That's all we need."

"No," said the man. "I'm looking for Kenneth Poole."

"Kenny?"

"I just saw his act. I'd like to talk to him and to you two," the man said looking at Liz and Charlotte.

"We've got a dead woman upstairs," said Vogel softly. "This is a bad time."

"Where is Kenny?" asked Charlotte as the pit band played *By the Sea* to accompany Scrimberger and his seals off the stage. The applause was the best of the night.

"What's with all the noise?" Scrimberger asked.

Both seals barked. Scrimberger threw each of them a fish from the bucket he was carrying.

"Corrine's dead," said Liz tearfully. "And Charlotte was almost killed."

"I wasn't almost killed," said Charlotte. "Someone tripped me."

"Can you still dance?" asked the white-haired man.

Charlotte looked at him and said, "By tomorrow I'll be perfect, unless I break my leg kicking the hell out of who-ever—"

"Where is Kenny?" asked Liz.

The stage door flew open, letting in a frozen blast of air. Standing in the doorway was a chubby little man in a black coat and derby hat wearing black gloves and carrying a black pebbled-leather satchel.

"Someone should be with the body," the chubby man said, closing the door behind him.

Scrimberger muttered something and led his seals past the stairs to the downstairs room reserved for animal acts so the cats, dogs, seals, parrots, and occasional chimp wouldn't have to go up and down stairs.

"Buddy Donald is upstairs with her," said Liz.

"For Chrissake," said Alf rubbing his forehead. "Buddy's supposed to be on next."

"Upstairs?" said the chubby man.

"Corrine's upstairs," said Liz pointing to the landing.

"Corrine?" asked the chubby man. "What in the blazes on a cold night in hell are you talking about? I'm Doctor Milton Frazier. Someone called about a dead body. I practically tripped over it right out there."

He pointed to the door through which he had come.

"And," he said. "It's no she. It's a he, and even though I've worked with you vaudeville people before, I don't think his name is Corrine. And what's he doing out there without a coat on a night like this and a little U.S. flag on his chest and . . ."

Alf dashed to the stage door, opened it, and ran out. Buddy Donald, short and wiry with very little hair, who had once been a tenor and was now a comic, came hurrying down the stairs saying, "I'm on."

He ignored everyone, adjusted his cuffs and walked onstage.

"It's Kenny," Alf said coming back through the stage door. "He's out there. He's dead."

"I just told you he was dead," Doctor Frazier said. "Close the door."

Alf closed the door.

"What happened to him?" Liz cried.

It was Charlotte's turn to comfort her sister.

"Looks to me like he slipped on a patch of ice by the steps," said the doctor. "Looks to me like he must have been in a hurry, which is not a good thing to do on ice, especially when, as I could see, you're wearing tap shoes. Left leg's broke. Hit his head on the ice. There's another body?"

"This way," said Vogel motioning for the doctor to follow him up the stairs.

The doctor stopped at the top of the stairs and said, "Call the police. And try to stay alive till they get here."

"Shame," said the white-haired man, buttoning his coat. "I'll come back and talk to you two young ladies tomorrow."

"About what?" Charlotte asked.

"About being in a movie," the man said. "My name is Lee DeForest. I have a studio here in Chicago. I'm starting to make movies with sound to show in theaters like this one, short movies with music. I'd like the two of you to do your act for my cameras and sound tomorrow."

"You're kidding?" said Charlotte.

"No," said Alf. "I heard of him. He makes movies with sounds. We're thinking of showing them here."

"I show them all around the country," he said. "You get paid well, I think, and people all over the country get to see you. I can assure you, you'll be famous."

The sisters looked at each other and simultaneously said, "Sure."

"I really came to see Mr. Poole," DeForest said with a sigh. "One of my people said he would be perfect for movies. Tap dancing. Music. Pity. Now if you tell me where you are staying, I'll have a car pick you up at, say, eleven tomorrow?"

"We'll miss the first show," said Liz.

"Miss the first show," said Alf with a wave of one hand and the other on his forehead. "We're three acts short. We'll show an extra movie."

About the Authors

Winner of the Agatha, Anthony, Macavity, and Shamus awards for her short stories, and Edgar-nominated twice for her Cass Jameson series, **Carolyn Wheat** embarked on a new venture with *How to Write Killer Fiction*. This unique approach to writing the crime novel explores "the funhouse of mystery and the roller coaster of suspense" so that the writer can create the ideal reader experience in either genre. She is currently at work on a book about detective characters as archetypes. She offers writing workshops and teaches regularly at UCSD.

Edward D. Hoch is a past president of the Mystery Writers of America and winner of its Edgar Award for best short story. In 2001 he was honored with MWA's Grand Master Award. He has been guest of honor at the annual Bouchercon mystery convention, two-time winner of its Anthony Award, and 2001 recipient of its Lifetime Achievement Award. He is also recipient of Life Achievement Awards from the Private Eye Writers of America and the Short Mystery Fiction Society. Author of over 875 published stories, as well as novels and collections, he has appeared in every issue of *Ellery Queen's Mystery Magazine* since 1973. Hoch resides with his wife Patricia in Rochester, New York.

Annette Meyers was born in New York, grew up on a chicken farm in New Jersey, and came running back to Manhattan as soon as she could. She has a long history on Broadway (assistant to Harold Prince) and Wall Street (headhunter and arbitrator, NASD). Her first novel, *The Big Killing,* featured Wall Street headhunters Xenia Smith and former dancer, Leslie Wetzon, who stumble over bodies on Wall Street and Broadway. There are now seven Smith and Wetzon novels and an eighth, *Hedging,* will be published in 2005. In *Free Love,* set in Greenwich Village in 1920, Meyers introduced poet/sleuth Olivia Brown and her bohemian friends. *Murder Me Now* followed. With husband Martin Meyers, using the pseudonym Maan Meyers, she has written six books in The Dutchman series of historical mysteries set in New York in the seventeenth, eighteenth, and nineteenth centuries. Both Annette Meyers's and Maan Meyers's short stories have appeared in numerous anthologies.

John Lutz is the author of more than thirty-five novels and approximately 250 short stories and articles. His work has been translated into virtually every language and adapted for almost every medium. He is a past president of both the Mystery Writers of America and the Private Eye Writers of America. Among his awards are the MWA Edgar, the PWA Shamus, the Trophee 813 Award for best mystery short story collection translated into the French language, the PWA Life Achievement Award, and the Short Mystery Fiction Society's Golden Derringer Lifetime Achievement Award. He is the author of two private eye series, the Nudger series, set in his home town of St. Louis, and the Carver series, set in Florida, as well as many non-series suspense novels. His *SWF Seeks Same* was made into the hit movie *Single White Female,* starring Bridget Fonda and Jennifer Jason Leigh, and his *The Ex* was made into the HBO original movie of the same title, for which he co-authored the screenplay. His latest book is a suspense novel, *The Night Watcher*.

"Janet Evanovich meets The Fugitive." That's what author Tim Dorsey calls **Elaine Viets**'s new Dead-End Job mystery series. *Shop Till You Drop* is the first in the Signet series. Elaine actually works those dead-end jobs in this South Florida series. She has been a dress-store clerk, a bookseller, and a telemarketer who called you at dinnertime. She was nominated for three Agatha Awards in 2003 for Best Traditional Mystery for Shop Till You Drop, and two short stories, "Red Meat" and "Sex and Bingo."

Angela Zeman, a former director of MWA, is the author of *The Witch and the Borscht Pearl* (Pendulum Press). The cozy novel, praised in reviews from *Publisher's Weekly* and other venues, features characters from the popular Mrs. Risk "witch" short story series. Mary Higgins Clark chose a Mrs. Risk story for her anthology, *The Night Awakens*. The second Mrs. Risk novel is expected to appear soon. Her suspense story in Nancy Pickard's anthology, *Mom, Apple Pie, and Murder,* was reviewed by PW as "magical." "Green Heat," her story in the MWA anthology *A Hot and Sultry Night for Crime,* also garnered high praise from *Publishers Weekly*. She also writes nonfiction articles about the mystery field, both alone and with her husband, Barry T. Zeman, who is an acknowledged authority on the history of the mystery and antiquarian book collecting. They contributed an article to MWA's 2003 handbook edited by Sue Grafton (Writer's Digest Books): *Writing Mysteries*. http://www.AngelaZeman.com.

Another original story by **David Bart** appeared in the 2003 Mystery Writers of America anthology, *A Hot and Sultry Night for Crime,* edited by Jeffery Deaver. David's work has also been published in *Ellery Queen's Mystery Magazine* and *Alfred Hitchcock's Mystery Magazine*. One of his many stories published in *AHMM* was translated and reprinted in a Paris anthology. He is presently working on a suspense novel in addition to short stories and is an active member of the Mystery Writers of America, SouthWest Writers, and PWA. David lives in New Mexico and can be reached at djbart@flash.net.

Bob Shayne has been nominated for two Edgars for his TV movie "The Return of Sherlock Holmes"—also nominated by the Writers Guild of America as Best TV Movie of the Year—and for "Ashes to Ashes and None Too Soon," one of twelve scripts he wrote for the popular 1980s TV series "Simon & Simon." Pierce Brosnan is attached to star in and produce Shayne's upcoming movie *Once a Thief*. This is his first short story. He is also developing a series of historical mystery novels featuring the Naomi Weinstein character.

Mark Terry is the author of two mystery series, one featuring Dr. Theo MacGreggor, a consulting forensic toxicologist, and one featuring Megan Malloy, a computer troubleshooter. He is also a frequent book reviewer, technical editor, and freelance writer. His work appears regularly in *Mystery Scene Magazine,* and has appeared in *The Armchair Detective* and *Orchard Press Mysteries*. He has published nearly one hundred book reviews, dozens of columns and articles, and even the occasional poem. His "day job" is in the field of genetics. He lives in Michigan with his wife and sons. Visit his website at *www.mark-terry.com*

Gary Phillips writes in various mediums from the short story form to comic books to scripts, as a general practitioner of mass media. And what few forays he's had into the arena of Hollywood has taught him that show bizness ain't a business for sissies.

Parnell Hall is the author of the Stanley Hastings private eye novels, the Puzzle Lady Crossword Puzzle mysteries, and the Steve Winslow courtroom dramas. His books have been nominated for Edgar and Shamus awards. Parnell is an actor, screenwriter, and former private investigator. He lives in New York City.

Susanne Shaphren's first nationally published mystery was *The Visit,* a Fiction Award story in the March 1972 issue of *Weight Watchers Magazine.* Her articles and short stories have been published in an eclectic alphabet soup of magazines including: *Authorship, Better Communication, Crosscurrents, Delta Scene, Golden Years, Hibiscus, Jack and Jill, Lady's Circle, Mike Shayne Mystery Magazine, Plot, Short Stuff,* and *The Writer.*

A transplant from Washington, D.C., **Libby Fischer Hellmann** has lived in the Chicago area twenty-five years. Her amateur sleuth series, featuring video producer Ellie Foreman, made its debut in 2002 with *An Eye for Murder,* published simultaneously by Poisoned Pen Press and Berkley Prime Crime. *A Picture of Guilt* was released in July, 2003, followed by *An Image of Death* in February 2004. Her short stories have appeared in both American and British publications. When not writing fiction, Libby writes and produces corporate videos. She is also a speech- and presentation-skills coach. She holds a BA from the University of Pennsylvania and an MFA in Film Production from New York University. She lives on the North Shore of Chicago with her family and a Beagle, shamelessly named Shiloh.

By the age of thirty, **Charles Ardai** had been a Shamus Award–nominated mystery writer, founder and CEO of a $2 billion Internet company, and a managing director at the investment and technology development firm *Fortune* magazine called "the most intriguing and mysterious force on Wall Street." His proudest accomplishment, however, is having appeared as an extra in Woody Allen's "Radio Days." Mr. Ardai lives in New York.

Gregg Hurwitz is the author of *The Tower, Minutes to Burn, Do No Harm,* and *The Kill Clause.* He holds a B.A. in English and psychology from Harvard University and a master's degree from Trinity College, Oxford. He lives in Los Angeles.

Show business may be murder, but somehow **Steve Hockensmith** has managed to survive his brushes with it—so far. A freelance journalist, he has covered pop culture and the film industry for *The Hollywood Reporter, The Chicago Tribune, Newsday, The Fort Worth Star-Telegram, Total Movie, Cinescape,* and other publications. He also recently sold the movie rights to his Derringer Award–winning story "Erie's Last Day," and a short film based on the story is in the works. His short fiction has appeared in *Ellery Queen's Mystery Magazine, Alfred Hitchcock's Mystery Magazine,* and *Analog.* But what he really wants to do is direct . . .

Shelley Freydont is the author of the Lindy Haggerty mystery series (*Backstage Murder, Midsummer Murder, A Merry Little Murder*). She has toured internationally with Twyla Tharp Dance and American Ballroom Theater and has choreographed for and appeared in films, television, and on Broadway. She is a member of MWA and Sisters in Crime (President of NY/TriState chapter 2001–2003).

Robert Lopresti is a librarian and songwriter in the Pacific Northwest. Thirty of his stories have been published in

Alfred Hitchcock's Mystery Magazine, and many other places. One of his stories was nominated for the Anthony Award in 1994.

Mat Coward is a British writer of crime, SF, horror, children's, and humorous fiction, whose stories have been broadcast on BBC Radio and published in numerous anthologies, magazines, and e-zines in the UK, US, and Europe. According to Ian Rankin, "Mat Coward's stories resemble distilled novels." His first non-distilled novel—a whodunit called *Up and Down*—was published in the USA in 2000 by Five Star Publishing. The same publisher produced his first single author collection, *Do the World a Favour and Other Stories* in 2003.

Stuart M. Kaminsky is the author of fifty-six published books, forty short stories, and five produced screenplays. He was one of the writers of the A & E Nero Wolfe television series. He won the Edgar for best novel in 1989 and the Prix De Roman D'Aventure of France in 1990. He has received a total of six Edgar nominations for his novels and short stories. Kaminsky writes the Toby Peters series, the Porfiry Rostnikov series, the Abe Lieberman series, and the Lew Fonesca series set in and around Sarasota. He has also written two "Rockford Files" novels. Kaminsky has a B.S. degree in Journalism and an M.A. in English Literature from the University of Illinois and a Ph.D. in Communications from Northwestern University. He taught film history, filmmaking, and creative writing at Northwestern University for sixteen years before going to Florida State University in 1988 to head the Graduate Conservatory in Film. He left FSU in 1994 to write full time. He now lives in Sarasota with his wife and family, and finds time to play a lot of softball.